A child like Jared—highly intelligent, deeply frustrated—is an inherently violent being, a crucible of emotion that could move from boil to freeze and back again in seconds. I knew it because I'd been such a child.

My mother had told me quite recently that I was incapable of killing. But what did she know of my fantasies at twelve when I was soft clay, the sculpting not going well? Would she have slept soundly, only a wall between us, if she'd seen my fist close on a carving knife as I crept out of my bed headed for hers? Never mind what happened or didn't; never mind whether the knife was gripped in fact or fantasy. How high was the inner wall between passion and action? That is the question. Was Jared's wall unscalable, no matter what the cue?

THE HOUSE ON SPRUCEWOOD LANE

"[A] very intelligent, smartly written novel with a bit of a new twist."

—Bookreporter.com

"A compelling read."

—Judith Rossner, author of
Looking for Mr. Goodbar

"[An] assured first novel. . . . Slate handles it deftly, rounding her characters so that the reader can hear their ragged breathing."

—*Publishers Weekly*

THE
HOUSE
ON
SPRUCEWOOD
LANE

CAROLINE SLATE

POCKET STAR BOOKS
New York   London   Toronto   Sydney   Singapore

This book is a work of fiction. Names, characters, places and incidents are products of the author's imagination or are used fictitiously. Any resemblance to actual events or locales or persons, living or dead, is entirely coincidental.

 A Pocket Star Book published by
POCKET BOOKS, a division of Simon & Schuster, Inc.
1230 Avenue of the Americas, New York, NY 10020

ISBN: 0-7434-1889-1

First Pocket Books paperback printing July 2003

10 9 8 7 6 5 4 3 2 1

POCKET STAR BOOKS and colophon are registered
trademarks of Simon & Schuster, Inc.

For information regarding special discounts for bulk purchases,
please contact Simon & Schuster Special Sales at 1-800-456-6798
or business@simonandschuster.com

Cover art by Shasti O'Leary Soudant

Printed in the U.S.A.

TO MY SISTER PAULA,
THE ONE AND ONLY

ACKNOWLEDGMENTS

Strong, smart, optimistic: Loretta Barrett is the agent a writer hopes for. My editor, Amy Pierpont, sparked to this book, climbed into Lex's head with me, and never made a wrong suggestion. Thanks!

Nancy Lucas, the ideal intuitive reader, Linda Wallace, the sharpest knife in the drawer, and Sandy Silverman, way more than Ms. Make-nice, are key among the friends who helped keep the lights on during the dark time of my mother's death.

Finally Eamon. Always Himself. I wouldn't dream of asking for more . . .

Let the liberties I've taken with Westport and environs be on my head alone.

PROLOGUE

It's a warmer than usual Halloween, the air clear but listless, lacking the apple bite of prime fall. Along Sprucewood Lane, jack-o'-lanterns, angel-hair cobwebs, dried-vegetation still lifes, adorn porches and front windows of houses that sit confidently on two or three acres of landscaped lot. Comfortable homes. This is Fairfield County, Westport, a town where people of newish means, seeking the burnish of old money, choose the words *home* over *house, comfortable* over *rich*—and can afford their luxuries of understatement.

Clusters of costumed children bounce from house to house, collecting whimsically wrapped favors. Householders here don't resort to improvised handouts of small change, random jelly beans, ad hoc apples. Halloween treats, like Christmas gifts, are selected and packaged to display taste, imagination, love of children.

A boy dressed in everyday jeans and sweater hunches forward, pulling behind him a red wagon that looks brand-new. Actually, the wagon is three years old, or will be come Christmas, but unused. It had been his mother's idea, a movie-inspired fantasy: red wagons, green trees, white houses, and happy boys. But Jared McQuade is no red wagon kind of boy.

He is a genius, teacher after teacher tells his parents, each outlining a fresh September strategy to "reach him," "tap that potential." But along about Halloween, the honeymoon is over: the stubbornly unresponsive object of all this reaching and tapping has won again. It's been that way since first grade.

"Duh," is the internal comment of Jared himself, Olympic gold medalist in the category of hollow victories. He wonders why they bother. As far as he's concerned, it's a waste of everybody's time, and he knows they wouldn't keep at it, except for his oversized IQ, which is bullshit. What he is, is a boy-shaped computer, software coded in hypertext by a programmer with a sick sense of humor. So the creature can multiply numbers in his head really fast; so some pretty fancy physics seems to him plain common sense—so what? So Goddamned *what*, when the fool can hardly get past hello without fucking up, while boys who puzzle over the sum of two and two goof with each other as easy as turning on a water faucet.

He is twelve and a half, tall for his age and scrawny, the navy sweater bags on him. Funny-looking: a cartoon of a boy, all ears, spiked dark hair, and braced teeth. His inner eye catches a personal resemblance to the snaggle-toothed pumpkin heads grinning in those lit windows—a perception highly inaccurate, not least because Jared, never mind grinning, seldom smiles. When he does, his face takes on a vulnerable innocence that would embarrass him painfully were he aware of it. Certainly he is not smiling tonight as he drags his wagon from house to house, hating dumb-ass Halloween, hating his humiliating task, hating his mother for forcing it on him.

Inside the wagon lounges a mermaid, iridescent green from neck to forked tail, each sequin hand-sewn by that same mother. The mermaid's head is tossed back, one thin arm held with apparent ease at an angle uncomfortable for most mortals, as she rakes her long red-gold hair with a silver comb. Her other hand holds a round silver vanity mirror, of delicately chased design.

Calista. *Goddamned* Calista.

He remembers how when he was a little kid and Calista was a baby, Lex would make him laugh when he felt like crying. "Ihaychoo! It's okay to say it, Jared. It's like a sneeze—you get it out and then you feel better." *Ihaychoo, Calista!*

It is hard to believe that this glamorous child is Jared's sister, but she is. Her name, the Greek word for "the best," was chosen by her mother from one of those baby naming books. It suits her. This is a girl of extraordinary talent. Her body, arched now, classic mermaid-style, is supple to the point of appearing boneless. Calista, recently turned ten, is a gymnast, as her mother had been at the same age. But daughter surpassed mother years ago. Melanie would tell you that herself. Giving Calista a little pat on the behind, she'd say in that drawl of hers, more southern than one might expect after two decades up north, "This baby's been Olympic bound since she could walk. She was born with a star on her soul!"

Calista's face is arresting, rather than beautiful. Her features jump the bounds of prettiness: gray eyes a bit overlarge; small chin, too abruptly pointed; upper lip long and tilted at its ends, smiling by default. From time to time, she flick-turns the mirror to catch the streetlights and flash them in the eyes of other trick-or-treaters, who seem to enjoy the attention.

"Hi, Calista," they call, and stop to admire her costume: "Cool." "What about you, Jared?" one asks, his friends laughing in chorus. "Forget to put on your King Neptune suit?" Which was actually what his mother had had in mind for him, but Jared's "No" had been flat and final enough that she'd believed it and quit while she was ahead, settling for sullen, plainclothes boy-power to pull Calista's wagon. Her parting shot, "Go naked for all I care. You will drive me to *drink*, Jared; I swear you will!"

"Stop fucking with that mirror, Calista," Jared says through gritted teeth, "or I'll leave you right in the road. First car comes along'll squash you flat."

She laughs, a sound musically light, yet anchored by undertones suggesting a prior life heavy with smoke and brandy. "You won't leave me," she singsongs knowingly, "because I'm your sister and you love me."

Jared jerks the wagon hard enough to disarrange her, and feels a ripple of satisfaction as he hears the clank of metal on metal: the comb falling from her hand; the damn mirror would've been louder. Love. *Lovlovlove*: the more you said it, the sillier it sounded. Just like *Ihaychoo*, except there's no Lex round to make any of it funny. There is no one Jared can tell. No one.

It feels like he's swallowed poison, and it's burning his stomach out. That's probably why he's been thinking about Lex so much recently—missing her again, which is pretty stupid. How can you miss someone you don't know anymore? Someone who doesn't give a damn about you anyway? Someone you haven't seen since you were six? But he could tell her; he's sure of that. And she'd know what to do.

His stranglehold on the neck of the bulging orange loot sack tightens as he trudges up the steps of the corner house to collect another pair of treats—and yet one more version of, "Calista, well, aren't *you* the most . . . George, come look at Calista. She's a *mermaid!*" It is enough to make him want to puke.

On to the next house; only six more by his count. "Jared, I have to pee." The voice, stripped of its showy teasing now, comes from a little girl trapped helplessly in nylon and sequins.

"Well, let 'er rip," he says not unkindly. "That's what the astronauts do when they're suited up. Anyway, natural habitat for mermaids is water, isn't it?"

"HI, THERE!" Melanie calls from the porch, determinedly cheerful as she strides out the front door to meet her children. Long arms outstretched, long legs sleek in black leather pants, she moves like a dancer, if a bit stiffly. The fact is, her back hurts fiercely, as it often does. For this reason, her step is extra-brisk. Pain is an enemy, and Melanie fights enemies by ignoring them, a strategy that takes at least as much grit as hand-to-hand combat. You can see the effort in her heart-shaped face, its determined bones no longer in hiding beneath a girlish roundness of cheek, its mouth thinned with self-restraint. At forty-two, she is strikingly good looking, and just as strikingly tense: a taut wire waiting to snap, or be clipped.

She motions back at her guests, grouped in the doorway. "Come on out and have a look at my enchanted creature of the deep. Ja*red!* Now, careful. Not so rough with her up those steps." From in the wagon, Calista favors the clustered adults with her mirror-flash routine. "Trick or treat?" her voice sings out. That's my girl,

Melanie thinks, her heart expanding with hope that the rest of the night will go well.

EIGHT HOURS GONE: late night blurring into early morning now. Melanie skims the stubborn surface of sleep, enveloped by an occasional wave, only to emerge again into wakefulness, the back tightening with pain, as she tries too hard to dive through into oblivion. Finally, just as her limbs begin to liquefy into the warm dark sea, she hears—thinks she hears—a throaty growl, a sharp croak. She startles full awake and, a shaved second later, realizes that the feral sounds came from her own open mouth.

Six feet to her right, over at the other side of the king-sized bed, lies Tom, who, sometime during the night—who knows when?—slipped into his accustomed slot. Tom was not at home Halloween evening, as he was not at home most evenings. Melanie no longer expects that he will be. She ignores his absences as she does her backaches, applying her considerable ingenuity to filling the empty spaces. Mind over matter is her philosophy here: if she doesn't mind about Tom, he will not matter.

Tom McQuade lies perfectly still, giving no sign of having heard his wife's animal cries. But, then again, he might have and decided to pretend unconsciousness. You never knew with Tom. Melanie no longer trusts her husband, even in so trivial a thing.

She seriously craves a pill, though no pill except for a vitamin has passed her lips in a long while. They used to. Oh, did they ever! Red, white, yellow—the tiniest ones always, oddly, the most potent. Starting when she was fifteen, way before she'd ever known a back could hurt, the little pellets, obtained by hook and crook both, became her defending army, little soldiers combating loneliness and anger and guilt. But ten years ago all that changed. Eight months pregnant, she lay hemorrhaging, semi-conscious, while fragments of tense, official talk fired back and forth across her broken body: *"What was she on?" "Insane to be behind a wheel." "How could you allow . . . ?" "I didn't allow. I was . . . away. Look, what are their chances?"* This last from Tom, his deep voice clogged with shock and fury. *"We'll do our best, but . . ."*

Her mind had asserted itself suddenly, like a rock jutting out of the mist, and in a moment of utter inner clarity, Melanie offered God a very simple deal: my life and my baby's, and I'll never swallow even an aspirin again. Come on, I've picked out her *name!* She felt Him weighing her offer. Hey, I promise—not even an aspirin. Afterward, she'd swear His hand had touched hers, sealing the bargain. Though Melanie and God had always maintained a good working relationship, she had never felt closer to Him than she did right then.

She wishes for His attention now, but cannot summon Him up. Something is going terribly wrong, she knows, spinning out of control somehow, right under her eyes, which have watched but failed to see . . . something. Calista is not Calista, and hasn't been for months. Her daughter—her delightful, headed-for-the-gold-medal daughter; her dream-come-true, best friend daughter—has begun to bounce like a pinball: sunny to sullen to snotty to silent to spiteful, and back to sunny again. "The five *S*'s," Nate calls them, his sandpapery New York sound as comforting as the words. "She's turned ten. Girls that age can strike quick as a snake, Mel. It's the will muscle—they start to flex it, mostly in their mother's face."

Normal, he's assured her. She believes him. It is, after all, his job to know such things. And she trusts him:

Nate's the only shrink who's come close to reaching Jared, not to mention the life-saver he's been for Melanie personally. Of course he's right. And yet . . . She's meant to speak to God about all this, but somehow has shied from broaching any of it.

Halloween night had been going better than well: the shiny red wagon crunching up the pebbled walk; her new poet's shirt billowing at her back like a white silk sail as she hurried to meet her children. The moment had been perfect. No sad woman she, alone with her children on Halloween, her husband elsewhere, as usual. Quite the contrary, Melanie had invited friends over, setting a scene that Martha Stewart (her own house up until recently a mere ten minutes south, and not a bit nicer) would have envied: pine fragrant fire, its blaze winking brilliantly off accents of polished brass; Chinese vases filled with bittersweet; old brandy, mulled cider, good cheeses on the big Georgian silver tray for the grown-ups, hot chocolate in a tiger-shaped pot with matching mugs for the kids. Enter Calista sounding like her best self, calling out, "Trick or treat?" And Melanie even thought she spotted the beginnings of a smile on Jared's face.

But about half an hour later, she happened to glance at him, skulking in a corner, eyes fixed on his sister with a hatred so pure, so strong, as to be unmistakable. At the same moment, Calista, who'd been giggling as the guests passed her from lap to lap, rolled off onto the floor with a dull thump—laughter all gone. "I want to go to bed," she said nastily, and began to pull hard at her mermaid's tail, trying to rip it to shreds. Quickly, Melanie stooped beside her, taking over, easing the costume down gently over Calista's hips, to preserve the delicate, hand-sewn sequins.

The sharp lemony acid smell hit her nostrils, even

before her fingers felt the dampness. No point in taking care now, the damned thing would have to be thrown out—soaked with pee! She clenched her teeth, monitored the hand that itched to slap Calista, really whack her. (Slap Calista? Even the thought was . . .) "Get up to bed, you two," she said quietly. The children hesitated, checking out an unfamiliar cat growl in her tone. "Better get moving. I *mean* it!"

Now she peers across Tom's tousled dark head at the clock dial: ten to five. Absurdly early to get up, yet she can't lie there one more minute. Cannot. For the first time, it strikes her as dangerous to be sharing a bed, however large, with an enemy, a man who'd wanted to leave her, take her son away, split the children up. He had never come out and said it, but she'd gotten the signals loud and clear. That's what her husband had wanted to do: go off with Lex, take Jared. Melanie knew Tom's ways a lot better than he dreamed she did. She could remember a time when she used to feel downright tender about that remoteness of his, thought she could see the hurt little orphan boy hiding inside sarcasm and silences, peeking out from time to time, trusting only her to see him. But that time was long gone. For all she cared, Tom—past, present, and future—could go straight to hell.

Six years ago, he had grinned the grin of a man newly in love. And in love with what? Incredibly, with Lex (as she called herself now; to Melanie she'd always be Allie), odd scrap of a thing, all bones and prickles, more like a girl than a woman—Melanie's own sister, and yet not a real sister at all. But, proof of the pudding, Lex was gone and Tom was here. The family was together. That was important on any terms—any terms at all. Still, in a house this size they could have moved to separate rooms. They hadn't, though. Neither had suggested it.

She bounds out of the bed, the sharp pain in her back curiously satisfying in its clarity, pulls on a sunny cashmere robe, slips her feet into matching yellow high-heeled mules. Her face is plaster-stiff with sleeplessness and grief. She is losing Calista. Whatever Nate says, this child is slipping away from her. The signs are unmistakable, the sheer *spite* the hardest to bear: Calista was toilet trained at sixteen months, for heaven's sake!

Her thoughts take a side leap to Jared. She doesn't focus on him much, except to be peeved with his ugly manners, rotten temper, his refusal to cooperate one *bit*, his . . . lack of any shred of charm. From time to time, she blames herself for Jared's mess, but mostly she blames him. A boy with his brains, talk about spiteful! Even so, that look in his eyes last night was different . . . and scary.

Her mules make a lonely clack on the polished wood of the hall. The house's faint hums and creaks accent the early morning stillness, underline her anxiety. She walks past the square center hall toward the children's wing. The nest of my unrest, she thinks. Nate has sensitized her to wordplay, at which he is expert, and she decidedly is not. But she does try. Melanie is a devout trier. All is quiet; the cause of her sleeplessness, fast asleep. A swirl of relief and guilt, like cream into acid-strong coffee, softens the bitter edge of her fearful resentment. Children, she thinks. They are just children, every day a new day for them. They are *your* children to watch after and mold. They will grow up; they will be fine—if you do your job properly.

Her mules clack past Jared's closed door, past the bathroom. Then comes Calista's door. It is wide open . . .

CHAPTER
I

Lex:

This is a love story, of sorts. Perhaps passion play is more accurate, except that the classic passion play finishes off with a clear, ringing moral, which is missing here.

I was not present that Halloween night in Connecticut, nor the following morning. I was not inside Melanie's head, nor Jared's, so what you've just read is the view from my mind's eye: Jared, isolated in his fury, frightened; Melanie, frightened as well, struggling to control her own instincts. I think I've gotten it right. I believe this partly because recording shards of human behavior is my job, partly because I know these particular people in my blood and bone. They are (and the cozy oatmeal-and-bananas feel of the word can still turn to glue in my mouth) my family.

When it happened, I was an ocean away from them, six years out of contact. I'd constructed a life insulated against strong feeling for anything but my work. Since passion had, in my hands, inflicted deep damage, I abstained, much like a so-called recovering alcoholic or gambler, supported by an *Anonymous* organization of one. Safer for everyone, or so I'd thought . . .

THE COLD, WET KEY slipped from my hand, and since the bulb above my front door had burned out weeks ago, I found myself on all fours in the rainy dark, panning for a bit of metal, to the accompaniment of more metal—eighties rock—blaring from above. The volume rose as the parlor window swung open. "Charades, is it, Lex?" Colin shouted. Half his face was painted green, his lower lip a luscious purple. Not Halloween any longer—past the witching hour two nights later, in fact. Apparently, the boys had decided to extend the revels. "Pig after truffles, that what you are?" David, this time "See, I've guessed, so you can quit snuffing about the ground and come on up for a pint."

We lived in St. Augustine's Road, Camden Town. Colin and his band, Sussed Out, shared the main house; I lived alone in the basement flat. Nice boys. Oxford and good lineage, all five, which they tried intermittently and unsuccessfully to obfuscate with multiple orifice rings, working-class accents, and Australian beer binges. "Thanks, no," I hollered back. "And it's not truffles. I'm searching for my inner child."

Not altogether untrue. I'd been working a straight eighteen hours and had my own sort of binge on tap, if only I could lay hands on the damned key. I groped the ground faster as my nose caught the fragrance of the wet plastic carry bag on the ground beside me: *doner kebab*, pilaf, *poori*, and the hottest of the onion chutneys. It was overeagerness for the food that had made me drop the key in the first place. Furthermore, if I did not find it very soon, I knew I would sit my bottom down on the muddied concrete step and, drenched in front of a locked door, scoop Indian takeout into my mouth with my bare hands. That's the thing with passion: leaves you in the mud every time.

My thumb touched a serrated edge. My hand pounced to grab the key before it could escape. I barely managed to get inside the door before ripping open the bag and teasing my mouth with a chunk of the kebab, prelude to an ecstasy of tastes and textures, strong, assertive, substantial . . .

I've examined these eating orgies not only because they're mine, but because, as I've mentioned, observing odd human behavior is what I do—not cataclysmically odd human behavior, not wars, or genocide, or even serial killing, but small, offbeat aberrations, which seem to beckon and draw me inside them. And there I shelter myself, entirely absorbed for the months it takes to complete my work, something like a camper in a sleeping bag. I'm not in the business of passing judgment or dispensing remedies; I try to record accurately and comprehend what it is I'm recording. To be more specific, I make my living producing short films about, for example, grannies who cover their bodies in erotic tattoos, men who hunt crocodiles in sewer systems, children trained to commune with long-dead ancestors. This is fare for which British television has a reliable, if not voracious, appetite.

My own appetite, only sporadically voracious, is equally reliable in its way. Since childhood, it has come roaring in, usually to mark certain endings. I well remember being twelve, becoming ravenous on the train home from school for summer holiday, beginning to think of treats to stockpile; equally so twenty years later, following final-cut editing sessions, like tonight, and other endings, too, less neutral ones with consequences far more devastating. I eat at home alone, and urgently. I eat highly spiced food, aggressive food. I eat until I'm stuffed and faintly ill and thoroughly exhausted. Then I sleep for many hours. When I can keep from it, which is only some of the time, I do not throw up. In my grogged, overstuffed state, it seems to me like an unspecified win of sorts if the food stays put.

The panel of experts who have written on the subject judge me to be the classic "overinvestor," one who is emotionally decimated when her portfolio of hopes vaporizes. I gorge myself so as to fill the void, which turns out to be unfillable. Let me mention that I have never sought to cure myself of this "eating disorder."

Though in some essential but unspecific way I feel American, most of my attitudes are English, and so I give a wide berth to therapies that claim to heal anything other than a broken bone or infected appendix. Besides, I'd grown to find my binges useful, as well as troublesome: I would write *finis* to the teenaged mediums or the tattooed elders and go home to eat myself into oblivion; then, it would be over until the next time—usually some months later. The useful bit was that each occasion worked as a kick up the arse, a sharp *aide-mémoire* to mind my graver disorders and keep my emotional valuables tucked safely in a lockbox.

Now, as I sat on a flowered sofa, shoveling food into my impatient cavities, it occurred to me how futile is the action of clean logic upon murky need. Trying to match the two resembles arranging a bad blind date—the couple engaging perhaps for the length of an introductory drink, before realizing they could never dine together.

When the phone rang, it was as though the interruption had come during sex—if I remembered sex well enough to be accurate. I likely would not have answered, except that I thought the caller must be Clive, whom I'd left two hours ago, still bent over a viewer at the editing studio. Though food was a sometime addiction, work was my rock and redeemer: life jacket and teddy bear; mate, lover. So when it called, no matter what, I responded.

The voice wasn't Clive's, though. "I need you to come. Don't you read your . . . ?" Then a cutoff, as though someone else had taken the phone and hung it up.

Just those few words, a child's voice, a boy's. No way to recognize it, not after six years. Not likely he'd even know how to reach me. But despite those odds, my pounding heart insisted this was not a chance wrong number. A mouthful of curried meat barely made it through my constricting gullet and landed hard. The appetite went stone cold, shoved aside by surprise and apprehension and the tickling of my recalled feeling for a little boy, lost to me through my own fault—a boy who'd suffered because of my unchecked passion.

When I first met my nephew, he was three. I fell for him instantly. How could one not fall for a three-year-old who'd look up at a stranger dispensing preserved fruit at Fortnums, a stranger he'd just been told was his aunt, and greet her by asking if she knew the difference between eternity and infinity? But shortly after falling for Jared, I fell for his father. That's the précis. There is, of course, a longer version, complete with mitigating details: Melanie and Tom's souring marriage; her obsession with the hard-born baby girl; Jared's increasing dependence on me; my absorbing late-night delves with Tom into film and journalism turning into delves far more personal, causing us before long to dive at one another like suddenly impassioned snails.

Oh, I could go on and on, but why? The unseen jury has ruled: Reckless abandonment. I plunged straight ahead, no thought for anything but my own cravings—certainly none for Melanie, who had taken me into her home while her husband sent me to film school in New York, nor for Jared, who had every reason to count on me.

At the end of my great love affair—three years, start to finish—the field was strewn with more wounded than the last act of *Macbeth,* and I hied myself back home to London, alone. As I said, when the fit is upon me, I wind up in the mud every time. *Don't you read your . . . ?*

Don't I read my . . . what? I stood and began to pace the flat. It was a space tailor-made for an isolate, streamlined, nothing hidden from view, no secret enclaves: a few pieces of functional furniture for sitting and lying about; a great many books spilling out of shelves to cover tabletops; computer rig and file bins occupying pride of place on the longest wall. Don't I read my *what?*

And then I knew, or felt I did. Jared was twelve, his birthday last March: the ninth. I'd thought, as I did every year, about sending something, something that would intrigue and delight him, that would make him laugh—he'd had such an uproarious hoot of a laugh. But, same as every year, I didn't. This was a kind of self-imposed penance. A long-delayed, palliative gift would be self-indulgent, no more, no less. I'd failed to provide what he really needed from me, had left him with barely a good-bye and no reason he could understand for why I'd gone—why I couldn't come back.

In any case, the gift I'd fantasized sending Jared this time was a just-released computer game with gorgeous animation and the astronomy theme he'd always cottoned to. He would be a real hacker by now, of course he would. I rushed to switch on the computer and dial up. "You've got mail," it announced. And so I did, dated November 1.

> *This is from me, Jared. Calista got killed last night, and everything here is weird. You probably think it's also weird to hear from me all of a sudden, but I want you to come. I said to my dad that I wish Lex was here and I think he said, Me too, but his face was turned the other way and he said it so low that I wasn't sure.*
>
> *I saw your show on A&E about the family who lives with that monkey colony. It was cool. That's when I searched for your E-mail address. I've had it for a while now. I wanted to mail you right away, but I was too much of a wuss to do it. Look, I need you here really badly. Don't call first, okay? If you do, I bet my mom will say to stay in London. So just come!*

I stared at the screen, but the message didn't change. Calista killed. It must have only just happened, or I'd have heard. Tom was well-known, you might say a celebrity; the death of his child would certainly . . . Then again, I'd been incommunicado for most of the past two days—no television, no newspaper, no Web.

Melanie's little girl dead. She'd be ten now—just— but what my mind flashed was a butter-blonde toddler, amazing at cartwheels, remarkable at memorizing song lyrics, singing them out more or less on-key, but most notably, rendering songs of lost love with a bluesy, seeming comprehension that was unsettling. There were other things about Calista I'd found unsettling as well, not the least of which was her uncanny resemblance—not simply in features, but in a kind of intrinsic magnetism—to my mother. I wondered whether Melanie saw it too, but never summoned up the nerve to ask.

I stared at Jared's words, but didn't fathom them. A moment, half an hour, out of Melanie's sight, what calamity might have struck Calista? Hit and run? Freak fall? Botched kidnapping?

My mouse darted and clicked a few times and there was the answer, worse than anything I was prepared for. Much worse. The E-mail had been matter of fact, artless truth-telling from a child up to his eyes in a horror that required no embellishment. It's been my experience that, by and large, children are straightforward. They dramatize only when they intend to manipulate or deceive, in which case they play an audience like veteran troupers.

The words on the screen began to sink in, my sense of unbelief evaporating with each new headline. I scrolled through a welter of news stories, some stark, others deeply purpled. I read them all. Absent the tabloid tinting, this is what they said:

At seven forty-five A.M., November 1, local police had responded to a call from Tom reporting Calista missing, apparently as of sometime between two A.M., when he arrived home and looked in on the children before going to bed, and seven-fifteen that morning, when Melanie found her bed empty. Melanie had a look round the house and then awoke Tom and Jared. There seemed to have been no break-in, nor had anyone in the family seen or heard anything out of the ordinary. The previous evening the children had been out together trick-or-treating and returned home at about nine-thirty, after which they'd spent about half an hour with

Melanie's Halloween guests, before going up to their rooms. The guests—four: Calista's gymnastics coach and his wife, Calista's fourth grade teacher, and a family friend who was an educational psychologist—stayed until just before midnight.

At about noon, in a more thorough search, Calista's body had been found in the initially overlooked basement wine cellar, half-hidden behind a rack of cabernets. She had been strangled with an improvised garrote. She was fully clothed in red gym shorts, white T-shirt with a gold star on its front, and tiger-striped slippers, one half off her foot. No obvious signs of sexual molestation, but the autopsy had not been completed and preliminary findings had not been released. A broken bottle of cabernet was found on the floor close by; bits of glass had inflicted minor cuts on her legs, and the wine had stained the seat of her shorts.

The journalistic brotherhood was taking little pain to conceal its collective *schadenfreude* over Tom's turnabout position. Tom was a newsman with a fuck-you bearing and a blemished past. No, he'd been a newsman, but that term did not accurately describe his current occupation. If one admired the host of *Inside Straight*, he was the keenest of bold investigative reporters; if one didn't, he was the most abrasive of crass television hacks. Now he had become a quarry on his own preserve. A *New York Post* columnist, in a piece thinly cloaked in requisite sympathy, pointed out that since most murdered children die at the hands of their nearest and dearest, if an outsider was not arrested promptly, Tom was about to bask in some of the brightest lights of his career.

The coverage mentioned that the McQuades lived in a sprawling fourteen-room house on four acres in Westport; that Calista was an accomplished gymnast with a shelf full of trophies and Olympic aspirations, and a good student, besides; that there was an older brother with some reported school problems; that the family was in seclusion and unavailable to the media.

Oh, and that Calista had done her trick-or-treat rounds as a mermaid. A spiky, sequined headband, part of the elaborate costume made by her mother, was in place crowning her long fair hair when she died.

Suddenly, the smell of the food in the flat was pervasive and sickening. I stuffed the carryout containers back into their bags, twist tied them neatly, and walked them out the door, down the alleyway to the garbage bin at the curb. The rain was coming down steadily—the kind of unlovely rain that derives its bullying power from insistence: seeming to be without beginning or end. I stood awhile, glad to submit to its chilly sting.

CHAPTER

2

An hour later, I did what Jared asked: I just went. To abruptly pick up and go off was not on the face of it all that different from my usual mode. The way I work is, a story gets caught in my head, and if it burrows in, starts to rearrange the mental furniture, there comes a point at which I just follow after it. This moment has occurred more than once in an airport, causing a spur-of-the-moment shift in tickets—Alaska instead of Istanbul. The monkey colony that Jared liked so well captured me as I was leaving Heathrow in a minicab to go home, after a two-week shoot in Israel. I told the driver to take a U-turn and was on a Kenya Airways flight to Nairobi two hours later.

Those impulses have always been electric with possibility, and cutting through the clouds to follow them, to be surprised, has given me joy. Perhaps in that way, if in few others, I resemble my mother. She had responded to such an inner call herself once, a grandly romantic escape, only to realize, too late, that she'd taken part of what she was escaping with her. Me.

Now, at Heathrow, six in the morning, waiting for my flight to New York, the electricity was present, but in brute force: a shock to the system, overloading the circuitry, causing the brain to throb inside my skull, begging for a change of message. For good measure, the prospect of this trip made me feel like a dry drunk setting out on a pub crawl. I was giddy with fear. But I did need to go there, and not only for Jared.

Cheesy headlines shouted from the airport newsstands, pawed like insistent rug merchants hawking exclusive wares. The tabloids were settling in for a good old-fashioned ghoul-fest, reporters' knives sharpened to a fine edge to have at one of their own. But actually, Tom was not one of their own: he was a TV Yank who'd disgraced himself during his brief London stint, and who, incidentally, earned far more money than they did. So "McQuade Daughter Slain in Halloween Crown" had progressed to "Inside Straight: Was McQuade Daughter Raped?" And from there to, "Police: No Intruder Killed Calista."

I scanned a few front pages, but didn't reach for my wallet. For all the flash, they were privy to no more hard information than I'd already learned off the Web. The foamy fill was lavish speculation, and the eagerly chatty maunderings of former cleaners, disgruntled colleagues, and catty neighbors infuriated me. The photos stabbed at my innards: Calista in her gym clothes, flying through a pole vault, smiling my mother's brilliant smile. No photos of Jared, which against all reason, provided me momentary relief, as though he were safe, out of it.

Actually, absent any hyperbole, the facts themselves led down a bad road, and I knew it. No apparent break-in; the body discovered in the obscure wine cellar room (dusty bottles for the occasional fancy dinner—neither Tom nor Melanie cared for wine); Calista raped perhaps, and yet fully clothed, no obvious genital violence; strangled. Why strangled? If raped, then why redressed, except possibly by a remorseful parent? And what about that crown set just so on her head?

No *apparent* break-in, which is not to say *no* break-in (a hopeful note, if anything about this could qualify as hopeful). But I did call it hopeful, since it was the single element that might point to someone outside the family.

The boarding announcement for Flight 22 came. At the last second, shard-gathering instinct prevailed over emotion and I handed over a couple of pounds for the *Mirror, Sun,* and the rest, shouldered my backpack and computer case, and joined the queue.

Fortunately, the flight was not close to full and the seat beside me was empty.

After takeoff, I removed my boots, hunted up a couple of British Air pillows and a blanket, flipped up the center seat arm, and settled myself across the two. In normal circumstances, it's a pretty good sleeping arrangement for a person like me, one of the few advantages that comes with being abbreviated at two inches under five feet tall and two pounds shy of a hundred. But I did not think I would sleep on this trip. I was too frightened of what might visit were I unconscious and unable to resist.

When the flight attendants made their breakfast rounds, I took only a tepid tea and lay back in my improvised bunk to sip it. My eyes, burning with canned air and exhaustion, begged to shut themselves. When they did, it was neither Jared nor Tom who was behind them, but Melanie. Not the grown Melanie, not the way she was when I last saw her, but Melanie, in the time I think of as Before. She was fifteen then, the best person in my world, a world not awfully large—I was six years old.

But I was aware of a feeling for her that I did not feel for my parents. Later I would identify it as love. My mother (admittedly, it's hard to know how deeply early memories are colored by later ones) always found me a dish she hadn't ordered, but had decided gamely not to send back. My father was something short of an actual memory, more like an impression—an impression of distance, silence. In contrast, Melanie seemed to enjoy me. My inner ear recalled the ring of her ice-cube laugh as she'd swoop me up and spin round fast, making me laugh along with her.

Her tall, adept body was in constant, quicksilver motion, even when she wasn't at the gym. I could see it now, dropping to kneel on the floor beside me, as she tried to teach me the rudiments of gymnastics, how to stretch and fold myself. "You'll be the star of hide-and-seek, Allie," she said, appealing to my then passion, "if you can learn to make yourself into this tiny ball. No, honey, *this* way." My body did not move "this way" easily; though small for my age, I tended to be clumsy.

One July morning, not days after that, I awoke at some still-dark hour to hear footsteps in the hall and some shuffling noise. I opened my bedroom door a crack to glimpse my mother, wearing a gardenia-printed dress, large suitcases in both hands, carefully descending the stairs. Something, probably a zest for my favorite game, kept me from calling to her. Instead, after she'd gotten downstairs, I followed, sneaking barefoot in my nightgown, sticking close to the wall, to see what she was up to. I heard her on the kitchen phone, though she spoke softly; I picked up the words "leaving now" and "see you." I knew that leaving meant the car. When she turned her attention to some last-minute fiddling with her cases, I slipped out the laundry room door to the garage and folded myself up on the floor of the backseat, just the way Melanie had taught me.

After a while, lulled by the motion, and perhaps the dreamlike quality of the whole thing, I fell fast asleep. A sharp sound awakened me, not a moment too soon, in what turned out to be the long-term parking garage at Dulles Airport. It was the slamming shut of the driver's door.

"Mom! *Mommeee!*" I screamed, banging my fist against the window.

She stopped and stared, and for stretched seconds, considered—I swear; I saw it in her face—taking her cases and just walking away. Then, the seconds were over. She unlocked the door, grabbed me, and pulled me along—still barefoot, still in my nightgown.

An hour later, we were on a plane to Los Angeles: she and I and the man she was running off with—a tall, swarthy man called Uncle Tilt who, with his round wife, Aunt Phyllis, would come to the house for dinner, now and then. Curiously, I do remember that he wore fancier clothes than my father did, and smelled different.

At the time, I had no sense of days or weeks or months. It was simply that on a certain July Wednesday, I'd been Allie Miller, who lived with her parents and sister in Norfolk, Virginia (street address forgotten) and by Thursday, none of that was so anymore. Tilt Schwartz, my mother, and I, lived in a pink apartment somewhere in North Hollywood.

At first, the whole thing had a thrilling edge to it, except for the moments when I recalled my mother's face on finding me stowed in her car. Those aside, here was Allie, the dark little outsider, taken along on a secret vacation, while Daddy and Melanie were left at home. But after some time—days?—I wanted the vacation to be over. I cried and screamed and kicked and threw things, and was, for the first time in my life, spanked. It was Uncle Tilt's hand, quite vigorous. The surprise of it more than the pain stung me into an extended silence.

Ultimately, the vacation *was* over, having nothing to do with my wishes. Beginning to end, the interlude had lasted four months. The day he left: that was the end of Before.

"Allie, we are going to London," my mother said, as she might have announced we were going to the supermarket. "New deck of cards; new life. Now, look, you'll never be a beauty, but I think you're smart. So I hope you'll have the brains to make the most of this chance."

"Don't want this chance," I said, studying my shoes. "Wanna go home now. I want Melanie."

"Sit down. Alexis, I *said* sit down!" She pointed to the pink hassock that matched the armchair where she was sitting. I sat. "You are going to stay with me." She spoke one word at a time in the southern accent she would no doubt retain full-strength until her dying day: exotic music to which two subsequent decades of assorted well-off Englishmen had been charmed to dance. "And I am moving across the ocean. To London. No more tacky furnished rooms like this. No, sir, none of that for us! We will have a gracious home and a gracious life over there, on a lot less money than we're spending here. And we'll need to be pretty clever with money, I can tell you. Professor Leonard Miller is not precisely what's called a generous man. That's always been his problem, one of many."

"You could send me back to Melanie and go 'cross the gracious ocean yourself," I suggested hopefully. "She's big enough to mind me."

"Oh, she's big enough for a lot of things." Her voice slid round when she said that, like she was making a joke. Then it got dead serious. "But she's part of your past, understand? *Do you understand?*" I did. Oh, I did. I was a six-year-old with a past now—something that belonged to *me*. But she could grab it away and I was powerless to stop her.

She reached out for my shoulders and cupped them, as though to square them up for action. "You and me, you little scrap. You and me, we're going to be English ladies."

I realized as I got older that she had a company of stock characters waiting in the wings to be called on stage as needed: English lady, Southern belle, society decorator, canny real estate broker, helpless waif, and so on. In my Cambridge years, I summed this up as the affectations of a criminally banal woman. But it was nothing that simple. The stereotypes were indispensable to her most successful Operation Bootstrap: if she could visualize the persona, she could *be* it, quite convincingly, as long as the role remained useful.

In any case, the transition to English lady was swift and radical: a whirlwind revolution in time, place, action. The particulars of how it all happened remain an oil-slicked blur in my mind. What I do remember vividly is that I began to steal food, largely from the Chinese restaurants my mother adored. Egg rolls I tucked surreptitiously into my pockets, spareribs disappeared up my skirt into my underpants. I recall finding satisfaction in the knowledge that hours later I would savor these treats privately in my darkened room, away from her scrutiny. I couldn't have said why I was doing this odd thing, but I knew that the whole exercise helped me win some undefined game. And while I was winning, I did not miss my sister quite as painfully.

Meanwhile, my mother was busy becoming Frances Cavanaugh (her maiden name), frequent dinner guest at "good tables." She was an amusing new companion for bored Chelsea and Mayfair wives, this fine-boned American southerner, who wore a tasteful strand of pearls round the neck of her heathery cashmere and made them giggle with her quips and gossip. And she became even more amusing to their husbands, as her kisses edged over from cheek to mouth and her bottom twitched at strategic moments in a skirt cut to reveal the movement.

Under maternal instruction, "Mom" gave way to proper English "Mum," as Allie Miller was crafted into a marginally suitable accessory. Hair bobbed, spandy navy-and-white uniform with the right school emblem, I became Lex Cavanaugh, the last of the fatherly detritus jettisoned—except for the monthly child support he was bound to pay. I of course comprehended nothing of money then, but later on I came to realize that the "pittance" my mother periodically complained about was at least in part the reason I had not been packed up and sent back to Virginia. For starters, the pittance paid for a small flat at the southernmost end of Chelsea, not quite in Pimlico, just before the area began to become fashionable.

She had what her friends called "the eye," Mum did. The console table she'd picked up at Oxfam and lacquered red, the jacket on final markdown at Harvey Nic and tricked out with new buttons: whatever the item was, everyone else instantly wanted one like it, no matter that they could buy and sell her ten times over.

That's how she was able to edge into decorating other people's homes for pay.

But with the eye came standards, strict ones, that reached well beyond furniture and clothing to govern all elements of her environment. Her lovers and certainly her daughter were subject to them. In some instances, this worked well: I was sent to good schools, where I was a good student. In most other respects though, I was ill-suited to a woman of Frannie Cavanaugh's impeccable taste—abnormally small, awkward, surly, able to make the costliest outfit appear scruffy.

I had, however, inherited some of her stubborn will, which I used to hone guerrilla skills: I won only the occasional battle, but did manage to sabotage the occupying forces fairly frequently.

"You've been eating in your bed again. I want every crumb cleaned out of that room. If I see so much as one . . ."

"Smile. No, not like that. Like this. That's not funny, Lex. I swear you have zero instinct!"

"Left Cambridge? Left! Is this your idea of a joke? Ungrateful doesn't surprise me, but stupid does."

"You have betrayed my trust. I never want to set eyes on you again . . ."

The plane gave a rolling lurch—startling me out of what must have been a semi-doze. I opened my eyes and knew that the last voice I'd heard, the talk about trust, was not my mother's at all, but Melanie's. Spoken six years ago, to my back, as I walked out of her house carrying two suitcases.

A nighttime departure carrying a bag in each hand. Like mother, like daughter—except that the purloined husband had not come with me.

CHAPTER
3

I made my way from JFK to Connecticut in a rented compact, a blue one of the sort that Tom always called an old-man-in-a-peaked-cap car. He'd think up draconian punishments for the wizened drivers, traffic hazards because they crept the highway. I was a match for my car this morning, proceeding in the outside lane at fifty miles an hour, ignoring the honkers, letting the passers pass. Driving here always resembled a stage trick with mirrors at first, everything on the wrong side. And jet lag: face and limbs felt rusted over, while the eyes swam as though from a virulent allergy. When I'd been to America two years ago to film the child mediums of Montana, I had managed to avoid the east coast entirely. Now the route to Connecticut stretched out before me, at once strange and not strange enough—another reason to take it slow.

I drank from the container of cooling coffee in the dashboard beverage ring, and forced myself to eat the packaged pastry, all of it, the first food I'd had since the aborted Indian feast. Then, I turned the radio to an all-news station, which, as I'd known it would, offered Calista's murder in two-minute morsels every eight minutes.

None of it included fresh information. The police were not prepared to release detailed postmortem findings; Calista's body and clothing were being tested for traces of DNA other than her own, but results would take a while—and likely yield nothing definitive. It appeared as though she would be carrying the DNA of her family plus half of Fairfield County. She'd touched many neighbors in the course of trick-or-treat rounds, and afterward, the little mermaid had been passed from lap to lap among the group at Melanie's Halloween party.

The newsreader's tone was starchy: "According to Tom McQuade, his daughter was killed during the five-hour period between two A.M., when he last saw her, and seven A.M., when his wife found her bed empty. McQuade says he arrived home just before two from an evening spent alone, working at the brownstone apartment he keeps in Manhattan. He stopped by the children's rooms, he says, to kiss them good night, and found both in their beds asleep. His wife did not hear him come in; she was asleep, too." Translation: *McQuade: No Alibi.*

I happened to know from my three years in residence that Tom often came home quite late and did look in on the children every night, no matter how late it was. His lips brushing a small, white forehead; square, sinewy hand cupping a round, soft cheek: I'd stood beside him many times, watching, suppressing the urge—once or twice, surrendering to it—to stroke his cheek, kiss his forehead. Melanie used to blame him for making affection to his children "a dry old habit, 'bout as warm and spontaneous as brushing your teeth." His answer: "Yeah, well don't knock habit. You brush the teeth every day and, guess what? they don't go rotten."

This was one half of a lesson gleaned from Tom's own childhood, in which too much adult spontaneity had produced a chaotic patchwork of foster homes, institutions, and brief stretches with his mother, a woman always at the sharp edge of the moment. The lesson's other half was: Never strike your children. Not ever, for any reason.

There followed a series of sound bites: a police spokesman's assurance that "a statement will be issued very soon"; a neighbor's perceptions of the family (Melanie: "pleasant, but stiff—you know? Always in a rush." Tom: "one cold customer, just like on TV." Jared: "really peculiar kid—never looks you in the eye." Calista: "poise, you wouldn't believe; a real winner, that girl."); and expert commentary from the requisite retired FBI profiler ("odds are on the family—that's the first port of call in a case like this").

"Callie was a gift." A man's voice, husky. "Coaching her, shaping that talent, helping it grow . . . Well, let me say this: There was no better thing in my life—and that includes being on the 1976 U.S. Olympic Team. Callie was . . . would've been . . . I'm sorry . . ." Tears took over. So this was Vincent Anacleto, who'd been with Tom when he found Calista's body. His words were so heavily freighted with feeling that it felt mean to notice that they were mainly about him rather than Calista and to suspect that the U.S. Olympic Team, 1976, would be hauled into any subject he might be discussing, including the weather.

Next bite: "The McQuade family has no comment to

make at this time." This voice was small but authoritative. It reminded me of one of those hostess bells my mother's Mayfair friends had within toe reach at table to summon the maid.

"That," explained the newsreader, "was Rima Silverstone, Tom McQuade's television producer. We've just learned that she'll be speaking for the family." I remembered Rima. Six years ago, I hadn't liked her. Six years ago, she'd been an evening-news fact checker, not all that long out of Vassar, big-breasted and pretty and bright enough to capture Tom's attention. And six years ago, I'd been in love and jealous, with reason.

Rima continued: "They are, as I'm sure you can all understand, in shock over what's happened to Calista. They've asked me to be their public voice, for the moment, and I've agreed to do that." A clamor of reporter questions. "No. No comment right now. They're giving the police every bit of help they can. But Tom, Melanie—and Jared, too—they trust you to understand their grief and respect their privacy while they begin to mourn a little girl." Theatrical, that. Too theatrical, Rima, my friend.

Then, just as I was passing the Westchester border into Connecticut, a storm blew up inside my skull. The morning sunlight darkened, the broad ribbon of road before me blurred. The roaring sound grew louder. I jerked the wheel sharply to the right to get onto the shoulder of the highway and stopped the car fast enough to yank the top half of me forward. I sat there a long time, I think, head down, barely able to breathe.

A little girl was to be mourned. But no ordinary little girl. Calista had been a treasure, a thoroughbred being fashioned for championship; so much riding on her for Melanie, for the Anacleto man, for God knew who else.

What had it been like to be Calista? Had all those hopes and dreams inflated her for confident flight or weighed her down like a sack of stones?

Days before my departure from Connecticut, she had entertained the crowd at Melanie's dinner party singing "Stand By Your Man." Four-year-old Calista in violet velvet bell-bottoms and silver hair band, her arms stretching out toward the group of mostly adults in rehearsed gestures timed to underline key phrases of the song. Melanie accompanied her at the piano with basic chords and silently mouthed the lyrics. I'd been struck at the time by the utter femaleness of this little female—so apparent it made one believe in spiritualist talk about prior lives, old souls. One would swear she comprehended the shades of prideful melancholy in the anthem. I'd watched Tom wince at her precocious womanliness, at Melanie's obvious delight in it. Afterward, when Calista had run over to him for a congratulatory hug, he'd made it quick and silent, and then left the room.

He had been deeply uneasy with his daughter at four. Six years later . . . ?

I lifted my head and concentrated on obliterating shadowy pictures beginning to lodge themselves inside my brain. They would do no one any good. But as I started the car and pulled back onto the highway, I could not help pondering just how much time it might have taken. How long had this singular little girl had to experience terror, before someone had succeeded in choking the life out of her?

"I'M MELANIE MCQUADE'S sister." I'd repeated this to five separate cops and a private guard before I got anywhere near the front door. By the time I reached it, the phrase had become as much a mantra for me as a password into the sanctum. *I'm Melanie McQuade's sister.*

The door opened a crack. ". . . and get her out of here!" Melanie.

"No, you *can't!* I need her to—" Jared. I felt my muscles tense, ready to run to him—not that there was a chance I could get past the large policeman in my path.

"To *what?*" Melanie: like the yelp of an injured dog.

"Easy, pal. You stay put. I'll take care of it." Tom: more audible than the other two. He was inches from the partly opened door, but I couldn't see him. And then I did.

He looked worse than I might have imagined if I had let myself imagine. The vertical creases down each side of his face and the single one between his dark eyes were like three scars hacked into gray stone. But worse were the eyes themselves. They had a look that was at once wild and resigned—a predatory creature knowing it has been caught.

"So you came," Tom said. He stepped outside to join me, shutting the door firmly behind him.

"Jared." I was needing to attend to breathing. What gripped me was powerful, but whether it was love or recollected love or craven cowardice, I could not say.

"Yeah. Figured." His long, lean mouth curled up on one side, in an economical expression of bitter amusement millions of television viewers would recognize as well as I did. "Damnedest kid, isn't he?"

"I'm certain he is," I said. "I don't know him anymore, of course," which was the bleak truth. So what was I really doing here, except maybe complicating all their lives? "Oh, God, Tom. I'm . . . Melanie must be . . ." The English language surely contained appropriate words, but not ones I was able to find.

"Look, you just happened to catch us picking up some things here. Anacletos', that's where we've been staying since . . . the other day. Not a great arrangement—he's kind of an asshole and she can set your teeth grinding—but then there's not much choice. Can't be here, crime scene. Can't do a hotel or my hidey-hole in the city, no security. We'd be eaten alive—ladies and gentlemen of the press doing exactly what I'd be doing in their place."

"I gather Rima's speaking for you?"

"Seemed like the right fit. Show's on hold, she's free, I trust her."

Tom spoke as he always did, in a kind of Kansas-syncopated shorthand, which regarded articles and pronouns as largely useless. He had the sound and the look of a hybrid: cowboy crossed with newsman, both as depicted in old black-and-white films, where you knew a man's character by his jaw, his hat, and his talk. Tom didn't sport a hat, but he had the squarest of jaws and spoke in those laconic bullets. In the early years of his career, he was considered tough and fresh. After the London disaster and his switch to inquisitional television, the verdict shifted toward brash and treacherous: as it stood, the viewers still tuned him in, but the hat they saw on his head had turned from white to black.

"Jolt for Melanie," he said, "you showing up."

"The last thing she needs just now. Is that what you mean?"

"Probably. But you may be just what Jared needs, and . . ." His eyes shut. I had the idea he was going to say that he needed me, too. I hoped he wouldn't. I didn't think I could stand to hear it. "And she'll manage it."

"How is she? Managing, I mean."

He took a moment to answer. "Head's above water. Just. She's dog-paddling fast. Your sister comes through in the clutch, though. Always." I saw the corner of his mouth tick up and wondered which of several instances was in his mind. He held out a hand. I pushed myself past an inclination not to take it. I reached out to his grip and returned it with equal firmness. The sky did not fall, nor did the earth move. "Come on in, Lex," he said, looking down at our clasped hands for a moment before he opened the door.

Cartons, shopping bags, leather and canvas cases littered the large, sunny living room. People stood, sat, pointedly not talking, waiting edgily to go. Despite the opulent setting, it was somehow reminiscent of news photos we've all seen and pitied—second-tier casualties of war: a family, numb with disaster, having had to quickly select what to take, what to leave behind as they prepare to flee. My eyes, searching for Jared, found Melanie first. She sat in a green wing chair, wearing green tweed, cashmere, and pearls, a pair of fully packed Vuitton satchels at her neat, ankle-crossed feet: the best-groomed refugee in recorded history. Then I took a keener look at her face and saw that the premises behind it had already been vacated: no one at home there.

Jared stood in a far corner, tensed like a threatened fawn, ready to bolt. Just above his head was a grouping of photos of Calista: flying in mid pole vault; bent backward into a perfect semicircle; smiling in triumph, a silver winner's cup held high. No photos of Jared were in immediate evidence. I suppressed an impulse to make straight for him, fearing to scare him off. God, he was skinny and so tall! He'd grown literally like a weed, its parts not in tidy concert the way a cultivated flower develops, but every which way—ears and teeth ahead of the pack. His eyes, dark like his father's, reviewed me.

"Hello," I said foolishly.

He pointed down to a computer case on the floor beside him. "Dad got me a ThinkPad to take to the Anacletos'. I've copied everything on it already—everything important. You never know what the cops might mess round with."

"Sounds like a good idea," I said, "the laptop—the copying, too."

He moved out of his corner in my general direction. "You, uh, want to go outside?"

"Jared," Melanie said, a warning edge in her tone, "you know you can't wander round outdoors. They're all out there, guards or not, just waiting to pounce, itching to snap their pictures, shove a microphone at you."

"Mom. I just meant in the back*yard*. You've got a fence six feet high, for Christ's sake."

"Don't swear. Besides, we're leaving in a minute, aren't we, Vin?"

"Whenever you say, Melanie. We're here for *you*." It was not Vin who answered, but a woman, sturdy and majesterial in her solicitousness. Vin, all muscle, cord, and leathery tan, was obviously the 1976 Olympian, and the woman must be his wife: his rich wife. I had learned many things (wildly varied in their levels of utility) from my mother, among them to recognize a certain blend of dowdiness and self-assurance that derived entirely from seasoned money.

Melanie murmured, "Thank you, honey," but didn't look at her.

"Maybe Jared and I could . . ." I began, and knew the words would be wrong. I forced myself to walk over to my sister—not too close. "Melanie, I am so sorry." I heard my voice falter. I knew not to touch her.

She rose and smiled at me, almost a parody of the welcoming hostess. "Thank you," she said, slick as butter, making no move to touch me either. "I surely appreciate your coming. Vin, Courtney, this is my sister, Alexis, from London."

Two cops with "Crime Scene" badges round their necks appeared in the entrance hall, coming from upstairs. We all watched as they disappeared into the kitchen, most likely headed for the basement. "Go ahead, Jared," Tom said. "Take Lex out to the yard. But not too long. We need to get out of here."

"Jared," Melanie called to his back. She waited until he had turned to face her. "Remember, not too long." He pivoted fast and grabbed my hand, the gesture more for his mother's benefit than for mine, I thought.

"I didn't realize you'd be so little," he said once we were outdoors.

And I didn't realize you'd be so big, I thought but did not say. He'd spoken in a kind of jokey tone, but I sensed a note of real concern, as though he feared the protection he'd summoned would prove inadequate. "Well, I did take some tae kwon do classes last year." I had done, but not for any reason Jared would find reassuring. In fact, one morning after a bad binge, I'd awoken weak in the limbs with a visceral sense that my physical existence was vanishing. It was my alarm over this that sent me scampering to a martial arts studio in Camden Road—one floor above my favorite Indian carryout place. "I wasn't half bad, really," I said, almost truthfully. "Have you ever tried it?"

"I wanted to do karate, but Mom wouldn't let me: 'You are warlike enough, thank you.'" He had Melanie down to near perfection, accent, pitch, and all. I laughed.

"And are you?" I asked. "Hostile?"

"It's funny how you English say it—haw-*style*."

"Well, you people, you play fast and loose with our vowels, switch them round: *hah*-stl; *vye*-tamin. Remember, the language *is* called English. Anyway, technically at least, I'm an American, like you. Just look at my passport." But I could see he'd gone. For a few moments, when he was imitating Melanie, absorbed in language quirks, he was there with me: six-year-old Jared become twelve and a half. Now his face was shut down. "Jared, this is all terrifying for you."

He looked at me sharply. "Why do you say that?"

"Because your sister was murdered, because your parents are devastated, because there's so much you don't know. And they don't know," I added, perhaps more loudly than was necessary.

He stared at me and then looked down at the grass. "You mean was she raped and who killed her?" His voice gave no clue to his thoughts. But thoughts meander like water; they go anywhere at all. So, is the unthinkable what one cannot think, or what one will not think, or what one *does* think but won't own up to thinking?

"Yes," I said, "both those, of course. But I also mean knowing how you're supposed to feel, how you're supposed to *be*. In your place, I couldn't grab hold of it, and I can't imagine you can, either. The closer you are to people, the more complicated the feelings you have, not all of them good. So when something dreadful happens to . . ." When Calista was maybe a year old, I'd told Jared about sneezing out *Ihaychoo*, getting rid of it, having it over. I had to tread gingerly with him, not only because he'd just lost his sister in luridly terrifying circumstances, but because, however keenly he remembered our past, I was a stranger now. He could not possibly trust me, and was wise not to.

"We have to go inside," he said coldly. "Are you going to be staying round?"

I could have turned it back on him with a quick Do you want me to? But the question would have been unfair. More important, as a barrister I once knew briefly, but well, was fond of saying, "Never ask a key question to which you do not already know the answer." I touched his shoulder, just very lightly. "Yes, I am going to be staying round," I said.

"Want to know a fact?" he asked over his shoulder as he jogged toward the house. "Halley's comet is coming round to Earth's neighborhood again in 2061."

CHAPTER
4

I went with them to the Anacletos', about half an hour away in Southport. Melanie did not offer an objection to my joining them, though I thought I saw her readying to; the rest of the group seemed to assume I'd come along. Jared accompanied me in my pokey blue compact. Our eyes met briefly, twice perhaps, during the drive, and we talked little. I followed his lead that way, mostly answering questions about films I'd made. I reckoned he believed me about staying and therefore knew he could take his time. I felt the back of my neck chill. I realized after a moment it was damp with sweat.

As soon as we reached our destination, I was taken over and put to bed by Courtney Anacleto. There'd been a games mistress in a posh school I'd attended for two terms during one of Mum's palmier periods. I recalled her meaty hand at my back, shooing me along the field hockey ground as though I were a malingering puppy. I could feel that touch in Courtney's.

"Come on, Lex. It's sleep you need. I don't want to be inhospitable, but I'm going to insist you get some. You'll be no good to your sister or Jared if you let yourself get sick." I considered punching her jaw, though to do that, I'd have had to ask her to lean down and let me reach it. The truly annoying thing was, Yankee bray, heavy hand, and all, she was right—as bossy people too often are. "Now, you're going to march upstairs, young lady." I do get spoken to like a child rather more often than taller thirty-two-year-olds. "You'll thank me for it later."

As in fact I had reason to, because I slept soundly and, to my knowledge, dreamlessly for many hours. I awoke early the next morning and took some time muddling through to why I happened to be lying under a cedar-fragrant patchwork quilt peering at a triangulated dormer window. One's first waking moments are defenseless, the body assuming that a good sleep in a comfortable bed has put the world to rights, so when the reason for my pleasant surroundings clubbed me, the blow hit extra hard.

Here was how the day went. Tom had left for the city early; I did not see him. Courtney was in and out of the house on various errands, and Vin spent most of his time working out in his basement gym. The remaining three of us, by tacit agreement housebound, performed a kind of ballet: Jared and I drawing intermittently close; he and Melanie huddling briefly, then abruptly breaking apart; Melanie and I whirling and stretching as much as necessary to stay out of each other's way.

The ringing phone was constant punctuation, the maid fielding the calls. Most of them were for Melanie, and mostly she refused them, except for several from Tom. Not long after one of these, we happened to be in the same section of downstairs hallway. She came toward me fast, white-faced, so deep in her thoughts she failed to see me, then stumbled as our bodies brushed. When I reached out a hand automatically to steady her, her arm drew back as though preparing to deliver a slap, but dropped to her side instead. "I am *fine*," she said. I think I began to say something, but whatever that might have turned out to be, she would not have heard it. She was up the stairs, gone.

I saw no television sets round the house; no newspapers were in evidence either (confiscated, I suspected, by Courtney for the greater good—and again, perhaps she was right). During the hours Jared and I browsed the Web together on his new ThinkPad, we stuck to astronomy sites, picking up tidbits about a new comet due to streak by in several weeks—brighter than Halley's, it was to be; perhaps brighter than the recent Hale-Bopp, as well. If Jared clicked into news, he did it when he was alone—as I did. Periodically, in the privacy of my dormer room, I hooked cell phone into laptop and scrolled round. No new answers (the police were not releasing autopsy reports, so the matter of rape, among others, remained unresolved), but some new questions—among them, why were the McQuades "stonewalling" the police? Why had they engaged legal counsel: separate legal counsel? In a brief press conference, Rima maintained that Tom and Melanie were continuing to offer "every cooperation" to the police, and that legal counsel was a "formality" to cope with "multiple technicalities."

Jabberwocky-speak. Christ, why didn't she simply say that the justice system was run by coppers and lawyers, and since the McQuades were neither, they needed a tour guide—an interpreter? But almost immediately, I knew that my improved statement was no improvement at all, merely disingenuous blather. Tom had engaged lawyers for only one reason: He and Melanie were suspects. And the longer it took for credible alternative suspects to turn up, the more intense the pressure would become. That sweat again at the back of my neck. It's the way my particular organism insists that I acknowledge fear: a boggy wetness hidden behind a dark curtain of hair. What, I asked myself, if there weren't other suspects?

I AM GOOD at waiting, and long accustomed to it. That first sharp smack on the bum from my so-called uncle introduced a Pavlovian conditioning; sharper flicks from my mother's tongue furthered the training. I learned that I was powerless to affect my environment; I learned that straightforward assertion, complaint, rage, called down pain. And so I developed patience: a watchful, lizardly patience that, as it happens, has proved indispensable in making the sort of films I make. Wait and watch, blend into the landscape while you do it. People will unfold before your eye, letting you record what is true. But the landscape I'd placed myself in now was a minefield—waiting came hard, and my eye refracted what it saw through too much history.

At about four, I went downstairs and sat in a conservatory room at the rear of the house, looking out on a walled garden. It was a beautiful room, huge and bright even in the fading late afternoon sunlight. It was filled, as the rest of the house was, with old, good furniture—each stick of it standing with unassuming grace, likely in the precise spot where it had stood when Courtney grew up here. My mother had aspired for most of her life to get her hands on such a house and never did, except briefly when we moved in with some pinhead of a lord who'd inherited a spread in Surrey. But he shrieked like a hyena if she so much as rearranged a chair. Mum lived now, and had for the past seven years—quite happily, according to her occasional letters—in a trim condo in Sydney, Australia, with a view of the water and a virtually penniless young lover. She was "glad to be free," she'd written me on a picture postcard, "of all that stuff!" Things change.

Vin Anacleto jogged into the room, wearing fresh khakis and T-shirt, smelling of soap and lotion, his close-mown hair damp. He perched on the rolled arm of a blue sofa, catercorner to my chair, and leaned in at me. Vin, I'd noticed, wasn't much of a sitter. He tended to prop his taut arse on the edges of things briefly, between bouts of pacing.

"Callie would've qualified nationally this year in a walk," he said, as though picking up a conversation in its middle. His eyes had not shared the refreshment benefits of his shower; they looked red-rimmed and sore. "I told Melanie, I said, this year's her year—ten years old and we go for national." His large hand made a washing motion across plummy lips. "Oh, Christ. Christ. Christ. Christ."

"Had you been coaching Calista a long time?" I asked gently.

"Two and a half years." The energy returned to his voice. "And it was a good thing I got hold of her then, believe it! She was getting into some bad habits. I mean *bad*. You know, breaking a run-up off short, sloppy spotting. If she kept that going, she was gonna wind up with a broken leg—or worse." No touch of irony in the man, not a corpuscle in the entire body beautiful.

"And how did you happen to get hold of her?"

"Courtney, of course." I raised my brows in question. "Hey, it's Courtney's world. We're just here so she can help us across the street, even when we don't want to go. No, no, only kidding," he rushed to add. "Court's a good girl; great instincts, you know? Well, Court met Melanie, who was having serious doubts—and rightly so—about that putz who was coaching Callie then. See, Melanie knows her way round a gym. She had an Olympic dream or two herself, as a kid." His hands reached out at me, palms up. "Jesus, look who I'm telling about Melanie—like you didn't know." Rump up off sofa arm, pacing resumed.

"You could probably tell me a lot about Melanie," I said. "We haven't been what you might call close." Sometimes you have to prime the pump. "We grew up apart, after our parents divorced."

He lit on the edge of a tawny maple table and smiled engagingly. "One thing about us gymnasts, we're good at sticking a foot in our mouths." Well, perhaps an ironic corpuscle. He waited for me to smile back, and I did. "The truth is, until you showed up, I didn't know Melanie had a sister. Not a lot of family resemblance—and of course the different accents." Up and ready for motion.

"So, tell me about my sister," I said.

"I could do that for hours. Gorgeous, smart, strong. Hey, she wasn't strong, he'd flatten her like a pancake. But she doesn't give him an inch."

He'd got that right: not an inch. They had their deal, Melanie and Tom, and I used to fancy I knew what it was: Two people abandoned as children had built themselves a shelter called home and made a blood oath to stay there, even though its boards were splintered and its roof let in the rain. It took some time after my affair with Tom was over for it to dawn that there was more between them than that. I remained unsure of precisely what, but it was something to do with causing and braving pain. I had nothing I cared to say to Vin on the subject, so I gave him a vague nod.

"Ask Court and she'll tell you I've got a crush on Melanie," he said. "Her idea of a joke—well, at least partly a joke. But, see, I'm a very affectionate guy, Lex, which Court doesn't always understand. I'm physical, you know? That's what athletes are: body people. Hell, she used to say I had a crush on Callie." He stopped his walking, let out a long breath, and turned away from me. "Jesus," he mumbled, and shoved his hands into his pockets.

"Calista was an especially . . . appealing child," I said carefully, willing him to show me his face. I looked at his fists clenching and unclenching themselves inside the cloth. It wasn't hard to imagine those large hands on her small, flexing body—molding its form, guiding its motion. Had his pulse quickened as he'd spread her thighs, cupped her buttocks?

Then he did face me. "Hey, look, Callie and I . . . She was an athlete; I was her coach. That's about as close as two people get. It's like you breathe together, okay? Thirty years ago, it was me and my coach—and that bond was what put me into the '76 Olympics. Melanie understood perfectly, because she was a gym rat for a couple of years herself when she was a kid. She knew what it was for Callie and me: *athlete* and *coach*; period, the end." The olive of his complexion looked a bit darker. He was blushing. I wondered whether the police had broached this line of questioning with him yet, or whether he was gearing up for the day they would. It was hard to look him in the eye and hope that he had murdered his star pupil, but I realized I was doing exactly that.

"You and Courtney," I said, sensing that he'd jog himself out of the room if the subject didn't take a benign turn, "did you meet during your . . . Olympic period?"

"Nah. Long time later. I broke my leg in '77. It never was really right after that, not right enough for Olympic competition. No, I met Courtney, summer of '83. I was a tennis pro up in Newport. That's where her family went summers. Poor Portagee stud; moneybags Southport lady. Bet you think that's why I married her."

"Is it?"

He returned to the sofa arm where he'd first perched. "Beats the hell out of me." Suddenly, he laughed. "At the time I'd've said we got married because she wanted to so bad there was nothing I could say except yes. But, hey"—he held out his arms like a tenor ready to try the high note—"I *like* all this, can't say I don't."

Jared appeared at the door and stood there, one thin leg crossed round the other in the aimless, edgy stance of a child who doesn't know what to do with himself. It had been, what?, four days since Calista's death, not even. There were autopsy results as yet unknown, a body as yet unreleased for burial. Meantime, the family was interned—parrying, waiting. And Jared had been sentenced to solitary confinement while the world finished collapsing about his ears, however long that took. "How would you like to go for a ride and find some pizza?" I asked him. His eyebrows rose, giving his face a lift. "That'd be good," he said.

"You know, Lex," Vin said, "it's not my business exactly, but that may *not* be good. Melanie won't like him going out, wandering round." I knew that as well as he did, and didn't care. This was jail, luxurious, but still jail. Jared needed a break; so did I.

"I'll take responsibility," I said. "We won't be long."

A couple of cameras snapped and whirred as we left, a few questions were called at us. "Keep your head down, and don't speak," I'd instructed Jared. Once in the car, nobody followed, as far as I could tell. And what if a *paparazzo* or two had? Their prize would be photos of us eating pizza, is what. Jared knew a place not far from the beach; that's where I headed.

"You know about this English guy Rupert Sheldrake, Lex? He did a bunch of experiments with homing pigeons, like moving their base miles and miles away. But the pigeons always knew."

"Sheldrake called it morphic resonance, Jared. The pigeons communicate instantly through a kinship of pigeonness—pigeonality—no one knows quite how. It permeates the atmosphere if you're a pigeon; perhaps it has to do with common experience and trust."

He let a beat go by. "I like *pigeonality* better than *pigeonness*," he said.

"What do you think about trust?" I knew it was a risk.

"Don't go there." I didn't; I shut up. "I think it's bullshit," he said after a moment.

And why would he not? "Well then, tell me more about Sheldrake and his pigeons." He did, at length, pausing for a gulp of breath now and again. So bright and so scared. I wanted to stop the car, hold him very tight, promise him that he'd be all right in the end no matter what else wasn't. But I couldn't tell him that lie, so I kept driving and let him keep talking.

By the time we returned, perhaps two hours later, he'd switched from Sheldrake and resonant pigeons to Stephen Jay Gould and apes with opposable thumbs. Somewhere along the line I'd joined in and found my own spirits lifting as I told him about working with

Gould, how he would plunge into talking of American baseball, the New York Yankees, with the same vigor he brought to his other passions.

"You mean you did another monkey film, one with *Gould* in it?" Jared asked.

"I did, yes. My last, I've just finished the editing. You'll hear Gould's voice, actually, just for a three-minute cut. Otherwise, no humans, only the apes. We shot it in Brazil, the Rain Forest. Oh, you'd love the Rain Forest, Jared. It's fascinating and spooky. It reminded me of eternity, and so naturally it reminded me of you. Do you remember that first time we met? Your mother took you into Fortnums to buy sweets."

"I don't know if I really remember it, or if I just remember you telling me about it when I was a little kid. But my mom and dad don't talk about the England time. We were living there, right?"

"Briefly. Your dad was on assignment for the network, and your mother . . ." I didn't want to skirt it, ". . . was pregnant with Calista. Melanie and I hadn't seen each other for more than fifteen years."

"And you recognized her?"

"Oh, yes. She'd been everything to me until I was six." We acknowledged the parallel by not acknowledging it. "I wouldn't be likely to forget her."

"Then how come you didn't see her for fifteen years?"

"When I was growing up, my mother wouldn't let me. And later . . . Well, I'd had a rough time at Cambridge, and then dropped out. I wasn't in very good shape then" (an understatement: I'd been in a full-fledged state of bulimia, gorging and purging almost daily), "and I was far too ashamed of myself to go on the hunt for Melanie. You know, 'Hello, here's your long-lost sister, barely holding herself together, tricked out in a serving maid costume, scooping preserved fruit at Fortnums.' So, unless one believes in fate, it was a huge coincidence, the two of you marching in there."

"Do *you* believe in fate?" he asked seriously.

"I think not. But then, strange things do happen— like a funny kid turning up wanting to know about eternity and infinity." It filled my heart to see him grin. He *would* look like Tom, once his features had caught up with each other. I was about to say this, but I recalled the raw, diffuse guilt I had seen in Tom's eyes, and it occurred to me that the resemblance might not turn out to be a blessing for Jared.

"Do *you* believe in fate?" I asked him back

"Yes," he said, the heaviness back in his voice.

"It was not your sister's fate to die that way, Jared. A person killed her; a person who will be caught and punished."

"You don't *know* that," he said furiously. "What makes you think you know anything?"

"You're right. I don't know anything," Pause. "Do you?" I tossed it up like a shuttlecock, half hoping it would fall straight down.

"No," he mumbled. I glanced over and saw the back of his head. He was turned away, huddled close against the door, as far from me as he could manage.

WHEN WE GOT BACK to the house and Melanie opened the door to us, I expected a severe scolding, which I was prepared to counter with cool reason. All I got was an icy appraisal over Jared's bent head, as she hugged him to her hard enough to make him squirm, asking his cowlick, "You okay, honey?"

"I'm fine, Mom, *fine*," he said, the tight-voiced mimic

of her inadvertent this time. "Lex was telling me about her new ape TV movie. Could we get a tape, do you think?" He meant, I understood, to let her know that I had overstepped no bounds during the illicit outing—to shield me from her anger. Another weight on those bony shoulders.

"Sure we can," I said. "We'll have to have it converted so it'll play on an American set, but sure. I'll call about it tomorrow."

"We've already sat down to dinner," was all Melanie said.

A man joined us in the entrance hall, coming from the direction of the dining room. "Hi," he said, holding out a hand to me. "Nate Grumbach." He had a good handshake, firm but not crushing, and a creased, irregularly pouched face that reminded one of an unmade bed—a friendly unmade bed, the sort you'd like to curl into and read the Sunday papers. An iron gray thatch, thick as a summer lawn, covered his head. He was perhaps sixty, but exuded an energy that was ageless.

I recalled his name from the papers: one of the small Halloween group at Melanie's the eve of Calista's death. "I'm a friend of Mel's," he said in a voice richly textured with New York gravel. "And of Jared's," he added, thick gray-black brows raising, while his eyes, their irises dark as the pupils, fixed on Jared. "How are you, Jared?"

"Okay." I watched Jared edge toward the stairs. He had that fawn-about-to-bolt stance again. "We just had pizza; I'm full," he said to his mother. "I don't want any dinner." And bolt he did.

CHAPTER
5

I pushed some overcooked pork roast, potatoes, and green beans round a pretty plate and took in the scene. There were five of us—Courtney, Vin, Nate, Melanie, and me—dotted round a mahogany table that could have accommodated twenty. Nobody said much; nobody other than the Anacletos ate much. Even in less dreadful circumstances, conversation would have been impeded by having to project one's voice like a stage performer. Courtney asked me whether my jet lag was over, and I told her it was, thanks. Vin asked Melanie if her back felt better, and she said it was fine, thanks.

"So, you're in television, Lex?" Nate asked across the ten-foot diagonal that separated us. "Does that make you and Tom colleagues?" The question was bland enough, but something in his tone, or in my blemished soul, convinced me that Melanie had given him a more specific idea of Tom's and my relationship.

"No," I said. "I've nothing to do with news. I make films—very small ones."

"Ah." He nodded as though having registered something significant.

"Yes," Courtney chimed in, "Lex's films would strike a professional chord with you, Nate. Some of them are about people who could really profit from therapy." She chuckled loudly: the games mistress promoting team spirit.

His smart eyes smiled at me. "That would cover almost everyone, or almost no one," he said, "depending on your point of view. Some think the only ones who profit from therapy are the ones who cash the checks." A close enough approximation of my own point of view—which I was certain he must know. In fact, I felt that Nate Grumbach recognized me, knew me to a depth he couldn't possibly. My own reaction was quite uncharacteristic: I found being known by him rather comforting.

Melanie turned her head side to side gingerly, as though testing a movement that hurt. Then her hand went to her mouth to cover a wide yawn. Nate moved quickly down table, not rising, but sliding his bottom from chair to chair to chair until he was beside her. It was a kind of comic turn, an ironic comment on the size and population of the banquet table. And it was funny, without being in the least offensive. He clasped Melanie's shoulder and then began to massage the back of her neck. Her head dropped forward to receive his touch; she didn't bother to mask the next yawn. "Atta girl," he said softly. "I know it's early, but why don't you do something good for yourself? Go on up to bed."

"Mmmm," she mumbled. "Can't go to sleep yet, though; Tom's coming back later. We need to talk."

"Tom's idea of 'later' is elastic and you know it," Nate

said. "Suppose you talk in the morning? Come on, Mel, you're dead on your feet."

She laughed. The sound of it was desolate. "Don't I just wish?" She blew out a long breath. "You're right, as usual. I couldn't swallow another bite of food. Walk me up?"

"You got it," he said. His eyes scanned the table as his fingers continued to work at Melanie's neck. "Excuse us. I'll be back in a little while. When you pour the coffee, Courtney, I'd thank you for saving me a cup."

"I'll save you several," she said. We wished Melanie a good sleep, and they left—my brokenhearted sister and a warm-blooded man from whom she was willing to accept comfort. "He's an unusual man," Courtney said to me, after the footfalls had faded. "I like him, myself. I like him very well, but he does have that . . . side to him. Sometimes, you feel he's laughing at you."

"That's because he is," Vin said flatly. "And maybe we deserve it."

"But be honest, you don't care for it, Vin dear," she said. "It bothers you more than it does me. You shut up like a clam when Nate's round. At least you do recently." She sighed deeply. "I'm not sure what I even mean by 'recently.' Lord, time has become so tricky since it happened! Four days; five? It seems like months ago—but sometimes, only hours. And then it feels as though there'll be no ending. Ever." For a moment, I quite liked Courtney, but knew that was bound to pass the next time she brayed out an edict.

"Is Nate Melanie's psychotherapist?" I asked carefully. *Lover* was the word on my mind, but not of course on my tongue.

"No," Vin said, a bit sharply, I thought. Was I hearing the beat of simple sexual jealousy or of something more complex? Fear of Nate's high-beam insight? With some effort I forced myself to admit that I just might be overscrutinizing Vin Anacleto, self-identified body person. "He used to be Jared's shrink. But that's over."

"And a pity it is," Courtney added, her confidence back in force. "He was doing Jared a world of good. His specialty is children with learning disabilities—and of course all the psychological problems that accrete on top of the disability."

"What part of Jared's learning is considered disabled?" I asked, feeling the blood of combat rise to my cheeks. "He's possibly the brightest child I've ever met."

"Nobody denies that!" Courtney said. "But the child obviously has *issues*. He has never performed anywhere near his potential in school, hardly bothers handing in assignments. And he's far from easy at home." She raised her fingers one by one to tick off Jared's faults. "Taciturn, sarcastic, prone to tantrums—not all that often, but severe is my impression." The three fingers went down, and then back up, this time standing for, "Oppositional disorder, attention deficit disorder, hyperactive disorder: some combination of those, I'd guess. I've never gone into the specifics with Melanie, and Nate of course is the soul of professional discretion. But I can tell you that in addition to everything else, Jared could not have found it easy to be Calista's brother. Though you could never say such a thing to Melanie, of course."

I was unacquainted with the disorder triplets, which to my ear rang of late coinage, but I had no quarrel with the last part of her ad hoc diagnosis—except perhaps hearing it from someone who considered Jared a mental case. I cast my eyes down at the starched white cloth and tried to effect a short-term separation from him. Without a bit of distance, *I* would be learning disabled, tripped up every step of the way, as I trod on my own emotional toes.

"Nate was able to . . . uh . . . help Jared?" I asked.

"Oh, yes," Courtney said, her voice charging with enthusiasm. "Definitely. Only about three months, stem to stern, but the difference was remarkable. The child actually took exams, did homework—Melanie herself told me."

"Court was the one who arranged the whole thing," Vin said, giving me a look meant to remind me that arranging things was her specialty, and noteworthy.

"Yes," she said, taking her cue with no reluctance, "Nate's a consultant to our school system here in Southport. I'm on the board; I head the Learning Disabilities Task Force, so I've had occasion to work closely with him. I'd stopped by Melanie's one afternoon and happened to see Jared in one of his . . . episodes. The issue was homework. At any rate, he shattered a flow blue bowl, one his mother particularly liked, needless to say. So, I thought: Nate Grumbach—why, he even lives in Westport, no more than five minutes away from them."

"But the therapy stopped," I said. "Why, if it was going so well?"

"That's a question, isn't it?" Courtney's tone was its own underline. "Jared suddenly just refused. Of course, I don't know for certain why, but if you were to ask me"—as I just had—"I believe it might relate to how very close Nate and Melanie became."

"That's horseshit, Court!" Vin's palm slapped the table hard enough to make his place setting give a glass-jingling jump. "Couldn't you stop after 'I don't know'? Can't you *ever* just do that? Because sometimes you *don't* know!"

"I seem to have stepped on a corn," Courtney said with a tight smile.

Footsteps came down the stairs—a slow, subdued pace, not the tread of the Nate Grumbach I had met. When he came back into the dining room, his face had lost its animation and settled into a wattled sadness. "I think she'll sleep for a while."

"We've waited the coffee for you, Nate. I'll have Tonya bring it now," Courtney said. "Come, sit down." She patted the chair seat beside her.

"You know," he said, "I'm going to back out on you. My apologies, but I feel kind of beat myself. I need to get home." He turned to me. "I'm glad you're here, Lex." Words from his mouth were intensely flavored with meaning, stimulating my appetite for them. "I'd like it very much if you found the time to pay me a visit. Courtney'll give you my number. Good night all."

NOT SO LONG AFTER, I retreated to my room, where I booted up for a look at the late news and saw nothing but rehash frosted with blather. Then, as they will do, my cell phone dropped into a coma and kicked me off-line. I turned off the laptop and crept under the quilt too sapped of energy suddenly to remove my jeans or shirt. I wondered whether I'd hear Tom when he came in—if he came in. I pictured his face fuzzed round the edges like an old photo, and realized that it *was* an old photo I was seeing: a London *Times* headshot, circa 1989, that went with a feature on the American who'd just been appointed his network's London bureau chief . . .

THE MCQUADES LIVED in Hampstead, in a Tudor-style house. "Not anything like fixed up yet, but I am *learning*," Melanie had said to me, laughing as she led me from pretty room to pretty room. That ice-cube laugh rang, incredibly, with the same vibrancy I'd remembered. "I'm a sight, though. Just look at me, pregnant out to here, dashing three-minute miles from auction to auction." *As Mum used to do.*

I laughed back, recognizing that she must be nervous, too. It had been one thing, sharing the euphoric shock of yesterday's unlikely meeting at Fortnums: me staring across the counter at the stylish blonde in the perfect maternity dress—answering her "Miss, can you help me with the stuffed apricots?" with an almost voiceless, "Melanie?" But it was quite something else to be here on her turf, by appointment, down off the spontaneous high, uncertain of what should come next for us.

I jittered inside my skin, burning with shame at who I was: a twenty-two-year-old university dropout who spent her days gift-wrapping preserved fruits and too many of her evenings gorging on curry in an East End bed-sit imagining how she would film this creature she had become—wondering between gulps whether or not she was real.

What I did not understand, certainly not that first evening at Melanie's, was how essential my sorry state was to any reunion with her. I was balm to my sister's mother-inflicted wounds, a reflecting mirror for her victories. Had I been a fellow Fortnums' shopper in a well-tailored suit, smart briefcase hanging from my shoulder, rather than a serving girl, things would have ended right there. After half an hour, she would have kissed my cheek and taken her leave with promises of a phone call, never to be placed.

"Where's Daddy?" Jared asked. "He said we could look at stars through the telescope." Even at three, Jared had been fascinated by the stars—how far away they were, why we could see their shine, what kept them up there without falling. His curiosity was voracious about all sorts of things. I was quite mad about him.

"No stars tonight; it's raining. But he'll be here soon, pumpkin," Melanie said. "Now, stop playing with those potato chips; no one'll want to eat them with your hands all over them. Jared, I said *stop!* A drink, Allie? Oh, I do have to remember, you're *Lex* now, you said. God, Tom's work hours are un*real!*"

"I don't mind if you call me Allie," I lied. I minded very much. My old name prompted the ache that had keynoted my childhood. I wanted to cry; I wanted to eat—and could let myself do neither. "I'd love a drink," I said.

She drank bourbon and I joined her. An hour later: no Tom. Jared, protesting that stars were *too* still there when it was raining, had been put to bed with assurances of telescope tomorrow, and one from me about a boat ride up to Greenwich.

When we were alone, drinks freshened and refreshened, I pumped my courage up and asked, "Melanie, how is . . . could you tell me about Dad?"

"He died two years ago." Then her mouth clamped tight, a little dimple appearing at the left corner of it. That dimple, I was to learn, meant "no trespassing."

The information floored me to a degree beyond logic. My recollection of the man was less than sketchy. What was he to me, after all, but an idea labeled "Father"? And not even an idea I'd recently considered. A virtual stranger has died, I told myself. Is it more than a conceit to fancy I miss him? Half of me was so deeply absorbed by this question, that it did not know the other half was about to speak. I heard my voice seconds before realizing it belonged to me. "Mum's alive and kicking," it said, "anything within foot's reach."

Alcohol and pent-up emotion can hoist one to pinnacles of insensitive stupidity.

"*Mum?* Can't you cut all that English *crap!*" She shot up from her chair and stood towering over me. I looked up at her, feeling like a misbehaving seven-year-old, punished for the wrong offense. Then Melanie stepped back, her face softening a bit. "Oh, Allie, 'course you can't. It's the way you talk, isn't it?"

"Shit, I'm sorry for being so thick! It was a surprise to hear about . . . him. And of course I know how you must feel about . . . our mother."

"Look," she said, a small, tight smile fixed in place. "You don't know how I must feel about *your* mother, and I'm not gonna discuss it. As far as I am concerned, she is dead—as dead as my daddy. Deader. That's it. Now, if you and I are gonna be friends or sisters or whatever, I don't want to hear about her. Not a word."

I nodded the way one does when one means the opposite. "Do you . . . Might I see a photo of him?" I asked.

"There are no photos," she said flatly. "And I prefer not to talk with you about that subject, either." Which effectively embargoed discussion of all but the rather recent past.

But I had found my sister, and was determined not to lose her again. So the protests caught in my craw were washed down with the next bourbon, which helped me soldier on, trying to amuse with anecdotes about growing up English—all of them heavily edited to excise mention of Mum. It was a bit like displaying an album of photos with one central face carefully snipped out of each group shot. For me, it had the depressing effect of underscoring how influential my mother had been at every turn of what I called my life.

Melanie held up her end by telling me that after her second year at university, she too had dropped out. ("May not've been the brightest thing I ever did." An arpeggio of laughter. "But I was so impatient to get on with things!") She'd become a flight attendant, rising in record time to head stewardess in the first-class cabin, which was how she'd met Tom.

"It was kind of romantic, really. He was right behind me in the security-check line at JFK, and we started chatting and it turned out he was on my flight. When I told him I served first class, he went and upgraded, out of his own pocket. Now, he couldn't really afford the first-class ticket, you know. I mean he had this great reputation from being a reporter in Vietnam and all, but no real money yet. But then, here's the kicker, he *slept* through most of the flight, so he hardly knew I was there!

"Finally I woke him up. I said, 'Sir, I do apologize, but I can't permit you to fly my cabin to Paris without taking a glass of champagne.' I made him laugh, see. That wasn't easy."

At almost ten, she went ahead and put dinner on the table without him, and nary a complaining word. Instead, she chatted up his brilliance, his intensity, his drive for success. Yet, at the same time, with a word here, an eye roll there, she half deprecated precisely what she was praising. The implicit wink in her undertone said, "Of course he's a little silly, stubborn, selfish; we know how men are and that is our upper hand." This was music I'd grown up hearing. I hadn't liked my mother's rendition, and hearing the same tune from Melanie thrummed a sour note.

Suddenly, in mid-sentence, she rose and ran from the room, like a highly trained dog responding to a whistle beyond my hearing—in this case, a key turning in a lock.

"*You could have called.*" The hiss of angry whispers carries well. I heard Melanie's from the entrance foyer, never mind walls and carpets. Yet, a moment later, as she pulled him into the dining room, her voice was bright, if hyper-southern with nerves and drink. "This is my li'l sister, Allie, Tom." She stood close beside him, her hand forming an epaulet on his shoulder. "You 'member, dahlin," she said. "I told you, Jared and I found her behind a *candy* counter in Fortnums."

"Hi, li'l sister," he said, flat and sharp-edged as a skimming stone. Black Irish, slim, and no taller than Melanie, he sent a certain power charge into the air. I can't claim to have known that the fossil fuel at its core was rage, but I do believe I sensed it. Rage and I have had a closer than nodding acquaintance.

I stood, swaying a bit, as his dark eyes took my measure and kept their own counsel. I managed a return "Hi," swallowed hard, and tasted bourbon trying to rise back up in my throat. I felt in the dock, hauled before a judge and ordered to explain myself, following which, I would be weighed up, likely found wanting. "I left Cambridge, you see," I said, the words falling out like a cascade of beach pebbles. "Just packed up and left. I wasn't doing all that well there, farting away my time, barely hanging on to a second, but still . . . It's not even as though I had a grand alternative plan—just damned moviemaking fantasies and nasty habits! The only satisfaction in the whole fiasco was seeing my mother's face when I told her. So, that's the lot: I've fucked up my life." My hand rushed to my mouth to stifle a potentially dangerous belch and, when that crisis passed, reached down to the table for the cut crystal glass half full of bourbon. I raised it in his direction. "Cheers, then!"

"Like to hear about the damned movie fantasies sometime," he said with a faint smile that spoke of suspended sentence, if not reprieve. "Not tonight, though. You're going to bed now, li'l sister." His tone roughened up. "And you, too, Mother of the Year." Abruptly, he stepped away from Melanie, dislodging her hand from his shoulder. "Christ, you *wanted* this baby, remember? Are you trying to get it born without ears or knees?"

And Melanie didn't say a word, just smiled her shiny smile, tears brightening her already bright eyes, while she braved the humiliation. Or so it had seemed.

I leapt like an impaired d'Artagnan to her defense. "We may be shit-faced drunk, but you're a real bastard, aren't you? Do you treat the population at large this badly, or do you reserve it especially for your wife?"

His head cocked a bit to one side as he nodded. "Yes to all that. Yeah, guess I do store a supply of proprietor's reserve for her. Unfortunately, there's plenty to go round. Tell you what, let's all get to bed and wake up perfect in the morning."

We did all go to bed. Two visits later, I brought my backpack and satchel of belongings from the East End squat and came to live with them. It was Tom who proposed it, and in fact the arrangement suited us all. It suited exceedingly well . . .

Now I ROLLED myself tight inside the quilt and wept—for them, for me; for then, for now; for illusions shattered, for hopes realized: I wept what Virgil called the tears of things. But mostly I wept for Calista, on the brink of life that night, dead this one.

And not by Tom's hand. Surely not. Please, not!

CHAPTER
6

I heard the crunch of gravel under car wheels. I had not been quite asleep, just lying there, never having got round to undressing—staring at the ceiling, face sore and swollen from the unaccustomed tears, trying to find some vantage point from which to make out the shape of this tragedy.

I got out of bed and went to the window. Tom emerged from the passenger's side and a dark-haired woman from the driver's. The woman was Rima Silverstone, spokeswoman *extraordinaire*. My watch said it was just shy of four A.M. I hurried into the loo, then gave my face and mouth an icy wash and stole silent and barefoot down the stairs. An impulse, certainly: some might say I had never lost my child's taste for hide-and-seek. But the game here seemed more reminiscent of blindman's buff, and I was consumed with an urgency to see. Something. Anything would do, so long as the damned kerchief came off my eyes.

I heard them settle themselves in the kitchen, which was connected through a butler's pantry to the dining room. I entered the pantry this way and crouched, knees to chest, beneath a butcher-block countertop, safely hidden by its depth and shadow. For what seemed endless moments, I listened to the sounds of coffee in the making. Then finally, Rima:

"However we slice and dice, we come back to the same place. You didn't like my last statement. So you didn't; I'm sorry. But what else could I have said? The fact is you've lawyered up—you and Melanie both—as you had to do under the circumstances. The media know that damned well; they're not stupid. But they're playing to the stands, and the folk out there get suspicious when grieving parents do anything but grieve. I just tried to give the thing a little spin back our way. Look, Tom, you have to give them something to satisfy—"

"No, *you* look, Rima. I don't have to give them shit. I've got to protect my own—and I've sure done a superb job of that so far." The scorn-tipped dart was one of Tom's most potent weapons. His aim was no more forgiving of his own skin than anyone else's. "Now, here's the drill: I will retain *twenty* lawyers, standing on each other's shoulders, if that's how many it takes to build a wall for us. We will move to Arizona, or Oregon, or Liechtenstein or the South fucking Pole."

"Tom, no! You're coming at it wrong. There is nowhere to hide. Running won't work, even if the police would let you right now, which they won't—and being that cavalier about the media may help get your rocks off, but you know how self-defeating it is. For God's sake, you're *one* of them!"

"Right—exactly why I know not to give the bastards half an inch."

"But by the time the sun is up they'll know about the FBI consultants being called in—polygraphs and profilers and the whole schmear. So how high can you build your wall?"

"You don't get it. They are going after Melanie now, the cops and the Feebs. And they can't have her!"

Melanie? My breath caught in a gasp loud enough to hear, were anyone listening. Melanie?

"What are you saying, Tom?" Rima asked, with an insinuating twang. "That *you* think she did it?"

It sounded like the crack of a rifle: palm slashed cheek, confirmed by the yelp of pain, which immediately followed. Then nothing. "I don't need your smartass mouth," he said after some time.

"Sorry," said Rima, sounding suddenly very young.

"Me, too," he said, almost inaudible from where I was sitting. "Want out? You should. Guy belts you, you run the other way is what you do, if you have any sense. You ought to do that anyhow. What do you need this for?"

"I don't have any sense, Tommy. All I have is the way I feel about you. That's what I need this for." Why is it that everyone's most heartfelt love talk sounds as trite as everyone else's, and all of it like a lift from some old film? Been there; done that—yes, indeed, I had. No sound. I deserved to be slapped harder than Rima for wondering whether they were mending their tiff with a kiss.

"Don't, Rima." Tom's voice, ragged as ripped canvas. "Just knock it off. Don't you understand? I can't pat your head, dry your tears—or take you to bed. None of it matters to me now. It's chickenshit, all of it." Another long pause, punctuated by clicks of crockery: cups refilled.

"So, where do we go from here?" She sounded restored: a brisk Noo Yawk gal, notepad in hand, taking a meeting—or perhaps that's the other coast. "Not us personally," she hurried to add. "I mean the strategy."

"No comment. The McQuades have no new information and feel that public statements from them right now would serve no purpose. Their single interest is finding the person who . . . murdered their daughter. That's your strategy." He might have been speaking from the bottom of a well.

"Add 'helping each other and their son to get through the shock and pain,' and I'll buy it." She was a trouper; I had to give her that.

"Yeah, okay. Probably better leave out that McQuade intends to wring the necks of the helpful citizens who suggested to the police that Melanie 'overidentified' with Calista, pushed her too hard to be perfect, went ballistic about some bed-wetting."

"Ex*cuse* me? You know damned well that all those things are true."

"Why would I want to wring necks if they weren't?" he asked grimly.

I rode his train of thought: the police would go back a decade to uncover a pregnancy rife with pills and emotional eruption, culminating in an almost fatal auto accident. FBI experts would process that and come up with a profile of reckless instability: a perfectionist who, under sufficient stress, might jump the rails again, perhaps turn violent against the very person she most loved. But how did that theory square with suspicion of rape?

I did not have to wait long for an answer. Tom said, "Tomorrow they're going to release that there was no rape, at least not with a penis—no semen. And not with anything else that size. But they say they found some inflammation, irritation. Could be nothing—tight leotard, bubble bath. What they're really thinking is maybe a finger." The unflinching remove with which he said these things was likely what enabled him to say them at all.

"Why didn't you *tell* me that?" Rima asked, like a child demanding candy.

"Just did," he said flatly.

"So it could be a woman," she said meaningfully.

"Rima, go home. Thanks for dropping me off. Good luck with your media buddies."

"But, Tom, we—"

"Go. Now. Barring five minutes ago, I haven't raised a hand to anybody in ten years. Don't want to break my record twice in one night."

I waited to hear the front door shut and her car start, before leaving my hiding place. I stepped out into the hallway and intercepted Tom on his way back to the kitchen.

"Somebody rub a lamp and make you appear?" he asked. His eyes were bloodshot and narrowed with exhaustion. He was wearing a dark gray business suit and white shirt open at the neck. A bit of blue tie hung outside the flap of his jacket pocket, where he'd stuffed it no doubt after a volley of meetings with lawyers. Tom didn't care beans about clothes, but he was quite aware of the politics that went with them, the value of dressing the part, if you wanted the part.

A Tom vignette. Seven years back.

He (standing at front door): "Jacket?"

Me (in a rush to catch a train to New York to interview for my first production assistant job): "It's not about clothes. Turtleneck and pants will do fine."

He: "Fine, after they hire you. Today, a jacket'll put

you one up; and if they're not wearing jackets, it'll put you two up." Perhaps he had been right: I did wear the jacket; I did get the job.

"No lamp, no genie," I said, "I was doing a bit of eavesdropping, actually." I put some effort into keeping my voice steady.

I saw his jaw grind. "Guess you're up to speed then."

"No, Tom, I shouldn't say I was up to speed at all."

"There's plenty of coffee left. If you were listening, you know it's fresh."

He rinsed out his mug and got one down for me. Rima, I remembered, did not drink coffee, only Coke. "I still take it with a bit of milk."

"Yes," he said and poured. We sat at right angles to one another at the scrubbed pine kitchen table. "Your show," he said. "Point your Steadicam and shoot."

We used to sit this way late into the night in his kitchen—his and Melanie's. I looked at him and fought a clog in my throat. It was not nostalgia, not desire choking me, but some viscous tincture of distrust and anger and pity. "Why did you hit her?"

He nodded, as though I were answering a question, rather than asking one. It was a thing he did. It had to do with being the one in control, of course. I'd always understood that, and hadn't minded. Now, the mannerism annoyed me. "Was it because Rima struck a nerve? *Do you think Melanie did this, Tom?*"

His eyes closed and his thumb worried his lower lip. "It's not about what I think or don't think," he said. "I hit her because I'm a street fighter, Lex. Graze a street fighter, he swings first, thinks about it later. Melanie had my number ten years ago: gutter trash. All I did was prove her right. Again. Christ, I never figured I'd do a repeat, not after the other time."

The other time had been in London, the night of Calista's untimely birth. Just before Sunday supper that evening, Tom had announced abruptly that he had a flight to catch and might not be back for a day or two. Melanie, surprised, hurt, and high, had launched herself at him, spat in his face. She'd shrieked, *"Gutter trash alley cat. You'd bring us all down, wouldn't you?"* The flare was so sudden that I hadn't got Jared out of the room in time to prevent his witnessing it, or the slap that jerked her face ninety degrees round and knocked his heavily pregnant mother sideways. Tom had left for Heathrow—or somewhere—without a word.

Later, after Jared and I were asleep, and I thought Melanie was too, she went out for a drive. The police phone call came in the dark hours of the morning.

Melanie and the baby hung in the balance in hospital for two weeks, during which time Tom stuck close to her bedside, not speaking but sometimes holding her hand for hours. He stared at tiny Calista through glass only occasionally; the few times I stood beside him doing it, he seemed dazed as though from a clout on the skull. He would come home to Hampstead unpredictably, and when he did, Jared would cling to me like a limpet, refusing to let his father within ten feet of him. Now the memory of that time swallowed me up like Jonah's whale, and for the seconds I spent in its belly, I felt what I'd felt back then.

"You *are* a street fighter," I said. "And decidedly an alley cat, but anyone who calls you gutter trash will have *me* to contend with!" I stuck out my chin and held up balled fists boxer style. He managed a pallid laugh.

"I've missed you, Lexalot."

"Don't call me that, okay?" I was spewed back into

cold, rough seas; the moment was over. And I was grateful for that.

"Sorry."

"Forgiven." I sipped coffee, wondered if I was speaking truth and decided that it didn't matter. So I said what was on my mind, no garnish. "Tom, I was crouching in a cupboard hoping to pick up some notion of what's really going on here. I have no interest in spying on you and Rima otherwise, do you understand?" Economical nod of his head. "I promise you I can be better for Jared if I know what's knowable, good or bad. Tell me." Long seconds, no response. "You know me; we haven't just met, Tom."

"Yeah," he said quietly into his coffee cup. He looked up. "How much of the coverage have you read?"

"Updates on the Web, as of, oh, six, seven hours ago."

"Supermarket tabs?"

"No, not these last two days. Just what was on the stands at Heathrow."

"*Enquirer, Star*—after you finish gagging and intoning the PC litany about what shit-rakers they are, know this: they often get the beat on a story precisely because they are who they are."

"And in this case?"

"Haven't told Rima, or anybody—swore to my leak I wouldn't—but the *Star* is coming out with photos day after tomorrow, photos that haven't been officially released. Photos of Calista, the way she was when she died and when they did the autopsy." He swallowed twice and continued. "The autopsy report's there, too. Cops were holding it back. Massive abrasion on her neck from the garrote, abrasion on the back of her right hand from who knows what, genital irritation, which could be . . . You already know about that."

"I didn't know about the hand. Do the police have the garrote?"

"Yes. It was there hidden in a corner; I never even saw it. Homemade thing, they say. No way to tell whose home."

"How does the *Star* get these beats? As if I didn't know."

"Little cash goes a long way. A lot goes farther."

"What else has the cash bought?" I asked.

"A leak that Melanie and I told the police different stories about the burglar alarm." He said it deadpan into my face, his voice altogether toneless. The effect was ominous, and meant to be. It was a moment before he continued. "They questioned us separately, of course. I said the alarm was off when I got home, which seemed strange, because Melanie turns it on before she goes to sleep. So I set it, went up to look in on the kids, and went to bed. But when Melanie was questioned, she said that she *had* set the alarm before going to bed, and then early in the morning, when she found Calista missing from her room and started to look for her, it was off."

"Well, what's so damaging about that? It would seem to mean that some outside person, who knew how to work your alarm system, came in to the house . . . and left."

"Except that after Melanie found out what I'd told the police, she quickly changed her version and said that, no, she'd just remembered: it was *off* when she went to bed—she'd forgotten to set it before going up. And it was definitely off in the morning."

"That doesn't mean she's lying. Or that you are," I added, with some spite. "I assume there's an alarm here in *this* house. I don't have a clue whether it's on or off or gone to hell, do you?"

"It's off while we're staying here. Courtney's security guards make the place safe enough. You know as well as I do that perception is nine tenths of the law, Lex. The cops perceive that Melanie's engineering her alarm story to support the impression of an outside killer. And once the Feebs get started on it—"

"And what do *you* perceive?" I asked, temper nearing a boiling point, because he sounded as skeptical of her as he said the police were. "Did all this police questioning take place before or after Calista's body was found? Do you perceive Melanie may have been so distraught about Calista being missing—let alone murdered—that matters like alarm switches were perhaps not at the top of her mind?"

"Whoa! Been studying for the bar while I wasn't looking?" He pushed his chair back from the table, stretched his legs out straight and examined the ceiling. "The buckshot you just fired is a good part of the reason we need lawyers."

Right. *Separate* lawyers. So that he could protect Melanie, or the opposite? He was evading me, giving me the facts I'd entreated for, but at the same time ducking away. A sudden emptiness growled inside me, bringing with it a crave for the rich taste of chili—very hot chili. This sensation was quite familiar. I tightened my gut in resolve: I could not do this now. "Is she perhaps trying to protect you?" I asked slowly, deliberately.

His eyes quit the ceiling to meet mine. "Do you think she would do that, protect me? Do you think she'd have cause to?"

Melanie had lied to protect Tom before, and we both knew it. As for the questions he'd just asked, what I truly thought was that if Melanie suspected Tom of Calista's murder, he'd better acquire some bulletproof clothing and grow eyes in the back of his head. I did not care to say that, so I did some bobbing of my own. "What's your impression of our host?"

"Vin?" He laughed—the variety of laugh that serves as the universal human discomfort default position: a hiccup of anger, derision, fear, despair, embarrassment, relief. "I think he's as simple as he looks: a not-so-bright jock who married money and pays daily interest on it, though maybe the rates aren't so high—under her bullshit Courtney's pretty decent. Look, Vin pushed Calista way too hard, but he had Melanie with him every step of the way, day in, day out. That kid was going to be an Olympic star, top of the charts, a celebrity, no matter what it took out of her hide. Melanie was hell-bent. Didn't like it, but didn't like much of anything about the way my wife brought up her daughter. Who would know that better than you?" He reached across the table and began to trace a question mark on my palm with his index finger. The palm is loaded with nerve endings. I shuddered and jerked my hand away.

"Your daughter, too, Tom. Whether or not you cared a damn for her. Or do for anybody." I aimed to wound and I did.

"I'll take charge of blaming myself, thanks," he said frostily. "The indictment's a long one and I know the particulars by heart." He rose and put his coffee mug into the sink. "For what it's worth to you, I think Vin's sexual taste runs more toward Melanie than Calista and, convenient as it would be, I don't read him as a killer, certainly not of a little girl who was the single shining hope in his limited life. What is it you're doing, Lex, going through that Halloween party list hoping to hit pay dirt? I wish you well, but they all went home and Melanie says nobody had a house key or knew the alarm code. Nobody at that party; nobody period—not even the cleaning lady. You know how Melanie is about privacy."

I sat looking up at him as though at a stranger. And perhaps he was one. My fingertips, same hand that Tom had teased moments ago, began to drum on the pine tabletop, a single bit of echoing sound in the large, high-ceilinged kitchen. Despite all that had been said and left unsaid, Tom had not denied that he suspected Melanie or that she suspected him. Nor could I swear for his innocence. But of one thing I was certain: I was no longer in love with him.

My stomach quivered like an infant's, whose entire consciousness is an emptiness demanding to be filled. I was quite aware of a large fridge ten feet away, but neither its locale nor its contents were of the remotest interest to me. I patted my jeans pocket, checking for car keys and wallet, both present. I pushed my chair back and stood. "I'm going out for a drive," I said. "I may be gone for a while. Tell Jared I haven't done a bunk, okay? If he doesn't believe you, he can peek into my room. I'd never run off without my laptop."

CHAPTER
7

She stood in the doorway, hands on her hips. "You hang that phone up now, young lady. I said now!" She waited for me to comply, which I did. "You will not try to telephone anyone in the States again. You hear me? You understand?"

"Yes." I felt my stomach begin to twitch.

"Because if you do, I wash my hands of you." Her elegant hands pantomimed along. "I am gone. You will have no mother."

My store of scenarios for abandonment was plentiful, varied, and highly colored. In one, she would drive me out to the west of England, force me from the car on the cliffs of Cheshire, and speed away; in another, she would disappear into a restaurant's ladies' lounge and never come back. In yet another, she would stow me in a closet, bound and gagged, and rent the flat to tenants. What they had in common was the terror they provoked—terror that whipped my insides to a jelly. It was curious, this terror. Though she could charm me on occasion with her sheer zest for new experience, I neither liked nor trusted my mother. Moreover, in some way I believe I knew, even at age seven or eight, that if she did abandon me, I would in fact get what I said I wanted: to be sent back to Virginia—to my father, to Melanie. Yet, the threat remained potent until I was thirteen. The first time I summoned up the nerve to say, "Leave me, if you like, I don't care," the words came out past teeth about to chatter. I was not a courageous child. Sneaked food was the closest I came to defiance.

Now, as I drove speedily along Route 1 toward Westport, searching for an open diner or market, I pondered an old question: If I could but figure out a way to delete film clips like this one from my brain, might I once and for all be rid of this stupid, highly inconvenient compulsion? I felt my gut shiver and thought, probably not. Psychological magic never pulls itself off that neatly, except in ancient movies. Think of *Spellbound,* with its seductive moment of truth about swizzle sticks and ski tracks. Oh, I do honor Hollywood of a certain vintage. Life was so clean round the edges!

My mouth watered, anticipating tastes. Chili was still front and center, but sausage would do . . . In London, I'd have known precisely where to go. Not much in Camden Town was open at six A.M., but a few places were. Here, I hadn't a clue anymore. After some wrong turns, I located the site of a truck-stop diner I remembered, but it was gone—replaced by a shop selling exorbitant sneakers to joggers and those who meant to jog. I was beginning to sweat, when up the road I saw a lighted storefront, its white marquee lettered in pink and orange. I approached it with high hope, which flagged when I saw it was a Dunkin' Donuts. But after a quick assessment of probabilities, birds in hand, and my own thumping heart, I pulled into the curb and parked.

"A dozen bagels with cream cheese, three large orange juice, four coffees with milk. Um, and a dozen doughnuts—six chocolate, six cinnamon. Oh, and where's the salt and pepper?" It wasn't chili; it wasn't anything I craved—but with enough salt and pepper, the bagels would do, they'd have to. The doughnuts were insurance.

"You must be feeding a hungry crew, kiddo," the man behind the counter said. He was small and stringy and naked-faced, like an old bird, plucked of most of its feathers—a tough old bird. "That's a lotta food for four people."

"Yes." Years ago, I'd have explained how it was really more than four, but some of the group didn't drink coffee. More recently, I would have said that it was all for me, and perversely enjoyed his reaction. These days, I said yes and paid the bill.

I placed the flat gray boxes carefully on the backseat and U-turned back toward Compo Beach, past the place where Jared and I had eaten pizza last evening. The beach was as deserted as nontropical beaches are in November and all beaches are at six in the morning. I parked and carried my food over to a jetty rock, which provided a bit of shelter. I knew this spot: Tom and I used to come here sometimes. I'd visited it on my own with a large parcel of Hunan food the day before I took my ruptured life back to London. This morning, the air was cool and damp and my Shetland not very warm, but my body stoked enough of its own heat so that I hardly noticed. I slathered the first bagel thick with cream cheese, salted it lightly, and covered the white surface with enough pepper to turn it black . . .

I awoke sometime later, much later, I guessed. The

wind was gusty, the sun full. I was freezing and numb in the hands and feet. I felt stuffed to the point of pain and nauseous. I don't often throw up the food I've gorged, but this time I needed to. I stuck my finger deep into my throat and leaned in toward the large rock. On the third go, a mischievous puff of wind attacked and blew a spray of vomit back onto my sweater and jeans. After a few more heaves, my innards settled enough to allow me to clean my face and hands in the icy water and dab the worst off my clothing with a wet Dunkin' Donuts paper napkin. I gathered the debris and disposed of it in a large trash barrel, noting with only passing interest that I'd consumed seven of the dozen bagels and four insurance doughnuts, all chocolate, as well as an orange juice and two coffees. I checked my watch: it read eleven-forty.

I got back into the car, turned on the heater, and let it run on high until I could feel my extremities begin to thaw. Then I trolled Route 1 for one of those huge American drugstores and found it. In short order, I left with a toothbrush, toothpaste, plastic packet of underpants, size small, and black sweat suit, child-size large. Catching a look at myself in the driver's mirror was enough to send me back inside for a comb, compact of pressed powder makeup, blush, and tinted lip gloss. I am far from vain of my appearance, but neither am I masochistic about it. In an Exxon station ladies' I scrubbed up, changed clothes, and did a bit of cosmetic repair. When I pulled the car back onto the highway, the stained clothing, last vestige of my debauch, stayed behind in the Exxon's bin.

Apart from the sore muscles in my middle, a clean, astringent sort of ache, I was all right, and would be until the next time—which, I hoped, would not come as bloody closely timed as this episode had been to its predecessor. Extraordinary, isn't it, how one does get accustomed to anything? Or perhaps *ordinary* is the more accurate word. Move an elephant into the drawing room and soon enough you're using its trunk as a coatrack and taking automatic care to step round the shit. New job, new lover, delusion, compulsion, amputation, murder—*voilà*, with astonishing speed the decor regroups to accommodate the altered state and life rolls along. After a bit, it begins to feel normal.

Normal. The word rolled noisily in my alleyways. What might have been normal for the child who lay dead now in some chilled official compartment? Within a small circle, Calista seemed to have become an icon and so, ultimately, a commodity: the power by which she ruled had put her in thrall to her subjects and rendered her powerless.

But parsing the nature of celebrity told me little. The large canvas of concepts overwhelms me; particulars can speak to me. What had Calista's days been like? School, of course; gym and more gym, Vin and Melanie in constant attendance. "Try it again." "No, not that way, *this* way." "Come on, one more time . . ." Flashbulb pops; video camera whirr the ever-present background noise. Calista must have been one of the world's most photographed infants. Judging by what I'd seen on display in the McQuade and Anacleto homes, that pace had not slackened. I thought of the photos soon to appear in the *Star*, medical examiner's shots that had fetched their seller a fancy price. Had the feel of someone's finger inside her become normal for Calista, too? Such a finger would not have been Tom's; I knew that—thought I did.

I was unaware where I'd driven myself until I turned up Sprucewood Lane and saw the house, wrapped like a parcel in yellow police tape, a single uniformed sentinel patrolling against curiosity seekers. I did not stop; there was no hope of getting inside. I was surprised to note how much that disappointed me. Prints of fingers and feet, blood, DNA, and the like—police clues—would be entirely useless to someone like me with no capacity to read or interpret them. But Calista's bedroom, a look round there might tell me something about her I could understand. Since that opportunity was not readily available, I would need to tap one that was . . .

A surge of energy let me know that I was back at work. I felt on firmer ground than I had since my arrival: work was what I did well.

I turned the car's heater off, lowered the window, and circled round back to the house. I got out of the car and approached the policewoman guarding the house. She was not much taller than I, but a good deal wider; she walked back and forth with the military precision of a Buckingham Palace guard. "Excuse me, I'm Mrs. McQuade's sister, and—"

"Sorry, you can't come in." Small smile. "Even if you are who you say you are."

"Rather than a reporter, is that what you mean?"

"That's what I mean."

"Perhaps you could answer a question for me. My sister asked me to go round to Calista's school to collect some things, but didn't give me directions. Do you know where it is?"

"Sure. Hit Route 1, go three quarters of a mile north, hang a right onto Cherry. It's the Nathan Hale School, white building—all white, with columns. Tara," she added, her dark face less than heartily amused.

"Thanks." I began to turn away.

"Look, I got no idea who you are: what my nose

smells is reporter—if you're McQuade's sister, you sure don't look or sound like her. But, hey, you could get directions to the school at the nearest gas station. So don't thank me, I didn't give you squat."

"Right," I said pleasantly.

The Nathan Hale grounds were sweeping, well-landscaped, and filled with children—white children—some just milling, most involved in a scramble of running, jumping, chasing, tagging, throwing, catching—a hectic fight against the clock to spend the small change of their physical energy against the confined afternoon ahead—a long two hours of sitting and behaving themselves. I felt the memory of school playgrounds in my limbs, breathed it in the air. At ten, I'd worn the requisite navy blazer, white blouse, and gray skirt to school (which resulted in many more skinned knees than these sensibly trousered girls likely suffered). But other than the difference in costumes, this might have been lunchtime recess at Westminster, except for a TV van with the Eyewitness News logo on its side.

Calista had been in fourth grade. Her teacher was named Barney Warden. He had been mentioned in the coverage as one of Melanie's Halloween guests. I scanned the playground and saw several adults on duty, two of them men. I parked the car and approached one of several guards at the playground entrance.

"I'm here to see Mr. Warden," I said briskly. "I'm Melanie McQuade's sister, just in from London. She asked me to stop by and talk with him." Like the policewoman at the house, his stare was not friendly. He was no folksy neighborhood school volunteer, but an agency professional, laid on to protect the teachers and children from media harassment. And Godspeed to him. "I am not a reporter."

"You got ID?" he asked. I flipped my wallet open to show my driver's license and handed it to him. "Doesn't tell me nuthin'. Got a note from your sister?"

"That wouldn't tell you nu . . . anything either, unless you knew her handwriting. I appreciate you have a job to do, sir, but I must ask you to tell Mr. Warden I'm here. Our family is going through quite a lot at the moment. Do not add to it." I'd learned the imperious approach at my mother's knee. Chin high, tone cold and crisp, it had worked surprisingly well with angry creditors, especially.

"I'll get him," he snapped. "You wait here. And I mean *right* here."

I suppressed the desire to salute, or give him the bird. He returned minutes later with one of the men I'd glimpsed: a very tall redhead, mustached and bearded, dressed in tan chino pants and a thick black pullover. The lanky body and the neat, but not all that neat, facial hair brought to mind a farmer in a nineteenth-century painting.

Barney Warden stopped a good eight feet away, well inside the school fence, and waited for me to speak. "I'm sorry to interrupt you," I said, treading carefully, and gave my bona fides. "I'm Lex Cavanaugh, Melanie's sister. I'm staying at the Anacletos' with the family."

"Condolences. What can I do for you?" But he did not move forward.

"I need to talk with you in private."

"What about?" He had a pleasant tenor voice and a manner that was direct without being challenging—in combination, I thought, a decided advantage for a primary school teacher.

"Jared," I said. The idea struck me there on the spot, and seemed quite a sound one on its own terms. "Tutoring him. He's not in school at the moment and may not be for some time . . ."

"Shouldn't you be talking to *his* teacher?" The question was asked straight; it was the pale green eyes that added irony—or perhaps it was just the way the sun hit them.

"Jared's not had an easy time with his teacher," I said, knowing it must be true, "and Melanie knows you better. She has confidence in you." He looked hard at me. It was not an effect of the light I was seeing now. I'd gone too far.

The school bell sounded, and the children scurried to form themselves into class rows. A pair of girls sidled over to where we were standing, giggling at a private joke, the way girlfriends do. These girls were likely Calista's classmates—her friends, as well? Had she had any friends her own age to laugh and whisper with? I'd had a special friend when I was about that age; Miranda, freckled all over and quiet, so quiet most adults missed her flair for the subversive: she'd set off a cherry bomb in the teachers' ladies' loo once, and managed to be the only girl at school not suspected of it. Her confiding it to me, trusting I wouldn't rat on her, had been the highlight of my year. She'd left at term end; her dad was transferred—France, I think.

One of the girls poked at the other; the poked designee stepped forward and said in the tones of a small wife, "Mr. Warden, the bell." I gave my cause a last-ditch push. "Look, I know you can't now, but do you suppose we might meet after school?"

"All right," he said, but not immediately. "I'll meet you right here. Three-thirty." Which gave me some two hours to spend at the Westport Public Library.

I'd visited this red brick building often during my

three years here, a comfortable small-town resource, circa nineteen-fifty-something, frequented mostly by children and their mothers—and in some cases, grandmothers—who remembered the library when it was new. Nothing elaborate here, no microfiche archives or the like, certainly no supermarket tabloids. I did spy two computer stations, but decided I'd rather browse the papers themselves, since it was not hard news I was after. No, now that I was in a work mode, fragments of ancillary fact and comment were my quarry. I was on the dig for oddments that might fit together into some sort of human archeology—though what sort usually remained an open question until late in the game. So I settled myself at a blond wood table with a stack of dailies and the most recent weekly newsmagazines.

It was the local paper I found most useful: the *Westport News*. While all Melanie's Halloween guests except Vin had refused to talk to the media, some other locals were quite eager to do so. A former housecleaner for Melanie: "I wouldn't put nothing past that one—except hurting her little girl. No way! The sun came up and set down over that child's head—and she was a nice little girl, too, nicer than the boy." The woman went on to say that she'd worked there for more than a year, "a record working for her—talk about demanding . . ." and been fired two months ago in a dispute about laundry. "I stripped Calista's bed and the sheet was wet. Mrs. McQuade was mad as hell that I seen, you know, that the child peed her bed, her being a big girl and all. Next thing, I'm gone!"

A mother of one of Calista's classmates said, "The kids liked her, though I don't think she was close with any of them. My Beth tried a few times to make play dates, but Calista wasn't ever available, what with her gym schedule every day and stuff her mother had planned for her on the weekends. I gave Melanie a call once to ask her directly, but she ducked me. I couldn't call her rude, but definitely standoffish. Girls' play dates were not on her screen. Far be it from me to tell anyone how to be a mom, but . . ."

None of what I was reading was a surprise, including comments on Tom from people who counted him a mean bastard, but seemed to be regular viewers of *Inside Straight,* nonetheless, judging by their ease at quoting specific segments verbatim. Allusions to Jared as a "weird kid" with a "bushel of problems": too much talk of that for my liking . . .

The paper carried thumbnail profiles on each of the Halloween houseguests, under the headline: "Last to See Calista Alive." I learned that Vin was forty-eight, had been a creditable supporting player in the 1976 Olympics and might have gone on to a bigger career but for the leg injury. He coached gymnasts one at a time— implicit was the fact that he did not need to make his living at it. He was apparently a good coach, too: Calista's predecessor was now twenty-three and retired, with an Olympic trophy on her shelf.

In addition to a daunting list of boards and committees she served on and chaired, I found two interesting bits about Courtney: she had completed two years of medical school at Harvard, before dropping out, and she was distantly related to Barney Warden. Their fathers had been second cousins and for a time partners in an investment brokerage that had been acquired fifteen years ago by J. P. Morgan, after the death of Courtney's father.

So Mr. Warden was no itinerant farmer, but a local aristocrat *manqué.* His squib was on the vague side. It said that his father, Bernard senior, now resided in Palm

Beach. His mother was dead. Barney (technically, Bernard junior), thirty, was a graduate of the University of California at Berkeley and had taught school in California, New Orleans, and Florida. He had only just returned to Connecticut last summer, after an eleven-year absence, and was staying at the home of a friend who was in Germany on an extended business assignment. Translation: rather than being squire of an estate similar to Courtney's, her cousin was house-sitting.

I wondered whether the decision to forgo a career in high finance for elementary math had been his, or made for him by Bernard senior—and what, after all this time, might have brought him back to Westport.

Disappointingly, nothing illuminating was on offer about Nathan Grumbach. He was sixty-one, a widower, childless. He was a graduate of New York's City College and Columbia University, and had consulted to the city's board of education and the New Lincoln School, as well as maintaining a private practice in Manhattan. He'd moved here following his wife's death, four years ago, and established a practice specializing in children with learning disabilities. As Courtney had told me, he was a consultant to the Southport schools.

My neck was stiff and my mouth felt parched. I rotated my head slowly to release the tension and then held my finger under my tongue until my mouth watered. As I was doing them, I realized that these were tricks of the trade Tom had taught me to use during all-nighters working on film school projects. "The three R's: reporter's refreshment regimen," he'd called it—learned from old news hands back in the Vietnam days.

Like it or not, Tom McQuade's fingerprints were in evidence all over my life, and always would be. That was a fact; I don't argue with facts.

CHAPTER 8

I returned to Nathan Hale a bit early, early enough to see Barney Warden towering like a flagpole over a swarm of boys, ages perhaps eight to ten. The boys were kicking a soccer ball; he was directing traffic, demonstrating technique, and now and then clapping a shoulder in encouragement or praise, as well as providing the occasional verbal boot to the bum. "Way to go, Matthew!" "Yo, Billy. No sulking. It got past you. Look sharp so next time it won't." Man and boys seemed to be having a fine time. At half past three, he blew the whistle round his neck, and after a bit of lingering, the last boy was gone. Barney gave his forehead a wipe and loped over to the gate.

"Might we go somewhere for a cup of, uh, anything you'd like," I said.

"My dog's waiting for a run," he said, mild speculation in his eyes, which were, I now noticed, the same color as Courtney's, though the family resemblance ended there. "How're you at running?"

"Not bad."

I followed his red Jeep, a survivor of many seasons, hash-marked with nicks and bruises. Quarter of an hour later, on North Avenue, he pulled into the driveway of a sizable, storm blue Victorian with white trim, black shutters, and a red door. It was overhung by very old trees.

Seeing it, I was struck with an odd pang of nostalgia. Not that I'd ever lived in such a house or even entered one; I hadn't. Nevertheless, as a child, I'd imagined the house—well enough so that every time a teacher said, "Draw a house," my hand had drawn this one, down to the red door and the dominating trees.

"Nice house," I said, more to puncture the moment with sound than any other reason.

He was already up the front steps, unlocking the red door. As soon as it was open, a large German shepherd bounded out on the porch. He caught it by the collar. "Whoa, boy; whoa, Jasper. Leash time: this is suburbia." He reached inside the house with his free hand and retrieved a long, leather lead, which the dog allowed him to attach with good grace—more or less. Then the two began their run down the sidewalk. I kept pace, barely, needing to work my legs double time to do it. It felt good, though, the wind filling my lungs, as the limbs pumped away. I'd had virtually no exercise these weeks, what with wrapping and editing the monkey film. I tend to be sporadic about exercise, in any case, as I am about work, food, and too much else. The *sensei*—"teacher"—at the tae kwon do studio had admonished me for extended absence, pointing out that control and consistency were what that art was all about. No question he was right.

We ran for perhaps forty minutes. Neither of us

attempted conversation, even when the dog paused to relieve itself. Back at the house Barney stopped, one foot on the lowest porch step. He scratched Jasper's head absently while turning his attention to me, as though I were a new arrival. "Okay, Lex, what's the deal?"

"I told you that—"

"I know what you told me. You're Melanie's sister. Let's say I believe that. What's really on your mind?"

"I thought you might have vetted me by now—called your cousin and asked whether an English dwarf was in temporary residence there."

"No, I didn't. Let's say you are Melanie's sister. She did not send you to see me because of her confidence in me. I'm betting she did not send you to see me at all. So why did you come?" Jasper stared at me, his pennant of a tongue waving as he panted. He was a very good looking dog, if you fancy dogs. His owner waited, teacherlike, for an elementary answer.

"I *am* Melanie's sister; I *am* staying with the Anacletos. And you're right. I did come to the school on my own hook. I haven't the least idea what Melanie might think of you. I can tell you she doesn't care much for me."

"That's a good start," he said, his feet planted just where they'd been, on the bottom step.

"Look, Jared really *is* the reason I'm here—I mean, he's what brought me over from London. He E-mailed me, asking me to come. We . . . we get on, him and me. And I *do* think you might be a help to him. I admit a tutor is only a bit of what he needs just now, but it's a bit that can be given him. Most of what he needs can't. Does he like you?"

"I have no idea," he said. "He's strange enough for me to like him, though." His eyes narrowed as they had over at the school. Now, in the darkening late afternoon, there was no question of the mocking look being a trick of light. It was there, but seemed to be directed inward rather than at me, a private Chekhovian rumination. "Tutoring him would be a possibility on my end, but I'm not sure I'd be your sister's choice."

"Oh, why not?"

"Look, the proximate cause for your visit is to talk about Calista, not about Jared. Isn't that true?"

"Yes, it is. Are you going to tell me to bugger off? Get lost?"

"I don't know. Maybe."

"Then might we go inside while you make up your mind? It is getting a bit cold, and I'd welcome a chance to sit down."

He mounted the remaining steps and unlocked the door.

We sat in a square living room furnished mainly with books and utilitarian things to put one's bottom or feet on—a comfortable room. I reminded myself that the room was no testament to the depth and quality of Barney Warden, but reflected his absent host. Nonetheless, Barney's presence seemed to permeate this room with a demand for truth. I was going to have to give it to get it. I sat in a small oak rocking chair, while he moved a stack of books and papers from sofa to floor to clear a space for himself.

"I didn't really know Calista, you see," I began. "I'd been out of touch with my . . . the family for six years. There's so much I don't understand. I thought that if I could only . . . this is difficult, because I think *you'll* misunderstand . . ."

"Just say whatever it is, and if I misunderstand, tell me I'm misunderstanding. And if I *still* misunderstand—

well, maybe that shows I'm understanding more than you want me to."

There was a transparency about him that reminded me of water. Water, of course, is known to be invitingly simple and suddenly treacherous. I said, "I'm a documentary filmmaker of sorts, that's what I do; it's pretty much my entire life, which tends to make me rather obsessed with understanding properly."

"And what I'm supposed to misunderstand here is your intention, right?" He smiled, sort of. "No, I don't think you're wanting to pump me for a film you're making about your niece's murder. Did I pass?"

"Yes. And thanks. I'm not lying when I say I'm here for Jared. But Calista is at the center and I have no grasp of her at all, which leaves me with only platitudes and diversions to give him. He can't talk about her, so he talks nonstop about astronomy and black holes and the like. Melanie won't talk to me at all. Vin effuses about the Olympics. Courtney makes pronouncements and runs about telling everyone what to do. So aside from the fact she was killed and the media skew on it, I know nothing."

"And you thought my skew might add something. What about her father's skew? What does he have to say?" The green eyes and the face round them sharpened with appetite to fix blame: another person joining the long queue ready to indict Tom.

"I'm sure your skew will be different," I said quietly. "That's why I want to hear it."

The dog was stretched out at his feet. He leaned over to massage its neck. When he looked back up, it was to say, "I'm going to make tea. Want some?"

"Yes. Black, no sugar, please. Would you like any help?"

"To boil water? I think I can manage."

The dog did not follow him, but stayed where it was, rolling its eyes up at me as if to say, "I know what you're up to." Well, if it did, it knew more than I. *Not "it," "him,"* I could hear Mum say. She affected the British enthusiasm for dogs (up to but never including ownership of one), and found my indifference to them yet another embarrassment. I looked back at *him.* He yawned, showing an array of large sawteeth, and turned away. When I heard a growl, it was not Jasper but my stomach. I felt scared: the binges I'd come to regard as normal were episodic, separated by months. I had not ridden out an extended loop-the-loop of bulimia in six years. It threatened now at a most inopportune time. Holding it in check would take discipline and luck—neither had ever been a personal strong suit.

Barney set a very large mug of dark amber tea on the low sea trunk in front of me. "Have you a biscuit or something handy?" I asked. "Nothing major, but . . . something?"

He returned with a half-gone box of gingersnaps. I took one and ate it with no appetite, but because it was the prudent thing to do: eat small amounts frequently; do not think about food. I'd always considered that second bit fatuous, formulated perhaps by someone who'd never had the experience of trying to not think of something.

"You can turn your chair round and put your feet up on that other one, if you want," he said. "Jasper and I are just squatters here, but I've known Chazz since kindergarten. He encourages feet on furniture—makes him forget he grew up to be a bond trader. You look beat. You look bone weary."

"Thanks." I raised my feet onto the improvised stool

and took a generous sip of the tea, followed by another bite of biscuit. "Introduce me to Calista, would you?"

He shook his head slowly. "I knew her two months. Just two months."

"All the better in a way." His red eyebrows doubted it. "No, I mean that. You don't have preconceptions, loyalties—no emotional hostages to deal with. How did she strike you?"

"As an easy winner, too aware for her age that she had a lot to lose. She was like a smart politician running for reelection. She knew how to keep the crowds happy with her but still hold them at arm's length. Look, maybe this'll give you the idea. At the end of lunch recess one day, I went to herd my class back in and saw all the girls and some of the boys in a cluster. Right in the center of it was Calista standing on a bench. She had her arm raised like the Statue of Liberty. I hung back for a minute, wanted to see what it was about. She paused for a minute and down came the arm with the index finger pointed at a girl—Carrie Neubach, a plump, asthmatic kid who's absent a lot, bit of an outsider—and Calista said, 'I choose . . . No, sorry.' And she turned pretty fast and pointed at another kid, Linda Wallace, this time—probably the highest IQ in the class. 'I choose you.' Poor Carrie was devastated. What The Chosen got to do was to put her hands under Calista's back while she did some kind of amazing backbend. That was it, no big deal. But I remember thinking that for Calista it was like grabbing a cookie, a snack. She got so damned much attention that her stomach for it expanded. Follow that?"

"I think so, yes." *Most definitely yes.*

"But she also struck me as a kid in over her head, beginning to panic."

"Panic?"

"Yeah, panic. She didn't show it often. Hell, Calista was much too polished to let rough stuff come through, but a couple of times I called on her in class and caught her with that deer-in-the-headlights look in her eye and I could tell she was someplace else, someplace not good. And she wet herself once in class. I don't think the other kids noticed. She covered like a seasoned trouper, foot out in the aisle, just enough to hide the spot on the floor, some plausible excuse or another to stay in her seat until after the room was emptied, backing her way to the closet for her coat, which was fortunately about knee-length. But I got what had happened."

"Did you say anything to her?"

"About wetting herself? I'd never embarrass a kid that way. But I did ask her if anything was wrong, an upset at home or maybe life just getting her down. She grinned at me. 'Mr. Warden,' she said. 'My life is straight up; I've got nothing to be down about. But thank you for asking.' "

"And that was it?"

"Not quite. It ate at me, you know? It was so unchildish, so careful: the smile, too charming; the 'thank you for asking' . . . Jesus! I didn't believe her. I'm not confident about much, and for good reason, but when it comes to kids, I do see at least an inch or so below the surface."

"Any ideas what the panic might have been about?"

"You always think of sexual abuse."

"And when you think of sexual abuse, your thoughts turn to the father?"

"It's a logical turn."

"True, but logic has been known to lead down a wrong path. Calista did have other men in her life."

"And two of them, from what I hear, saw way more of her than her father did, if you're talking about Vin and me."

"Is that what you told the police? I mean about suspecting Tom."

"Hold on. I'm taking the Fifth here. What I told the police is between them and me."

"Isn't the Fifth to do with *self*-incrimination?" His face blushed in the hectic way peculiar to redheads. "Sorry," I said, meaning it, "that was uncalled for. You . . . had me going is all."

He stood. Jasper, who'd been snoozing at his feet, did, too. "Maybe you'd better—be going, that is."

"Look, my damned mouth has been known to run off on its own. I *am* sorry, truly. It was just . . . Tom could be drawn and quartered so easily over this; there's such public enthusiasm for it."

"Tom seems to be top of your mind, right up there with Jared."

"Barney, please don't make me go just yet."

"Finish your tea." His long legs folded, and his seat went back down into the sofa cushion. "You're going to ask me what I did after I tried to talk to Calista about what was biting her. The answer is, not much, not enough. I called the parents in for a conference—I did do that. Melanie came; not him. I've never met the man, to this day. I told Melanie that at times Calista seemed tense—see how tactful I can be? And I asked her how things were at home. She said that they couldn't be better, except for Tom's demanding work schedule. That smile of hers—you know, the smile of denial—wasn't so different from Calista's. I mean you could see where Calista got it from." He scratched at his beard while nursing a thought. "Women like Melanie see everything and admit nothing."

His perceptiveness gave me pause. "Did you get specific with her?" I asked carefully.

"You mean did I ask her if she thought someone was fiddling with her daughter? No, I didn't. But I did ask her if there'd been any incidents of bed-wetting and such. The answer was a resounding, 'Absolutely not!' It rang so positive that it registered as a lie. To cut to the chase, I got exactly nowhere with her. The reason she asked me to that damned Halloween party was to showcase Calista, how perfect, how just fine she was. I knew it at the time, and I didn't want to go; for once my instincts were right."

"Why *did* you go?"

He flipped his hands, open palms up. "Who knows? I think I had some notion that the mythical Tom would be there and I could talk with him, maybe get through to him—or at least get some idea what was going on. But of course he wasn't there."

"Your cousin," I said. "Did you discuss any of this with Courtney?"

"Courtney and I don't discuss. 'Cousin' sounds very clubby and all—childhood memories of long summers, tennis, swimming, et cetera. It wasn't like that with us. Court's ten years older, but that's not the main reason. See, our fathers were at each other's throats daily. They managed to run a business together for better than fifteen years, make even more money than their respective dads had left them, but outside the office, *nada*. Court's father was a mean son of a bitch, the kind of guy who'd rag his daughter about her fat behind and tease her about what a bust she'd be as a doctor. And then tell the audience that he was only kidding.

"My dad's just . . . just your garden-variety dictator, but other than that, he isn't what you'd call a bad guy.

Point is, Court and I didn't see all that much of each other growing up; we haven't since and we don't now. She did make some calls to help me get this gig at Nathan Hale, and I was grateful for that. You know, Court's damned good in her way: a great advocate in real need of a great cause. So what's she got instead? Vin. It's a shame she gave up on med school; she'd've been a *good* doctor. No, I didn't bring the Calista problem up with her. Wish I had, though. She'd have grabbed on to it like a pit bull, shook it in her teeth till something fell out."

I had to agree but didn't say so. "The Halloween party. How did it go?"

"It started off okay. Calista and Jared were out doing trick-or-treat. Good food, good drink, everyone in a good mood, Melanie hostessing her heart out—no Tom. Spent a lot of time talking to Grumbach. He's a really perceptive guy and not just about kids. Plus, he's the opposite of pompous. I'd give him a high S.Q. That's *shrink quotient,* in the jargon of a certain select group.

"And then the children came home. Jared looked depressed and pissed off—and no wonder: it must have been fun and a half, dragging a wagon full of princess mermaid. Anyway, Calista was head to toe sequins, laughing, waving herself round, getting passed lap to lap, breathing all the air in the room, as usual. All of a sudden, somehow she landed on the floor and started to pull at her costume. She was upset. I don't know what happened, but right then she was a real kid, mad as hell about something, yanking at that tail, dying to get if off her. Melanie was there like a shot to take over—she'd sewn the damned thing herself and didn't want it to get ripped. And then Melanie went stone-faced. I saw her look at me and then look away fast. Calista had peed in the mermaid outfit; I could tell that was it. Melanie was just about flipped out, so furious she could hardly talk."

And how not? Humiliation may be the most exquisite form of torture yet devised: the fall from grace, the desecration of one's crafted, cherished public self. Think Malvolio. Never mind that the play purports to be comedy rather than tragedy, his final torment is tragic, the underlying rage made almost unbearably poignant by the need to hide it behind repentance, forced graces. To picture Melanie's pride in Calista publicly soiled made me cringe for her.

"What happened then?" I asked.

"The party died on the spot. She sent the kids to bed with one of those frozen social grins, stretched lips and gritted teeth—you know the kind. I'm no big fan of Melanie's, but I felt rotten. It's not easy to see a woman like her brought down that way, no matter what the reason. Watching it, you're kind of a voyeur. I don't think I stayed another ten minutes," he said. "I gather the others didn't stay long, either."

For a moment, I simply enjoyed liking him. "Do I dare ask you how much of this you've told the police?" I asked.

"Pretty much all of it, with editorial comment omitted." He hadn't been looking at me while he talked, but he did now. "For what it's worth, I can't think your sister murdered Calista because she wet her pants."

"Good. Neither can I."

"That kind of cuts down on the possibilities, doesn't it?"

"The possibilities are broader than you think," I said. A fortune cookie insert, but I hung on to it for my own purposes. It also happened to be true; possibilities always run beyond the fences our preconceptions impose. I glanced at my watch. It was coming up on seven. I eased myself off the chair. "I'll get out of your way now, but I'd really appreciate it if you gave a thought to working with Jared. You'd be good for him."

"What makes you think that?"

"I watched you coaching the soccer practice. And I've formed my own opinion in the time since then."

He stood. "You don't know near enough about me to have an opinion," he said evenly, his transparency turning opaque suddenly. "But I will consider helping out with Jared, if you can sell your notion to his parents. And you might want to talk to Grumbach. He knows the kid pretty well, not to mention the mother. Come on, Jasper and I'll walk out with you. We're going down to the marina." I looked at his aquatic eyes and thought a marina would be a logical destination for him.

"Have you a boat, then?" I asked.

"I do. Like sailing?"

"I think so. I've only been a few times."

"I'll take you one day, if you want to go."

"I might. I might want to."

CHAPTER
9

I drove up this street, down that, in no rush to return to Southport. The prospect of the Anacleto house appealed to me as much as a cell in Reading Gaol, which says something about the limits of my commitment to Jared, or to anyone—something not flattering. Though it took me years to own up to it, I am one of nature's isolates: by definition not expansive, not social, and not generous. I thought of Barney's Jasper: perhaps I don't fancy pets because I am simply too selfish to contemplate tending one. Odd how people will easily admit to virtually any personal deficiency except lack of a sense of humor or a generosity of spirit.

As I turned the car finally in the right direction for Southport, I took these thoughts by the scruff, threw them to the back of the storage bin, and focused on Calista . . .

Calista Brooke McQuade (*Brooke* simply because Melanie had liked the sound of it), born at the Royal

National Hospital two months premature on August 15, 1989. The previous evening, an IRA bomb had blown up two maintenance workers in a Fleet Street news office building—secondary casualties: her father's career and her parents' marriage.

At the time, I'd been living with the McQuades almost six weeks. Days after our first inauspicious meeting, I had been invited to move into the Hampstead house and, as Tom put it, "help Melanie out with things." "I'd take it as a favor," he'd said to me privately. "London's strange territory for her and Jared, and I'm going to be tied up a lot of the time." I had accepted on the spot, as one does an unanticipated piece of good luck, especially when one's life has been on the downward spiral. I was loopy about Jared, and though Melanie and I were not precisely soul mates, I found her resolute energy more bracing than irritating, as long as we played by her rules. And I did occasionally catch a glimpse of the irrepressible girl I'd adored as a child—occasionally was better than nothing by a long chalk.

As for Tom, if my lust for him was flexing its muscles, preparing for a gallop out of the barn, it was doing so in secret. I trusted his rough honesty; I admired his success; I loved the challenge of his company. To the extent I knew, that was all.

But in those days my capacity to see, to interpret, to comprehend much beyond, as well as behind, my own nose was severely limited. And so, until the men arrived at the door to question his whereabouts on certain days and nights, I never suspected that Tom might be involved with Sinn Fein in any way different than his news colleagues.

There had been clues, if one had been alert to clues. There was, for example, the erratic pattern of sudden absences. Then there were the telephone quirks: wrong numbers and hang-ups, too many of them. All this could simply have meant another woman, which is what I'd vaguely supposed. In the final days there were the clicks on the phone line, which can indicate it's tapped. But by then, things were near their climax.

Melanie knew something extraordinary was going on. She never said a word about it, not to me, and perhaps not even to Tom himself. But I became certain she did know.

I remember with a sharp-edged specificity every detail of the morning the men showed up. The door chime rang just before eight. I was in the kitchen scrambling eggs for Jared, who preferred them, like his toast, quite browned, almost burnt. He was at the table, eyes glued to an American cartoon on the small telly. Melanie and the baby, who'd been home from hospital only a few days, were still asleep. No nurse or nanny. Someone came to clean several hours a day, but that was all. Neither Tom nor Melanie was partial to live-in servants, and besides, Melanie wanted no hands on Calista but her own. Even though she was far from strong, and sleeping badly, having given up her accustomed arsenal of pharmaceuticals, she attended to Calista, while I saw to Jared.

When I cracked the door open, the shorter of the two men wished me cheerful good morning as he flipped his badge at me. "Sorry to disturb you this early, miss. MI6."

"Yes," I said, "so I see."

"You the nanny, then?" the taller one asked.

"Not really. I'm Melanie McQuade's sister. Look, I expect you've come to see Tom, but you're out of luck. He's not home at the moment."

"No," he said, "we know that. We've come to see your sister, actually."

"She's asleep, I'm afraid. She's just had a baby, and—"

"Apologies," said the short one, "but you will need to wake her."

"Not allowed to wake Mommy," said Jared, drawn by his ineffable curiosity even from cartoons.

But further debate on waking Melanie was unnecessary. She appeared on the stairs, combed and kempt, wearing a purple plush dressing gown and cradling Calista in the crook of her arm. "Good morning," she said, neutral but far from unfriendly. "Is there somethin' Ah can do for you?" The only sign that she might be anything other than fully composed was the extra helping of drawl.

"Sorry to disturb you, Mrs. McQuade. MI6. My name is Struthers," said the tall one as he watched Melanie descend the stairs like royalty, "and my colleague here is called Carmody. We've some questions to ask, rather important. They've to do with your husband." I glanced at Jared, whose eyes were round, as though he were watching an alternative cartoon. "Is there someplace where we might talk?"

"Has something happened to Tom?" Melanie asked quietly.

"Not as far as we know," Carmody said, his undertone loaded with subtext.

"Then Ah must ask you what it is we might have to talk about."

Struthers's head gave a small shake. "You've just recently given birth, haven't you, Mrs. McQuade?"

"Ah have. August fifteenth. Mah daughter's name is Calista. It's from the Greek—means 'the best.' "

"Lovely," said Carmody with a cursory look. "We

understand that you were . . . uh suffered a bit of an accident that evening."

Melanie's eyes nailed him. "Ah went out for a late-night drive by mahself, and had the bad judgment to crash mah car. Ah'm a very good driver, we southern girls begin young, but Ah'm not used to drivin' on the wrong side. Not yet."

"Quite," said Struthers. By then, even I had realized that Struthers knew all about the crash and its cause. "Your husband was out of town that night?"

I saw Melanie hesitate for just a second. "Yes, that's correct. He flew right back, of course."

"Of course," Struthers said. "The preceding evening," he asked mildly, "what about that?"

"We had dinner at home, Mr. Struthers," she said. "I cooked a chicken pot pie. That's Tom's favorite." Two items presented themselves: the southern accent had receded to minimal, and Melanie was lying. Tom had not been at home that evening—not for dinner, not for many hours afterward. "Now, I *do* think I must ask you to leave," she said. The two men exchanged eye signals and decided not to push further right then.

"Give Jared his breakfast, Lex," she said a moment after the door had closed behind them. "Calista and I are going back to bed." She mounted the first few steps and stopped, looking down at Jared and me as though from a far greater distance. Her face was as grim as a soldier's in a losing battle, but I thought I saw tears welling in her blue eyes. "If Tom happens to turn up, wake me."

In the end, her audacity had made no difference; an informer later placed Tom at a meeting where no newsman belonged. But the point was that Melanie had dared tell the lie and had told it flawlessly, gauging on the spot what Struthers knew, as opposed to what he surmised.

As I pointed the car toward Southport, I felt in rather daunting awe of my sister. It had been easy for me to denigrate the adult Melanie—calculated, materialistic, distressingly like my mother in those ways; a far cry from the blithe girl I'd idealized. But she was also a woman of principles and nerve. Though I did not share the principles or always know what they were, I had to admire the nerve.

Melanie was capable of anything she deemed necessary. I did not believe that she could have killed Calista in any circumstance, but suddenly I was certain she was lying as coolly as she had that morning in Hampstead. About something . . .

I pulled into the Anacleto driveway just in time to see Nate Grumbach preparing to get into his Volvo, a stately wine-colored wagon, perhaps a decade old. He walked over to my car and extended his hand to help me out—a nice gesture, stately, like the old Volvo.

"Lex. I was just asking about you. No one seemed to know where you'd gone."

"I didn't say. But I did tell Tom to let Jared know I'd be back." He nodded in what looked like approval. "Who's inside? All of them?"

"Vin and Courtney are out. I think she was on the edge of stir crazy. Jared's holed up in his room. I came over to keep Melanie company and maybe coax a little food into her. Tom had her out lawyering most of the day."

"And where's Tom?"

"At the moment? I don't know, Lex. Where is Tom ever?" The eyebrows raised, pleating his already rumpled forehead.

"Look, Nate," I said quickly. "I really would like to talk with you."

"For you, pro bono." We both laughed. "Sorry. These last few days I find I need to laugh as badly as I need to cry: department of sanitation for the human infrastructure, messy but it works. Seriously, Lex, I'd be glad to talk with you. I've already told you that I'd welcome a visit. Tomorrow's Saturday; I don't have hours. Suppose you take yourself over to my place; I'll give you lunch. How's that?"

"That's good. Good," I repeated. He gave me address, phone number, and directions.

He moved toward the Volvo and then turned back to me. "I know all of this is tough on you. But tough isn't altogether bad. It builds muscles you don't know you have until you need to use them." He nodded almost imperceptibly, as though confirming something for himself. "And I'll bet you're gonna need to use them."

As I watched him drive off, it occurred to me that what I labored awfully hard to achieve came naturally to him: insight. It was like a musician's ear or an artist's vision—part of one's hard wiring or not. Sure, you could cultivate it to a point, but a natural is a natural. He was able to read people, and people desire to be read—a desire that draws them to astrology, to palmistry, to religion—and to shrinkers.

I rang the door chime. Almost instantly, Melanie opened the door herself. The openness of her face told me she'd thought it must be Nate returning, perhaps to say another word, bestow a kiss, collect something he had left behind. Her expression congealed when she saw me. She began to turn away.

"Melanie," I said, weary of our pantomime yet again, "come on. Can't we put it away? I have no excuse for what I did six years ago. None. I was a puerile bitch. Think of me as a sort of Monica Lewinsky."

"Don't give yourself airs," she said dryly. "Monica Lewinsky was pretty—chunky, but pretty—and sexy as hell. And Hillary Clinton was no kin of hers."

"Direct hit. Look, I can't erase it or make it all right, but I am sorry for . . ." The sentence had no good end. I was sorry I'd betrayed her, sorry I'd abandoned Jared. But it was equally true I had been sorry that I'd failed to take her husband from her. And even now, my heat for Tom stone cold, I could not be sorry for the experience of having loved him, not for a single minute of it.

"No, you can never make it all right." She quick-marched into the foyer. I followed behind her.

"Fair enough. What was between Tom and me was. It's long gone. Hate me if you need to."

"Don't you dare to talk to me about what you *think* there was between you and Tom. I'm bored with the whole issue of his cattin' round with you or Rima or any of the others." She turned and gave me a bitter smile. "What's the matter, you self-important little scrap? You still think you were the one and only true love?" The taunt had the satisfying sting of a whipping deserved.

"I'd say that title is yours, Melanie, for what it's worth. And it seems to have great worth, for you and Tom both. He always comes home; you never change the locks."

"Well, maybe I should've," she said softly, as though her mind were half on something else, "years ago, way before your time. Anyway, it's all just a load of dirty laundry now, with everybody in the world peeking at the stains." Melanie and her privacy; Melanie, who'd never wanted full-time help living in her house, looking, scrutinizing. She threw her arms up, open wide. "I couldn't care anymore. Let 'em look. Doesn't matter."

I reached out and held on to one of her arms on its way down. "I *am* a self-important scrap. Perhaps loners like me become excessively important to themselves because they're so unimportant to anyone else. Melanie, I am sorry for causing you pain."

"I don't want to say or hear one more word about it." But she didn't shake my hand off her arm. "I'm tired. Very tired." Her hand went to her neck and began to rub it absently.

"Can I make you a cup of tea or a drink?"

"I want to sleep." It was a plea—made not to me. Her face had the sunken-eyed look of the sleep-starved.

"Do you think that in the circumstances a pill might be okay?"

"No," she said. "No, I don't. I gave my word about that. I stick to my word." She laughed and it was a sound almost bell-pure. "A brandy might be all right, though."

We went into the conservatory, which contained a generously stocked bar. I poured us each a liberal tot, and we sat ourselves at opposite ends of a long sofa, like the mismatched pair of cushions we were, and began to sip. Sisters, but known to each other in patchwork fragments only. Our mother and father had shared us in a most Solomonic way, split right down the middle. The notion made me begin to giggle. "Don't mind me," I said. "It's probably alcohol on an almost empty gut. Courtney stocks good grog. I think the bottle said twenty-five years old."

"Vin," she said. "Vin is in charge of the bar. It's something he's good at—he did a little bartending B.C.

Courtney couldn't care; she wouldn't know twenty-five years from twenty-five minutes. These old-money families, the women, anyway, they fall into two groups, far as drinking: the ones who'll sip a little sherry, and the ones who'd swig paint thinner if nothing else was round." It felt good to chuckle at something.

"Do you . . . Do you trust Vin and Courtney, Melanie?" I asked on the heels of it.

"I don't trust anyone." It was like a ball fired hard and fast at my face, the jokey mood of a moment ago gone for us both. She looked away. "I trusted my daddy," she said into her glass, like a girl mumbling a prayer. "I trust Calista." She met my eyes again. "I suppose I trust Nate." She took another swallow of the brandy. "Anyway, Vin thinks he's in love with me, and Courtney knows it. Nothing I need to trust them for. I don't give a damn about them. I've got other things on my mind."

"Melanie, what about Jared?"

She snapped to attention and put her glass down on the table beside her. "Say what you mean," she said sharply.

"I mean that he can read, he can think. And he has all the time in the world to do both—day after day here, so many hours closeted with his computer and whatever's in his head. His sister was murdered; the police and the FBI are sniffing closely at his parents."

Her body seemed to relax itself. "PD, FBI, DA: the whole alphabet of them can sniff and bark as much as they want, but they can't prove what did not happen. They can't do anything to us," she said, her chin raising itself in emphasis. "You care so much about Jared, make him see that."

I said, "I'll try." I should bring up school now, I

thought. It would be the right time to mention Barney, the possibility of . . . But something made me say instead, "You know, in Hampstead, the morning the MI6 pair came? I admired the way you pulled it off. I never told you that, did I?"

Her ghost of a smile seemed to appreciate a private joke. "No, you didn't."

"You knew what he was up to. Even that night that he hit you and ran off. You knew it wasn't a woman. You hollered something about dragging us all down . . . You *knew*."

"That it must be something dangerous? Sure I did. That man would see us all in hell for a damned story. So I figured . . . You're a weird little spook, bringing this all up now. Daddy used to say you were a dark horse. He was right. You and Jared, peas in a pod."

"Da . . . He used to say that about me?"

"Well, for a while. Then we stopped saying anything." Metaphors about heartstrings are cliché with reason: mine were vibrating now in a Daddy chord, minor in key. "You know," she said, rising, "I think I'll be able to sleep now. Thanks, Allie." This was the first time since Hampstead she'd called me that. Slip of the tongue or intentional, tonight I warmed to the old name.

"My pleasure," I said. I followed her out to the foyer and watched her mount the stairs, as consciously straight-backed as though a book were balanced on her head.

I went into the kitchen and found the maid smoking a cigarette beside a partly opened back door. She snuffed it out on the sole of her shoe and gave me one of those looks, part guilt, part defiance and total resentment. "Don't mind me," I said. "I'm trespassing on your turf looking for a sandwich of some sort."

"She don't abide smokin'," she said.

"I expect there's a lot she doesn't abide. Anyway, my lips are sealed." I did the lock-and-tossed-key mime, and she smiled: gorgeous white teeth in a Nefertiti face. She was about my age, I thought. "What's your name?"

"Tonya. Ham and cheese all right?"

"Super," I said. She fetched ingredients from the fridge, turned her back, and set about assembling it. Her motions were as quick and efficient as a short order cook's. Neither of us spoke for a bit. "Hard work for you round here with all the extras in residence."

"Oh, yeah. My aunt's coming in tomorrow to help me out. She be stayin' for a while. She was Miz Courtney's nursemaid way back when."

"It sounds so *Gone with the Wind*," I said.

"Only difference between Southport and South Carolina is the weather—and the pay, which is *damn* good in this house, not to mention a free room and bath in one of the best pieces of real estate in Fairfield County. Courtney may be strict, but she's not stingy." The down-home patois came and went at will, I noticed. She nudged my sandwich from cutting board to plate and handed it to me. "Drink?"

"A Coca-Cola if you've got one. And by all means, do smoke, if you want to. Everybody does in London."

She considered the invitation and, after she'd fetched me the Coke, accepted. "Sorry about your niece," she said. "Callie was . . . a nice little girl."

I noted the brief hesitation. "Was she, Tonya? I only knew her as a baby."

"She was always sweet to me. Knew my name, and *how are you* and *please* and *thank you*. She was an old soul, Callie, so maybe she's just flown back home."

"How do you mean, an old soul?"

"Well, like she lived before, had the experience of being a grown person already. Maybe that's why she knew just how to handle the grown-ups, give them what they wanted so they'd give her what *she* wanted."

I bit into the sandwich and realized how hungry I was in an everyday way: the sort of manageable hunger that goes away after one has eaten a meal. "And what do you think she gave and got, Tonya?"

She took a long drag at her cigarette. Her sheer satisfaction in the act of smoking inspired a momentary desire to take up the habit. However, a new addiction seemed a poor idea. "It was love," she said. "Not just, you know, love like any kid wants, but like Callie was gonna win the Love Olympics—blow any competition right out of the water!"

"And what did she do to get it?"

"Well, against her brother she didn't have to do much of anything. Jared shoots himself in his own foot just fine! Callie had a clear field with the grown-ups, and it seemed to me like she learned just how to make folks feel special: her mama, Vin—I even heard her one time playing up to Courtney. 'Courtney, you're the smartest person I ever met!' Know what? It worked, had Courtney eating right out of her hand. She practiced those moves just the way she practiced in the gym downstairs here. Poor kid."

A poor kid and a seductress both: What could be much more seductive than a magic mirror reflecting back the viewer's best self lit by a pretty little girl's admiring eyes? Calista had sung for her supper. "You didn't mention her dad," I said.

"No. I don't know Mr. McQuade except from his show, which I don't care for: It's too mean. Never seen him over here, not until now. They're hintin' round in the paper, on the TV, that he might've messed with Callie and then killed her." The dark, liquid eyes fixed on mine waiting to hear what I'd say.

"I *do* know him, and I find that almost impossible to believe." Almost? Yes, almost—the qualifier would hurt Tom's feelings, but he'd approve it, despite that. I could see him leaning back in his Eames chair the way he used to do, blunt index finger pointing at me to emphasize the lesson he was about to deliver: *"And if you plan on making any film about humans that's worth shit, cross the word* impossible *out of your dictionary."*

"What about Vin?" I asked, sharper than I meant. "You think it's possible *he* might have messed round with Calista?"

She stubbed out her cigarette and stood. I knew before she spoke that I'd put a foot wrong, stamped it squarely into her patch of loyalties. "I *think* we're about done here," she said as she rinsed the saucer she'd been using as an ashtray. "You want any more to eat?" Her face dared me to say yes.

"No. No, thank you. And . . . anything we talked about is private."

"We didn't talk about anything at all, Miz Cavanaugh." She opened the kitchen door; a gusty breeze blew in, chasing the vestige of cigarette smoke. Tonya stepped outside.

I made my way upstairs, tired in the way that makes every fiber, especially brain tissue, feel half melted. I stopped before Jared's closed door, wanting to tell him a casual "Hi, I'm back; see you in the morning." My knuckles drew back, but before they touched wood, I heard something inside that did not sound like a CD. A cat, was my first thought—he's got an animal in there. My second was something else: Jared sobbing. I knocked. "Jared, it's Lex."

"Go *'way!*" I opened the door, and ducked not quite in time to dodge a large book shied at my head. It caught my shoulder smartly. Jared's crying paused for a second; he stood looking at me, tears rolling down his blotched, red face.

"You got me," I said.

"Good!" he shot back furiously.

"Mad at me for going off? I told your dad to tell you I'd be back. Did he?"

"Didn't see him; he's never here. The two of you could go and fuck your . . . Who the hell cares anyway?"

I stepped over the threshold, kicking the book inside ahead of me, and closed the door. "Evidently, you do," I said. "Look, your father and I are in-laws and friends; that's all we are now. Sometimes, I badly need to be alone, so I will go off. But I won't leave. You have my word." He didn't move, but the fists at his side began to unclench. I did not debate the advisability of touching him. I went to him and wrapped my arms round him tight as a swaddling cloth round a baby. We stayed that way for some time, his gasping sobs and the throb in my shoulder marking seconds like a metronome. I felt his body grow less rigid as he cried himself out. Finally, he was still.

"You're ch . . . choking me."

"Sorry." I turned him loose. His breathing was still syncopated. I saw a box of tissues, handed it over to him, and sat on his bed, near the foot, leaning against the polished brass frame. Shortly, he joined me, but up near the head, keeping his distance now.

"I wasn't blubbering about you, not mainly," he said, froggy hoarse.

"Oh, I know that," I said.

"Blubbering, that's what he calls it, my dad. He can make you feel like . . . like a bug. Worse than a bug."

"In England they call it blubbing. My mum wasn't awfully sympathetic about it either. She'd imitate me; laugh at me. So I took care to blub alone in my room. I did it for hours. I remember rather looking forward to it. I'd blub and then I'd eat all sorts of food by myself, then perhaps blub some more. And it *did* make me feel better."

"What . . . what was the reason?"

"Nothing as good as yours."

"And you still did it when you were twelve?"

"Unfortunately, just about then I stopped crying altogether for quite a few years. I'm not just sure why, probably to spite my mother but I think it would have been better for me if I hadn't. It's awful not to be able to cry. I'm glad you can. Talk to me about Calista. She must have been tough to have for a sister."

"That's a poem: Calister, tough sister. Dumb poem. Did you mean to make a poem?" He forced a laugh, a jagged one. "She was okay," he mumbled, and blew his nose. "She was a fucking asshole," I heard him mumble more softly into the tissue. He drew a broken breath. "I don't want to talk about anything. Want to know a fact? Jupiter has just about a thousandth the mass of the sun. They call it 'the star that failed.'" He repeated it slowly, listening to the words. "The star that failed."

I looked at him: shaken, scared, with all the reason in the world to be so. *Disturbed, weird:* those crackling words lobbed carelessly at him like small fireworks set to explode.

"Did I hurt your shoulder?" he asked, looking back at me.

"A bit." I reached my feet off the bed, captured the

thrown book between them, and raised it up to hand level. *"A Wrinkle in Time."* If I had opened it, I'd have seen on the flyeaf, "To Jared from Lex. I'll read it to you while you're still 6, but by 7 I'll bet you won't need my help. Happy Birthday." But by the time he turned seven I was gone.

"I am so sorry," I said, holding the book out to him.

He took it. Then he yawned. "I guess I want to go to sleep," he said quietly.

"Give me a knock when you wake, okay? No matter how early. Maybe we'll be able to go off somewhere." I leaned over and kissed his forehead. He let me do it.

CHAPTER
10

The story Tom had expected in the *Star* next week in fact surfaced earlier. It was on the Net when I awoke the following morning, graphic photos purloined from the coroner's office: Calista's dark, strangled neck, her splayed naked legs, vacant face. Surrounding this pornography, sprouted lush weeds of tropical prose: speculation and innuendo. Calista's genital and vaginal irritation could have been . . . Tom and Melanie's stories about the burglar alarm sounded like . . . Asphyxia to enhance sexual sensation was sometimes achieved through a ligature like the one . . . The back of her right hand had been abraded with soap and brush—an effort to scrub away what proved to be black and red ink from felt-tipped pens. Part of a murky ritual that . . . ?

The gist was that Macbeth and his Lady were in cahoots in a cover-up, because one or both of them had done the murder—either him in the heat of sexual passion or her in the heat of jealous rage (or pique over pants-wetting?). Or perhaps Lady M was a bit sexually wonky herself.

I sat in bed, legs tented before me, eyes glued to the screen as the computer warmed in my lap like a malevolent cat. The sight of Calista's ruined neck chilled the marrow, and the thought of Jared seeing on his screen what I was seeing on mine was in some way worse. I pictured him gazing, fascinated, furious, terrified, wondering—if he allowed himself that latitude—whether he'd been born to monsters, and what might happen to him if left in their care.

How well can one know another person? For whom can one swear? To what extent? I thought of the teenaged snake charmer I'd filmed in Bali two years earlier. Briefly, in my heart I had become him, had felt course through my veins the hot blood that coursed through his as he dominated a cobra, bent the lethal creature to his will. The blood was heated by a sense of power almost indistinguishable from love. His bond with the snake was the most important element in his life. Had a snake been killed in that village, it could not have died at Yoshi's hands, no matter what the evidence against him. During those six weeks I would have sworn to that.

But only that. I'd met his widowed mother, an ill-tempered crone of whom he was inordinately fond, and his macho elder brother, of whom he wasn't. If one of them had turned up murdered, I could have sworn to nothing.

Tom: there had been a time when I was sure that I uniquely knew every cranny in this most crannied of men simply because I was in love with him. As Melanie had pointed out, what a piece of hubris. Certainly I pitied the risky childhood he'd spent bouncing from place to place, none of them safe. Certainly I exulted in cosseting the wounded boy inside the hard-shelled man. Certainly I was thrilled by his audacity, charmed by the range of his knowledge, eager to accrete as much of it as I could, flattered by the privilege of sharing intimate moments with a man not given to easy intimacy.

I remembered the play of his hands on my skin, his mouth biting sometimes, the pleasured pain of my spine rubbing itself raw, getting shagged on a shag carpet. I remembered the private signals, his calling me Lexalot, which meant we would have sex that night. I remembered the night he told me how the rough stranger who was his mother, assisted by a social worker, had dislocated his arm when dragging him from the foster home where he'd lived from infancy to four years old. I remembered him teaching me, often sternly, his principles of integrity in journalism. I remembered the jolt of learning how far he'd stretch them for a story, the shock of seeing his hand slash Melanie's face. And I remembered the wounding surprise of discovering that he'd begun to cheat on me with Rima.

Nothing I had ever glimpsed in Tom jibed with a man who would wrap a cord round his little girl's neck and violate her with a finger while he watched her die. My heart wanted to swear that that was impossible, but the pernicious "almost" intruded itself once more. Years of conditioning against swallowing absolutes whole had scoured from my soul any aptitude for pure faith.

Jared, I will protect you as best I can, but I cannot promise your parents are innocent.

I opened the dormer window and breathed in cold, gray air. It seemed quite appropriate. Fifteen minutes later, showered and dressed in my drugstore sweat suit, the clothing closest at hand, I knocked at Jared's door.

He did not respond and I heard no sound. After a second knock and a third, I opened the door. He was not there. Seven-thirty in the morning; perhaps he'd gone down to breakfast. Perhaps . . . A pounding in my chest began hard and fast, and left me breathless. He was meant to wake me, so where was he? It was absurd, of course, to be this scared—hysterical, illogical, womanish . . .

My eyes darted up and down the hall. There were only the two guest rooms, Jared's and mine, in this top floor wing. I stood poised on the stair pondering what to do. I thought of Melanie, the wild panic she must have felt waking in a house as dead quiet as this one to find Calista's room empty.

I bolted down the first flight. "Jared," I called out, then, "Jared!" not caring a toss about making an ass of myself. I would tear the place apart if necessary to find him.

And find him I did. I caught a glimpse of the back of his yellow shirt in the doorway of Melanie and Tom's room. "Mom," I heard him almost moan. "Mom. No, Mom, *no!*" He took a step backward.

Her arms reached out beyond the doorframe for him. From where I stood, I could not see the rest of her. "The Internet, right?" Her voice grated. "I bet you've been reading garbage on the damned Internet. I will rip the phone out of that room. I will *smash* that computer—"

His head turned and he saw me. "Lex . . . ?" That was as far as he got before the arms wrapped themselves round him and pulled him inside. The door shut behind them.

I stayed put, trying to calm down. He had run to his mother. Did that mean he trusted her, or just the opposite? Was Tom there inside that room? Throughout their marriage, as far as I knew, Melanie and Tom had shared a bedroom, never mind that he was seldom in it. I could not quite bring myself to crouch before the door and keyhole peep, though the temptation was there.

I felt off-balance, impotent—a rotten combination. There in the roomy, square hall, lined with oil-painted landscapes and closed doors, I found myself dropping into a knee bend, then another. Before I knew it, I'd done a dozen. I pictured my *sensei* in the Chalk Farm Road studio nodding in restrained approval. My foot kicked out high. After five or six goes it achieved a smooth, reliable ninety degrees. Then I attempted a whirl. I gave myself a full ten minutes of these shake-out routines, and somewhat calmed, I went downstairs.

Courtney was in the breakfast room, suited up for business, head lowered into a newspaper, which was, I imagined, the *New York Times*. I paused before entering to take a look at her for a bit unawares. She was a woman constructed of squares: flat, square face; wide, square body. In my books, *plain* is not a euphemism for *ugly*. Courtney was plain—as was the tan herringbone jacket she wore today; as was her tan hair, side parted, fastened with a tortoise barrette, the way it must have been for close to forty years. Her head did not move, nor did she turn the paper's page. Either she was utterly absorbed in what she was reading, or she was not reading at all.

As I would have with a film subject, I ticked off her items: One of the last people to see Calista alive; married to a man with whom Calista had spent perhaps a third of her waking hours every day, much of it in the gym in this house; had been at least mildly jealous of Calista, perhaps more so of Melanie—but that information came at second hand from a not-awfully-bright man with a tendency to preen. Barney had told of a brutish father hacking away at her confidence until she'd quit medical school to run the beaches of Newport in pursuit of a strutting tennis pro.

What I knew at first hand was that Courtney, with her battering-ram persistence, had initiated important changes in the McQuades' lives: she'd introduced Vin as a new coach for Calista and Nate as a therapist for Jared. My impression was of a woman generous but only on her own terms; observant, if not intuitive.

I was so focused on my inventory taking that I'd failed to see its object look up from her newspaper to notice my presence.

"Good morning, Lex," she said. "You're up early."

"Not so early. *You're* up, after all."

"True. Orange juice, coffee, and toast on the sideboard. If you'd like one of your English breakfasts, I'll have Tonya make you something more substantial."

"Thanks, no. This'll be fine."

We performed the country house dialogue like a light tennis volley, both of us preparing for the real game. It was clear from the look in her eyes that she wanted to talk. So did I.

"You know about what's in the *Star*," I said, once I'd seated myself at her left hand. "Have you seen it?"

"I do know. It was on the television news. Mercifully, the channel I was watching didn't show the photos. I don't need or want to see those pictures." She spoke briskly as always, but at the same time her cheeks flushed deep pink. Though she was not redheaded like Barney, she had a redhead's skin, the thin sort that shows turmoil beneath it, even when the face is apparently in repose. "I had all the TV sets but the one in my bedroom removed and stored in the basement before the

McQuades came to stay—some silly idea that I could shield Jared from just this kind of thing. Pointless, what with his computer up there and a phone. He's probably been treated to an advance look at the *Star* already."

"I think so, yes."

"Their story, I gather, is aggressive in going after Tom and Melanie both."

"Scattershot pellets, nothing like hard evidence. And nothing like a motive." I paused and added, "Unless you're willing to buy a history of sexual abuse."

"And are you?" she asked. Her eyes appraised mine keenly.

"Actually, Courtney, I was going to ask you that question. You see, I've been out of the picture entirely for most of Calista's life, so my opinions are apt to be quite outdated."

For the first time since I'd met her, she had nothing to say. She peered at me as though my face might hold a clue to her own thoughts. I'd expected a spontaneously hearty "Nonsense!" Instead, she said, "It was something I'd begun to wonder about. That is to say . . . As you know, children are my interest. I volunteer in the courts as a guardian *ad litem*—a third party who monitors custody, adoption, abuse cases to represent best interests of the child." I nodded, not wanting to break in with anything that would divert her. "I get to spend some concentrated time with these children. Now, they don't usually come from homes like Calista's—not from Westport or Southport. Norwalk, Bridgeport, towns like that, more likely. Black, many of them; poor, most of them. What I'm saying is, the children I see are less sophisticated than Calista, less poised. I've noticed something about them, the ones who've been sexually abused. There's a way they can look at you and then look away fast when you look back—as though they're ashamed of themselves. This is only an impression, mind you, but recently, I thought I saw that in Calista."

"How recently?"

"The last time I saw her. Halloween." Her cheeks colored again. She lifted her cup and took two deliberate sips of coffee. Self-discipline, I thought—product of good breeding. I worried that an excess of good breeding might lead her to just drop the subject.

"What happened that night, Courtney?" I prompted. "How did the evening strike you?"

"Is this the way you interview people for your films?" She smiled like a polite patient in a dentist's chair.

"Sometimes. It's what I know how to do. In a crisis we all do what we know how to do, and hope it's of some use. Look, I think you're an observant person and a compassionate one. You care for children. I care a great deal for Jared."

"Yes, I can see that, and good for you! Poor Jared, God knows he needs someone on his side. But he's such a difficult boy to like."

"I find him quite easy to like," I shot back, and was immediately sorry for it. The last thing I wanted was to steer us into a cul-de-sac for a debate on the winning qualities of Jared's personality. "But that's neither here nor there," I said quickly. "Look, I'm *his* volunteer guardian *ad litem*, if you can see it that way, and I'm asking you to help me grasp what I need to grasp."

"You haven't touched your toast, Lex." Enter the games mistress. "And the other night you only moved your food round on the plate. No wonder you're so thin." A sure conversation stopper. "Seriously, if you're undertaking what you say you are, you're going to need to keep your strength up." I began on the toast. It was easier all round than arranging to barter bites for stories like a toddler in its high chair. "I've been over some of this with the police, of course," she said.

"Some of it?" I coughed as toast crumbs took a turn down the wrong path.

"Are you all right?" I nodded and downed some coffee. "I didn't mention to them what I just told you," she said with a meaningful look. But what its meaning was, I couldn't say.

"Why not?"

"I thought about it and . . . Don't forget, they questioned us so soon after . . . It was not exactly clear in my . . . I didn't want to make mischief . . ." This bobbling of hers was so at odds with any Courtney I'd seen that it made me wonder whether she was certain of her husband's innocence—or thought the police were. I waited, figuring she'd go on talking.

"It really was sad," she said. "Calista was an utterly engaging child, but she dominated life in that house. Your Jared was like a stepchild, and that was Melanie's doing, all Melanie. I mean, my God, just look at that wall of Calista's photos, first thing you see when you walk in. It's as though the child were a movie star." Her head wagged slowly side to side in disapproval. "Or an only child."

"Anyway, when Jared wheeled Calista up the front walk in that absurd wagon, she flashed a hand mirror at us and called out, 'Trick or treat?' She was smiling and being charming as all get-out, but I happened to catch her eye—no, I caught it on purpose, I suppose—and she got that look I told you about, and then she looked away fast.

"Then we all went inside. Melanie and Calista seemed in top form and everyone was having a high old time, except of course Jared, who stood by the doorway looking ready to explode. No one else seemed to notice him, but after the murder I mentioned it to Nate, and he said he'd also thought Jared seemed especially agitated that night. I tried to talk to him a little, but he didn't really respond." Her mouth moved into a rueful almost smile. "I admit that for all my goodwill, I don't really have a lot of rapport with children, I mean one-on-one." She pulled the smile wider and added, "But, as you said before, Lex, you do what you know how to do."

"I understand the evening fell apart rather abruptly."

"Who told you that? Nate?"

"No, actually. Barney Warden did. I went over to the school yesterday."

"Did you?" She studied my face as though readying to tell me something. But it underwent a sea change and turned out to be, "Lex, are you sure you wouldn't like a fried egg, some bacon. Really, it's no trouble."

"I'll just take another piece of toast. That's all I can manage." I reeled this off very quickly and jumped up to fetch the damned toast. It was either that or clap her a good one.

She waited until my mouth was filled and said, "I was in the bathroom when the storm broke. It all must have happened very fast. When I came out, the kids and I almost collided head-on. They'd been ordered upstairs and they really sprinted. Vin told me what had happened, but he couldn't fathom why. One minute everything was fine, the next Calista threw herself on the floor—she was trapped in that ridiculous tail, you know, had been for hours. Barney thinks she had an accident, wet herself. I can't imagine that would be a major catastrophe."

"Isn't that sort of thing meant to be common among sexually abused children?" I asked.

"Yes. Yes, as a matter of fact it is," she said, and looked away, reluctant suddenly, I thought, to discuss that issue further.

"Since you were out of the room, I suppose you don't know whose lap Calista pitched herself off."

"No. Was she on someone's lap at that point? She'd sat on everyone's, including mine. Melanie tended to pass the child round like a box of chocolates."

"You don't like Melanie much," I said, "and yet you arranged for Vin to coach her daughter, for Nate to work with her son, and now you've taken her in."

"You don't like her either," she replied, not missing a beat, "and yet you're here." She drained her coffee cup and stood with the jacket-straightening moves of someone about to leave. "We all have our reasons. Maybe our lives are defined by more reasons than are good. I'll say to you simply that my husband and I operate together in what you might call a delicate balance. He is a gymnast, of course, so in many ways that comes more easily to him than to me. I work hard, though. I work hard for everything I have, other than money—and certain aspects of being rich have not been as easy as you might think. You never know if you're doing enough for others or too much . . .

"Melanie and her family are here in part because Vin needs them to be. Their presence—more precisely, Melanie's presence—is keeping him from falling apart. But if there were no Vin, I might have opened my home to them anyway. Like or dislike is not the issue: this is what my minister calls an obligation in charity. Now, I really must go. A rather stubborn judge has agreed to delay his Saturday golf game to meet with me. I can't keep him waiting."

I stood, too. The top of my head reached almost to her shoulder. "I appreciate your candor, Courtney. Might we talk some more—later perhaps?"

"Perhaps." She was holding a gold compact open, angled to catch the light so that she could apply her pink lipstick accurately. She cared, I realized as I watched her take the time to do it. She cared very much how she looked. The compact snapped shut. "Well," she said in the ringing, take-charge tone, "one thing I suggest you think about. Jared will need to go back to school, and soon. This is apt to drag out a long time. It will be a disaster for him to hunch over a computer all day and watch it happen. Now, there's a challenge for you: convincing your sister of that. But you like a challenge, Lex, don't you?" She hoisted the strap of her briefcase onto her shoulder and left.

I watched Courtney's sturdy, brave back readying for a day of volunteering her goodwill and intelligence to do worthy things—and irritating the pants off people while she did them. I wondered whether the real reason for failing to mention her suspicions of sexual abuse to police was that the person she suspected off the bat was her husband.

"Lex." Tom's voice behind me. When I turned, the effect was peculiar. He had during the past day and night loomed so hulking large in my mind that I was startled to see him reduced to human scale: a slim man in chino pants and a brown pullover, his face older than the one that lived in my mind. It was rather like a first sighting of Robert Redford or Paul Newman, both of whom I had met back in my production assistant days: the huge film stars were astonishingly small.

"I won't say good morning; it isn't one. I saw it on the Web."

He said, straight-faced, "Geraldo has tendered an invitation to tell my side of it on his show."

"Jesus."

"Can't blame a guy for trying. I would in his shoes."

"How's Jared?" I asked. "I saw him go into your room."

"Not my room," he said tightly. "I'm down the hall. Melanie's choice; who can blame her?"

It passed belief, didn't it? A philanderer like Tom hurt—as I could see he was—at being evicted from the marital bed. I said, "Jared caught the *Star* coverage too, I think. He looked distraught."

His eyes shone with rage or incipient tears; it was impossible to tell. "I would hack off my arm to make it easier for that boy if that would do any good," he said quietly. "But it wouldn't, of course. I'm not much good to him anyway you look at it. Aside from some crazy superstition I've got about a good-night kiss, I hardly see my son, don't really know him. Didn't know my daughter well enough to find a way to love her. Not ever." He reached out to me. "Hand, please. Just let me squeeze it, okay?"

I held it out and he did, hard, as though his other arm, the one he'd volunteered for Jared's sake, were actually being hacked off. I wanted to give him sustenance . . . something. But I did not have what he needed.

After a moment, he released my hand, slowly. "Thanks. You're a good girl, always were, Lexalot. Warm hands. You know, the bitch of it is I've wanted to touch Jared these last few days, just . . . touch him, the way men do their sons. And I can't seem to make the old arms move. Ironic, huh? Who you can touch, who you can't."

Any good girl with warm hands, a rounded behind, and some sass to her walk, but not your son. How about your wife? Can you touch her, or did you stop ten years ago? I never asked you that, Tom. "You could begin by talking to him," I said flatly.

"Could. Should. Maybe sometime when Melanie's not round," he said with a sour smile. "She runs interference on him these days like an all-American tackle. Haven't you noticed? Those big eyes of yours see every damned thing." I thought of Jared as I'd seen him half an hour ago, being swallowed up into his mother's room. Overprotective? Exactly how protective was the mother of a murdered child meant to be of her surviving one?

A phone rang twice and stopped.

"He can't just stay locked up in this house, Tom, isolated with no end in sight. Even if he can't go back to school just yet, he needs to be able to take a walk, ride a bicycle. Breathe!"

He stepped back and looked at me, suddenly the ice-eyed predator of *Inside Straight*. "You don't buy that a killer could be waiting to catch him out alone, huh? I guess you're with the majority, who think Jared's completely safe, except from his mother and father."

Just then, a black woman, older than Tonya but handsome in the same strong-boned way, entered the room. The aunt, no doubt.

"Miz Cavanaugh?"

"Yes," I said, glad for this or any interruption.

"Telephone for you. You want to take it upstairs or in the library? It's your mother—from *Australia*."

CHAPTER
11

"How did you know where to find me, Mum?"

"You serious, Lex? We have newspapers in Sydney, and Patrick's on-line with his damned computer half the night—these boys with their toys. One way or another, I learned that you were there and where y'all were staying. I got the phone number from information." Some blessings do come with my mother. The absence of admonitions for failing to keep in touch is among them. "Now, look, I took the trouble to do that because I need to talk to you about all this."

"*All this*'s name was Calista. She was ten."

"I can manage without the snotty talk, thank you." *Ah, but I can't, Mum. I fight you like a porcupine: quills out even at a distance of ten thousand miles by telephone.* "I know you think I fly round on a broomstick, but I am not a woman without feelings—and I feel sick about what's happened to that poor child. Everyone does."

"Everyone is not that poor child's grandmother."

"And neither am I," she said, sounding for all the world like Melanie at her most steely, "because I do not choose to be. Let's be very clear about that. Melanie McQuade is no daughter of mine—and please do not give me hearts and flowers about the power of blood ties."

"I wasn't about to."

"You were thinking it. I am far from stupid, and I know you like a book."

"What I was thinking was just the opposite. I was thinking how *little* power such ties have over you. I've read *your* book, as well. In the original version I was meant to be no daughter of yours, either."

"Well, that's not how it worked out, is it? It's what happens that matters—what you do, not what you think. And you better hope, young lady, that we none of us have to hang for the thoughts that fly through our head. If we did, the world would suddenly become a very empty place, I can tell you." I didn't respond, sick suddenly of my own part in our long-term, long-distance, ham-handed jousting match. What did I want from her after all these years, a bogus protestation that what I knew to be true was not?

"Let it go, Lex," she said. "It's over. So you didn't have the mother of your dreams and I didn't have the daughter of mine. Well, so what? You had it pretty good. Why, I'd have kissed the ground to have the chances I gave you, never mind you threw 'em all away. Your childhood was—"

"Right, Rebecca of Sunnybrook Farm."

Her laugh rang with a black undertone. "You are lucky that reading some old book's as close as you came to living on a farm. Forget about your sunshine and rolling fields. You get up at five in the morning's what you do, in all kinds of damn weather and you mess round with chickens and cows and pigs—and they all smell. It is hard and dirty work. Farm men live with the animals and off the animals; they smell like the animals and act like the animals." This was new. I had not heard any of it, nor had I heard this particular chord in her voice: its component notes were loathing and pain.

"I didn't know you'd grown up on a farm, Mum." She'd never said anything more specific than, "in the country," but then, I hadn't really inquired.

"There's a lot about me you don't know, but that's not what I called to discuss. I just got carried away there for a minute. There's also a lot about your so-called sister you don't know, and that *is* why I'm sitting here on this phone."

Now. After decades when you wouldn't say a word, punished me when I persisted in asking. Now. "I'm all ears, Mum," was all I said, and I tried to make it neutral.

"Melanie is a vixen and a cheat." *Very much the words I would use to describe you, Mother.* "She cannot help herself. True, she is talented—was talented—and she can be charming. But notice how she has no friends, how guarded and suspicious she is. She's always scheming, that's why. Melanie is a person who'll carve your heart out, if it suits her." Dead air.

"Is that it? Is that what you wanted to tell me? Might you want to add some specifics perhaps to make it sound less like an anonymous poison-pen letter out of a third-rate thriller?"

She laughed full out. "You are such a Brit, Lex! I did that for you. You have that toney Cambridge accent because of your mummy. Now that I've paid you a compliment, what're you gonna do, start talking Cockney to spite me? Specifics, you want? She's a nympho and a thief. That girl was spreadin' her legs by the time she was twelve and stealin' even younger. Plus, she was the best damned liar in the state of Virginia, and maybe by now in all of America. You mark these words: Some way or another Melanie is involved in that little girl's murder, just like you see in the papers. I can't say she did it herself; I don't know that. But she *is* mixed up in it, and it has to do with a man. And if you ask me, you ought to get the hell out of there."

"I'm not asking, and I'm not leaving, either. You walked out on Melanie when she was fifteen. For most of her life you haven't known her at all."

"By fifteen, my friend, the die is cast. I am telling you what you need to know, specially if you really do care about what happened to that little girl."

"Stop calling her 'that little girl'!" I screamed into the phone, control vanished. But almost at once, on the crest of a thought, I fought to grab hold. "You listen to me," I said, almost whispering to keep the shake out of my voice, "if you have any inkling of blabbing this shit to a tabloid or chat show, I will fly to bloody Sydney and personally cut your vicious heart out."

"You could never do that," she said, giving serious consideration to the possibility, "you know, cut a heart out. But Melanie could. Oh, yeah, she could. She is Old Testament, comes from having a Jewish father, probably. They are very vengeful people." What I'd heard growing up was that they were very near with money. "Now, don't say I didn't warn you. And since I sense you're about to hang up on me, I will say good-bye and good luck."

The phone remained pressed to my ear while I stood behind Courtney's ornate old desk, listening to the purr of the dial tone as though it had something to tell me. It didn't, except to underline that she'd had the last word as usual, and that I was left holding a bag of hot, windy anger—as usual.

I puzzled whether she was right about my being unable to kill and hoped she was not, before hoping just the opposite. Then I wondered whether any particle of what she'd said about Melanie was relevant to Calista's death. Finally I wondered whether my mother would, out of some late-flowering notion of moral responsibility or sheer malice, spew her imprecations out to a wider audience—or whether she already had.

The dial tone hushed itself into silence. I replaced the receiver in its cradle. My hand was not steady and my stomach shimmied with the beginnings of desire.

When I left the study, I heard Melanie's voice coming from the breakfast room and walked toward it. I found her and Tom sitting beside each other drinking coffee, while Jared, across the table, ate pancakes with what appeared to be a hearty appetite. At first glance, they might have been an advertisement for any of a dozen home products: good-looking, affluent, suburban American family, enjoying a weekend breakfast together.

"Good morning, Lex," Tom said. Fresh start. "Join us for some breakfast?"

"Good morning." I looked at Jared. His return gaze resembled that of a puppy trapped inside an animal shelter cage. Or perhaps that was merely what I imagined, given my indifference to animals and ignorance of children. He lifted his fork and downed another bite of pancake. "I'll have some coffee, thanks," I said to Tom and got myself an unwanted cup of the stuff from the sideboard urn and a piece of toast for prophylactic eating. "Well, Jared, are we going to go off somewhere today?" I asked, hoping he'd want to, hoping they'd let him go with me. Hoping foolishly.

"Jared's going with *us* today, Lex," Melanie said, her voice rippling to a meringue peak as it hit "us," and her tone guarded: our encounter last night had gone underground, leaving no trace. Her makeup was perfect, fair hair freshly washed and blow-dried. She looked terribly pretty in a silk shirt, the color of good butter. I noticed that Jared and Tom, too, were spandily dressed for an outing. Everyone seemed almost fine, if you ignored a slightly stunned quality their faces shared.

I glanced over at Tom, and knew. They were going to walk the gauntlet of photographers and reporters. The family, brave and united in its grief, its public face beaming wholesome rays of sunlight at the dark forces of satanic speculation.

"Maybe we could, uh . . . you know, tomorrow?" Jared asked.

"Of course we can," I said heartily, though my heart was badly out of sorts.

The maid walked in from the kitchen—the older woman again, Tonya's aunt. In her hand was a FedEx pouch. "This came for you, Miz Cavanaugh."

I thanked her, opened it, pocketed an enclosed note from Clive, and handed the pouch to Jared. "The tape of my monkey film." He smiled a wide, real grin. I smiled back—the first good moment in a while. "Maybe we can plug in and see it tonight, if Courtney can be persuaded to haul out some of her visual equipment."

"Why'd she hide it?" asked Jared. "To keep the poor baby from seeing the news? Like, duh."

"We're leaving soon, Jared," Melanie said. "Now, scoot upstairs and brush your teeth. And while you're at it, brush out any smart remarks you find in that mouth.

You hear me?" I'd been pleased to hear his smart remark. Personally, I find sarcasm a useful pain drain, vastly preferable to silent suffering or self-injury. But this was not the time to offer that view to my sister. Nor was it the time to mention the warheaded missile, perhaps already launched off the coast of Australia and heading her way.

As Jared passed near him, Tom reached his arm out awkwardly, as though guiding a newly grown limb, and tousled his son's hair. "I'll watch Lex's movie with you, buddy. I've always had a thing for monkeys."

CHAPTER
12

I rushed to get out of the house before the McQuades. I did not want to watch their performance for the media, some of whom were already at their stations just beyond the gates when I nosed my little blue car out of the drive. My comings and goings no longer got more than a halfhearted flurry of reaction. The men and women of the press knew by now that I was a dry well.

It was a quarter to ten. Nate Grumbach was not expecting me until twelve-thirty or so. If I'd been able to conjure a good excuse to land myself on his doorstep immediately, I would have, but excuses, I reckoned, were unwise strategy with someone as acute as Nate. Better to stick to the plan. I headed for Compo Beach again, for no bingeing purpose this time, simply because I like beaches for contemplation—and on gray out-of-season days such as this one, I like them best of all.

I parked, zipped my jacket up to the chin, rammed

my hands into its pockets, and began to walk. My fingers felt the crackle of paper: Clive's letter that had come with the videotape. I opened it and held the single sheet up into the wind like a small sail. It was brief.

> Pet [Clive on the page sounded reassuringly like Clive in person: a middle-aged, East End bred, happily married father of five.]: Our bottom-feeding press are making a banquet of your family disaster, as I'm sure you know. They still do hate McQuade something fierce here. In case you haven't cocked a snook, the tale-spinning ranges from your sister killing Calista under orders from God, speaking through her wisdom tooth, to your brother-in-law, member of a secret Irish cult, performing a Black Church sacrifice slaughter. And those are only two. Here's your tape. Hope it diverts the boy, if even for an hour. Post-production on the new film is going fine. I'll E-mail only if I need to. Keep your head on straight. Godspeed.

The Brits hated Tom with ample reason if one happens to think like a Brit: While a guest in their country, he exhibited the outrageously bad manners to consort with their enemies; the English ruling class do not forgive bad manners except amongst themselves. Accordingly, in some quarters, the prevailing version of the incident is that Tom McQuade, dating back to his checkered childhood, maintained ties to American IRA agents and was recruited by them while still in his teens. Tom supposedly wangled a London assignment in order to be on hand to participate in terrorist strikes, using his position as an American bureau chief as a cover.

The bare facts were that Tom was placed at several top-secret meetings where plans were made to bomb the offices of a certain Tory newspaper in Fleet Street—the bombing that resulted in the deaths of two night maintenance workers.

In the clamor of aftershock, it was the IRA agents themselves who turned Tom over to MI6 in exchange for more lenient prosecution and immunity for some higher-ups in Ireland. They swore to Tom's presence at the meetings, to his knowledge of the bombing plans— all in all, sufficient to support a half-cooked case of collaboration against him. Absent Melanie's artful lies about some other key nights, he might in fact have been formally prosecuted.

"It was a story," Tom told me. We were drinking whiskey in the Hampstead kitchen. He'd spent the day in an MI6 interrogation and arrived home quite late. Melanie, displaying her fury through utter silence, had taken herself off to bed at the sight of him. "The biggest damned story I'd had a crack at since Nam. One I'll never get to write now."

"Two people died," I said. "One was pushing a broom and the other was in the loo. The one in the loo was nineteen."

"No one was supposed to be there," he said. "The thing was going to go off in a top floor at a time when . . . Not how it happened. Obviously. It all got fucked up and two people *did* die. You want to beat me up? Take your licks; make 'em hard, make 'em hurt. There was nothing I could do."

"MI6 thinks you could have alerted them to the plan," I said—a tentative lick, a lick all the same.

He scrubbed his eyes with his fists and downed some drink. "I said there was nothing *I* could do—I being I.

I'm a reporter with a confidential source. The deal was that I could be a fly on the wall and two weeks after the fact I could do my report, no facts barred, no names mentioned. In the end, all bets were off on their side. Giving me up was their best shot to save their skins, so I guess we're even. I was using them; they used me. Wouldn't you say that's even, Lex?" He looked at me hard, demanding an answer.

"Dunno," I mumbled, then added, "Not that I have much experience, but I've never seen anything come out even, have you?"

"No, you're right." It was not what he had expected to hear. He nodded a sort of surprised approval. "Very sharp."

Flattered, I was so flattered, flattered enough to brush aside questions of ethics and blame. I was twenty-two then, and appallingly young for my age. I didn't normally talk back much in those early months; I listened and looked. Melanie and Tom, so recently installed as the cornerstones of my life, had taken on a film-noir glamour: the tarnished couple, perhaps doomed ultimately, but riveting meanwhile. In short, I watched the movie, goggle-eyed, and hoped against hope that they'd come out alive.

"Now, here's the question," I said in a surge of self-confidence. "If you'd been willing to sacrifice your story, couldn't you have stopped that bombing?"

"I'll never know, and neither will you. The difference is I'll live with those deaths for the rest of my life; you won't. Also, if I had broken faith and informed on them, I could be a dead reporter instead of an unemployed, potentially imprisoned one. Melanie and the kids might be dead, too. And a bombing would have happened anyway, maybe not that day, but the next.

"If you want the straightest answer, what fucking burns my ass is not those two poor bastards and what I maybe could have done and didn't do to prevent their deaths; it's not how much blame I own—plenty, and I know it—it's not even losing the job and maybe doing jail time. No, what really burns my sorry ass is my still-born story: 'Inside the IRA,' or some such. No one'll use it now, except the sleaziest of the sleazoids, the ones who cover Martian kidnappings. And I won't let them have it. So that's that." He raised his jelly glass. "Pip pip, cheerio, old thing!"

He did look burned at that moment. His face was gleaming as red as the face of a devil lit by live fire.

"You collaborated with the IRA for a story?" I asked, a word at a time, more awed than repelled at the idea. "You'd do it again tomorrow, wouldn't you?"

"Yeah, I'd do it again tomorrow. But outside of a bed, my friend, I never collaborated with anyone about anything in my life. I operate strictly solo, and I'm a pure-bred reporter, no idealogue." He grinned at me, a grin that mocked and encouraged. "You're getting it, about the lure of the story, aren't you? Don't bother to deny it"—I'd made no move to do that—"I'm looking at your face and I see it. Maybe you *will* make your films."

I was getting it.

The affair began in Westport two months later. I stipulate that the term *affair,* with its suggestion of frosty martinis sipped behind tall potted palms in the lounges of illicit hotels, is ridiculous. But try to come up with a better one. *Liaison,* perhaps? Not, Lord help us, *relationship.* So, *affair,* it is.

Ours began at just past midnight in the kitchen of the house on Sprucewood Lane. (Tom and my milestones always seemed to happen late at night in kitchens.) The two of us drank beer and contemplated my future.

Instead of indictment and trial for Tom, a deal had been struck with MI6 for his immediate *persona non grata* expulsion from Britain. When Melanie and the children left for America, I joined them—never a question of my not. The process of departure and resettlement progressed with extraordinary speed. Melanie had the Hampstead house and its contents sold within a week's time. Though it pained her to let go of her carefully selected treasures, she did—except for a certain small inlaid chest she could not bear to part with.

"I want nothing from this damned country, 'cept never to see it again." She claimed to feel similarly about Tom. However, when we landed in New York, we joined him at the Warwick Hotel, where they shared a room. With Tom's proxy, she chose Westport, Connecticut, as the place they ought to live, selected the house (in a smart neighborhood adjacent to the Hunt Club and recently vacated by a transferred executive), engaged painters and such, rented temporary furnishings, and achieved occupancy, largely furnished, within three weeks.

Tom wrote the checks, learned the layout of rooms, and made himself at home—as at home as he was anywhere, which was, at once, entirely and not at all. This dichotomy rang a responsive chime in me. Perhaps it lies at the heart of the reason people become journalists.

"They've got a good film school at NYU. I'll grubstake you, but getting in is up to you," he said. "My name would be a death kiss just now, so we won't mention it. Cambridge should help you, even if you did drop out."

"I dunno." I'd reverted to an inarticulate mumble. I

felt my pulse quicken, my neck begin to sweat. I recognized it as fear of an especially galling sort: the fear of getting what you've said you want, having your bluff called and then being unable to deliver the goods. "Melanie's going to need me here. Jared . . ."

"Scared, huh? That's okay, as long as you don't let yourself give in to it. If you do, you will hate yourself; I promise you that. This is November, new term begins in January. Hey, look, if you went under the wheels of a truck, my wife and son would manage, right?"

"And what about you, Tom?" The musky hoarseness in my throat knew where I was headed, even if I were to claim innocence. "Would you manage, too?"

His face darkened with that devilish look, teeth gorgeously white in a tight crescent-moon smile. "Badly— especially badly if we'd never found our way into a bed together. I've thought about that. Have you?"

I combusted spontaneously, my body ready to shoot straight to hell just to keep the fire roaring. The heat made my singed ears pop. I slid down off the step stool where I'd been sitting and went to him. "Oh, yes, I have thought about that."

We did not find our way to a bed, only as far as the carpet of his snug study, which fortunately was adjacent to the kitchen . . .

THE TAPE CUT off at this point. I had not allowed myself these memories for years. Now, taking them out of their vault for inspection left me in an odd state of peace. They were my souvenirs, precious to me—the more precious because they were complete, attached to no current ache of desire, no plans, no daydreams.

The sky darkened fast to slate color. The temperature had fallen since I'd begun my walk, which had brought me unawares to the far end of the beach, site of the recent bagel orgy. I took a deep breath and blew out a cartoon's white speech balloon, blank of any words. Then suddenly there were words: *Tom could not have done that to his daughter.* Those were the words.

I checked my watch. Eleven-forty. I began a jog back toward my car. I'd almost reached it when fat drops began to fall from the sky slowly, then faster. I looked up and smiled as they pelted my face. Responding to a craving of the body, I kicked my leg out and up at a sharp right angle and felt the hamstring pull just short of pain. I did a fast whirl, synchronized with a downward slash of stiffened arm, which my *sensei* would have rated marginal but not hopeless in timing and technique. I tried some splits and got almost to the ground. The next half hour was more than bracing; it was exhilarating. For the first time I experienced the harmony of body, mind, and nature that is said to define tae kwon do. I laughed, surprised by a surge of physical joy, as I practiced "the art of unarmed combat" alone on a rainy beach.

CHAPTER
13

Nate Grumbach's house was a neat green-and-white cape, dwarfed by its roll of land and majestic old trees—as though someone had bought up the two acres back in the 1920s, then run out of cash and skimped on building the house. It was raining hard as I pulled in to the long, curved drive and parked behind. The place was, I saw, actually larger than it looked, a separate wing tacked onto the back, invisible from the front.

I got out of the car. My leather jacket, a thrift shop relic designed by the Royal Air Force to withstand rigors tougher than November rain in Connecticut had kept my top half dry during my beach workout, but my feet were quite damp, my bottom a good deal damper, and my hair drenched.

He was standing at the half-opened back door, motioning me inside. "When I was your age, walking in the rain was considered seriously romantic, but I gotta say you look like a cat someone tried to drown."

"That's rather romantic in its way, the cat escaping, some of its lives still left." I squished up the couple of steps to a square of porch and went inside. "Sorry to be dripping on your floor," I said.

"Floor doesn't mind; it's brick and it's withstood a lot worse than water. Tell you what, I'll get you something to put on and stick your things in the dryer." I hung my jacket on a peg, removed my sneakers and socks, and followed him barefoot through an over-warm kitchen, where something baked itself in garlicky eminence, and up a narrow staircase. When we reached the top he said, "Now, just a second, be right back, okay?"

I waited in a small hall while he entered a room at its end, presumably a bedroom, and shut the door behind him. Moments later, he returned holding a storm blue toweling robe that looked to be about right for someone my size. "It was my wife's," he said, answering an unasked question. "She was built small." He smiled in a way that brought to mind the word *quaint,* a step shy of *shy.* "I know better than you do," he said, "that it's eccentric, bordering on peculiar, for me to hang on to her clothes this long. But I figure a moment will come when I'm ready to get rid of them and then I'll do it." He held the robe out to me. I hesitated. The transaction felt intimate in a way I seemed to like enough to make me question why.

"Thanks," I said, as I reached out for it: the robe was warm and dry; I was cold and wet.

"Why don't you hit the bathroom, warm up, dry off, and use it in good health—towels in there are clean. I'll see you downstairs."

Behind the closed door, I stripped naked. I began to reach for a towel to dry my hair, but somewhere on the way, my attention locked in on the room itself. It was small, square, and sober, and except for a book-filled wooden rack alongside the toilet, entirely spartan, the appliances clean, but half a century old, the porcelain as dull as overly brushed false teeth. The room smelled astringent yet oddly lush: leather, lemon, clove—a scent that tweaked memories beyond my grasp. Without deciding to, I found myself touching surfaces, bottles, tubes, jars, brushes. As I fingered these objects, the skin all over my body prickled to gooseflesh. My hand reached up toward a high, glass shelf, and suddenly my eyes began to blur . . .

A naked little girl, a young voyeur alone inside a forbidden domain, the thrill of it pungent in its naughtiness. Six, she is six. She reaches high up—too high— unable to grasp the object she's set her sights on, sending it instead clattering to the tiles, smashed apart, filling the room with choking fragrance. Then the man: suddenly he's there staring at her, naked and damp and cold. He is tall and dark and very angry. He says . . .

I did not know what it was he said. He had no voice, no face.

A rap at the door made me jump as though my bare skin had been flicked with a whip. "Lex? You okay in there?"

It took me a moment to answer. My chest was heaving, laboring to capture air, which seemed in short supply. "Yes. Yes, Nate," I managed. "Sorry. Be right with you." Caught in the jam jar, I thought. But what jam jar? I grabbed the towel off its hook and pummeled my wet hair.

He had a fire going nicely in the fireplace of a generous, beamed-ceiling room off the kitchen. This was part of the rear extension that made the little house a full third larger than originally built. As I padded in, his wife's blue robe wrapped and tied round me, the hem brushing at my ankles, he looked at me with bassett hound eyes. Quickly the eyes sharpened and narrowed as he smiled. In approval? Not wholly: it seemed more speculative than that, more complex.

"Drink?" he asked. "It's a good day for red wine. I'm having some."

"That would be fine." I sat on one of two facing caramel leather sofas. My legs raised themselves up and curled under me in the position of a comfortable cat. Against all odds, I felt myself subsiding into the sense of reflexive well-being induced by orange fire, red wine, and the rich brown tones of Nate Grumbach. But I was not here to enjoy. I unfolded my legs and brought them back down to dangle in air, since they did not reach the floor. The world's accoutrements are not designed for people under five feet tall, so we become accustomed to certain indignities.

He returned with a glass and a plate of crackers and cheddar. "You know," he said as he set them down on the wood slab table separating the sofas, "when I was a boy in the Bronx, my favorite food was specials. Maybe that was just my *bubbeh*'s name for them. Double-size kosher hot dogs is what they were, and she'd boil them up in a big dented aluminum pot on Thursdays, baked beans out of a can on the side and coleslaw. Fresh rye bread, mustard—the best: Grumbach's madeleines." He sat himself on the sofa opposite mine and leaned back into the cushions, wineglass in hand. "No, that isn't what we're having for lunch, but you'd probably enjoy it if we did. Anyway, something about how you're sitting there reminds me of the way those specials would bounce round in the boiling pot, some of them would split their skin. *Bubbeh* used to say that those were ones that were too anxious to get on the plate. My point is, you'll get on the plate, Lex. *We'll* get on the plate. We will talk about all the things we need to talk about— some of them today, others not. Hang on, hang in; we've got time. Lean back and tuck your legs up the way you had 'em. You know you're uncomfortable as hell perched the way you are."

"Is that part of the short course from your wife?"

"What?" For a second he was befuddled. It was just a stupid pun, an antimacassar to cover my impatience, but the allusion to his wife had caught him unawares and landed hard. After half a beat, he laughed. "You might say that." I'd been rude in my awkwardness— also jealous, no doubt, at not having had a *bubbeh* to boil sausages for me and make up tales about them.

My legs continued to dangle before me. "Nate, I'm sorry. Look, it's tempting for me to sit here with you going on about the rain and the Bronx and London and madeleines and specials. I sense that I could so easily, well, tuck up my legs and my worries and simply have a good time here today. But afterward I *would* pop my skin for not having gotten to what's important."

He nodded, lips compressed, my image of a working shrink. "Important? Lots of things are important, not always in the order they seem to be. But okay, here's the deal: Get yourself seated in a way that doesn't make *me* uncomfortable, and fire when ready."

I curled myself back up, took a long sip of substantial wine, and said, "You appear to be the best friend my sister has; you were Jared's therapist; you were there at Halloween. You know all the players—all the apparent ones and maybe some who are less apparent."

His smile drew up, wrinkling his face like soft, old leather. Did I remember my father looking like that?

No, not possible: the father I had known would have been twenty-five years younger. "Are you asking my opinion on who killed Calista? Because I have none to give you."

No opinion he wanted to give me: I admired the precision of his language. "Any thoughts on who *didn't* kill her, then?"

"Melanie didn't," he said almost grudgingly.

"But Tom might've?"

"Lay off, Lex. If you're waiting for Godot to come and reveal some universal truth, forget it. I'm no mind reader or fortune-teller or guru. But I am a guy who's spent a lotta years in the people business. I know there are mothers who smite their children out of rage, out of psychosis, out of despair. Melanie, in my professional opinion, could not be one of them. Item two: Tom is a willful, self-absorbed, risk addict, with a wide streak of violence in him. He did not have a clue about how to love that child, not paternally—nor sexually either, I would think. Could he have killed her? Not impossible. Why would he? I have no idea. And I don't think I want to walk any farther down this road now."

"All right," I said reluctantly, eager to know where the road would lead. "But here's the thing: If I'm to be of any use, I do need to understand these people I call my family, and six years of estrangement, which I imagine Melanie's told you about, has left me rather ill-equipped. The way it is, I lurch through a maze of dark tunnels, if you see what I mean. I keep coming up against walls, bashing my head, not able to see where to turn for an opening. I could use some navigational guidance. I think no one can help me better than you."

"Fortunately or not, I think you may be right," he said, the gravel in his voice thick. "I *can* help you. And I think you just might be able to understand—which does not mean that we'll see things the same way. Let's both acknowledge that. Agreed?"

"Agreed."

"Then I'll tell you something for openers: This being mugged by the media, hounded by the cops, all of it is *good* for Melanie—for Tom, too, though I don't happen to give a rat's ass about Tom."

I've always admired whoever coined "a rat's ass" to exemplify the lowest possible unit of regard. I quashed an impulse to get off track and tell him that. "I think I see what you mean by good for her," I said, "but spell it out anyway, would you?"

"See, Melanie is a fighter. A fighter wants to win, no matter what the fight is. An attack gets her blood up, the hardest punches make her want to punch back just as hard. I think that absent this outside enemy—which, by the way, gives her common cause with Tom and may resuscitate something in that marriage—but without that, she might just curl up inside herself and get lost, go under with the grief. I would hate to watch that happen," he said slowly, "because I care for your sister. I love her toughness and her nerve and her loyalty."

"What about the stubborn optimism, the faith that anything can be yours if you set your will to it? Do you love that?" My question tumbled out with the excitement of discovery, of seeing what my buoyant big sister and the woman who'd survived Calista's birth and gone on to create a dream daughter might have in common: the forge-ahead, damn-the-torpedoes-and-anything-else-in-your-path optimism I'd just named.

"I do love it, and I admire it," he said, "and I also envy the hell out of it. See, I have to work hard at optimism myself; it's a requirement in my line of work—pessimistic therapists better pack it in and take up podiatry. And, no, I'm not her lover, which I'll bet you were wondering—though, strictly speaking, it is none of your business." He cut himself a large slab of cheese and popped it into his mouth. While he chewed, his eyes waited as frankly as a chess opponent's for my next move.

"I'd say the boundaries of what might be whose business have recently been redrawn, haven't they? I mean, every detail of Melanie's life and Tom's is up for grabs or sale. It's only a matter of time before the *Star* or some spicy chat show asks you a battery of questions—and offers to pay you for the right answers. If they haven't already."

"Sure the calls've come, some more creative than others. I expect that soon they'll begin to invent their own answers about where I fit in. And I don't give a—"

"A rat's *ass*," I completed in my best American accent. We laughed, both of us.

"Old army expression," he said. "I had an uncle in World War Two, stationed in Guadalcanal. He taught me chapter and verse on barracks patois. I was an eager student, I can tell you. You like it, I'll give you the short course sometime." His inflection barely altered on the words "short course," just enough to let me know that we were sharing a private joke.

I let him have the smile he was looking for; it came easily. "I'll take you up on it, when all this is over. If all this *ever* is over," I added with a sudden sense that we were treading water in a sea with no horizon visible and destruction close by. Jared, Melanie, and Tom would be sucked down one after another into a whirlpool, me along with them.

"You're a fighter, too, in your way, aren't you, Lex?" Nate asked, not casually.

"Dunno," I mumbled, breaking eye contact. "I try. A great deal of the time I lose."

"Anyone who fights loses sometimes. But it's yourself you're fighting mostly. That *is* what you do—and why you suffer more damage than you need to. You're a small country occupied by big emotional artillery. Sometimes, it's better to surrender."

"Do shut *up!*" I was apparently less comfortable being known than I'd thought. I wanted to cut off his words with a sharp chop to the windpipe. And I wanted to weep, because his observation was too true and his advice too dangerous. "What gives you the damned right to poke at me? I'm no patient of yours."

"Sorry," he said quietly. "I was overstepping." A ghost of a smile flickered. "But wasn't it you who pointed out that the privacy boundaries had been redrawn?"

"I didn't mean mine," I said sourly, skewered fair and square.

"Only us suspects, eh?" He shrugged, that malleable face reconfiguring into humorous mug. "You had nothing to do with anything; you were an ocean away, right?"

"You've made your point, let's drop it, okay? You . . . you trod on a sore toe is all—more accurately, a sore foot. More accurately still . . ." My tension broke into a weak laugh. "Good Lord, *I'd* better be the one to shut up. I'm a mess talking about myself."

"Aren't we all? Shrinks included." His eyes were graver than the words or their tone. "I make a pretty good lasagna," he said, rising. "And I'm starved, even if you're not. Lunch is served in five minutes. In the kitchen or here? I give you the choice."

"The fire's nice," I said. "I vote for here." While he

was off in the kitchen preparing, I stared into it watching the flames dance and zig. I was conscious, too conscious, of the terry cloth against my bare skin. I wondered about Nate's dead wife. Had she died suddenly, or had she lingered, while he'd nursed her, brought her meals into this warm room, she lounging like Elizabeth Barrett Browning on this sofa in this robe? But no, that picture was wrong. Nate had not come to Westport until after she'd died, according to the *Westport News*. Only then had he moved here: he and her clothes. A shudder ran through me, despite the cozy warmth of the room. I wanted the dead woman's damned garment off my body.

Nate marched back in bearing a large, laden wood tray, which he set onto the coffee table with a professional flick of wrist. *"Prego,"* he said, like an Italian waiter, placing within my easy reach a serious portion of lasagna, its sauce a glistening, regal red against a plain white plate. "Americans don't much cotton to that refinement the Italians have, saying 'please' when they serve. Myself, I like it."

"Old-line British waiters say 'Thank you' when they serve. The English cotton to it very well; they reckon it's their due." Which brought my mother to mind: she'd always maintained that this sense of their own importance was what made the Brits such easy pickings for a skilled picker. "Gorgeous food," I said, leaning forward for better access to it. My mouth watered with appetite—unusual for me in company. Mostly, except on a binge, food was just food and I cared little about it. He topped up the wineglasses and reseated himself across the table.

"Wonderful," I said, the first bite barely swallowed, the second on my fork. *Slowly, now,* I reminded myself.

This is a meal; don't let it be anything more. He was studying me again, the look on his face not quite a smile. He knew somehow, I thought, about food and me—which meant Melanie had told him. "Who taught you to cook?" I asked. "Your grandmother?"

"A book—a lotta books, actually." His arm went up, index finger pointed for emphasis, "Beware the man of one book!" he pronounced in a Yiddish accent, which amused as intended. "You can read, you can cook. All you have to do is like food enough to want to bother. Calista liked my lasagna. She especially liked that." It was almost a throwaway but quite deliberate. It was the first time since I'd arrived that her name had been mentioned.

"Did you cook for her often?"

"She and Melanie would stop over for a bite, maybe a couple of times a week, after gym. Calista was fun to cook for, or do anything for. She'd call me Grumpa sometimes, to make me laugh. Melanie got a kick out of that. Look, I can quote you textbook language about overachievers, natural born stars: seductive kids, in the broadest sense of that fraught word. Calista was all those things, and it led her to . . ." The vibrancy quit his face, leaving it bloodless and slack and old. "The label *tragedy*'s become banal with overuse, so I'm not gonna . . ." He seemed about to continue, but then shook his head, telling us both no. "If you don't mind, that's it for now."

"Jared. Did he come to dinner, as well?"

"Sometimes. He stopped wanting to," Nate said flatly. I noticed his inner lamp was switched back on. "Look, Lex, I know what you're thinking, but it's a fine line I walk. I'm an educational therapist, not a Freudian shrink. Jared was my patient, yes. It's true Melanie and I got to be close, it's true that I was fond of Calista, and it's true Jared resented the hell out of both those facts. Now, you could drum up a corps of orthodox believers who'd beat me bloody over lack of professional distance, but I'm not about to give them that permission and *certainly* not about to join in and help them."

So logical; so pat: Was it possible he didn't *see?* I felt my fist clench. "Tell me, is that your one-size-fits-all guidance, Doctor: 'Surrender to your emotions and don't punish yourself'?"

"It's never that simple, but it fits more sizes than you might think. A lot depends on motivation, of course. If you don't act from malice, if you satisfy your standards of personal integrity . . . makes all the difference. For me, self-flagellation is not my sport. I am a widower who enjoys a lot of his own company. What social life I have comes one way or another through my work— Courtney, Melanie, a few others. The friendship with Melanie mattered, *matters* to me." He sipped at his wine. For once, his face offered no clue as to what was behind it.

"And what about Jared?"

"The work Jared and I did together was not compromised by that. I helped him, I really did. It began to make a difference in school; Melanie started to see some improvement at home. And I never once betrayed a confidence. He knew that, but he got the idea I didn't like him—one of his problems: he feels disliked, by himself for a start. I tried to get him to see that, but he chose to quit our work together, and he chose to grudge on it. I'm not telling you anything you don't know when I say Jared is one angry, hurting kid. None of that began or is going to end with me."

This was no gossiping neighbor, no grandstanding

journalist I was hearing, and with every word he said, my fear for Jared intensified. I stiffened my spine and jumped in. "Of *course* he must have felt jealous, rejected—your becoming his mother's best mate, his sister's great fan. Did you like him—as a person? *Do* you? That is relevant, isn't it?"

"Maybe less than you think. He's a boy with major intelligence and major problems that prevent him from making the most of his gifts, not to mention screw up his life. The truth? I liked him well enough to do him a great deal of good."

I said, "You talk about small countries occupied by heavy artillery. Do you think Jared ought to surrender to his emotions?"

"No, Lex. No I don't. In Jared's case, that could be dangerous. See, his emotions are poisoned—they're so toxic with envy and self-loathing that they run a risk of annihilating him, or someone else. That make any sense to you?"

What made a chilling sort of sense was Nate's implication that Jared could kill. Was his opinion informed by something he knew, one of those confidences he'd pledged to keep? Who else, I wondered, might harbor similar suspicions. Jared: downy-faced, awkward, brilliant, funny, sad, angry. Was this child poisoned? I thought of the way he'd looked this morning—the trapped-animal resignation, replaced for a spontaneous moment by a smile of glee when the film cassette arrived. If Jared was an embattled country, I was a patriot in its cause. "No," I said. "It does not make sense to me. I see all sorts of other things in Jared. I see someone stronger and healthier than you describe."

"And *I* see someone overidentified to a point where she could do him damage instead of good. I worry about Jared, especially now. But there's nothing I can do for him directly, because in his mind I'm an enemy. I talk to Melanie. Within the bounds of confidentiality I tell her how I see things. But it's less than ideal. Maybe you can do more. After all, in crisis *you're* the one he reached out to, right? I'd say he trusts you as much as he can trust anyone."

To love somebody is one thing; to bear the weight of that person's primary trust is quite another, especially when the person is a child, not yours: responsibility with no authority, no time limits. I felt a quick wash of panic. I, the short-distance runner, dealer in the brief intimacies intrinsic to my sort of film: in thirty-two years of life, I had committed myself long-term to no one.

Nate picked up his fork, took a first taste of lasagna and chewed it ruminatively. "You're wondering how far Jared can really trust you—and how far you can trust me."

I laughed in some mixture of consternation and relief. Being read, especially for one unused to it, has its ups and downs.

He nodded as though I'd spoken. "I'm gonna guess you'll come through for him, Lex. And you can trust me as far as you need to. Now, remember both those things." I took the time to make sure I did just that. I had the feeling I would want to replay his words.

CHAPTER 14

It was mid-evening, almost eight, when I left Nate's, after sampling the excellent coffee he ground from the bean, brewed slowly through filter paper in a glass Chemex, and drank lots of. He had not wanted to talk about Jared any further, so we didn't, with one exception: I'd broached the notion of Barney Warden as a tutor and asked Nate what he thought.

He did not answer immediately. I watched him register surprise that I'd met Barney, watched his brows beetle as he mulled the idea, and supposed that people in his business were often actors in some sense: signifying, communicating all their working hours. "Good idea," he said, finally. "Barney is one of nature's teachers, I'd think, despite his history." I knew I was meant to take that bait. However, some impulse refused me permission to pursue the nature of Barney's personal strife with a third person, even Nate Grumbach.

I turned on the car radio and learned that the

McQuade family in its first public outing since the murder had visited Banana Republic and The Gap, lunched at The Peppermill, and then gone to see some movie I didn't catch the name of. The family spokeswoman had asked the media to "respect the family's privacy," so apparently they'd refrained from thrusting mikes in faces. The newsreader reported that Tom and Melanie had held hands and Tom had kept an arm round Jared's shoulder. She also said that the police were working on several promising leads, not to be disclosed for the moment, and expected to release Calista's body to her parents for burial soon.

That sounded like good news—a vindicating signal. In contrast to the fervid media speculations, the authorities had kept theirs quiet so far. On second thought I saw the official silence as ominous. Were the police, like Nate, moving past Melanie and Tom to consider whether the jealousy and hate of a twelve-year-old was to be taken less seriously than an adult's as a motive for murder?

As I drove down the Anacletos' road, a woman and a man got out of an innocuous brown car parked just to the left of the long driveway. I recognized them for who they were: police.

"Ms. Cavanaugh?" the woman inquired, pro forma. She knew who I was. "I'm Detective Domingo; my partner is Detective Bixby." Domingo was an East Indian, not much older than I, whose soft, earnest voice and dark, level gaze communicated intelligence. But the assessment may simply reflect my own bias in favor of such voices and gazes. That sort of coin has another side: some of the stupidest British twits ever to draw breath pass as intellectuals solely on the strength of the up-market accents and self-admiring miens inculcated in their nursery years. The partner, Bixby, was spreading into middle age, his body padded in hard fat, his face suggesting acid indigestion.

"Has something happened?" I asked quickly.

She saw the fear in my face and said, "No, no, your family's all okay."

"You were waiting here for *me,* then?"

"Yeah, we were," Bixby said, taking my measure in a frank stare. "Thought we might have a few words with you."

"I don't know what those words would be, Detective. As you must know, I only arrived days after Calista was killed, and I've been out of touch for years."

Domingo took back the ball. "Look, you've known the family, as a family, closely over a period of time. No one else seems to. They're a remote group. Even the inside factions seem to have kept their distance from one another."

"Factions?" I asked, though her meaning was clear, and on the mark.

"Yes. Three subgroups is the way we see it. Calista and Melanie is one. Then Tom, then Jared—each of them a stand-alone." The rain had slowed to an intermittent drizzle, but as we stood there, it began to renew its resolve. "Let's duck into our car, before we're all drenched," Bixby suggested. "That okay with you, Ms. Cavanaugh?"

"Why not just go into the house?" I asked disingenuously.

"Easier this way," he said. Certainly so from their point of view, with no Tom round to intervene, insisting I "lawyer up" before speaking a syllable.

"Fine with me," I said. I had my own reasons for wanting to talk with them unfettered by objections of counsel. Admitted, they were trained interviewers, but so was I.

The smell inside their car suggested a history heavy in cigarettes, coffee, and sugar. Domingo and I sat in back, Bixby in the front passenger seat swiveled to face us.

"Are you two the main investigators in this case?" I asked.

"Part of a growing team," she said. "I was lead officer in responding to Mr. McQuade's phone call, so I was there when the body was found. Dennis"—she gestured at Bixby—"came on board later. Lex—may I call you Lex?—how did you learn about the murder? Did your brother-in-law phone you? Your sister?"

Trick question? I felt the sweat begin at the back of my neck. Pretend you're Melanie, I told myself. Figure out the best option and be cool. "Jared," I said. "Jared let me know. It was almost two days after the fact; I'd been incommunicado editing a film. I came at once, of course. Why do you ask?"

"I don't know," she said. "In light of your past relationship with Mr. McQuade, I wondered whether you thought you'd be welcome." *You have no secrets from us; we're onto you.*

I shrugged. "I'm here. I've been invited to stay. But talking of Tom, we all know he's controversial and abrasive, someone who's made enemies, justifiably. I assume you're looking at who might bear him a grudge."

"Pretty extreme way to settle a grudge," Bixby muttered.

"Of course we are." Domingo jumped in before he'd gotten the last word out. "We're looking at all possibilities." *And pigs can fly.*

"It's hard to look at all possibilities, isn't it?" I asked

mildly. "Such a global concept, all. Far simpler to focus on her family, right?"

"When a child is killed, looking at the family is routine, Ms. Cavanaugh," she said. "I'm sure you know that. Don't confuse what the media's doing with what we're doing. By the way, the medical tech who leaked those autopsy photos is going to have to find a new job, if he can. We would be only too happy to rule out the family, if they're innocent. Maybe you can help us." She made it sound logical as ABC, easy as pie.

"Now, how might I do that?" I asked. *What sort of treachery do you have in mind?*

No answer. Instead, Bixby asked, "How old are you, Lex?" his narrow-eyed gaze freighting the question with enough significance to make me reluctant to answer.

"Why do you want to know?"

"You look very young, you know—I guess part of it's your being small, no makeup on your face, those big eyes, long hair. Hey, I'll bet that from, say, fifteen, twenty feet, you could pass for a kid." He turned to Domingo. "Would you agree with that, Anna?"

"I see what you mean, Dennis. You must hear that all the time, Lex, don't you?"

This all rang of rehearsed dialogue. I wanted to slap the "Lex" from their mouths, insist they return to "Ms. Cavanaugh"; more important, the back of my neck didn't like where this playlet seemed to be headed. I kept still.

"Six, seven years ago," Bixby said, "you must have looked even younger."

"Do you think," Domingo asked quietly, "that a youthful—you could say childlike—appearance might have been especially attractive to Tom McQuade?"

I exploded in a harsh laugh. "Tom McQuade's tastes

in sex are eclectic. But to my knowledge, they have without exception run to women—short, tall; young, old—*women,* whom he well and truly *fucks,* adult to adult. I can attest personally to that. He is not a likely candidate to finger a little girl—his own or anyone else's. Now, can we ring the curtain down on this little performance?"

"Really sorry we upset you, Lex," Bixby said. "But we did have to raise the issue. And we appreciate your input."

"You're quite welcome," I replied, and reached for the door handle.

"We aren't quite finished yet," Domingo said. "We'll need a few more minutes."

"I'm afraid our needs don't match." I opened the door an inch or so. But there were arrows left in her quiver, and the next one she fired off stopped me cold.

"We've had a call from your mother."

I shut the door and sat back down. "So did I," I said, "early this morning. I should tell you that my mother is a charming, venomous bitch, with the extraordinary ability to sail through life untouched by any form of self-blame. And her ingenious technique for accomplishing this feat is to fling filth at her victims. She ran out on a fifteen-year-old daughter. I think that about says it—except to point out that, as she has had no contact with Melanie for a quarter of a century, anything she says is on its face uninformed—at best." I forced a smile at Bixby. "Are you by any chance the father of teenagers? You look as though you might be—but, then again, it may be simply that you appear old for your age."

"Ouch," he said, his smile a lot easier than the one I'd proffered, "you got me right in the heart. Yeah, I got two—girls, as a matter of fact. Look, what did your mother tell you on the phone this morning? And how much of it was news to you?"

"Not much in the way of specifics, and all of it was news. My mother never talked about Melanie when I was growing up. She wouldn't allow me to, either. Can you imagine what it might be like, Detective, to lose your sister and father when you're six, and be forbidden to mention them in front of your mother?" I said this to him coolly, not out of any need for his sympathy, but as a character reference for Frannie Cavanaugh.

He nodded knowingly, compressing his lips into disappearance. "Your mother told us how she left the family, took you with her. 'Rescued' was the word she used."

"Now that *is* a laugh. Want to know how it happened? She ran off with her boyfriend, I hid on the floor in the back of the car. She had no intention whatever of taking me along. In any case, if we're sorting old news from new, that part's very old news to me." Bixby slewed his glance over at Domingo.

"Maybe we can tell you some new news, then," she said. "Melanie was pregnant when your mother left with you."

I was too stunned to feel even surprise. "Would you do that, Bixby?" I asked. "Would your wife? Leave a pregnant daughter on her own."

"No," he admitted. "But she wasn't alone. She was with her father." I didn't like the curly tail he put on the word father. "Your mother says they were a pretty tight pair, Melanie and her father."

"Are you saying," I began to ask, surprised at how little breath seemed to be supporting my voice, "that my . . . her father made her pregnant?"

"Well, here's where we're not a hundred percent sure," Domingo said. "Melanie wouldn't say, according to your mother. But from what she observed between the two of them, she did assume that was the case."

"Did she? Quite easy to blame a dead man, isn't it? Normally, my mother prefers a more sporting challenge."

"Again, this is unsubstantiated," Domingo said. "But what your mother claims is that your father stopped talking to her entirely at that time—not one word, after telling her that she could go straight to hell, and that he would take care of Melanie."

I had the sensation of riding a carousel at wildly accelerated speed, my vision blurring as the platform spun round. I gave a laugh, which punctuated itself with a hiccup. "All happy families are alike," I said giddily. "Are we about done now, Detectives? Because *I* say we are." This time I got the car door fully open and one leg out.

Domingo stopped me with her soft voice. "About Jared," was all she said.

Here it was. Like an ice cube applied to an angry burn, it chilled my overheated nerves. "What about Jared?" I asked, turning toward her, as vocally cool now as she.

"He was the one who contacted you, you said."

"Yes." I clamped my jaws shut. I had talked too much, I saw—given more than I'd got.

"He's a high-strung kind of boy, we understand," Bixby said. "Damned smart, but problems in school. Kind of a loner. Given to tantrums. No star like his sister." There was a long pause while I said nothing. "Speaking of stars, astronomy's a hobby with him, no?"

"He has lots of interests, Bixby," I said. "Bright kids

do. Astronomy's one of them. Why do you ask?" I wondered for a second whether he could hear my heart pound, and knew he could not.

"Just something we wondered about," he said casually. "Well, we've kept you from your family long enough. Thanks, Lex; you've been a big help."

I sat in my car and watched theirs disappear down the road. My hand trembled as I turned the key in the ignition. I felt like a victim; in a sense I was. I had allowed myself to be mugged by a pair of assailants more adept than they looked. The after-burn smarted, a sting to my pride: I had told them nothing they did not already know, but they had been less concerned with gaining information than with giving it. Using hints of pedophilia, suggestions of incest, teases about astronomy, they'd meant to shock-prod me into response, into running their errand: shaking the family tree to see what incriminating bits of fruit might fall out. I had too willingly turned out my emotional pockets to them. I promised myself it would not happen twice.

WHEN I ENTERED the house, about an hour later, my hands were steady, my mind dead quiet. Three years ago, I'd filmed an Austrian family of circus performers: tightrope walkers they were. They'd talked a great deal about the early training they had in a certain kind of hyperconcentration used to focus on a spot at the end of the skinny path ahead. One of them had given me some beginning instruction in the technique. Tonight, I used it: I sat in my car and strained to recapture that absolute focus that would lead me through the next few hours without making an impulsive misstep. It came, slowly, not easily.

What was hardest to blank out was a brand-new

mental flash photo of leggy, blonde, teenaged Melanie, forehead to forehead in embrace with a tall, dark, craggy man, who bore an uncanny resemblance to Nate Grumbach.

I FOUND MELANIE, Tom, and Jared together in the conservatory involved in a spirited game of Scrabble. "Oh, Lex," Melanie said, "come join us. You were always good at words with no vowels." Tom: "Cambridge had its uses." Jared: "I want to see your monkey tape. The TVs are back, and the one in the den has a VCR."

The dialogue and their faces suggested the possibility that Austrian tightrope walkers had been teaching the tricks of their trade on both sides of the Atlantic.

We collaborated in batting a feather-light conversational ball back and forth across an invisible net for the next few hours and repaired to our separate rooms rather early—each of us escaping the others with skin intact.

I awoke with a shuddering start sometime in the night, lurching out of a dream I could not quite remember. Something about a body, male, with no head. Suddenly, I found myself enveloped in the sort of blubbing Jared had been doing the previous night, the sort that seems without beginning or end. And I knew its cause. Incredibly, against all odds, I was blubbing the blub of an orphaned child.

My cheek burrowed into the wet pillow, knees drew up to touch my chin. The fetal position helped ease the throb inside my gut, which was not empty but felt empty. I do not say it made any sense, since I had disliked and distrusted and feared my mother for most of my life. But now I could no longer have a mother. That she had sabotaged Melanie was no surprise, but an act need not surprise in order to shock. This one shocked me through to the core—perhaps because it stepped outside the bounds of our personal battleground, perhaps because I was powerless to strike back in any way that would wound her; all I could do was withdraw. Her games had always been winner take all. She was no one's mother: perhaps that was finally what she'd won.

My mouth watered, asking not for curry or chili or Szechuan peppers, but for the thick kosher sausages Nate's grandmother had cooked—the ones that could not wait to get on the plate. I shoved my knuckles between my teeth and sobbed myself back to sleep.

C H A P T E R
15

Calista's funeral was held in an Episcopal church, a lovely old white frame building—a picture book Sunday place where the amply affluent congregate to worship the God responsible for their luck in life, encouraging Him to keep up the good work.

Melanie chose this church quite soon after moving to Westport, with the same diligent research she had applied to house-hunting. Sometimes she and Calista had attended it, for frankly social, rather than spiritual reasons: to see and be seen. Formal religious observance had never taken hold in Melanie, had likely never been planted. Her relationship with God was hyperreal: intense, direct, and private—she and He both talked, both listened; any third party would have been an intrusion, not to say a competitor.

Tom, who'd been born a Roman Catholic and raised on and off by its institutions, abhorred that Church and all the others. He affected to be amused as well as appalled by the staggering popularity of a God who "is a senile psychotic with one ugly sense of humor." Jared had early on begun to mimic his dad in this verbiage, enjoying the words before he was old enough to know what they meant.

Blue and white flowers covered a white coffin not much larger than a good-sized wedding cake. The three McQuades and me, the Anacletos, Nate, and Barney—he, only because a fourth pallbearer was required—no one else was permitted at the private service. The minister did the one thing Tom had demanded he do, be quick. Jared held my hand and squeezed it hard throughout the five to seven minutes of ceremony. I did what I do: I observed the minutiae. Tom's arm wrapped Melanie's shoulder, while her own arms hugged herself, as though against a freezing cold. Nate sat alone. The several times I glanced at him, his eyes were shut, his face as immobile as a dead man's. Vin was the only person openly weeping. I saw Courtney's fingers begin to rub his sleeve, and watched him jerk his arm away. And I saw Barney watching me watch. Our eyes engaged for a moment. I looked away because . . . I don't quite know why I looked away—perhaps because I liked his eyes, which seemed a frivolous thing to be registering just then.

The drive behind the hearse in a hired funeral car with tinted windows took a bad, silent hour. Melanie's eyes hid behind large, black sunglasses. Tom's stared out the brown window. Jared sat beside me, as he had in church, his eyes down. Once, he raised them and peered my way. I mouthed at him, "It'll be over soon." His lips parted, starting to say something back, then didn't.

The burial was surreal, its utter sadness intensified some way by the glare of unforgiving November sun glinting off the sugar whiteness of the coffin that Tom and Vin and Nate and Barney carried from the hearse. While they were giving it over to the professionals, Melanie knelt down at the edge of the hole that would in moments become her daughter's grave and looked down into it. We knew, all of us, to give her a wide berth. She watched intently as the men began to lower the coffin. She seemed quite composed and worlds removed, head nodding, lips moving, in what looked less like prayer than earnest conversation—whether with Calista or with God was impossible to tell.

Jared gave a sudden yank at my arm, urgently pulling me away from the gravesite. His face was simmering with emotion. I went where he led. When we reached the parking lot, he boiled over, fist raising high and bashing down hard against the fender of the funeral car we'd come in. It didn't hurt the polished steel any, but it did his knuckles.

"Hey!" a liveried driver began.

"Do you think you could give us some privacy," I said coldly. The man gave us a dark and dirty look and walked off on stumpy legs.

I took Jared's damaged hand in both of mine. "You don't want to fight with cars, they do tend to win."

"I *hate* . . . !" he screamed, and stopped short.

"It's okay, darling. Who? You can say who it is you hate."

"All of them," he muttered. And no wonder. Quite obviously, the child that mattered was dead, and the one who was alive may as well have been, for all the attention his parents had paid him today. "And her, too," he said. "It was her own fucking fault!"

"How was it her fault?" I managed to ask, hoping I would be able to cope with the answer.

"Dunno," he said, looking at the tarmac.

"How was it her fault?" I persisted, Nate on the subject of Jared fresh in my mind.

Finally, he met my eyes, his begging me to back off. Grief. Anger. Fear. Guilt? But don't survivors often feel guilty simply for having survived?

"I really don't. I . . . just said that. I . . . I *really* . . ." His voice trailed off, and his flushed face went suddenly quite pale. "You'll watch the meteor shower with me tonight?" he asked weakly.

He had been talking about it for days, a new comet due to streak across the sky leaving a trail of glittering particles in its wake. If tonight's weather was as clear as this afternoon's, the light show would be glorious, more so viewed through the new telescope Tom had bought and handed over to Jared with a laconic, "Bet you'll put it to good use."

"Of course I'll watch it with you," I said. "We made a date, didn't we?" I cupped his cheeks with my hands. "She was your *sister.*" My need to stand with him, by him, was as strong as his to have me do it. "There is no wrong way for you to feel. Do you understand?"

"I understand." His voice was desolate: hopeless and bitter. "But it's not true, what you said. There *is* a wrong way."

At that moment, I would have traded anything in my life to become an eagle. I'd have gathered him up in my talons—carefully, so as not to hurt him—then, spread my strong wings and flown far away.

I turned round. I wasn't sure why, but when I did, I saw her: Detective Domingo, her hands thrust deep into the pockets of a bulky trench coat. She was standing at the far edge of the parking lot, keeping a respectful distance. But she could see us as well as I could see her. What she might have heard, I had no idea.

C H A P T E R
16

I had always thought the social rituals of condolence useful only to those who can be condoled, which is by way of saying that they ought to have been entirely useless in this case. Curiously, they weren't. Only twice before had I been involved in death ceremonies. The killer both times had been AIDS, the victims: a documentary filmmaker whose boots it would have been an honor for me to shine, and a production assistant who'd been as inept as he was charming. On those occasions, the hectic activity of grieving, the eating and drinking and talking and laughing and weeping—all magnified larger than life-size—had been a finale, which rang the curtain down in a way that the death itself had not. Closure, as the shrinkers call it.

Here, the post-burial hours had been bleak, and a cheat: there was no closure in sight. So the rituals of condolence merely filled some blank time, which was considerably better than nothing. Courtney bustled about

like a nanny at a nursery party, superintending the colla-
tion Melanie had allowed her to organize for a corps of
carefully vetted guests. A surprise to me, Nate had
begged off at the cemetery. As we were climbing back
into the funeral car, he'd kissed Melanie's cheek, and said
softly, "Mel, m'dear, I'll be no good to you back there.
I'm out of steam. I need to go home. Tomorrow: I'll see
you tomorrow." Tom also had decamped, left us at the
Anacletos' front door without explanation and gone off
alone in his car.

Absent Tom and Nate, Courtney had a brief go at
taking charge of Melanie. Instead, Melanie, her spine
regally stiff, face placid as a cameo, took firm charge of
herself and of center stage, artfully rendering Courtney's
presence redundant. She allowed her hand to be clasped,
listened to visitors' encomiums to Calista, murmured
her thanks to them for coming, steered them toward
food and drink. In a former life, I would have judged
my sister's performance weirdly plastic, corroborating
evidence of her shallowness.

It was my judgment that was wanting in depth. Now,
I saw valor, grit, will, exercised over searing pain, the
effort powered by forces deeper than I could fathom. I
spent the dragging hours trying to make myself useful,
and being largely useless. Jared had made an early
retreat upstairs to his room and did not want company.
Barney disappeared for a time, gone back to his house
with the respectable excuse of needing to walk the dog.

All the while, Vin had been quietly getting quite
drunk in a corner of the conservatory. He stood
propped against the wall, his arm lifting to pour, lifting
to drink, the motions progressively fluid, oiled with
scotch. As the last guests were leaving, he staggered to
Melanie's side and threw his arm heavily round her

shoulder. Courtney immediately materialized beside him with a "Vin, dear . . ." He swiveled his head and slurred, "Been thinking 'bout changing my name, I'm so sick of hearing you say it." I recognized the look on her face, the confused hurt of a publicly slapped child. I had personal experience with the feeling: a confusion of shame and blame, both directed inward. Melanie, meanwhile, plucked his arm off her as though ridding her back of a dead cat, and indeed the arm dropped lifelessly at his side. In a triumph of good manners over curiosity, the visitors hurried out the door.

While they were doing so, Barney, having recently returned, took over. When he spoke, the steady, sea-green eyes in his redhead's complexion added a certain gravitas. "You're going up to bed now, Vin," he said evenly. He might have been calling one of the soccer boys out of the game for bad behavior.

"My house, buster. Call me a kept man, but 's my house. Who's gonna make me go to bed? You?"

"Don't, Barney," Courtney said. But her protest was weak: she was about to cry. Barney didn't speak; he simply acted. Before Vin's scotch-dulled reflexes could respond, Barney's long body had moved from behind to trap his arms in a double hammerlock, the better to frog-march him up the stairs. A judo move, I recognized with surprise.

"Cool," said Jared, who was observing the action from halfway up the staircase. "Cool," I agreed.

Later, Barney joined Jared and me in the back garden. After a few tries, we positioned Jared's telescope just so. Then the three of us took turns getting the brilliant view of a newly discovered comet making its debut, streaking the sky, trailing a glittering wake of astral debris behind it.

CHAPTER
17

When the knock came at my door, it did not wake me. I was curled up on the window-seat cushion in my dormered room, gazing out the window. The comet and its tail were gone, but their greenish flash lingered in my mind, as it went walkabout backward through time . . .

I'd had a dormered bedroom once. Over the two-year period just before I was sent away to school, my mother had on and off lived with, of all things, a poet. He'd been, of course, a poet with family income: a kind of remittance poet. He had a small house in the Cotswolds, left to him by an uncle; that was where the room was.

His name was Ranald, a rather delicate man with pink-and-gold coloring and a temperament to match. I quite liked him, probably because he paid me notice and wrote me silly verses, which he read aloud with great relish. The two of us would laugh (he had an improbably high-pitched giggle, like the whinny of a high-strung horse), and Mum would say, "What a pair: a nine-year-old who sneaks greasy spareribs into her bed and a forty-year-old whose life's work is rhyming June with goon." His laugh would drop to a chuckle then, subdued and rueful. And he'd say, "Ah, Frannie, I do adore you. You're as good for me as a headmaster's cane." I remember pitying him then—marveling at why he put up with her when, unlike me, he had a choice. That was before I learned that the arse has its reasons which reason knows not. And the arse accustomed to a hiding does find its cane one way or another.

I suppose this woolgathering was to do with Courtney and Vin, and for that matter, Melanie and Tom, though the philosophical question of which arses were exposed and which hands held canes might be less simple than it looked. As I said, the knock at my door did not wake me.

"Come on in," I called, expecting a Jared as sleepless as I. But it was Melanie standing there.

She wore a long robe of yellow wool; she was partial to that color. With her face clear of makeup and her hair tied up into a bun, she looked both older and younger than the Melanie I was used to seeing, and different in another way, too—one hard to pin down, except to call it a kind of calm that seemed to come from the inside out rather than the reverse. "I thought you might be awake. You've always been a little night crawler." The sharp point on "crawler" inflicted a pinprick just to let me know my transgression would never be erased. She strode over to a small chintz-covered armchair and sat, but her back did not touch the cushion.

"I understand that your mother telephoned you here," she said, her narrowed eyes shooting blue darts at me. "You gave her this number?"

It had been four days now since the phone call, each of them begun with my resolving to tell her, and not making good. "Yes, she phoned me. No, I did *not* give her this number. Of course I didn't," I added, disproportionately irritated with her for thinking I might have. "Her boyfriend's a Net-surfer, so she learned where you were staying and that I was with you." We were in it now, for a penny or a pound. All things come to one who waits; the downside is that the waiter does not get her choice of venue, nor time to prepare. "She called the police, as well," I said. "She was more explicit with them than with me."

"Oh, I will just bet she was." Melanie's head cocked to one side. I thought I saw a trace of knife-blade smile. I wanted to speak, I really did, but a glut of words jammed my gullet, fighting one another for exit, leaving me effectively mute. I was surprised to see her expression soften round its edges. "Come on, Allie," she said in a voice warmly firm, a reminder of a half-forgotten dream: a big sister's voice, "better tell me what she said. If you think there's anything left in the world that can shock me, you're wrong. And, yeah, I called you Allie on purpose this time."

"She said that you were a vixen and a cheat and a thief—and that you were sexually rapacious."

She laughed, the sound brassy and jarring as a trumpet in the cozy chintz room. "Rapacious? She said *rapacious?*"

"No," I admitted, "*rapacious* wasn't her word, just my editorial summary. She said you'd begun having sex when you were twelve, with lots of men." The back of my neck dampened with the inevitable nervous sweat. *Fuck it! Say the hard bits. Just say them.* "She said that you were pregnant when she left. She implied strongly that you and our father were lovers, and that the baby might have been his."

"Thirteen, not twelve. And why should any of this interest the police?" Her tone was milk mild, but one could hear the milk starting to scald beneath its surface.

"She makes you out to be a disreputable character— sexually pathological." No response except a wide, blue stare. "She claims to be certain that you're involved in Calista's death, and that it's something to do with a man."

"Is that all?" she asked. A catch in her voice undercut its coolness.

"No. No, it isn't all." And before I knew what was happening, words began tumbling out of me, unprocessed, unmonitored. "Look, you think I don't know what she is? I do know. At least I fancied I did. But the truth is, I know nothing about her except the way she turned out. And the way she turned out has its resemblance to the way *you've* turned out: tough and wily. But then, I know nothing about you either, do I? No, that's not quite true. I *did* know you—until I was six, I did."

"Hell of a long time ago," she said dryly. "What makes you think that what you happen to remember was real?" Something in her voice suggested that her curiosity was more than casual.

"Because you hugged me," I said, as tenacious over a scrap of recalled affection as a Dickensian orphan over a crust of bread, "and you played with me and you threw me up into the air and you laughed. You had the best laugh! I loved you because you were the only person in that house who cared for me at all. You did and you showed it. I think it's hard to fool a kid, so I will *always* believe that was real, no matter what you say now. As . . . as real as the way I've always felt about Jared."

"Maybe," she said quietly. "Maybe. But what's real has a way of changing right while you're looking at it, or looking the other way." The air round us was dry as dust; it seemed textured with regret. "You were a funny little kid. You did make me laugh."

She had handed me a gift, a precious one. I'd have liked to thank her for it, but flooded in gratitude, I could not find words.

"I believe we were talking about your mother," she said, "not in the past, in the present."

"Right." The candy-colored part of memory lane was closed. "But you are like her," I said. "Your face freezes at the mention of her, and hers would freeze when I'd allude to you in any way at all. As I began to grow up, I got the idea she was afraid of you."

"Well, she'd have reason to be afraid of me now," Melanie said with a quiet more arresting than any rant. "I'd cut her throat soon as look at her." She pointed at the bedside table. "There's some Kleenex over there," she said not unkindly. Until then, I hadn't noticed that my face was wet. It wasn't that I was crying; it was just this march of tears trailing down my cheeks. I went and fetched a wad of tissues.

"Maybe we really are related. I made the same threat on the phone. I said that if she went to the media with this crap, I'd come over there and cut her heart out."

Melanie smiled back. "And what did she say to that?"

I spoke to her eyes. "She said I didn't have it in me to kill anyone, but you did."

She nodded and gave a small snort, not quite a laugh. Her hands held on to the chair arms the way some people do on airplane takeoff. Our eyes remained engaged. "Do you think I killed my little girl?" She said the words one at a time.

"No." I meant it. "I don't believe you could have, but—"

"I don't want to hear the 'but,'" she said quickly, her hands gripping the chair harder.

"Well, you're going to." It felt odd for me to override Melanie. From the look on her face it felt odd to her, too. "I think you are withholding something, lying, like you did with the MI6 men for Tom."

For seconds—so briefly that I might have imagined it—I saw her want to tell me what it was. Then that was over; she'd decided not to. "It's your mother who's a liar—a vindictive, jealous liar." Her voice echoed as it might have in a courtroom. "You say I'm like her, but you're wrong. She was a whore who never loved anyone in her life. This man, that man, the next man—all she really wanted was to pick their pockets."

"What about our father's pockets? Assuming he *is* my father." My mother had always referred to him in poisonous tones as "your father," and though I knew her to be a fluent liar, I had never questioned that. Now truths and lies were varicolored balloons tossed into the air: possibilities in play, all of them. "I gather he didn't have much money."

"No, college professors don't. She didn't only want money, you know. She wanted whatever they had that she didn't. She wanted their heirlooms, their prestige, their talents. But she could never get what Daddy had. He wasn't rich; he wasn't good-looking: what he had was in his mind, and no way was he about to let her in there. But she wanted it bad enough to make him marry her—and still he locked her out! And, yes, he is most definitely your father." Another smile: this one smug with knowledge. I didn't respond. "Hell, all you'd have to do is look in a mirror and you'd be sure of that."

"Could you tell me what you mean," I said, my insides feeling oddly liquid.

"He was short, pointy-faced—big, kind of Jewish eyes, same tortoiseshell color as yours. He was the spit of you, except he was getting bald and you've got all that which-way hair." The shiver that ran through me was the sort often described as a cat running over one's grave.

"Do you . . . Is there a photo I could see?" Years ago, she'd said no to that, but she'd also refused to talk about him. Now . . .

"We weren't a picture-taking family."

"But surely . . ." I craved to see; it would have made her words real.

"I have no photos. None." Her tone had the finality of a gavel. "I suppose you got your brains from him, too," she said quietly, just a trace of grudge. It was a compliment, and somewhere at the back of my mind I recognized it as such. But mainly I was otherwise engaged, gripped in the hectic activity of trying to erase and redraw shadowy images.

"I . . . I pictured him differently," I said.

"I thought you said you couldn't picture him at all."

That had been true until a few days ago. But following Domingo's family history lesson, I'd put flesh on the skeletal idea called Daddy. "I'm not sure. You see, I've remembered something . . . things." I saw them again, Melanie and the man, head to head, preparing to kiss, his hand making long strokes along her extended neck. "I recall him looking quite another way—tall, swarthy, with lots of dark wavy hair and heavy eyebrows."

"Oh, Lord!" She laughed, an almost merry sound this time. "The mind is a *wondrous* instrument." She sounded lyrically southern at that moment, the sound of my mother at her most charming. "That is not Daddy you're remembering at all, you ninny; that's Tilt."

Tilt. Tilt. Inside my skull the syllable seemed to bounce off frozen walls in a hollow echo, which made no sense. I bit down hard on my lower lip and tried to restart a train of thought. It came in fast, disjointed spurts. The synthetic smell of auto carpet as I lay curled on the backseat floor . . . My mother's mouth, a dark red O of dismayed surprise . . . Her quick "Dammit, come on then, Allie," my arm pulled along like a rag doll's . . . Inside the airport cavern, all the more unreal in cold, bright light, a tall man bearing down on us in fast, giant steps. "For Christ's sake, Frannie, we can't . . . !" Why was Uncle Tilt here? And where was Aunt Phyllis? And what . . . The searing needle of pain in my ears as the plane gained altitude; me, too scared to cry. Then the time later on, in the place called L.A., when I couldn't stop crying—and the whack of his hand—one, two, three—on my behind. *Tilt.* Yes. I could barely breathe.

"I'm not certain I understand," I said. But as the words left my tongue, I began to be appallingly certain that I understood quite clearly. "You and Tilt."

"That's right," she said, her mouth set in a foxlike smile. "H. Tilton Schwartz. His first name was Howard, but he hated to be called that. I used to tease him." Melanie had taken photos, after all, vivid ones—they were printed in her mind.

Fifteen, she'd been fifteen. Hardly unheard of, pretty teenaged daughter, mother's lover. I felt the queasy excitement of a certain kind of surprise, the kind that must be felt by adopted children who discover that fact late in the game: the world flipping over to reveal an utterly unsuspected other side; the sudden, darkly thrilling knowledge that now everything one knew was up for grabs.

"I told you she was jealous," Melanie said, the trace of satisfaction in her tone eaten away by acid content. "That's the key to it. She didn't give a hang that I was pregnant or how I was going to deal with that or if I'd have to drop out of school or give up gym, let alone any thought of the Olympics. All she cared about was that I stole her boyfriend; that he liked me better in bed than he liked her." Her hand gave the air a short, fisted jab. "She had that coming to her. Indeed she did!"

"Where was Da . . ." It was hard to know how to refer to the man. He wasn't "Daddy" to me and "*your* father" seemed . . . ". . . our father in all this? Did you and he . . ." *Oh, for Christ's sake, stop bobbling, Lex!* ". . . have sex, as well?"

"Daddy? Me and *Daddy*?! That's ridiculous. If you'd known him, you couldn't think such a thing. Daddy was shy about anything physical; why, he never so much as took his shirt off in front of me. He loved me as his *daughter*. And that was *all.*"

And me, I wondered, back into a Dickens novel, the pitiful orphan yearning before a sweetshop window. What about me? Did he feel nothing for the other daughter, the one who looked like him? And why, even after Melanie's description, could I still not see him?

Melanie continued, telling the story to herself as much as to me. "When he found out about her and Tilt—not to mention *me* and Tilt—he was, you'd have to say, horrified. See, he never knew squat about her affairs before, his nose was always in some book or another, and his head in Hegel or Sartre or one of those. That's where Daddy really lived—he wasn't a worldly kind of man at all. *I* was the one who knew about her. 'Mah little friend,' she used to call me, and she'd tell me all about the new love of her life, Mr. Whoever."

"How did our father find out?"

"I told him. I told him after Tilt got me pregnant."

"Did Tilt rape you?"

"*Hell,* no! He liked me in bed better than he liked her"—it was like a damned mantra—"and I liked him there, too. I wasn't exactly Miss Virgin. Tilt knew what he was doing; he beat out slobbery boys with pimples by a country mile—even college boys," she added, almost wistfully, "even the paper boy. But Tilt turned ugly after I let him know about the baby coming—said it wasn't his, when I *knew* it was. I despised him then. If he wasn't gonna protect me, I wasn't gonna protect him."

"So she took him and ran out on you. Did she want to leave, or did she get tossed out?"

"Some of both. She went under her own steam. She was mad as hell—not at Tilt, but at *me*. She wanted him for herself, and she also wanted to be rid of the whole humiliating thing. But Daddy wanted her gone. He told her to get out, told her he'd take care of his daughter. And he did—took me down to Planned Parenthood for the abortion and came by to pick me up after it was over." She tried to make this father of ours sound—well—fatherly, but even she could not bring that off: the dropping of one's daughter like soiled laundry to be collected after it was washed and folded sounded as frigidly minimal as it was.

"Tilt was boxed in; he *had* to go off with her," she said, her voice stronger now it was back on the ground she preferred. "He was scared to death the story would come out, maybe even that he'd get arrested for statutory rape. But Daddy wanted to keep it quiet as much as Tilt did, so . . . Anyway, when it all blew over, Phyllis took him back and he came running like a big old jackrabbit."

Trained at her mother's knee: eyes on the prize, she had thought to beat the champ at her own game. At root, Melanie was as motherless and mother-ridden as I—more so.

"I was never raped, but she was, you know. Your mother was," Melanie said. "On that pig farm in the boonies where she grew up."

"I only found out she'd grown up on a farm when she phoned up the other day. I said something about Rebecca of Sunnybrook Farm to irritate her, and it did. She let loose a diatribe about farm life versus my sheltered existence. Who raped her?"

"Her father," Melanie said casually, as though the subject had ceased to interest her. "You know, drinker, muddy boots, leather belt, whippin' and fuckin'—poor-white-trash story. Probably that's another thing she saw in Daddy—you know, how Jewish men are good providers, they don't screw round as much, they don't drink a whole lot, and they don't hit their wives. I probably should've married one," she said ruminatively.

"Tom doesn't rate so badly on that exam, maybe as high as three," I said, "depending on how you keep score."

"Suppose so. He did only hit me the once. He can be a mean bastard anyway, but you know that, don't you?" Her eyes gleamed, inviting, daring me to cross over into complicity. It was not precisely an olive branch but close enough. I sat briefly upon the tack of divided loyalties; then I thought, fuck it, that's the truth about Tom: he *can* be a mean bastard.

I smiled back. "I *do* know it. The problem is he's so much else besides."

"I am acquainted with the problem," she said with a dash of vinegar, "in all aspects."

The question boiling up into my throat was irrelevant, except to me. "Melanie, why do you suppose I can't remember my father? I was six; I ought to have some impression unless he boycotted me entirely. Did he?"

She sighed, like someone readying to handle a cumbersome, perhaps messy, chore. "You know, when you were a stringy, yowling baby, which you were, Daddy would roll up his eyes and ask, 'What's red and wet and mean as a pickled hot pepper?' "

My knees drew up close to my chest, perhaps in a move to shelter the stringy, yowling self who seemed at the moment most precious and endangered.

"He wasn't crazy about you," she said: a fact evenhandedly stated. Then her voice turned harsh. "Daddies don't automatically care all that much for their little girls." She referred to Tom's lack of love for Calista, of course. I had nothing to give her for the pain of that, nor could I block my own ache: Tom and my father had felt how they'd felt. I sat silent and hugged my knees tighter into me.

"He did not give you up," she said flatly, back to history. "He never would've done that. Daddy had a set of moral standards for people, himself included, and he was pretty damn strict about them. When I was eleven, I got caught stealing clothes in a boutique. Now, he didn't beat me—he'd never raise a hand—but he wouldn't talk to me or look at me for three months, not once. I was just crushed by that—see, I loved my daddy. In fact I was so crushed that I . . ." A flash of mischief crossed her face, and I saw the Melanie, sassy and gorgeous in her stewardess togs, who'd made Tom laugh. ". . . got a lot more clever about my stealing afterward.

"You're looking at me so funny, Allie, all scrounched up sitting there. What's on your mind?"

"You. Things. So you stole. I'd like to hear about that sometime. I go off and binge on food. I think you know I do that, though we've never talked about it. We've never talked about much, really."

"Sure I know. You lived with us, remember? I may be no genius, but I'm not slow. I've always thought it was crazy, your eating thing." She shrugged. "A little crazier than stealing. 'Course I don't steal anymore."

"And I still do eat. Does that mean you win?" I'd have given a lot for the ability to hoover the snippy words back in. "Sorry. That was a stupid thing to say, all things considered."

"You mean because my baby was killed? Let me tell you, there is nothing you or anyone else can say to make that any better or any worse than it is. Calista was my life. Now, you and some other people think that was a bad thing. You say I was overinvolved, et cetera, et cetera. But I don't give a damn what y'all think. My little girl is *still* my life—but now she's moved back inside me." Her hand went to her flat stomach and stroked it lightly. "It happened yesterday at the cemetery. God put her back. I can talk to her now. She sees . . . everything—understands."

Tears massed at the back of my nose; I swallowed hard until they receded, and stifled the urge to mention her other child, the one who was alive. "Understands what?" I dared ask. "Do you mean she understands why she was killed?" Fools rush in and so on.

"No!" It was like the crack of a semi-silenced pistol. "Look, we were talking about *you*, Allie," she said evenly. "We're gonna get back on that. See, here's the thing, you only got to be born because she lied to him about the birth control and waited to tell him till it was too late for an abortion. Otherwise, he'd've taken her to some doctor who was doing them then."

I recognized what she was doing, walling up fresh, urgent secrets behind the old ones I was perishing to learn. Nevertheless, what she offered was irresistibly rich, so much information on a tray before me after a scanted lifetime: pounds of chocolate truffles to wolf down. Likely I'd sicken on the surfeit, but I was more than ready to pay that penalty.

"And why did she want me?" I asked. "Well, not *me* of course, but some child? She never cared for children, and she obviously wasn't keen on him by then, either."

"She wanted to stay married for the moment. True, it was Old Dominion U, not Harvard, where he taught, but he was Professor of Philosophy, and she was Mrs. Professor, with more books in her house than in anyone else's and a husband who'd read them and understood what was in them. Remember, it was never only about money for her, it was about being different and *better*." A smile that managed to be both impish and sad. "And there were students who'd come over. The paper boy was there a lot."

"The boy who delivered the papers?"

"Not delivered: *owned*. His family did, for a couple of hundred years—First Families, all that. I'd call him Paper Boy and he'd laugh. He was sweet . . ." Her face hardened. "And naive."

She shifted position slightly in the chair, so that the lamp beside shone on her cheek. In the golden light, her skin had the texture and tint of a perfect peach. How eccentric that from the same basket of genes should have tumbled out our disparate selves: a peach and a hot pepper.

The peach appraised the pepper and seemed sufficiently satisfied with what she saw to continue. "I've told you, Daddy took commitments seriously. Before you arrived, his plan was to keep the marriage together till I went to college—and he was going to have me in college at sixteen if he could make me smart enough, push me hard enough." She gave a soft snort. "It didn't work, for a lot of reasons—a lot of reasons. He might've pulled it off with you, if you'd stayed round long enough. See, with me, it was my *body* that was smart. I wanted to be in that gym ten hours a day. I wanted to *fly!*"

Suddenly, she leapt from the chair and turned a cartwheel. As she went upside down, the yellow robe dropped to curtain her face, then to wave like a banner. Her long, pale legs, naked to the waist, sliced the air like a propeller tipped with high-heeled mules. It all lasted seconds: the cartwheel was flawless. When it was over, she stood rosy-faced with pride, electrified with the sense memory of flight, filled with joy. There was no sign of the stiffness, the back pain that plagued her, on and off. What she'd said earlier, about Calista being back inside her—it made one wonder.

I applauded, slow, loud claps. "Well done. I never could turn cartwheels or jump a rope properly," I said. "My body's fairly stupid, though my mind is good at certain parlor tricks. But if you're searching for your father's intellectual heir, look no farther than Jared."

"Yeah," she almost muttered. "Your idea of tutoring for him; Nate told me about it. He thinks it makes sense and so do I. I have my doubts about Barney Warden— funny duck, but then so's Jared. Nate says he's a good choice. I guess he'll do."

"I'm glad you see it that way," I said carefully.

"You think I'm the wrong mother for Jared, don't you?"

The answer was yes. For a start, she did not like him much. "The question's irrelevant and you know it, Melanie," I said. "You *are* his mother; he's your son. Right and wrong doesn't pertain." It was a longer answer than yes, but equally true.

Just then, a peremptory rap at the door. Immediately it opened to reveal Jared in green pajamas, his eyes slitty, face like curdled cream. Tom, still wearing the funeral suit absent its tie, stood beside him, a steadying arm about Jared's shoulder.

"His head's hot. I think he's sick," Tom said to Melanie. He had obviously just returned from wherever he'd been, and stopped by Jared's room to bestow the ritual good-night kiss. Never mind it was coming up on five in the morning.

Melanie rose and strode toward her son, palm outstretched to feel his head. "He is hot. Feels like a hundred two or so." Her hand brushed Jared's cheek. "What's the matter, honey? What hurts?" Universal motherspeak to a sick child. She did not often call him honey.

"Throat, neck . . . I dunno," Jared mumbled. "Think I have to throw up."

Tom relinquished his hold, and Melanie took over, leading Jared quickly back down the hall to his bathroom. Father, mother, child: I had a vague memory of a similar scene performed by my mother and me and someone male—but it was sufficiently amorphous to suggest that it might have been sketched in by my imagination. I looked up at Tom.

"Probably flu," he said. "Lot of it going round." He

sighed. "Melanie'll call the doctor, get some antibiotics into him. Poor kid, all he needed, right?"

"Sometimes it's a relief to get sick. You know, just burrow in under the covers and hide for a bit." As I said it, it sounded most appealing. "You look ready to drop, Tom. Where've you been?"

"Home."

"Oh." I felt like a trespasser.

"It's okay. Thanks for asking. I felt a need. Crazy, I know—I'm hardly a sentimental type. The cop on guard let me in. I guess even a suspected killer gets some kind of free pass on funeral day. I sat in Calista's room, just sat. Once it got dark, I dozed on and off on her bed. They had a cop watching me the whole time from the hallway, but it didn't matter. Didn't matter a bit."

"Did it help, going there?"

"Honestly, I don't know. All my landmarks are gone, Lex. I don't know a damned thing. I don't know who squeezed the life out of my daughter or why. I . . . Maybe it did help, a little."

"Tom!" Melanie's voice from down the hall. "Call Dr. Lineham's office, will you? They don't need to wake him up, but I need a callback as soon as he checks in with the service."

"I'll do it," he called back, Dad to Mom.

"How did you know you'd find Melanie in my room?" I asked.

"I didn't," he said, and walked away toward the stairs.

CHAPTER
18

I shut the door, faintly numb in body and spirit, but aching just the same, as though after a long night's eating. Perhaps the cause was lack of sleep, hours spent semireclined on a slim window-seat cushion. More likely it was the result of gorging on the previously forbidden past.

I plugged the computer into the cell phone and booted: this time I was seeking not late news about Calista's death, but fragments of my own life—not Allie's life, Lex's. As I performed the routine operation, my hands were ten thumbs, ungoverned by a mind. I had mail, thank God.

I found myself reading hungrily a note from the boys upstairs in St. Augustine's Road about some plumbing repairs for which access to my flat was needed—and was I okay, considering . . . ?; one from Clive about our next project and should he continue to block out the time in his schedule or, under the circumstances . . . ?;

my BBC contact wondering—just wondering, understand—whether I might care to do a film about my niece's murder, and if so . . . ; my bank manager, about my overdraft. There were several others: I had not checked E-mail for several days.

I responded to each at far greater length than is normal for me, feverishly typing to return color and texture to the existence of Lex Cavanaugh, moderately successful maker of small films—to prove that her pennant still waved, that dents, gashes, and all, she had in fact not decomposed into an unloved six-year-old. She had a flat that wanted its drains fixed; she had projects on her slate. She had . . .

But while the words took shape on my screen—the *yes*'s, the *no*'s, the *okay*'s, the *thanks for asking*'s—in the back of my mind sat two family groups, each posed for a photographer: the Millers and the McQuades. I appeared in neither of them. I worked the computer keys faster, but the uninvited visitors would not leave.

I closed down the computer. Speedily, I dressed myself in jeans and sneakers, and gave my teeth a hard brushing. The taste of mint, candy-sweet, made my stomach rumble in demand. In my head, a short man stood between his tall, pretty blonde wife and tall, pretty blonde daughter: the Miller family photo—the three of them. Despite what Melanie had said about a resemblance, his face was still a blur.

I wanted not to binge now, but I didn't think I could help it. I told myself that all I'd just learned had not been a loss, but a *gain*. But if that were true, why was I starved? And why did I feel angry enough to claw a live bear to death or cut the heads off everyone in that bloody picture?

I sprinted down the hall to Jared's room. His door

was open. He was propped on two pillows, reading a paperback with an iridescent sci-fi cover. Luckily, he was alone. "You feeling a bit better?" I asked.

"I guess. Mom gave me some aspirin and apple juice. My stomach's still yucky, though."

"I'm sure. Look, I'm going out for . . . not too long, couple of hours maybe. I wanted to give you notice this time."

He managed a smile. "So I wouldn't throw a book at you? This one's not very heavy."

The tiny joke, which said he trusted me to return, soothed my spirit. He looked so sweet and safe there under the covers. "See you later," I said, smiling back.

To my relief, I did not encounter Melanie or Tom or anyone else on my way out of the house. I closed the front door behind me and made for my car quickly. The cold predawn air hit my face with an odd, not entirely unpleasant sting, as though the skin were newborn. Just as I'd turned the ignition key, there was a knock at the window beside my head: Vin, in green-and-white jogging clothes, a sheepish half smile on his face. I lowered the window.

"Where you going, Lex?"

"Just for a drive," I said. "I couldn't sleep."

"Yeah, me, too. Look, I guess you think I'm some kind of a major asshole by now." I couldn't deny that and didn't affirm it. "Oh, sure you do," he said. "Guy gets smashed, gives it to his wife—his generous and loving wife, his rich wife. His wife from whom all blessings flow," he added. When sarcasm does not come naturally, it sounds mean and irritating rather than mean and witty.

"Why would you care what I think?" I asked. A bit disingenuous that: he cared what everyone thought.

"Probably because you're Melanie's sister, and I care a lot what she thinks. I may be in love with her."

"Can't help you there, friend." My hands gripped the wheel, my right foot itching to return to the gas pedal. "Why not speak to her directly? Though you'll find her hands a bit full at the moment. Jared seems to have come down with the flu."

"One unlucky kid, isn't he? All the way down the line."

"I wouldn't say so." My anger instantly rekindled itself, finding a handy focal point. "Except for the rotten luck of his sister's being murdered, Jared's quite fortunate. His sort of intelligence is one of the luckiest gifts I can imagine—just as lucky and a lot less fragile than athletic aptitude." Gratuitous. Worse, it was useless. The man I was out to hurt was my dead father. Using Vin as his whipping boy inflicted unjust pain and brought me no satisfaction.

"Now I've gone and offended you," he said. "Didn't mean to. It's just that these days my control's gone haywire. What's a gym coach with no control? I'll tell you what: Finished. And that's what I am. You won't be seeing me round here after today. I'm leaving."

"You are?"

"Yeah. I can't hack it. Barney wasn't wrong to let me have it. If I'd been sober, I'd've coldcocked him, but I was out of line, no question. Hey, Courtney means well—that's her emblem, ask anybody: Courtney Means Well. But believe me, even sixteen years ago, with all that money, there wasn't exactly a lineup of competition for her hand. Gave the old bastard a stroke, Court going after me the way she did. He dropped dead a week before the wedding. Funny, she didn't shed a tear at his funeral, but she cried her eyes out all through our ceremony. Go figure."

"I wouldn't begin to try," I said. "She's very fond of you, Courtney is."

"Crazy about me, I know that. But it's tough to live with someone who wants to do your breathing for you. When Callie was here, it didn't matter so much, any of it. Life was good. Melanie and me, we were like partners in Callie: shaping that talent; keeping her edge sharp, focused the right way." His face glowed as recent memory took him over. "Oh, we did need to keep a firm grip on her—you know how kids get; a little defiant as they get bigger, but we were handling it. We . . ." He heard himself, I suppose, and deflated back into the present. "But Callie's gone, and Melanie, too, in any way that matters. And Old Vin doesn't seem to have any . . . I guess you'd call it insulation left. Nothing between me and those grinding gears inside. Now, every time I hear 'Vin dear, don't you think you should . . .?' Or, 'Honestly, Vin, if you ask me . . .' I feel like I could strangle her, and—" Our eyes met for a glancing second and he looked like a dog who'd just shat on the carpet.

"It's an expression," I said, "a common one."

"That's correct," a new voice said. From the cover of dense shrubbery, her trench coat starkly pale, Domingo materialized like the ghost of Hamlet's father. The effect was easy to pull off in the shadowy dark, and it startled quite as much as it was meant to.

I enjoyed a brief fantasy of gunning the motor and cutting her down. "Do you have some sixth sense about people's comings and goings, Detective?" I asked. "Or do you just lurk about in hope?"

She laughed, a gentle ripple of a laugh that lied about her toughness of purpose. "Oh, no, nothing so dramatic. I know that Mr. Anacleto usually does his morning jog very early. I thought this might be a convenient time to have a word with him. I didn't expect to run into you. But since I have . . . Mr. Anacleto, would you mind if I had a private word with Lex first?"

I snapped the door locks shut. "I think Lex would mind," I said.

Vin looked at her, then me, deciding where his best interests lay. "I'll wait for you on the back patio, Detective," he said finally, looking now at the ground. "See you round, Lex." And with the wave of a boxer who's taken one punch too many, jogged himself off.

Domingo's head inserted itself into my still-open window. "Nobody—nobody broke into that house," she said with an urgency utterly at odds with her previous cool competence. I felt the steam of her breath on my cheek. "Someone who lived there killed her. Melanie, Tom, Jared. One of them did the murder, and the others have a damned good idea of which one. Think about that. *I want you to think about that.*" The quiet Indian lilt, electrified this way, was more menacing than a shout. Her round black eyes locked into mine; our faces were no more than a foot apart. If she believed that I had her answer lodged in my brain, she'd have split my skull to get at it.

"What is it you expect from me?"

"I think you know," she said. Her head withdrew from the car window, but the eyes stayed trained on my face. "You're a professional observer in an inside position. It happens I've seen one of your films—the one about the pack of wild children in Brazil. I thought it was sharp. I thought it showed a conscience. I'd say that's what I'm after: sharp observation, up close, interpreted with conscience."

"There's something extra for you in this case, isn't there, Domingo?" I asked. "Something personal, something beyond a dedicated cop investigating a particularly awful crime."

"A crime like this is its own motivation. No extras are required, believe me."

"But somehow I don't believe you," I said, a flicker of something in her face making me certain I was on a right track. I shrugged. "As you said, I'm a professional observer. That's my professional observation. Are you going to tell me what else is going on for you? If you don't, this talk is over."

She nodded, but not immediately nor willingly: the nod of a consummate realist who wants something fiercely. "I have a daughter," she said. "Sirena. She's a bit older than Calista was. Eleven."

"And?"

"And she's the reason I left Bombay. When she was three, I walked in on my husband giving her a bath. He had his pants unzipped, one hand working on himself while his other worked on her. I think I knew from the way she sat there in the water—so still, her face all flushed, as though she wanted to wriggle away, to cry out, and had been told she mustn't—that it was not the first time. It occurred to me to kill him. Instead, I knelt down and took over, finished bathing her. I forced myself not to scream. I didn't want to scare her any more than she was already."

She was feeling pain: hot, present, alive. It was the kind of pain I knew quite well: the kind that does not soften with time. She and I understood each other. Perhaps that was the potential she'd seen in me from the first.

"Sirena and I were on a flight to New York the following morning with four suitcases, everything we needed. He didn't dare make waves; he was a politician on the way up and terrified of what I'd do. My silence bought my daughter and me uncontested freedom. Fortunately, I had some family in Connecticut, an uncle in the Stamford PD. I have a law degree from University of Bombay, but police work suits me better."

Of course it did—hunting down villains, sending them to their punishments, as she hadn't her husband: an insight worthy of Nate Grumbach. "You raised the issue of my conscience," I said. "How easy is yours about overlaying your own experience on the McQuades. Has it, for example, been established absolutely that Calista was sexually abused?"

"The M.E. won't commit to definite. Manipulated with a finger, is his best guess. But the garrote round her neck—you know damned well that could have been a try at erotic asphyxiation, a sex game gone wrong."

"It's been mentioned in the media—along with imaginary voices and devil worship."

"Pencils tied to the ends of a piece of twine. Pencils like them were in Jared's room and in the study. No match for the twine in the house, I'll give you that. And by the way," she added, too carefully casual, "this information has *not* been in the media."

Her surprise punch had landed square, but I was determined not to show her that. "Don't you think erotic asphyxiation would be a bit sophisticated for Jared? And pencils are pencils. I assume the pencils were not distinctive or incriminating."

"No. Garden-variety yellow wood pencils, unsharpened and wiped clean of fingerprints. But they'd been tied to that twine for a while the lab says; the grooves were deep. Needless to say, the McQuades denied ownership of the garrote." I tried to think of other uses for a pair of pencils connected with a length of twine. Surely there were dozens, but at the moment, I could not think of one.

"I'd like to point out," I said, "that there are possibilities other than those you mentioned: that someone else had a key to the house and knew the alarm code; that someone was let in, perhaps inadvertently, by one of the family. Do you admit that either of those is possible?"

"I'm an investigator," she said tightly. "I sort out the credible from the incredible. If you ask what I *believe* after two weeks, twenty-four seven, on this case, I believe that one of them killed her and the others know it—or as good as know it."

"But why?" I pitched the syllables carefully, striving for an objective note that was sham. "Have you come up with a motive you find credible?"

"Their team of cute lawyers won't let us near enough to do our job. But sex, jealousy—other than money, those are the triggers for murder." She let out a long breath and continued, calmer now, more like a guest lecturer in sociology. "The parents both have traumatic sexual histories. Melanie was involved with men, probably including her father, before she was thirteen. She was obsessed with her daughter, who knows to what degree? Tom grew up in a string of settings where abuse would have been likely. As an adult, he's a violent risk-taker who constantly cheats with much younger women. And Jared . . ." she paused while my heart rattled inside its box. "Jared is an angry, emotionally unstable boy who took a constant backseat to his sister. He is also a boy on the brink of adolescence, a boy with an extremely inquiring mind and a computer. There's a lot to explore on the Web—some of it is enough to turn your stomach."

I could have tossed the argument back at her, done a few more volleys, but there is no real point in trying to refute a missionary's beliefs through debate, certainly not when you've no hard facts to cite. Calista's murder had struck Domingo's nerve center, transforming a level-headed detective into a Mother Teresa, armed with badge and gun, and also with a library of professional blather to support her emotional predilections.

As she stood awaiting my response, I knew that the McQuades, and only they, were in her sights. She would look neither right nor left, but continue to shake this tree until something dropped to the ground. And I knew equally well that she did not intend to let up on me until I was goaded into some blunder that would help her. I wondered in earnest whether I'd have served Jared better by staying put in London, doing no harm. At least that.

I started the motor, then turned to her. "I will think about what you've said. But I want you to think about this: Professional you may be, but you come with a bias that makes the alternative possibilities straw men. They're not straw men for *me*, though." I pressed the button to close the window. We exchanged stares, silently restating our positions while the glass rose to cut us apart. Then I shot out of the driveway intent on getting from here to there as fast as possible.

But I did not know where "there" might be, except that I knew it mustn't be Dunkin' Donuts again. Not now.

As I drove past the lighted storefront, I imagined Nate Grumbach there beside me in the front seat, and found myself comforted by his presence. Talking with Melanie, my tongue had balked at the word *Daddy*: I could not in fact recall ever having said it in my life, though I must have done. *Dad-dy*. No matter that it was Tilt, not my father, whom Nate summoned up for me, I wondered how it might feel to curl up in his lap while he stroked my head until I fell asleep. His lap would be warm, his swarthy face faintly fragrant of shave lotion. Shave lotion: The camera rolled, zooming in on a shot of me naked in his bathroom only a few days ago, in thrall to a far older freeze-frame, one marred with blank spots: a small girl naked in another bathroom, a faceless man standing over her.

But now the blank and blurred faces filled themselves in; a picture came to life . . .

The smell of shave lotion—lemon and leather and sawn wood—filled the girl's nostrils, making her choke and cough. She looked up at the man. He was sharp-featured, dark-eyed, balding. The cold fluorescent light cast a glistening halo on his bald head. She was under-sized for six, on the scrawny side. At the moment, she was cold and wet and scared. Her thigh burned something fierce where some of the shattering glass had nicked it. Her hand went to the small wound and came away bloody.

"Do you do these things through clumsiness or on purpose, Allie?" His voice was larger than he was—resonant, rather beautiful, seeming to come from an instrument larger, grander than he. She didn't know what to say to it. She never did. "Well, you think about it. I have told you to stay away from my things. That row of bottles is mine. Mine. Do you understand?"

"Yes," she whispered. The blood was running down her leg in a tickling path. She wanted to call out for Melanie, who'd come and wash it clean and put on a Band-Aid and rub her wet, shivery body dry in a big warm towel. Instead, she simply stood there, beginning to shiver, wanting to cry.

He held up a stubby finger. Its nail was chewed. Mommy always made fun of that, called him Nervous Nellie. "Now, we will reason this out. You needed to climb up there to disturb my things, my bottles, didn't you?"

"Yes."

"So, you took your clothes off, God knows why, and pulled over that stool and climbed up to touch things you were not supposed to touch. On purpose, correct?"

"Yes."

"Say it, then. 'I did it on purpose.' "

"I did it on purpose," she repeated. Magically, her shivering had stopped, nor did she want to cry anymore. On her own, she added, "And I hate you."

His face changed, broadening into something close to a smile, as though what he'd just heard had pleased him. "Well, I hate you, too," he said almost jovially, "so that gives us something in common, finally."

How on earth could I have forgotten Professor Leonard J. Miller?

The slice of memory had absorbed me utterly. Arms and legs continued to drive the car, but where they chose to drive it was no conscious choice of mine. When I found myself turning the corner, not onto Pinebrook, where Nate lived, but rather North Avenue, I let out a long breath I hadn't realized I was holding. Blue house, red shutters: the home of my childhood scribblings. That's where I'd brought myself.

I pulled to the curb and parked—and waited. It never for a moment crossed my mind that he wouldn't appear. It took perhaps twenty minutes for the front door to swing open and Jasper to come bounding out. Barney, in a black hooded sweatshirt, looking like a police sketch of someone armed and dangerous, was right behind him. I got out of the car.

"Hi." Neither surprise nor pleasure nor alarm was evident in his expression. Nothing was evident in his expression except despair. Something about him was terribly different. His eyes were red-rimmed and sunken; he looked thin-faced, almost gaunt. This was not the man who'd so neatly quelled an unruly drunk, who'd positioned Jared's telescope just so for the meteor shower, and yipped in excitement at the view. This was not the man I'd been with yesterday.

"Hi," I said. "Do you suppose I might run with you?" My voice had an unaccustomed treble ring.

"If you want to." He leaned down to clip the leash on Jasper's collar. His eyes moved back to me. "Should I ask you if you're okay? You don't look okay."

"I'm not exactly okay," I said. "You don't look okay, either."

"Yeah. Well. You want to run or not? This is going to be a short one." I saw him swallow hard, as though staving off tears.

"Barney, what is it?"

"I'm not up for talk," he said tonelessly. "Could we just get started here?"

"Suits me," I shot back in kind. "Let's go."

We did. I ran a bit behind—the difference between short legs and longer ones. His loping body, at least, did not appear to have changed. The damned dog seemed exuberant, overjoyed as it galloped, or whatever it is dogs do: the only happy member of this trio.

My thick rubber soles were buoyant against hard ground; my cheeks burned with wind-rush. I felt an inner eruption of freedom—a cupboard door blown open, bulging shoe boxes of memories tumbling from their shelves, spilling their contents into my every thought: his precision in all things, from the way his shirts were ironed to the way food was arranged on the dinner plates; his chilly scorn for my mother, "whose brain resides some three—no, maybe four—feet due south of her forehead." And I remembered his nagging at Melanie, exaggeratedly patient, always more regretful than angry, the way you might talk to someone irredeemably stupid.

Professor Leonard J. had cut me loose early; he'd done his worst and could do no more. Melanie had been less fortunate. The qualifications for his approval were too numerous, the hurdles too high even for a gymnast.

The cold air was tonic in my lungs. I felt keenly alive. And I was glad the old bastard was dead. It was a frustration not to believe in hell . . .

The sight of the blue house interrupted the bursts of recollection. We were back. Jasper's tongue flapped out in a doggy smile. I panted back at him. Barney seemed barely out of breath. "Feel better, Lex?" he asked, his mouth curled downward, as though asking the question was a difficult chore.

"I do, actually. Do you?" I asked a bit idiotically.

"Afraid not," he said, the bite of irony sharp in his voice. "No runner's high for me."

His face had a stony set; the eyes avoided mine, looked straight past me into the middle distance. I'd fled the Anacleto house with Daddy on the brain, but my hands and feet had hatched a different idea and driven the car toward the sheltering comfort of friendship.

"Are you ill? Jared's just come down with flu; perhaps you've caught a touch." I hated my own hypocrisy. I knew I was less concerned over the state of his health than thwarted by it, irritated at not getting what I wanted from him. Selfish. Perhaps inveterate selfishness is the biggest penalty the unloved child pays—and inflicts.

My gut did a tap step of legitimate hunger—at least I thought it was legitimate; it's hard to know. "Do you have anything like breakfast inside?" I asked quickly. "Or any time to eat it with me? I'll prepare it for both of us. I'd explain, only . . ."

"I don't *want* you to explain," he snapped. "Whatever it is you're after, Lex, you won't find it here. I'm fresh out of it today. I'm sorry. I really am." Tears pooled in his eyes making them glitter like green glass.

What in hell happened to you since last night? Tell me, maybe I can help. I like you. That's what I might have wanted to say. What I did say was, "I landed on your curb at six in the morning, with no invitation. I'm the one who's sorry. Thanks for the run," and hightailed it back to my car.

CHAPTER
19

I found it hard to keep my eyes off the tall yellow pencil lying beside a spiral notebook on Jared's bedside table. Was it from this house or had he brought it from his? Was it a twin to the ones on the garrote? If so . . .

"Checkmate," he said. He'd beaten me three times running. It was the following evening. His fever was lower, but he remained nested in bed pillows, wearing bright blue pajamas imprinted with planets—brand-new ones Melanie had bought: that's what a mother does, isn't it? She buys pajamas and such that her children will enjoy. I thought of Calista's tiger-striped slippers, one not quite on the foot of her dead body. I knew Melanie must wake now with similar pictures in her mind and forgave her anything she needed to do to bear them and keep on living.

It didn't seem to me that Jared was minding the confinement a bit; a safe berth for him, I thought. For my part, I was jumpy and frayed from a couple of days spent taking long mental journeys down twisting dead-end paths.

"How about Monopoly?" he asked sourly. "Maybe you could pay attention to that."

"Monopoly doesn't require major attention," I said with some sourness of my own. "I'll play it if you want. Did you bring a set?"

"No. They have one downstairs, though. We used to play it sometimes while Calista was doing gym practice with Vin. Courtney, Mom, and me— It was Courtney's idea of 'helping poor Jared fit in.' I didn't exactly want to, but you know how Courtney is. She nags, and then she nags louder. It's easier just to go along."

Never mind Courtney, this was the first time he'd spoken Calista's name in an everyday sort of reference. I didn't want to spook him. "Courtney means well," I quoted the departed Vin. "At least I suppose she does."

"She's a pain in the butt," he said.

"That too."

"Why're you staring at my notebook?"

I looked for subtext in his eyes and found none. "I don't know," I said after seconds that stretched like putty.

"Want to know a fact?" he asked: his sometime touchstone in awkward moments. "The moon's diameter is 2.160 miles. Its density is three point three times the density of water, much less dense than the earth—five point five."

"That's two facts—or three, depending who's counting," I said. "Interesting though. Did you always tag along to Calista's gym sessions?" I slipped it in fast, and he didn't seem to mind.

"Nah, but Mom made me come when the cleaning

lady or someone wasn't home to baby-sit me. I mean, shit, I'm twelve. Do I look like I need a baby-sitter?"

"Well, mothers will be mothers, won't they?" He paid me for the banal comment with a disgusted glare. Fair enough. But as I regarded his drawn, clenched face, a faint blue vein visible beneath the translucent skin of his forehead, I realized that I wasn't at all certain what level of supervision he might require.

"She always wants me to have friends. 'Why don't you go visit a *friend,* Jared? Play *ball* or something?' Like I was some all-American movie boy, instead of . . . I don't have friends; I don't play ball. I'm fine with my meteors and comets and numbers. Why can't she just leave me alone with them? I'm not going to set the house on fire or something!" His white face flushed feverish red in the cheeks as he worked up a head of steam. "I wanted to take tae kwon do, I told you that, but she said it was 'too hostile a hobby, Jared.' I mean, *you* do it, Lex! I've seen you practice since you've been here. A lot. Tell her that. Make her let me."

"When was the last time anyone made your mother do anything? Tae kwon do isn't a hostile hobby, but you do need control to learn it and greater control to use it. You've got a problem with control, Jared, and . . ." The unaccustomed words had a starchy taste in my mouth; I had never before preached to Jared from the pulpit of adulthood. But I saw that doubt had begun its work, creating that fog where landmarks disappear, and nothing is certain because too much is possible.

"Jared, she *is* your mum," I said flatly, "and you're going to have to do as she says about a lot of things for the next six years. That is the truth."

"Duh."

"For such a smart kid, you say that a lot." A wisp of

smile, despite himself. "Jared, don't shut down on me, okay? I want to ask you something important. Might anyone in the family have let someone into the house the night Calista was killed?"

He stared at my face, his own a careful blank. The vein in his forehead seemed to darken, and looked ready to throb. "Maybe," he said softly. It verged on being a question—tentative, bordering on hopeful. Then a flat "No."

"How can you be so sure?" My voice hit the air like tearing paper, ragged enough to startle him—a lack of the very control I'd so sanctimoniously extolled moments ago.

His lips disappeared into a cartoon line, as his teeth bit them closed. After a beat he said, "I don't know anything that happened. I was fast asleep." This is a recording.

"Jared, look—" That was as far as I got.

A clatter of shoes climbing stairs, followed immediately by, "Hi, honey. Feeling better?" Melanie was calm, a bit of a spring to her step. She exuded a wholesome warmth—by-product perhaps of Jared's illness, which had thrust her into active mothering.

He shrugged at her. "Kind of. We're going to play Monopoly. Could you bring the set up?"

"Sure." She cast a look backward to her left, outside my view, and smiled too broadly. Suddenly, she looked nervous. "In . . . in a little while, honey. Meantime, you have a visitor."

CHAPTER
20

"Hello there, Jared, Lex." Nate appeared beside Melanie, his shoulders hunched slightly, while his palms rubbed together in the attitude of a doctor out of an old film: the house-calling medical man conscientiously warming his hands to avoid giving a feverish patient an unpleasant chill. I smelled his shave lotion across the room, and was startled to recall quite clearly that it was the one my father had favored; Canoe, it was called. Yes, that was it; simple, really: Nate resembled Tilt Schwartz, if only superficially, but his fragrance was Leonard Miller's.

Odd, this newborn ease at remembering, a bit like vision bestowed suddenly upon a person who'd got quite used to coping with blindness; a brilliant but bewildering gift, but so far, a limited one: a fragrance, a face, a household autocrat, cold words in a cold bathroom.

"You've got what my grandma used to call the

grippe." Nate's rumbling baritone filled the room with
warmth. "Best way in the world to take a time-out from
the world, when you need to." I forgave him the Canoe.

"Yeah," Jared said through clenched teeth, as his
gaze fixed, seemingly on nothing benevolent, but rather
on Caliban rising from the underworld.

"Ladies, mind if Jared and I spend a little time
alone?" Nate asked. It had obviously been prearranged
between Melanie and him.

"No!" Jared yelped. "I don't want to." He wriggled
out from under the covers, thumped onto the floor, and
ran to my side. "Fuck it! I *won't* be with him. I *hate*
him!" His faced flushed a deep red. While the adult in
me assumed that this was meant for Jared's good, nevertheless, I held him tight to me and wished desperately I
had the power to send Nate packing.

"Maybe this could wait until he's feeling better," I
said.

"Jared, you get back in that bed now." Melanie's no-
nonsense tone reminded me more than a little of my
mother's, so I knew she'd win the point. "I said *now*.
And we'll forget the language, because you've got the
flu. Do you understand me?" Of course he did. She
stared him down, and he gave up, his eyes brimming
with tears he fought to keep back. "Ten minutes,
honey," she said, the harshness gone. "You and Nate
haven't talked in a while. It used to be very helpful to
you. Remember? Just ten minutes. We'll be right outside. Then we can all play Monopoly."

As the door was shutting, I caught Jared's eye and
was reminded of caged rabbits I'd seen in French
provincial market squares. They knew their fate, knew
they could do nothing to escape it.

"Why is it he loathes Nate, Melanie?"

"Because Nate got too close to the bone. That's what therapy's about, you know," she said. I wondered if she spoke from any direct personal experience and decided probably not. We were tough cases, my sister and I, neither of us quick off the mark to slit herself open to the bone for any promised benefit. "In the beginning, it was a such a help to Jared, you can't imagine," she said. "Then . . . well, he turned on a dime. Sullen, outrageous—just plain mean. Wouldn't see Nate anymore, wouldn't talk about it. Classic self-defeating behavior." Polly wants a cracker.

"Don't you think he might have been worried about how close you and Nate had become. Jealous, perhaps?" I trod gingerly here.

"Nate is a good man," she said slowly. "His friendship has helped me be better for Jared, whether Jared knows it or not, or whether you do. He explained boundaries and patient confidentiality to Jared—and anybody bright enough to understand all the astronomy stuff he gobbles up is bright enough to understand about that. Now, Nate wouldn't tell me anything Jared confided to him, but I did finally pry out of him that it was all about hate. Oh, I can imagine how much Jared must hate us—Tom for never being round and . . . things; me for being tough on him, for not loving him as much as . . . And I guess he hated Calista for . . ." Her voice caught and cracked. ". . . for being who she was. See, it scared Jared how he felt. He was furious at Nate for getting him to say things, and for hearing them."

"I see." The thing about a tower of psychological supposition is that it builds in such reasonable fashion, block upon hypothetical block. Its patterns of formula absent fact tend to make my skin itch. I remembered so clearly talking with Jared about sneezing it out: *"Ihay-*

choo, Calista," which hadn't seemed to faze him a bit. Of course, he'd been only six at the time.

"Anyway," she said, "Jared's in awful shape, and I thought maybe Nate could somehow break through to him now, you know, while he was in a kind of weakened condition—talk to him that confidential way like he used to. Well, maybe he'd get certain things off his chest, begin to . . . to heal, so he could *live* again."

I put my arm round her at about elbow level. She did not pull away, just stood there, her head bowed like a sunflower at dusk. Words of fealty, resurgent sisterhood, failed to spring to my tongue. "Maybe you're right," I said awkwardly. My ears strained to pick up what might be going on in Jared's room, but I heard no definable sound, only the suggestion of Nate's rumble. "He uses the same shave lotion as . . . our father did."

Her head raised. I could feel her body stiffen under my hand. "Yes, I know." She looked at me, waiting, I thought, to see what I had to say about that.

"I've had some experience in hating," I said quietly, removing my hand from round her, as I sensed she was wanting me to. "I knocked a bottle of the stuff off his bathroom shelf. I think it must've been shortly before Mum and I left, but I'm not certain. Anyway, we agreed we hated each other, he and I. It was out there in the open, and quite real. But you know, I think it's not the same with Jared."

"You mean not out in the open?"

"No, I mean I don't think he hates you. Or Tom."

Her eyes narrowed, ready to disbelieve. But hope was in them, too. "You trying to be nice?"

"No. I'm saying that Jared knows that you don't hate *him*. He knows that you look after him, tend him when he's sick, buy him interplanetary pajamas because he'll like them—and he knows that Tom comes and kisses him good night every night, no matter what. I'm saying that, bad as it's been for you all, terrible as it is now, Jared has something *there* with his parents. You and Tom may disappoint him, hurt his feelings, piss him right off, but he doesn't hate you, not the way I did my father. Believe me, I know the difference."

"And Calista?" she asked. "Did he hate her?"

"How would I know?" I said quickly. Then, "Melanie, look, I love Jared very much, which admittedly makes me no neutral observer. But still, I do not believe that boy is a killer." My voice rang back at me with a tinny sound, while her silence confirmed that she thought otherwise. Feared otherwise? Knew?

I said very quietly, "As far as the police are concerned, charging any one of the three of you will satisfy them."

Her face stayed still, but her eyes mulled actively. Her pointed pink tongue licked at her upper lip, catlike. Licking off an unexpected bonus of cream or preparing to pounce at an attacker? Why didn't I simply tell her about Domingo's daughter and the tunnel-vision it produced? I didn't know then and I don't know now. The strands of loyalty we spin for ourselves can be temporary, illogical, even counterproductive. But while they last, they last.

I said, "Domingo won't take seriously that someone else might have got into the house, or was let in."

"I didn't give out keys, not to anyone, ever. And I didn't let anyone in."

"Did Tom?"

"Why don't you ask him? You thinking Ms. Cuteass Rima sneaked into my house and murdered my daughter?"

"Let's say she could've. Why would she?"

"Beats the hell out of me." She let out a long breath. "Maybe Courtney, maybe Vin, maybe Nate, maybe your good buddy Barney. Maybe . . ." She'd been chanting it, like a rap song, tapping the rhythm with her toe. Suddenly, she stopped and stared at me hard. "I'm no police deputy and neither are you," she said coldly. "It is my job to protect the family I have left. I don't know what you think your job is."

"But, Melanie . . ." I began.

"But *nuthin'!*" Her hands sliced the air, orchestrating finality. "Things are hard enough without you dreaming up movie plots. Can't you understand that?"

The door opened and Nate walked out. "A start," he said to Melanie. "But a start's a start."

"Thanks," she said, giving a brief touch to his cheek. It was an understated gesture but one of deep intimacy. I thought of the way he'd massaged her neck at Courtney's dinner table last week, how he'd helped her upstairs to bed that night. Nate had volunteered they were not lovers. Perhaps their bond was stronger for that.

I walked past them to Jared's room and found him in bed, the quilt pulled up tight, nose-high. "Ready to come on down and buy Boardwalk and Park Place?" I asked, falsely hopeful. What I could see of his face was chalky.

"Tired," he said, through the muffle of quilt. "Just want to go to sleep."

"What if I bring the Monopoly set up here?"

"I said no."

"Time for your medicine, Jared," Melanie said, striding to the bureau, where she busied herself with the pouring of orange juice from carafe into drinking glass and the shaking of pills from their container. She did not look at Jared. "These antibiotics are really doing the trick," she said with overly brisk, false cheer. "If you get enough rest, you'll be in shape to start your lessons with Mr. Warden. He phoned today with a list of books he wants me to buy. Bet you'll like them." He'd phoned, had he? I was both relieved and troubled. I'd kept thoughts of Barney at bay these two days. Now I recalled an oblique reference Nate had made to his "history," and wondered what that might be. The last thing in the world Jared needed now was to be subjected to someone unreliable.

Melanie approached the bed and held out the glass. "C'mon now. Sit up and take the pills." He did after a moment. They exchanged looks, which I observed quite closely from the opposite side of the bed, where I stood. Hers might have been a plea for forgiveness; his was an unmistakable indictment for betrayal. Betrayal seemed to be endemic to our family.

"Tell me a fact," I said a bit desperately. "Have you got one for me?"

He swallowed the pills and retreated back under the quilt. "Yeah. A fact: I want you to get out of my room," he said, "and go to hell. Both of you."

CHAPTER
21

Nate was waiting for us at the end of the hall. "How'd he seem, Mel?"

"Damned mad, of course," she said. "He wanted to be alone."

Nate nodded. "Try not to let it get to you too much. He's got a lot on his plate."

They were like a pair of parents speaking over my head in a foreign tongue meant to veil meaning. "And just *maybe*," I said, "what he doesn't need is therapy against his will. Not right now."

"You're here with my consent. That could change." Melanie's warning rang cold and clear.

Nate intercepted. "Lex, just *maybe* you don't have the whole picture."

"I'd welcome seeing a lot more of it," I said with the resentment of a child who'd just gotten her mouth slapped for impertinence by one parent and was promptly being offered a conciliatory treat by the other.

"I'm going to my room," Melanie said, looking suddenly bleak, drained of spirit. "Like son, like mother. I think I want to be alone, too." She made quickly for the stairs and disappeared down them, her back ramrod-stiff.

"Think we can commandeer the kitchen sans maids?" Nate asked. "I'll make you a cup of coffee."

We found Tonya taking dishes off a silver tray to load into the dishwasher and scowling about it. She brightened when she saw Nate. "Hi, Doctor. Everybody had room service tonight. You seen Courtney?"

"I did look in on her, yes."

"She still cryin' her eyes out? She didn't touch but a coupla bites of her chicken."

"I think she's feeling calmer, if not better."

She shook her head. "He didn't have to just up and walk out. You know? He coulda . . . Men."

"Ours is the weaker sex, Tonya," he said gravely, "and don't you ever forget it. Courtney's bruised but no way broken. Don't feel too bad; she'll figure it out. You just wait and see." Dr. Fortune Cookie; Dr. Pangloss: house calls, two for the price of one.

Tonya favored him with one of her fine smiles. "Fix something for you. Cuppa coffee?"

"Tell you what, I'm a nut about coffee—love to make it as much as I love to drink it. Would I be offending you if I offered a trade? You clear out of the kitchen and let me make a pot, and Lex and I will finish doing the dishes."

"Best deal I've heard in a while, a long while. You have a good night now." It was clear she meant him, not me.

"You have a good night, too, Tonya," I said a little louder than necessary for sincerity's sake.

"What's that about?" Nate asked, once she was gone.

"I asked her some tactless questions about Vin last week. She thought I was pumping her unfairly, and it got her back up. In her book I'm a troublemaker—an opinion widely held in these parts, I should think." He gave a brief chuckle. He'd begun pottering about the kitchen, opening and shutting cabinets, fridge, freezer. "What are you looking for?" I asked.

"Coffee beans, but I guess ground is the best I'm gonna do here," he said popping the plastic lid off a half-full tin. He put the ingredients into the coffeemaker and switched it on. "And were you—pumping her unfairly?"

"I suppose so," I said. "But look who's on about unfair pumping. You're trying to get Jared to admit that he did this, aren't you?" I'd said it. A wave of heat rolled through my body, making me feel weak. I held on to the back of a chair and then sat myself in it.

He held up his large palm. "Easy, Lex. Let's take it a step at a time. I give you my word that I am not pressing Jared to say anything that isn't true. But you need to consider this: If he is guilty, it is in his best interests to admit it, to himself for a start. Look, I'm not saying he should run off to turn himself in; I *am* saying that his parents need to know the truth—for his own good and theirs. If he's innocent, that knowledge will lighten their burden. If he's not . . . they'll need to decide what to do."

He was right; of course he was. And yet . . . "Jared has not said he did it," I said stubbornly, unwilling to let go a damaged fabric of faith and hope, heavily mended with my own embroidery.

"No, he has not."

"So what we're talking about here is psychology—his, as interpreted by you."

"You could say so."

I took a deep breath. The air, strong with brewing coffee, helped brace me. "Then there's no more reason to suspect him than there is to suspect his parents, or anyone else who might've gotten access to the house—people whose psyches are less familiar to you. Never mind about footprints and locks and alarms for the moment, other scenarios exist, don't they?"

"Yes, Lex, they do. But *that* one exists, too. You must recognize it."

"There seems to be a growing crowd recognizing it. I won't be missed."

His head did a small, slow shake. "The smart-ass quip comes easy to you, much too easy. You underrate yourself, you know. Why not give the bigger challenge a whirl? You're up to it." Spoken like a dad, I thought: *Study a bit harder, darling. You're up to algebra. It's not that hard. Here, I'll help you.* He placed a mug of coffee in front of me. I stared down at it, feeling that I might weep.

"All right," I said, meeting his eyes now, "how about this: I don't believe that Jared killed his sister, and so I am going to focus my attention on the alternatives. Then if I am proved wrong, I'll figure out a next step."

His face broke into a smile that looked quite spontaneous. "Now, that's better. I wish you luck. Let me ask you something. If you *are* proved wrong, will it change the way you feel about Jared?"

I lifted the mug to my lips and tasted the coffee. It was strong as tar. "I don't know, do I?"

"No, you don't. But these are the real questions, and if you don't mull them, the answers are liable to blindside you." We drank for a while, not talking, my mind filled with the rough straw of half-formed thoughts.

He said, "We're on the same side ultimately, you know."

"Are we?"

"We are. In some way, you could call our team the pragmatists. We win by making the best of a situation whose best is none too good." He brought his face closer to mine, just short of invasion—close enough so I felt not his breath, but the pull of his energy. The Canoe smell of him was fainter, but still there. "We can help Jared, Lex. And we can help each other do it."

I shifted my chair back a bit to a place outside his magnetic field. "What are you suggesting?"

He refilled his mug and held the pot out to me. I shook my head no. He drank before answering, as though pouring fuel into a thirsty tank. It occurred to me how much more convenient an addiction coffee is than food—as rotten, some might say, for one's health as the odd binge-purge, but convenient. "The way I see it, we've got a critical few weeks to work with Jared, each of us with a different job. He's promised to see me every day. In return, I've promised him fifteen-minute limits: no session will go on longer than fifteen minutes, unless he wants it to. Barney's going to be tutoring him for two, three hours an afternoon, I gather. You are his lodestar . . . let's call you Peter Pan crossed with Mary Poppins: you embody his hope for a future—for something good, a life past all this. And in that role, you'll be best off avoiding any head-to-head confrontation, if you see what I mean."

Oh, I saw; I saw. I saw also how against my nature it would be to carry off such a role. Weeks, he'd said weeks. I felt a familiar trickle of sweat at the back of my neck as I realized how tempted I was to cut and run. I could be in my flat in what, ten hours? Perhaps less if I were lucky with flight schedules. I was a damned poor excuse for a lodestar or an advocate, or anything else Jared needed, so what was I doing here other than getting in the way? I feared that the urge to flee was not noble, but a thinly cloaked yearning to nest once again in the shelter I'd built for myself: a life of intense, time-limited absorptions; a life where I set up the shots and held the camera, a life of isolation and safety.

Though the desire for motion twitched in my feet, they did not move themselves. I would not go. Even if it were best for Jared that I steal away again, I would not, could not: My vital organs were trapped here, entwined with his. The surgery to sever them might not kill me, but would render my life-support systems not worth the powder to blow them to hell.

"And his parents?" I asked. "What role for them in all this?"

"His parents are his parents. They love him after their fashion—which is the limit of love, anyone's. Here's the thing, if he is innocent, we can help him back into life, get him ready to return to school after New Year's with a strong support system in place so he won't fall off the rails. But if he's guilty . . ."

"I don't want to hear that part, Nate. Call me Pan or Poppins or anything you care to, I will not consider that now. And I warn you to look to your own refraction. You don't like Jared much. That continues to worry me."

"Lex, you can trust me as far as you need to. I've said it, and it still goes. I work with children. That's what I *do*. I wouldn't have lasted ten minutes in this profession if I didn't have empathy with them, or if I intruded my personal tastes into their treatment. And actually, there are things in Jared I feel a real kinship with." He let out a long breath, and seemed suddenly out of steam, all that energy depleted. "I've helped him before; I can help him now," he said. "And anything, anything he says to me is one hundred percent privileged. See, I can urge him to level with his parents; I can't force him to. And I can't tell them myself." He drained the last drop from his mug and stood. "I'm going home now."

I stood, too. "Does all that coffee ruin your sleep?"

He laughed, not so happily. "You mean at my age? There's not much sleep to ruin. Insomnia is an old friend of mine. We drink a lot of coffee together, have for years. My wife wasn't well and nights got to be hard." He shrugged. "That's how habits are born."

"Oh?" He had not mentioned before how his wife died or in fact anything about her, other than that she was small like me. A certain expectant set to his face said he wanted me to ask now. My own expectant face posed the question.

"MS. It's a long and lousy way to die—if you happen to be lucky enough to get to pick. After a while, I had to do everything for Zip. Everything." His eyes crinkled almost shut, like someone looking into full sun.

"Zip? That means zero in American, doesn't it?"

He laughed. "Yes, but, no, especially in her case. It also means verve, dash, tang. Zipporah—straight from the Bible, but everyone called her Zip. She was a dancer. Ever hear of Martha Graham, Paul Taylor?" I nodded. "Zip danced with Graham. She was in Paul's first company, moved like a little streak of greased lightning onstage. The disease . . . Ah, well." He'd been revivified talking about her, carefree and excited for a moment, as he remembered her well and dancing. Now the air seemed to seep from him, dropping him quickly back to earth; his loneliness was stark. He went to the sink and turned on the tap. "Gotta clean these things up before I go. I made Tonya a deal, and I'm a man of my word. I'll rinse, you load the dishwasher."

"I'm sorry," I said, "about Zip." I was sorry about so much, but not sorry that he was here—that he'd told me something important about himself.

"Don't be a stranger, Lex," he said softly, not looking at me. "We're a tonic for each other, especially now. And the coffee in my kitchen's ground fresh from the bean; it brews up a lot better than this."

I took his hand. It was dry and very warm. "I will try, Nate. I will try to be what Jared needs, though I don't think I'm up to the task."

He did an extraordinary thing: he lifted my hand, still holding his, to his mouth and brushed it against his lips. "You're a good girl. And you are up to anything you need to do."

CHAPTER
22

I stood in Courtney Anacleto's vestibule listening to Nate's car start up. I wanted to fling open the door and call him back. Perhaps, if I could summon up a bit of composure, I might press my case for Jared's innocence, let my arguments flex their muscles and grow stronger than they seemed at the moment. Perhaps . . . The fact was, whether I was taking in his immutable logic or pushing back at him, I felt less scared than I was and the road ahead appeared less treacherous than I knew it must be.

The last vestige of motor sounds was gone. What I had to admit in the privacy of my own mind was that if Jared had killed Calista, the weight of the lonely secret would infect every cell in his body, more virulent as more time passed: it would kill his spirit—snuff out his eager curiosity, preempt his capacity for joy. That was what Nate had been trying to tell me, and it was true. It was true.

Sore as a boil at having to live inside my own skin, I wandered Courtney's house aimlessly, room to room, moderately thankful that hunger pangs were not part of the picture at the moment. I glanced at my watch: ten past seven and all the public rooms were empty.

I walked upstairs and, after one flight, paused. I heard music coming from the direction I knew to be the family bedroom wing, though I had never been there. For no important reason I walked toward the music. As I got closer, I heard it was the Beatles, rollicking through "When I'm Sixty-four." I stopped outside the closed door of what must have been Courtney's room—Courtney and the Beatles: that unlikely pairing made me warm to her. *Will you still need me? Will you still feed me?* Poignant questions. The poignancy underlined itself when the song ended and I was able to hear her sobs.

She wanted her Vin, no matter he wasn't very bright and she was, no matter he had no money and she had lots, no matter he fancied himself in love, or at least in lust, with Melanie. No matter any of that. Her Vin was gone and she wept. Slowly, I walked back to the staircase and made my way to my room.

I WAS CERTAIN to be awake all night twisting the mental Rubik's Cube in hopes of stumbling upon a comprehensible pattern of who and how and why. In fact, the process got me nowhere except into the deepest of sleeps. I awoke seven hours later clutching the tail of some thought I couldn't recall, and with a sensation, too amazing to be frightening, that I'd been whipping through space like one of Jared's comets. I sat bolt upright in the bed alert with confidence that though I knew no more than I'd known last night, I knew enough to frame the right questions, sift through possible answers, and discard wrong ones. Eventually, I would get there.

Melanie believed that Jared had murdered Calista. Whatever else that meant, it meant that she had not given keys to any alternative killer—Melanie was not bloody likely to have handed out house keys, in any case. I could hear Domingo's voice cutting in to challenge: "Prove it wasn't *Melanie* who did the murder and is now scheming to put blame on Jared?" Answer: *I can't prove it; I just know it.*

Tom and Melanie's carefully managed public appearances, their press statements registering dissatisfaction with incompetent, lazy police work in hunting for Calista's killer, were proper and rather pallid. In private, both were consumed with "protecting my family." I knew what Melanie meant by that, and I felt now that Tom, too, suspected Jared. Tom was an obsessed reporter. If he'd believed in an outside killer, he would have been laser-focused on hunting that person down. And if Rima or any other girlfriend had house access (unlikely), he'd have swooped down on that lead like a hawk. Again, Domingo: "Prove Tom didn't kill her." *I can't, but he didn't.*

Jared. Here I didn't need to wait for Domingo's prompt. A child like Jared—highly intelligent, deeply frustrated—is an inherently violent being, a crucible of emotion that could move from boil to freeze and back again in seconds. I would have known this absent the bloody demonstrations of it that famously kept dotting the American landscape. I knew it because I'd been such a child.

My mother had complacently told me quite recently from her perch in Sydney that I was incapable of killing. But what did she know of my fantasies at twelve when I was soft clay, the sculpting not going well? Would she have slept soundly, only a wall between us, if she'd seen my fist close on a carving knife as I crept out of my bed headed for hers? Never mind what happened or didn't, never mind whether the knife was gripped in fact or fantasy. How high was the inner wall between passion and action? That was the question. Was Jared's wall unscalable, no matter what the cue?

In the cold north light of morning that cast no shadow through my dormer window, I considered simply asking him the way I'd asked whether he had given out a key or let anyone into the house. I believed his no about that. So what about the big question, straight, unvarnished? Laying aside for the moment how hearing it might make him feel: utterly abandoned? utterly relieved? Laying aside, too, how sending those words from my mouth to his ear might make *me* feel, supposing I did ask it. "Jared, did you kill Calista?" He would tell me the truth, or he would lie. I was certain I knew him well enough to discern the difference.

I would know what the truth was . . . if *he* knew what it was.

It dawned on me that he might not, and that to confront him precipitously could cause a disastrous crash. That's what Nate had tried to make me see: It would take weeks of us all working together to ease Jared into a place where he felt safe admitting to himself what had happened that night.

If there was anything to admit . . . Plotting, dissembling—manipulating, tormenting him for his own good: was that to become the core of my professed love for Jared? No such relationship between equals would survive that treatment. But adult and child are *not* equals— we are meant to protect them. Still, my instincts howled

236 • CAROLINE SLATE

in protest at the notion of protecting with coercion, with pretense. The howl was as loud as though I were agreeing to betray myself. I did not think I could go along with Nate's proposal for very long. I would not be able to bear it.

A long, hot shower neither refreshed me nor left me feeling clean.

I looked in on Jared, who appeared to be asleep still—to my relief. Was that how it would be then—all spontaneity gone in a roundelay of avoidance, chased by guilt, precipitating further avoidance? Would it be possible for me to look Jared in the eye and converse about *anything* . . . anything at all, even astronomy and board games?

I found Courtney downstairs in the breakfast room, splotch-eyed, red-nosed and parchment-faced, bashing open the top of a boiled egg as if her heart's desire lay inside its shell. I stood in the doorway watching her, aware that I ought to feel more sympathy than I did over her loss of a self-absorbed bore with half a brain, and that in one or another of his buttocks. "Good morning," was what I said.

She fiddled her spoon about in the soft egg, but made no move to raise it to her mouth. "Please don't bother to tell me how sorry you are," she said brusquely, "I can't stand pity."

"Seems to me you quite like dispensing it; you just don't care for swallowing it. Anyway, I don't pity you. You're an intelligent woman with money enough to do anything you damn please. So unless you have a wasting disease of some sort . . ." I broke off, not because what I'd said was untrue, but because I was being fatuous— applying simplified logic to what was neither simple nor logical. "Shit! Why don't I just shut up, okay?"

That drew the beginnings of a small smile, which died aborning. She gestured at the sideboard. "Take some breakfast for yourself . . . if you want to. Frankly, I don't care whether you do or not." I did, and sat myself opposite her. "The truth is," she said, "I've just swallowed something more distressful than pity: a dose of poetic justice. It was pretty bitter. I rushed to take in the McQuades because that's what I knew Vin needed, and God knows I've made it my life's mission to give people what they need, whether they want it or not."

The twang of irony in her voice was heightened by the nasal consequences of copious weeping. "Vin needed a student," she said. "He was bored and at loose ends. Calista needed a coach who knew enough not to let her cripple herself with bad technique. And what Calista needed Melanie needed even more. Oh, yes, I always know what people need, no matter how I feel about the people. Serves me right, I suppose, for being a know-it-all: Vin is gone and I'm stuck with the bunch of you. Serves me right, I suppose."

"Sorry about that," I said. "Toss us out, if you like."

She shook her head and finally downed a spoonful of gooey boiled egg, in my books the epitome of nasty nursery food. "I can't, of course. Maybe if it were just Melanie and Tom, but poor, weedy Jared lying up there with a fever, with God knows what running through his mind . . ."

"What do you suppose is?" I cut in.

"Is what?"

"Is running through Jared's mind?" I found myself eager to know what she thought.

"Probably a horse race between his parents: which one killed his sister." She'd been ready for another helping of egg, full spoon en route to her mouth, but she paused, didn't eat. "What do *you* think is going through his mind, Lex?"

"He isn't saying. Perhaps he's wondering whether Vin and his mother were having an affair."

"Perhaps he is," she said evenly. "We have that in common, Jared and I. My guess is no, Melanie's choice, not Vin's. Are you suggesting I tell Jared that to make him feel better?"

"No. Look, Courtney, suppose they *had* been having an affair, might Melanie have given Vin a house key?"

Her face reddened. "Well, wouldn't that be convenient for you! You are relentless; you'd push anyone under a train for your family, wouldn't you? Let me tell you something: in the daisy chain of what we call love—God, the word sounds so small and hackneyed to make such a fuss over—Melanie has next to zero interest in Vin. For her, everything was about her surrogate: Calista. Everything. And if this would-be stud had the capacity to make that child an Olympian medalist, he was welcome to a few extra motivating perks—a pat here and there, a fanny-wiggle in his direction, little private laugh, peck on the cheek. Melanie would toss them to him like quarters to a panhandler. But she would *never* have given him a key to her house."

As she talked of fanny-wiggles, pats, pecks, private laughs, my mind returned to a mental sketch of Vin I'd tried drawing when first I met him. "Might Calista have given him a key?" I asked.

"What are you suggesting?" She tried to screen emotion from her voice and almost succeeded.

"You know what I'm suggesting. Don't tell me you haven't thought of it. Perhaps the idea of a key is new to you, as it is to me, but I know you've wondered about Vin and Calista. You have, haven't you?" Her face did not give way. I shook my head. "Look at you! No matter that you spent the night blubbing over him, no matter he's just walked out on you, you're *still* trying to shield him."

"The way you try to shield Tom McQuade? I observe things, too, you know. Vin is my husband. I chose him for reasons that made sense to me then, and still do. Don't you think I know how he appears to you—an aging jock whose one triumphant moment was more than twenty years ago? A bit of a fool who struts and holds forth, and snaps at his meal-ticket wife when he's had too much to drink? But you can draw a cartoon of anyone—anyone—and make the person ridiculous. You can draw one of me as easily as you can of Vin, more easily perhaps. And I could draw one of you."

"No quarrel there." But I hoped she wasn't about to try her hand at it. The glint in her eye suggested that the result might be dead accurate.

Instead, she said, "Vin Anacleto is a very conventional, not very bright man. He enjoys flirting; he likes the look and feel of women's bodies; he is very good in bed. The reason he's so good is his thorough enjoyment of the athletic performance of his own body." She might have been delivering a report on the water table in Peru. "What I'm saying is that Vin enjoys acrobatic sex with women. Obsessed as he was with Calista, my husband would be literally the last man in the world to diddle with her sexually, or harm her for any reason. Don't you understand? She was his shot at being something again." She paused and smiled. "In addition, during the hours in question, Vin was fast asleep beside me after an extended session of what I just described."

I nodded. "I see. Weren't you asleep, too?"

"No, as a matter of fact." Her face colored, not the

angry red of moments ago, but coral pink like a
teenaged girl's. "That sort of thing tends to . . . stimu-
late me. I can never get to sleep." Funny, blunt as she'd
been about the sex romp itself, her afterglow was
closely held private territory; I'd embarrassed her. It was
this detail that made me believe her.

So, perhaps not Vin: but in my fishing, I'd put a hook
into Calista, and I was not willing to turn her loose. It
was a new idea, one that gripped me hard. Calista: flir-
tatious, spunky star-in-the-making, every moment of her
life programmed, supervised, mother-dominated. Calista: turned ten, turned a bit rebellious. I could see her
longing for a tiny corner of life all her own, private; I
could see her grown willful enough, strong enough to
claim it. Just to feel the surge of her new power, just to
spite her mother, just for the hell of it, might she, confident and clueless, have chosen a secret friend? Might
she as part of the game have handed over the key and
alarm code? Might she, at some prearranged signal,
have opened the door herself?

CHAPTER
23

Saturday: Jared and I—and, incredibly, Tom—were playing Scrabble, the board balanced not all that steadily on an emptied breakfast tray on Jared's bed. Jared was, it seemed to me, clinging to the bed like a shipwreck survivor to a life raft. He looked washed-out, exhausted rather than ill, and his forehead felt cool to my palm—though admittedly my palms are unversed in matters of motherly expertise.

He felt okay this morning, he insisted. "Really okay." But he wanted no more "dork talk from grown-ups about feelings." He would play Scrabble. Period. Until Mr. Warden got there. And when his teacher ("my teacher," uttered with a proprietary seriousness that only intensified my hope that Barney would not let him down) came, they'd be looking into the existence of dark matter in dwarf galaxies, on account of new research just out from American Astronomical Society. "I called him right after I got up this morning. I downloaded a bunch of stuff off the Net, and he's going to bring some books I don't have. He wasn't supposed to start with me till Monday after school, but he's coming today," he said proudly.

"Great," I said, less than wholeheartedly. My initial faith in Barney had been based in sheer instinct. But my instincts these days resembled light-mad moths zigging this way and that, not to be trusted. While I warmed to seeing Jared engaged, spirited, even if the diversion was to be fleeting, I worried that the tutoring scheme I'd advocated for his benefit might in fact prove merely another disappointment by another adult in whom he'd placed some trust. "Scrabble it is," I said. "Beat your bum off."

"And I'll beat *yours*." Tom, unshaven and haggard, his smile as gray as his face, appeared at the door.

"Daddy!" The universal trill of a child surprised and spontaneously glad to see its father. I watched Tom love the music. He'd heard it precious little. "You'll play Scrabble with us, too?" Tom tousled Jared's hair—the second or third time I'd seen him do that recently. Did his hand move a tad more easily into the gesture?

Tom caught my eye in a look at odds with the banter. "Sure I'll play," he said, "if you dare take me on."

One wonders if there is any truth in the notion that character is revealed through games or behind a driver's wheel. Myself, I tend to think not, but for whatever interest it is, Jared was an erratic player, flashy at the big scores, careless with the small stuff, while Tom was steady and lethal, making the most of each turn. I was somewhere between: less bravura than Jared, less doggedly resourceful than Tom.

Expertise—Jared had just made a major score with that word, landing the X smack on a triple point square, which for a lovely moment polished his face with pride.

Then Barney blew in like a sea breeze, eyes clear, almost no trace of the haunted churl of two mornings ago. Almost. But there was some indefinable cloud still hovering. My viscera were glad to see him; my cerebellum had its doubts. I could smell the outdoors on his clothing, leaves and earth and salt water—at least that's what I imagined. He carried a battered brown leather briefcase and three large, varicolored books under his arm. Melanie was right behind him. Barney gave me a quick but intense look I couldn't decipher, and then turned his attention to Jared. "These were the best I could do on short notice," he said, "great photos and some of the earlier studies—good background for the Kormendy-Freeman work you got off the Net."

Melanie stepped forward and held up her hand. "Let me say a word first? I think two hours would be about right for today." Jared's face began to screw up in protest. "No, you're still not up to par and you need your rest. And don't forget," she added, the words larded with meaning, "you have another appointment later." His face closed down, its animation of a moment ago gone. I stifled an impulse to hit her. She tried to recoup, but it didn't work. "So who was the Scrabble champ?" she asked. "Dad," he answered quietly, looking at his quilt.

"You going to be round when we're done, Lex?" Barney asked.

I nodded, afraid that if I uttered a syllable right then a burst of frustration would fire off right behind it. The first light I'd seen in Jared's eyes since I'd arrived, and Melanie had snuffed it out: Nate's purgative tasted bad, very bad, gagging bad.

"I'll meet you downstairs then," Barney said. "I want to talk to you." That was mutual.

"He thinks you're pretty cute," Melanie said to me, once the three of us had left student and teacher alone behind the closed door.

"Doesn't everyone?" I asked snarkily.

"I think you—'fancy him' is the way you Brits put it, no?" said Tom.

In a different humor, I might have teased back. "Friends is all," I said coldly.

Melanie raised her brows and began to bob down the stairs. Midway, she stopped and said over her shoulder, "I'm going to get changed, Tom. Meet you in the conservatory in twenty minutes. You need a good shave; you have that desperado look."

"Always thought you liked the desperado look."

"I do." Raunchy grin. "In its place."

Once the top of her bright head had disappeared, I said, "The two of you seem to be in an oddly good mood." A distinctly postcoital one, it seemed to me.

"You do what you do to keep going." *And we know what it is you do,* I thought. I've heard it said that one never relinquishes a certain dog-in-the-manger possessiveness about a former lover, that it's a reflex. The proposition displeases me, which does not mean it's untrue. "She has the best laugh," he said softly.

"Always did."

"She matters a hell of a lot to me, you know. No matter what lousy thing I do."

"I think I know that." I searched his face for a way in and found none. "Tom, how do you feel about this reinstitution of therapy for Jared?"

His head shook slowly. "I'm not sure. But I tell you what: it would be a relief to know. Just *know.* I'll stand by him, no matter what, so will Melanie."

"But you're beginning to think he did it, aren't you?

You didn't in the beginning. Was it Melanie changed your mind? Nate? Do you think . . . ?"

"I don't know what I think anymore," he said wearily.

"You and Melanie going out for a photo-op stroll?"

"Something like that."

"I think he didn't, Tom. I can't support that with facts. But I think he didn't."

"Let me tell you something the police haven't released. The raw spot on the back of Calista's hand, where it looked like something had been scrubbed? They have ultraviolet pictures of what it was: a drawing of planets and stars—a pretty sophisticated one." Domingo had a magician's sleeves; no end to what hid up them.

"So? It was Halloween. Seems an appropriate decoration."

"The drawing wasn't there earlier. Melanie'd told me it was, but I think she was trying to cover for Jared. It wasn't there when I went in to kiss Calista good night. Both her hands were on top of the covers, palms down, perfectly clean, no raw spot—I'd have noticed, just like you'd have noticed—we're reporters. When I found her body, I saw the scrubbed hand. It kind of registered, but there was . . . a lot else to register; I didn't think much about it. We'll both lie, of course, Melanie and I. We'll say what we have to for Jared." He'd spoken fast, fueled by what seemed a single breath. Now he took a deep one. "Here's the thing for you to understand, Lex. We are not some pair of monsters persecuting our kid. He's our only one now, and we'll keep him safe, no matter what." His jaw worked itself like a set of gears. "But we do need to know. That's the only reason I'm letting this Grumbach shit go on."

"Who scrubbed the drawing off her hand?" I asked carefully. "And why?"

"I—Don't—Know." He turned away from me, and then back. "I've trusted you with this. Don't do anything dumb."

I WAITED FOR Barney in the front hall near the foot of the stairs, in a spot where he couldn't leave without my knowing. Tom's news about the drawing on Calista's hand was the worst thing I'd heard since the news of the murder itself.

A scene played itself out in my mind, the logic of it crisp:

Brother and sister can't sleep for all the Halloween excitement, or perhaps one or the other is awakened by their father's late-night kiss. They go down to the wine cellar together—God knows why, but perhaps they've done it before. Children do all sorts of things their parents don't know about. Jared decorates Calista's hand. He . . . If I was going to be of any use, I would have to take the next steps. Domingo and her lot had taken them; Melanie and Tom had; Nate had. All right then . . .

He is twelve, a funny age for any boy, child one minute, young male the next, hormones raging all the while. And this particular susceptible twelve-year-old boy has a glamorous younger sister, a girl whose own hormones were likely still asleep, all the more deeply for the daily gymnastic rigors, but nevertheless, a seductive girl, a little girl with a big hunger—for love, according to Tonya; for admiration, according to Barney; for a sense of power, according to the sketch drawn in my mind. Somehow, the two begin sex play down there in the wine cellar. He touches her; perhaps she touches him first. Anyway, it begins. He pulls down her pants, or she does. He fingers her, maybe goes as far as trying it on with his penis. She pushes him away; she screams; she threatens; he, never strong on self-control, is out of control—scared, humiliated, horny. He must stop her screams. The garrote . . .

The awful thing about seeing it this way was that I *could* see it. It was entirely plausible, even as far as explaining why Calista seemed to have been violated with a finger, not a man's penis. And why would a jury-rigged garrote be ready at hand?

I had a thought then; wishful, one could say and not be too far off the mark, I suppose but powerful, nonetheless. I'd seen sadness in Jared these weeks. I'd seen rage; I'd seen evasion—lots of that. And I'd seen fear. What I had not observed was the stricken look of guilt in this boy who'd summoned me across an ocean because he needed me. I knew that was no guarantee of innocence, only a straw. And I was grasping at those now.

"Hi." The voice at my back startled me.

"How did it go, Barney?"

"Mixed. We got on track, but it took a while. The kid was ice for the first half hour. Then he kind of thawed out and we had a great session on the small galaxies. He's got an amazing mind. I've been teaching seven years; I think he's my first genius. It would be a pleasure, except for the hell he's going through. Melanie came in to ring the closing bell and he froze right back up. But just before he did, his face had the look of a fox with the dogs on his tail. It's a look I know better than I want to."

"I imagine you do. I saw it on you the other morning."

He didn't break eye contact, but I saw he was

tempted to. "Yes," he said. "About that . . ." His voice trailed off.

After a silent moment, I said, "I think I'd like to know about that, for Jared's sake. And maybe for my own."

"And maybe for *my* own," he said. He gave me the smile of a man on his way to the dentist. "You once allowed as how you might like to go sailing. What about coming with me now?"

CHAPTER
24

I knew about the Westport Marina and the Compo Beach boat slip. You did, if you'd lived in the area, whether or not you were a sailor. They were fairly big, home to some impressive craft. Ye Yacht Yard was new to me, a small curve of harbor tucked between Westport and Southport. In late November, the clutch of random masts, black against the white sky, had a naked, fossilized look to it.

"Which one is yours?" I asked as he parked the Jeep near the water's edge. They were almost the first words spoken since we'd left the house. My "Do you take him everywhere?" when I spotted Jasper in the back of the Jeep, and Barney's "Not everywhere" had been the other bits of chat. Those apart, traffic swish and Jasper's panting provided the only sound. I'd spent the short drive perusing Barney's profile. It was not handsome; the jaw and nose were too sharp for that, the forehead too high. But it was good, the mouth quite defined, no way stingy, and the aquatic eyes plentifully browed and lashed with hair paler than the red of his head and beard. Today the fiery hair seemed to have stolen all color from the face under it. This was not the profile of a killer, a child molester—not that mouth. But all sorts of people, I reminded myself, had all sorts of profiles, all sorts of mouths, and soft-cooked assumptions to the contrary were best left to writers of paperback romances and their readers.

"Come on," he said, "I'll show you." He got out of the Jeep and opened the back door to free Jasper and to retrieve some gear. "Here, you're going to need this—and these," he said, handing me a thick Aran sweater, pair of woolen gloves and watch cap, all outsize for me, though too small for him. I was certain they had belonged to a dead girlfriend, a dark flight of fancy based on nothing but my morbid state of mind—that and the recent experience of having worn a dead woman's blue bathrobe.

The boat was larger than I might have imagined, twenty-something feet long, with a cabin and plumbing and decks of rich, waxed wood. It had a name: *Homeward Bound*. I registered liking the sound of that, and realized almost immediately that I was on the verge of buying Barney Warden again, lock, stock, and good mouth, as though his peculiar behavior of the other morning had already been acceptably explained—as though I knew that Calista's putative secret friend could not have been her teacher.

"It's rather grand," I said.

"Yeah. Rich boy's toy." That self-mocking Russian look: the dark smudges under his eyes underscored the effect. "My only one, I swear. And it doesn't moor in a rich boy's slip."

Out of a clapboard shack, a grizzle-bearded, leather-skinned gnome of a man appeared and waved. "Hey, Barney, doin' okay, kiddo?"

Jasper pulled at his leash, wanting to return the greeting at closer range, but Barney stayed put. "Better, Sandy. Thanks. We're going out—just a couple of hours."

"Good deal. Hope you got something on board to warm the bones."

"Believe it, pal." He turned to me and took hold of my arm. "Welcome aboard," he said. I took the long step from slip to deck and Jasper, freed from the leash, leapt after me. Barney untied the boat and then joined us. "You do swim, don't you?" he asked.

"In this mess of garments, I wouldn't swear for it, but, yes, I'm a passable swimmer," I answered as I put on the yellow slicker he handed me.

The next half hour was spent performing boat routines, numerous, finicky, and dull, yet strangely satisfying in their precision. I admittedly felt disproportionately proud of myself when, once out on the open waters of Long Island Sound, I pulled, at captain's orders, a designated rope and the sail began to rise, flapping into the wind. Then the exciting bits: his getting the thing under control and on course through several smooth maneuvers involving calls of "Ready about" and "Coming about," which meant ducking your head fast to avoid it being whacked by a swiveling mast. Throughout, Jasper joined in the game, barking periodically, probably at the same cues as on every voyage.

Once we were pointed in the right direction and securely under sail, the old sea dog curled up beside a length of coiled rope and shut his eyes. "How you doing?" Barney asked me.

"Fine. You?"

"Better."

"So you said to your friend before we sailed. Better from *what*, precisely? A rotten mood?"

"All right, it's talk time. I . . ." His tongue flicked his lips nervously. "Do you ever find that talk fucks up just what you're hoping it'll fix?"

"Frequently."

"Good. I was just curious."

"But broken things don't repair very well no matter what you do—most of them don't."

"True." He made a visor of his hand and gazed at the water ahead of us. "We should be smooth on course for a while. Want to go into the cabin? You can take off some of that gear. You look like a kid in her big brother's snowsuit," he said, "can't even get your arms down straight."

"It's a recurring problem. Yes, let's go into the cabin."

We sat on benches on opposite sides of a varnished table, facing each other. For a moment, I imagined I was visiting someone in prison. The captain looked like a captive now, despite the fresh, windburned color in his cheeks.

I'd no idea how to begin, so I didn't. In any case, this was his to begin.

"I have an illness, a serious, chronic illness," he said with a grim smile. "Unpredictable and incurable."

The words slammed like a fist to the gut, the surprise as bad as the pain—the pain itself, a surprise. "AIDS?" I asked quietly.

"Nothing that pure and simple. They call it depression."

Relief whooshed through me, and in its wake an indignant anger. "Isn't that just a bit self-dramatizing? Depression's some sort of blood-chemistry thing. You take the pills and it stays in its box. How dare you compare it to AIDS!"

His face screwed in puzzlement. "I didn't compare it."

"I guess that was me filling in the blanks," I admitted. "You know, 'unpredictable and incurable.' But really, isn't depression like diabetes or something?"

He laughed, a mocking spike of sound that reminded me a bit of Tom's laugh. "Or something. Now, let me guess, you never did one of your films on this subject. Am I right?"

"Yes. So I don't know what I'm talking about, I suppose. But I *have* read the news coverage—Prozac and all. You take it and you level out. Your lows get higher and your highs get lower, isn't that it? I gather it's not perfect, and people miss their wild highs, but still . . ." My hands went out, palms up. I stopped my blather. "I *don't* know what I'm talking about. I think . . . I think I don't want you to be ill," I mumbled to the table. "But that's presumptuous; it's nothing to do with me. Sorry."

"Lex." After a beat, I looked up. "You don't know what you're talking about, but I *want* you to presume anyway. That's why I asked you to come sailing." No mock in his eyes. They were asking something of me. I recalled his words: *Whatever it is you're after, you won't find it here.* He was fresh out, he'd said. I felt that way now.

"When you showed up at the house wanting to run with me, you caught me on a slide—a steep one," he said. "It started right after I left Court's. Funny to say that, considering the occasion, but I was feeling so *fine* that evening. On top of my game, you know? Being able to kick Vin's ass was, shall we say, satisfying, something I've wanted to do for quite a while. And later, out there in the back garden, you, me, Jared riding that comet's tail together . . . that was better than satisfying." My throat lumped and didn't respond to swallowing.

I managed, "And?"

"And King Kong always lands on you when you're not looking. Just when you're finally saying, okay, got it: stay mellow, avoid stress—so far, so good. Been off the meds for six months, seven, eight . . . Hallelujah, coming up on a year! That's when you crash. I had less warning than usual this time. Or maybe I was paying less attention."

"You didn't figure that the murder counted as stress?"

"Don't do that," he said, the rueful tone going harsh; "don't try to make me feel stupid. That's a golden oldie for me, and the sound of it gives me hives."

"Don't *you* do that to *me*—edit what I say. You're not the only one subject to hives."

It made him laugh—not my primary intention, but a good fallout. "Truce. My hives begin to itch when my dad's in the vicinity for, say, two hours. And I can't even put the blame on him, hotshot businessman, calculator wired into his brain, and he's stuck with this big gawk of a kid who can't do math worth spit, not to mention physics or Spanish."

"Blame him. I would. *You* would, too, if you were talking about someone other than yourself. What would you say to that father across the desk at a parent-teacher conference? I've listened to you talk about Calista and Melanie. You're not all that pious when it comes to handing out blame."

"A little more pious than you, I bet." A clatter at the cabin door. Jasper's top half showed through the rectangle of glass as his claws rapped it for admittance in a fair imitation of the big bad wolf. "Think about that for a minute while I let him in and go check things out topside."

He was gone about five, during which time Jasper sat beside me as though I owed him a petting. So I complied. Irrespective of species, if one states expectations with sufficient confidence, the chances are excellent they'll be realized. Jasper had the confidence to pull it off; I never have had.

"We're in good shape," Barney said, returning in a gust of cold air. "You two seem to be getting along. How do ham sandwiches and lemon tea toddy sound?"

"Like some of the best words I've ever heard," I said, one hand still occupied in scratching the dense fur behind Jasper's ears. After he'd moved to the small galley area to make good on the offer, I asked his back, "Why ever stop taking the medicine?"

His body paused, but he didn't turn round. "I can't give you an answer you'll like."

"Well, give me one you've got then, because I truly don't understand. And I want to."

"All right. Because taking medicine means you're sick; because between bouts I can manage without it, if I'm careful; and because taking this kind of medicine is *not* like taking insulin. Even if no one else notices it, it does blunt your edges—it does change who you are."

"You're taking it now, are you?"

"Two days now. It's beginning to kick in. If you came to run with me, say, tomorrow, I'd be glad to have you. The way it was when you did come, I hadn't swallowed one dose yet—telling myself I could manage without, just this one time: we tend to do that, and it's dumb. Anyway, I wanted to annihilate you, vaporize you with a ray gun, whatever it took to make you disappear—either that or fall on the ground in front of you and cry all over your sneakers." He turned and handed me a large green mug, capped with a steam cloud of hot lemon and whiskey. "I'm evening out. I really am." He raised his mug as though to say cheers.

"Can you . . . Are you meant to have alcohol with your pills?"

"If I'm careful. The byword of life for someone like me: *careful*. Whether I'm on meds or off: careful. I hate that." He opened a small fridge and produced a stack of plastic-wrapped sandwiches, which he placed in the center of the table.

I reached for one and unwrapped it, taking care to be slow and deliberate, because my mouth was feeling a tad excessively eager. "I eat," I said.

"Pardon?"

"I eat. You go down your black hole; I go down mine. It's a fact of my life, ever since I was seven. Not all the time, but periodically—I can go months without it happening, and something trips the switch. I need to eat and I can't stop. Finally, either I fall into a stupor and sleep it off, or I throw it up and *then* fall into a stupor and sleep it off. That's why I turned up at your house the morning after the funeral. I'd been up all night, a lot of it talking with Melanie. I learned some things about my early life, things I hadn't known and some I hadn't remembered—doors opened, doors shut, the sort of thing that can . . . Anyway, when I asked you if you had any breakfast available, it was because I was afraid I was on the edge of another binge and I thought I'd trick it round the bend by eating in company. I can do that sometimes. It's my version of being careful—one of them. The other is to binge only in a safe place; my flat, preferably." I lifted a sandwich half to my mouth and found my hand was unsteady. I felt a tickle of regret at having exposed too much.

He sat, long legs wide apart, straddling the bench. Yards of blue denim leg: he was ridiculously tall. "Thanks. That was a generous thing to tell me. You didn't have to."

"Um, right. I know, it's okay," I said fast, looking away. Kind words, compliments are difficult for me. They turn me into a too-full tumbler, apt to spill its wetness all over the carpet.

"Don't do that; I didn't mean to embarrass you," he said. And after a moment, "What do you think you look like, Lex?"

My eyes met his. "A 'scrap' is Melanie's description. My mother's early verdict was, 'You'll never be pretty, so you'd better be smart.' And my long-lost father, I gather, thought I resembled a stringy hot pepper. What do I think I look like? I suppose functional would be a word. Bony, sharp-edged: the compact, stripped-down model—no space for grace notes."

"I like the way you look. You know Picasso's portrait of Dora Maar? There are a few of them, but one particular—I think it's in the Paris Picasso museum."

"Yes, I do know it."

"Sitting there that way, with your cheek resting on your hand, you look like that picture. I thought so first time I met you."

"Bit of poetic license you're taking there. Dora Maar was beautiful."

" 'Thanks' is all you need to say."

I don't think I had grinned in a long while; the necessary muscles felt rusted. "Thanks."

"Pair of us—the walking wounded," he said. He sipped from the green mug.

"The walking's important." An unusually optimistic

thought for me. I watched him hand down a piece of sandwich to Jasper, who seemed to enjoy it, but played the gentleman and did not ask for more. "How long have you had him?" I asked.

"Almost three years. I was in therapy at the time. I can sympathize with Jared—I hated every minute of it, too. But the shrink suggested to my father that having the responsibility of a pet would ground me in the real world, keep me from letting myself go under, all that shit. See, right before that, I had a bad episode; bad. I slid all the way down."

"Why didn't you take the magic pills and stop it happening?"

"Why indeed! I was living in Seattle at the time. Things were good. I had a job in a nice school, new relationship with a nice lady. When the slide started, I didn't want to know about it, so I didn't. I got through the school days, barely. But with her, I couldn't hack it. No way. After weeks of silence and resentment, marathon sleeping and no sex, she took off. By then, I was in over my head and I didn't care. I quit the job and rolled myself up on the floor in a big rag rug. I couldn't move, even to get to the john. The ex-girlfriend kept calling to check on me and got worried when I never answered the phone. Finally, she called my dad in Florida, and he came to get me. I wound up in a hospital down there for two months. I'm surprised some reporter hasn't gotten hold of that yet, but they will."

"Did you tell the police?"

"Yeah. Not the details, but yeah. The woman, Domingo, I told her I'd been hospitalized for depression." *But you and your pathology don't interest her, Barney. Her mind's made up.* "What, Lex? Why that look?"

"Barney, I wanted to ask you about something." I

was on the edge of laying out the scenario of Calista's late-night visitor, her secret friend. I was on the edge, but I did not go over it—a reflexive wariness: these weeks the air we'd all been breathing was permeated with the grit of shattered trust. After too long a pause, I said instead, "I wasn't sure you'd show up for Jared this morning, wasn't even sure I wanted you to. Do you think you'll be able to stay the course with him?"

"The answer is yes." I heard his voice frost over as he added, "If that's what's troubling you." "So," he said, businesslike, vulnerabilities hurriedly placed beyond the reach of untrustworthy hands. "Are you ready to go out on deck, or would you rather stay in here? I'm going to turn her round and head back." He opened the cabin door and started to leave, Jasper on his heels.

The disconnecting click was so defined as to leave behind it the lonely whine of dial tone in my ear. My fault, which only made me feel worse. "Right. I'm coming."

He handled the ropes and sheets and cleats by himself this time. His moves were economical in the way an expert's are. I felt proud of his skill, and sad a second later, when I realized I'd no right to pride in him. But the sight of the sail coming about, its belly filling with the stiff wind thrilled me anyway. After he'd tied the ropes in place, he sat, staring out at the water.

"Look," I said, and once I had his attention, had no words on hand to follow. I walked over to where he was and stood beside him. "Look," I repeated, "I am so . . . very sorry."

"What for?" His mouth was tight.

"For cutting off." He nodded, waiting for more. "How in hell do I know how far I can trust you?" I burst out, angry with myself, not him.

"You don't. That's a simple answer to a simple question. You don't, I don't, nobody does. But everybody checks their own yardsticks and makes these decisions; a lot of the time, they overshoot, or undershoot, and they're sorry. Back in the cabin you began to ask me something, then your face stiffened up and you switched to a different question—a real question, just not the one at the top of your mind. So what happened on the way?" This was Barney: the man who'd seemed to me on first meeting as clear as water.

"I couldn't read the numbers on my yardstick. But you see, these last few days especially, instincts, emotions, thoughts, second thoughts—I can't seem to sort them out. May I sit down beside you?"

"Yes." I did, keeping a good foot of space, a no-man's-land, between us. The white sky had clouded over with extravagant billows of dove gray; the water was a black mirror; no earth in sight. Seated in the pointed prow of a boat, wind-propelling itself into infinity, I could feel the passion for sailing. This was a film I hadn't done. I would do it, I thought now. I would, if . . .

I filled my lungs with moist salted air; they liked the feel of it. "Barney, I was going to ask you something about Calista. You've told me about the way she queened over her schoolmates and made them like it, and that she didn't have any special friends in class. But what about an *adult* friend—or a teenager, perhaps?"

He blew out a long, cold, white breath. "She had the juice to make her power plays work with the other kids, and with lots of adults, too . . ." He shook his head. "You have to keep in mind, up until she was killed, I hardly knew the McQuades, any of them. Calista was one of twenty-two in my class. As I've told you, she was a charismatic kid who seemed to me to be under heavy-duty emotional stress. I tried to pursue it with her mother and struck out. That's it."

"And as you've said, you and she weren't drawn to each other in any—"

"Where you going with this?"

"Do you want it all, or not?" I snapped. "Because if you do, you're going to have to hear a version of Calista's death that extends the suspect list beyond the family. And you could be on it. You were quite sharp in noticing that I didn't trust you enough to say it first time out. Do you trust me enough to listen now?"

He didn't answer immediately, just looked straight ahead. "I'm listening," he said quietly.

"The police closed in round the family from the first. They've got reason, I know—no sign of break-in, no people known to have keys, the fact that a casual intruder wouldn't have known the wine cellar, all of that. But even so, there are possibilities, and Domingo won't look at them. I think she's an honest, smart cop, but there's something in her own past that impairs her peripheral vision here: Melanie, Tom, Jared, they're all she can see. Period. Here's the point: It *doesn't* have to have been one of them."

"You mean it could be me instead if someone gave me a key and told me the alarm numbers."

"Yes. But could you put that aside for a moment and just follow me?"

"I'm right behind you."

"Calista was dominated, hemmed in by Melanie's ambitions for her. Day in, day out: Mummy's agenda. Right?"

"I thought so."

"And, as you've said, she was a powerful piece of

work herself, Calista. She was ten, growing rebellious. Maybe peeing her pants was part of that; she knew it would drive Melanie wild. What if there were other parts? Since every bloody moment of her day and evening was programmed for her, what if she claimed some late nights for herself? Just for herself, secret from her mum."

"You sound like you're talking from inside," he said mildly, shifting his bottom a bit closer to mine. "Did you claim late nights for yourself, secret from your mum?"

"Only to eat, I'm afraid. I'm far from being a powerful piece of work. But here's what I've begun wondering about Calista. What if . . ." I felt like someone mounting a staircase in the dark, groping for a grab bar, some credible support for the next step. "Suppose she took up with a friend no one knew about—an older friend, perhaps, say fifteen, sixteen—someone old enough to slip out of his own house without getting caught. And suppose she'd risked letting him in after everyone else was asleep. The wine cellar would be just where they'd go for privacy."

"Okay," he said with a teacher's neutrality, not meaning that he was buying my theory, just that he was hearing it out. "And this happened more than one time, you're suggesting?" he asked. "And what would they do in their privacy?"

"They'd . . . I don't know what they'd do actually . . ." But I did know, of *course* I did. A cold gust of wind slapped my face. Suddenly, my tiptoeing quit and I dashed straight ahead, not caring if I fell flat on my face. "Well, hell, why else would a teenage boy be skulking round a basement with a little girl in the middle of the night? And she thought she was in charge, the little idiot!"

"This is some pretty fancy supposing you're doing here. Your phantom friend could be way younger than teenage, could be Calista's age—could be another girl."

"I know. I know. I'm just telling you the way I'm seeing it. And I *can* see it. He touches her; she doesn't know what to do, so she smiles, flirts. Maybe it's a bit thrilling as well as scary for her at first. And then, maybe on a subsequent visit, more happens and it's not a thrill anymore: *only* scary. And she screams, tries to escape, and he . . ."

"Kills her with a handy garrote? I don't know how to respond, Lex. If you're asking do I find that version plausible, all I can say is that Calista would have had enough nerve to carry it off. But the only person your theory clears is Melanie; Calista could have stuck it to her mother by having secret confabs with her dad or her brother, just as well as with some outsider."

My heart rattled. Jared: that's where my fancy supposing would lead most people. Not to Tom but straight to Jared. I was encased in this thought when Barney said, "Of course, your secret friend could be thirty as well as fifteen." I turned to look at him, face windburned a rose red, eyes an almost electric green. He was right—and, ironically, the vivid scenes I'd imagined narrowed the very realm of possibilities I was striving to broaden. My brain was deadlocked at the moment, unsure of its every thought. "I'm going to tell you, Lex," he said, "that if any of what you've been spinning really happened, it did not happen with me. And you're going to have to decide whether you believe that."

"I feel I do, but that's 'feel,' not 'think.' I'm not impartial here, and my radar for truth seems to have gone way off. *That's* what I don't trust." I prepared for a storm as I asked him, "Tell me, don't depressed people also have wild highs, where they feel omnipotent, do crazy things?"

"You mean *manic*-depressives. The current politically correct term is *bipolar*. I have only one pole to offer you and it goes straight down." His arm round my shoulder came as a surprise. "I know you had to ask it. Here's what I want to do: I'm going to give you my doctor's name and number and written permission for him to talk to you. I want you to do that, because I *want* you to believe me."

"Me, too," I said, almost inaudible, as I let my body do what *it* wanted, relax against his.

"Lex, you asked me a while ago whether I could stay the course with Jared. I'm pretty sure I can, and I've never felt more motivated to do anything in my life. I'm less sure whether he can stay the course with me—or at all. I don't know, I'm no doctor, but he seems to me ready to fall apart or blow up—one of those two."

"Melanie's having Nate do some therapy with him. Only fifteen minutes a day, but Jared hates the whole idea. I mean, he *really* hates it." I was skirting the border, talking round my ultimate fear on the subject. Though he must have known damned well what it was, he didn't name it—for which I was grateful.

His hand, the touch surprisingly powerful, began to knead my shoulder. I could see why Jasper enjoyed a similar stroking between his ears. "Sick kids sometimes do hate what they need most," he said. "First time I got sent to therapy, I tried to set fire to the poor bastard's office."

"But then you realized the error of your ways and got some value from him?"

His laugh flew out into the clouds. "Probably a poor example. I never got squat from him. The guy was a pompous horse's ass."

CHAPTER
25

Over the next two weeks, Jared's anger disappeared, either burned away by emotions more powerful or gone underground to lie in wait while it built up a fresh head of steam. He'd recovered from his flu and had reluctantly given up his invalid state. Though he continued to spend much time closeted in his room with computer and books, he ventured downstairs now. Like a pet dog, he was sent outdoors, given the run of the grounds on his own, and then taken on a leash to chaperoned outings.

Flanked by his parents, he attended sports events, movies, and other vetted public family entertainments. News cameras typically caught shots of the trio, Jared in the middle, each of his hands held. He did not, as far as I knew, need to be bullied or scolded into going. He exhibited the best of manners, smiled on cue—an ideal accessory to the McQuade family image, which was heavily under televised reconstruction.

A reconstruction badly needed: Tom had been used for media target practice daily. Rounding out the Battle of Britain and the Infidelity Follies were Scenes from Boyhood: foster families he had lodged with briefly when he was ten, twelve, fourteen were delighted to hold forth (for money, sport, or both) on his diabolical contrariness and violent temper and to recall (with wise nods to the lens) their perspicacity in knowing even then that these twin flaws would lead to a bad end.

My mother's missile launched itself publicly in a *Newsweek* exclusive. Shrewdly, she'd gone for class over quick cash—the magazine's credibility would help her inflict maximum damage, and the cash would follow from subsequent milkings of the material. Basically, it was an embellishment of the story she'd told me on the phone: the teenaged nympho, who'd seduced every male with a pulse rate in Norfolk, including her own father, and made a hobby of shoplifting during the rare interstices when she was vertical. I was still inclined to believe Melanie, especially considering the liberties Frannie Cavanaugh took with portions of her story where the facts were well known to me. In her version of our fly-by-night departure, she became a sort of maternal Sydney Carton, doing the far, far better thing: giving up the incorrigible, but nonetheless loved, Melanie in favor of "making a better life for my little one, Lex." About one thing, she was proved accurate: I lacked the guts to board a Qantas flight and do her physical damage.

"There's a reason you never met a grandma, Jared," Melanie said to him wryly. "And considering the possibilities, you're lucky. Your father's mother was a crazy drunk, and I had the bad luck to be born to a scheming, evil liar. You don't believe me, you ask Lex about her."

The story itself did not get Melanie down—quite the contrary, she seemed almost to welcome it. And I reckoned I knew why: As long as the spotlight was trained on her, it would not turn its beam full force on Jared.

Which was not to say he was being altogether ignored by the press. Speculation about him had begun to trickle onto page and screen. A natural reluctance to toss grenades at a child slows things down, but it doesn't stop them. The police had not yet released the information I'd heard from Tom about the scrubbed drawing of stars and planets on Calista's hand; however, Jared's reputation as a troubled, mercurial boy with ample reason for jealousy of his sister sufficed for the moment.

Brass bands and bullshit to the side, the greatest danger to them lay not in the plausibility of Tom or Melanie or Jared as Calista's killer, but in the implausibility of anyone else.

There was a sort of film over Jared now, a faintly clouded plastic shield round him—you could see him through it, talk with him through it, but it was always there. The flashes of enthusiasm had disappeared; whatever strength he had was marshaled in the cause of self-protection. And why not: as far as he could see, no one cared what he wanted, including the person he'd summoned across an ocean.

The days were circumscribed: Barney tutored Jared Mondays, Wednesdays, and Fridays from four to six. Nate saw him from six to six-fifteen daily. Jared made no complaint; not to me, he didn't—he had stopped talking to me altogether about any personal matter. Once, I dropped my own guard and said to him, "You know, there's nothing that could make me stop loving you. Nothing." "Right," he replied, clearly meaning the opposite. "I mean it," I insisted. *Then why don't you get me out of this?* He didn't say the words; his eyes spoke for him. They looked at me often that way, those dark velvet eyes, and when they did, I found it hard to keep from just blurting, "Did you kill her?" But each time, my promise to Nate, or a failure of nerve, forced the question down my throat, where it would sit while we played a computer game instead.

Barney was convinced that Jared was heading into clinical depression and needed medication. Nate countered him, saying that Jared was "beginning to take real steps toward looking at reality, which is painful work," and that introducing chemicals just now could "leave the process dead in the water." Melanie thought what Nate thought, and Tom went along. I held my breath and did nothing.

Melanie and I had achieved a stasis, delicately balanced, but balanced nonetheless. As had always been the case with my sister, there were topics she placed strictly off limits—anything to do with Jared's emotional state headed her list now. Surprisingly, she was willing to talk with a tinge of nostalgia about her "wild youth."

"Want to know what the best thing I ever stole was? A pair of Calvin Klein pants, tawny colored suede, like browned butter. Boy, I wanted those things *sooo* much. I'd go to Wallenberg's—that was the good ladies' specialty shop, you were too little to remember it—and I'd visit them. No way I could've got hold of the money. But I was gonna have them! So one Saturday, I sashayed myself in there, wearing a pair of velveteen pants kind of a similar shade—cheapies, but new, manufacturer's label still hanging off 'em under my sweater—and I waited till it got real busy. Then I took myself into a dressing room with a few things, including a nice little

T-shirt that I *could* afford." Cheshire cat grin. "I came out, cool as you please, in my new Calvin Kleins, carrying the T-shirt. 'I'll take this, please,' I said to the saleslady, and I paid for it and off I went."

"And you left the cheapies behind on the hanger to substitute?"

"Uh-huh: five items into the booth, five out. The feeling I got paying for that little blue T-shirt, talking about the weather to the cashier, while all the time, that smooth suede was kissing my pussycat. The feeling was about as good as any orgasm you ever had, I can tell you. Pinked up my cheeks—both sets of 'em!" And she laughed the laugh of a winner, just the way she must have done as she sashayed out of the store that day.

I was riveted. For the moment, the woman was not my sister, not Jared's mother, but a subject. I climbed inside her, felt the throb of ecstasy in the crotch of my buttery, new Calvin Kleins.

"But other times you got caught. Wasn't it mortifying? Didn't it make you scared the next time?"

"Of *course* it did." We were in the living room, sipping late-night brandy—we seemed to get on best together late at night with a bit of alcohol in us. She leaned over and surprised me with a triple pat on the head. "That's part of it, Allie. Being scared gives you the edge. I used to tell Calista that before a competition. 'Stay just scared enough to make your butt do better than anyone else's, baby.'"

CHAPTER
26

The Friday before Thanksgiving, Melanie came down with Jared's flu. Tom, who'd taken to staying in some evenings, stepped in as her nurse—bearer of juice and pills and tea and toast—an unaccustomed role, which he filled with surprising dedication.

Early the following morning, skipping over the forethought that might have changed my mind, I took advantage of the pair of them being otherwise engaged and knocked at Jared's door. "Want to go sailing with Barney and me today?" I asked, half whispering, though there was no one to overhear. He might respond to the tonic of adventure. If Pan/Poppins couldn't provide that, what the hell good was she at all? "It'll have to be a secret if you come," I added. "Your mum wouldn't approve." Which I knew full well because I'd asked her the previous week and received a flat no on the grounds of cold weather and the danger of "relapse."

He hesitated, biting his lower lip, while a smile began to curl his upper one. "Okay," he said.

The day was chilly but clear—the sort of day when the air has no weight at all and the sky's emphatic cloudless blue seems overly self-confident. This would be my fifth time aboard the *Homeward Bound*. By now, I was feeling a bit proprietary. I'd learned which ropes to pull when, how to tie a few elementary knots, and even how to bring the boat about. I was excited at the prospect of Jared's learning them, too.

I'd also learned some other things: the small pleasure of sipping lemon tea with plenty of whiskey, not only in the shelter of a cabin, but out on deck, laughing while the cold salt wind slapped your face; the unfamiliar luxury of friendship with a man one finds sexually attractive. I'd had few friends as an adult (all of them males, come to think of it) and few lovers, but never both those connections with the same person.

Barney and I had bear-hugged on the boat, insulated by layers of clothing. He'd kissed me a big smack in congratulation the first time I brought the boat about on my own. We had barely touched hands inside his living room; neither of us had pushed for more than that. What we *had* pursued with abandon was each other's company: we'd seen each other daily since our first sail, some days only for an early morning run, others, for dinner or late-night pizza and beer at his house. Sometimes we talked a great deal; sometimes we talked not at all. Despite the magic pills, his moods could sink occasionally and without warning like a stone in water.

Not only had he arranged for me to vet the nature of his depression with his psychiatrist in Florida, but he was adamant that I make the call. "Purely selfish," he'd said.

"If you can't trust me, I won't be able to trust you." When I phoned up, the doctor said, "There's no mania in him, just the episodic depression. Look, Ms. Cavanaugh, I do know why you're calling, so I'll offer this: Barney's no danger to anyone, except sometimes himself. It's a tough disease he's got and it's somewhat controllable, but not curable. So if there's more than casual friendship in the offing between you, I hope you're a strong young lady and a bighearted one." I couldn't lay claim to either quality, nor was there anything casual about our friendship. I thanked him and hung up.

In our talking times, I'd learned more about the father who, figuratively—sometimes literally—had kicked Barney's arse through his childhood and teens. He was a man of bullish temper and a fierce tenacity about what was his: his business, his money, his wife, his son; all of them expected to perform to his standard, or he'd know the reason why. "But we haven't disowned each other yet," Barney was quick to point out. "Two hours together gives me hives and him heartburn—all told, probably harder on Dad than on me."

And I'd heard some mention of his mother, who'd acquiesced to death as she had to life, meekly and quietly. She'd gone overnight of heart failure in Barney's twelfth year. No trouble to anyone ever, she was a cipher to her only child, with one rather important exception: she'd left a small trust of which he got control when he reached twenty-five. Two days following that birthday, he'd withdrawn the fifty thousand dollars and bought the *Homeward Bound*. Dad was not best pleased, but for once, could do nothing about it.

WHEN MY BLUE CAR pulled into the marina with Jared seated beside me, Barney, who'd already arrived, stowed his surprise. What he said was, "Glad to have you. I see she's got you dressed warm enough. Here, take Jasper's leash—see if he leads you to the right boat." But once boy and dog were safely out of earshot, his face grew tense. "Is this okay?" he asked. "You've got Melanie's permission?"

"I don't have anyone's permission, but I say it's okay."

After a moment, he nodded. "How good a swimmer is he?"

The question hadn't occurred to me. I suppose I fancied that all American children of a certain class swam, in the same way they all ended up with straight teeth, as Jared would once the bands came off. But when we caught up to him, he answered truculently, "I don't know how to swim," the defiant Melanie-like raise of chin ineffective in masking his embarrassment.

"No problem," Barney said briskly, "strap yourself into this," and tossed him a life jacket.

"This really your boat? I mean . . . like *yours?*" Jared asked.

"Really is," said Barney. "Do you like boats?"

"I guess so. Cool looking. I've never been on one before. You know, except a ferry."

He did, as it turned out, like boats—this one, at least. This time, I sat over to the side with Jasper and watched Barney begin to apprentice Jared in the basic routines, enjoying the teamwork of gifted teacher and gifted student. Despite being a bit lumbered with the bulky orange jacket, Jared hopped to, intent on performing each task correctly, while Barney explained the whys and hows of sailing.

The hours whipped and glided by, eased on their way with facts and lore and jokes: an authentic good time, radiating optimism and all's right with the world. Not a lie, I told myself. This afternoon is not a lie—just not a whole truth.

Later on, after sandwiches and steaming tea, I noticed that Jared had removed himself from Barney's side. I found him standing in the boat's stern, his head lowered, staring hard into the water. I placed my hand lightly on his shoulder—perhaps he did not even feel it through all those insulating layers. "What are you thinking?" I asked quietly.

"How deep it is," he said, continuing to stare down. "About four hundred twenty feet here, Barney says, but it looks like no bottom at all. Just water forever."

"Does that scare you?"

"No." He sounded at once blank and wistful in a way he should have been too young for. *Oh, Jared, don't have killed her!*

We returned to the house just before three, a few minutes earlier than the time in the note I'd left for Melanie. When you're lying, best be scrupulous about the trimmings: I'd said we were taking him to the Bronx Zoo. "Elephants, Jared," I cautioned. "Tigers. A few words about our mini-safari should account for wind-burned faces." The morality of encouraging a child to lie to his mother disturbed me far less than it might have.

"When can we go again?" Jared asked.

"We'll work something out next weekend," Barney said. "Maybe Friday—school's closed day after Thanksgiving."

Thanksgiving: what a bizarre time for such a rite. I said as much to Nate later that day when he told me he was planning to host the turkey dinner for us all next Thursday.

"Bizarre times are the ones that call out for rites, aren't they, Lex? Ants to apes to humans, we're pattern makers, always hoping that the right design'll be a road map to salvation. If there's a time to ditch Thanksgiving, it sure isn't now."

"I suppose," I mumbled. He had asked me not to be a stranger, and during these weeks, I hadn't been—not exactly. But we had not been friends exactly, either. Yes, I had seen him almost daily after his fifteen minutes with Jared. Yes, I'd come to his house for the odd cup of good coffee from premium beans, well roasted, fresh ground. But the sense of intimacy that had put out shoots as we'd drunk lesser quality coffee together in the Anacleto kitchen had failed to flourish. His smell of Canoe still stirred a feeling in me. It was not nostalgia, not revulsion, not longing, but an odd amalgam of the three—a muted sort of feeling, secondhand, like a sensation stimulated by a film or a novel, rather than inside my own gut—perhaps because my gut was fully engaged in pumping up the strength to walk the agreed upon line with Jared, never stepping over.

The Catholics go on and on about way stations between earth, heaven, and hell. As I spent this dragged-out time in limbo, I thought that hell might be an improvement. I spent fruitless hours trying to make Calista's secret friend a three-dimensional figure, a reality even to myself. But the exercise stalled in my head, perhaps because I'd dreamed it up as an alternative to Jared; yet, absent any fresh information about personnel in Calista's universe, he might be the first figure my rampant imagination would enlist.

Nate had just left Jared's room, and it was Jared I wanted to talk about, not the social anthropology of holiday ritual. In the hours following the voyage of the

Homeward Bound, I'd watched him grow quiet, recede inside his skin, as he did every late afternoon, anticipating his quarter of an hour of therapy as though it were time tortured on the rack—which in a way it was.

Regularly, I tried to wheedle more information from Nate, and regularly I heard the word *confidentiality.* But last week, Nate had looked up from his mug with no prompting and said, "Stay with it, Lex. Stay the course. You, Barney, me, Melanie—even Tom: we're all helping him get from here to there. And he's such a bright boy. That's helping, too." It was the best I'd heard so far.

"Actually," Nate said now, returning to blasted Thanksgiving, "I was going to recruit you as my *sous chef.* Want to come to my place for a bite tonight and go over the menu?"

I blurted, "I've got a . . . I can't tonight. Can we go downstairs and have a cup of coffee now?"

He hesitated a few seconds, an expression on his face I could not read. "Sorry, I have to get back for a five-thirty patient. I gather the gallant Barney's on your agenda this evening?" I am ashamed to admit that I blushed like a girl, but I did. "I shouldn't tease you, Lex; you're too easy a mark."

"You shouldn't patronize me, either—bad form for a shrinker. You seem in a good mood this evening. Did things go well with Jared?"

His face folded up in that soft-leather-satchel way it had. He nodded slowly. "I'd say so."

I knew it would be useless to press him on the spot. "Is the dinner invitation still open to your *sous chef* tomorrow night?"

"It could be. Seven-thirty?" I said that would be fine.

"See you then. Come with your culinary imagination working—oh, and bring a good appetite." Another tease: this one on my eccentric relationship to food. We had never, so to speak, put it on the table, but it was clear that he wanted to remind me he knew.

I had the odd sense of being pulled along on a tide, over which I had no control. It did not frighten me, but in another of those once-removed reactions I'd been experiencing lately, I felt it should.

CHAPTER
27

Barney and I made love that night. We'd been sitting on the floor before the fireplace in his living room, having polished off a pizza with pepperoni and mushrooms—Barney was no more a cook than I—and a bottle of California red wine. We were talking about Courtney and Vin, and Melanie and Tom. "Sex makes strange bedfellows," he said, with the Chekhov smile that lifted only one corner of his mouth. Our eyes caught. Evasion might have been possible a second ago; it wasn't now.

"I've never done it with a friend," I said. "That would make strange bedfellows for me."

He didn't move in my direction, nor did he look away. "I don't know if I'm going to be able to," he said, "and I'll feel like whale's shit if I can't. How's that for erotic foreplay?"

"I'll try it on if you will. I haven't been to bed with anyone at all for close to two years—more than that. Maybe I can't, either."

He rose and held his hand out to me. "Upstairs, I think. We can close the door on Jasper, at least."

We each took off our own clothes, slowly, as though unwrapping gifts. Neither of us talked. His body was long and pale, the ribs like the slats of a ladder I might climb barefoot. I was glad he'd left the bedside lamp switched on, glad for white moonlight through the window. At his first touch, I shuddered and a kind of groan escaped me as my skin prickled to gooseflesh. After that single sound, we made each other's acquaintance in silence. Almost two years since I'd lain in a bed with a man, but three times as long since sex had been other than an exchange of sneezes with a stranger. His hands and mouth brought me along fast, the scratch of beard against my thigh a reminder that this was Barney—not Tom; not a nameless no one. This was Barney: teacher, sailor, man who thinks I look like a Picasso. My ride was lavish, smooth; I wanted it never to end. My tongue imagined taking its turn, running itself round his body, washing every inch of it like a mother cat. He'd grow hard in my mouth, and then . . .

An intruder moved into my mind as though she owned the place; perhaps she did. She lay there on the peach satin sheets she favored: Frannie Cavanaugh, back arched, legs spraddled apart while a dark male head supped on her, just as Barney was doing now. The bedroom door had been open about six inches' worth. I'd stood, staring, unable to look away. Her head raised just enough for eye contact. She smiled at me and raised her hand, a gesture part dismissal, part invitation. *Hello, isn't it early for you to be home? But you can see, darlin', I'm busy now, so get yourself lost for an hour or two. Or gawp if you must—hopeless as you are, you may learn something.* I was fourteen at the time.

Barney must have felt me tense. He sat up; so did I. "Not a good idea, huh?" he asked.

"I dunno," I mumbled, dazed, furious with myself. Then I looked at his face and saw the self-disgust that goes with failure. "No," I said. "No, not what you think. It was me. I . . . I thought of something and . . . God, I'm a pathetic cow!"

"Come on, don't go gallant on me. I've been here before. You wanted to know about the magic pills? Consider this a lab experiment—it's listed in small print: possible side effects. The damned worst thing is you never know *when*. Well, you can't say you weren't warned."

"But my checking out just now had nothing to do with your bloody side effects." His eyes rolled upward, not believing. "*Barney!* Think of the distribution of body parts. How could I have known the state of your willie at that moment? Your face was in my cunt, taking me round the bend. And then . . ." I made myself say it; he deserved the truth, and I the shame. "I pictured my mother doing that with one of her boyfriends. I'd watched them, you see."

He pushed my hair back from my face. "There was a two-masted schooner inside a bottle. It was in a seaport museum in Maine. I was maybe eight and I'd never seen one of those before. I couldn't stop thinking about the miracle of it—so small and so perfect, every single thing. You remind me of that boat, your body does." It was the first time in living memory I was charmed by something said about my size. "I loved being down there breathing into you. I . . . God, I want to fuck you so bad!"

"Lie down, Barney," I said. "Please lie down. Please-pleaseplease."

He sank back like a birch tree forced by a strong

wind. We wrestled the pills to the ground. Not easily, but in the end, they cried Uncle two falls out of three.

That was the image in my head as we lay together afterward, legs entangled, slick with sweat and pleased with ourselves. I said, "That was a judo hold you used on Vin, wasn't it? I was surprised you knew judo."

"Not the martial arts type, right?" He laughed and rolled over from back to belly, chin propped on his hands. "I was a fifteen-year-old wimp, and my father got the idea he'd make a man of me. Once he fastened onto something, he was prehensile—still is. I got the choice of judo lessons or military school. Well, what would you have picked? He hired a master to come to the house twice a week, so there was no question of my playing hooky—and he had my number, I would have. He always did have my number."

"No, he didn't. *I* have your number: You're as dad-ridden as I'm mum-ridden. How about I ride you instead?" I climbed aboard his back and began to rock. I felt drunk with joy, omnipotent. I could say anything, do anything, and it wouldn't go bad. "You've got a marvelous arse, you know?"

Some hours later, my eyes snapped open to a formless sense of dread and a window full of lightening sky. Barney was still beside me, sitting propped against the headboard looking at me. Jasper lay like a comforter across the bed's foot. "Hi," Barney said. He reached behind my head and began massaging my neck. "What's wrong?"

"I . . . I'm not sure. What time is it?"

"Six something. But it's Sunday. You can go back to sleep, if you want."

"No," I said through a yawn. "I have to . . ." In a flash I remembered why I'd awakened feeling bad rather than good. A dream: Stairs, a tall, winding staircase, without beginning or end to it. A loop of twine moves slowly upward from step to step, the pencil ends of it clutched in knobby fists—male fists, impossible to see whose. Suddenly, the pencils begin to grow and twist with a life of their own, stretching themselves to escape, their points flicking out like snakes' tongues, wanting to write . . . what?

I sat up fast and blurted what Domingo had told me about the construction of the garrote. "Oh God, Barney, do you think he could have done it?" The relief of voicing the question almost canceled the guilt of hearing myself say it.

"Funny, I was sitting here watching you sleep, wondering the same thing. Now, maybe it's simply that I like him so much, but you do get instincts about kids when you're round them all the time. What my instincts say about Jared McQuade is that if he lost it enough to kill someone, he wouldn't do it like that. Putting together a homemade garrote? Erotic strangulation? Squeezing the life out of her? I don't think so. Maybe a rock to her temple."

I sat up with him. The pencils: they'd bothered me, too—it seemed I was more perceptive asleep than awake. "That would suggest premeditation, wouldn't it, if he'd tied those pencils to the twine?"

"Premeditation of *something*, anyway. Lex, you know Jared better than I do. Do you think he's sexually precocious enough to try a kink like that?"

It would have been comforting to brush it off as absurd. "Jared is an explorer; he reads, he absorbs, he thinks. He's also just on the edge of puberty. Young for his age in some ways, but still . . . If he came upon some porn, would it excite him? Intrigue him? I expect it would," I said.

"You think he's talking to Nate about any of this?"

"I can't tell. But here's the thing, a part of me is hoping wildly that Jared *won't* confide in Nate. I keep feeling there's a crazy contest between them, a sort of duel to the death—and I want Jared to win."

"A shrink would say you're projecting your own issues about grown-ups and authority." He planted a quick, chaste kiss on my lips. "Maybe you are." He gave me a boy's smile. "I like that about you."

"Barney, do you know other children in Nate's care?"

"There are more than a few in the school. One of them's in my class."

"And?"

"And I'd have to say the man does good work. The kid I'm talking about, Fernanda Hodge, has ADD, attention deficit disorder—couldn't stay with a task for three minutes running, according to her third grade teacher. She started with Grumbach late in spring term last year and still sees him. She's reading now, staying on task long enough to complete an assignment, and she's way less disruptive than her third grade reports indicate. I don't know if you can give him all the credit, but he's probably entitled to some. The parents are thrilled. Look, I've always found the guy a little Rasputinish for my taste, but, as you know, charisma isn't my dish of choice. How about you? Having doubts about him?"

"I have doubts about everyone. Except you," I added. It was almost true.

"Liar. But keep your doubts handy; you may need 'em." His hand moved back up to my neck, strong fingers working the nape. My head dropped forward and my scalp began a delicious tingle.

I said, "Nate uses the same shave lotion my father did. And he looks a lot like my mother's boyfriend."

"Which of those two guys did you admire most?" he asked tartly, and kept the fingers going.

"Neither," I murmured. "Quite mutual. And therein lies the . . ."

"Hey." The masseur quit in mid-stroke. "I just thought of something. You asked me whether there was someone Calista might've developed a special feeling for. There was, in a way. Kind of a surprise." My body withdrew itself from under his arm and tensed, waiting for the nugget of information. "I gave the class an assignment last month, only a few weeks before the murder. I asked them to write about 'A Person I Admire.' Calista chose Tonya."

Kind of a surprise was accurate. "Tonya? Courtney's Tonya?"

"Tonya Baynes. Calista was very clear about what she admired. She admired Tonya's independence and outspokenness. If I remember right, the composition said, 'She works hard for her money, but nobody owns her.' And 'She has a fresh mouth and she makes me laugh and I think she is beautiful when she smiles.' It hurt me to chop the run-on sentence, because it was so charming."

"Tonya," was all I said. My mind was busy replaying a nighttime kitchen conversation, which had ended in hard feelings—very hard indeed.

CHAPTER
28

When I arrived back at the house, I saw Tom walking the grounds with Rima Silverstone. After two days shut in catering for his sick wife, he had the restless air of a junkyard dog on a chain. "Lex, Rima, you know each other," he said tonelessly. She gave me a curt nod, victor to vanquished. I observed ungenerously that orange makeup over a sleepless face fares poorly, lit by morning sun.

"Melanie better today?" I asked.

"Depends what you mean by better," Rima said. "She's well enough to have called *Newsweek*."

Tom threw her a silencing glance. "She's given them her version of your mother's departure from Norfolk," he said. "Old Tilt Schwartz'll be hiding his head in the sands of Miami Beach—either that or he'll be pining for the good old days." He grinned wolfishly.

Why would she do that? I wondered, and then thought I knew. The grin had not entirely left Tom's face; what was left of it had turned cold. He understood her reason, too, and likely approved, but he was not about to tell Rima that.

"We're going to have to do some serious damage control, Tom. Now here's . . ." I left them then. He would humor her. Whatever Rima was about to propose would be less clever by half than Melanie's move.

Melanie, propped and bed-jacketed, wore her white-rabbit mask, rosy eyes and nose, like a badge of privilege. "Good morning," I said. "Anything I can get you?"

"I don't think so. Sit, if you want to. I gather you slept out last night."

"The private coverage round here is almost as impressive as the public."

"I heard Jared knock at your door this morning and call out to you—no answer. Your room's right above mine. Have a good time?"

"Yes. Yes, I did."

"I'm glad. Not my type, Barney. Probably too nice for me."

"Probably. You and Tom suit each other very well."

"A pair of sexual predators?" What started as a cynical smile turned, in the end, sad. "We have our moments, but the loving cup's glued together—pour in some hot water and it leaks where the breaks were."

"I'd say the opposite. The hot water's been cascading in and the breaks seem to have sealed tighter." I rose from the foot of the bed, where I'd been perched, and walked nearer to her. "Melanie, are you that sure of Jared's guilt?"

"Say what you mean?" Her voice curled as though questioning.

"True confessions, twenty-five years old, one hundred proof, highly flammable. How lucky for you that she went public with her attack. The timing was perfect, wasn't it? And just in case the blaze might die down prematurely, you tossed your own fuel on it to make sure the smokescreen stays sufficiently thick—all with Tom's approval, while he keeps poor Rima running her tail off with damage control moves so that it all doesn't look too obvious. What's next, an appearance on *Oprah*? Perhaps you could get your mother to fly over and join you on the tube." She sneezed and reached for some tissues. After blowing her nose spiritedly, she laughed at me.

"Tell me, Melanie, how do you know it was Jared, not Tom? Because Nate thinks so? Do you believe *everything* Nate says?" My throat rasped with unaccustomed hollering, and blood pounded in my temples. God, it felt good to explode!

"If you're expecting answers from me, forget it," she said, almost offhandedly.

"I suppose the answer would be that you're protecting your child as you see fit. It's hard on Jared, though, all this fucking protection. It's tearing him apart."

"I can't help that," she said. "G'wan, get out of here now. I need a nap."

I FOUND JARED in his room, of course. "Want to go down to the beach this afternoon and have your first tae kwon do lesson?"

A full-braced grin. "I'm too *haw*-style."

"It's all right. I'm too much an amateur to teach you anything very dangerous. I understand you were looking for me earlier."

"My mom said you were sleeping over at Barney's. You're having sex with him, right?"

"Right," I said.

"Hey, better Barney than my father." Sarcasm requires

a bit of spirit; I was glad to hear him summon it up.

"Long time ago, Jared. I can apologize to you, but I promise it won't help."

"It's all right. Everybody in this sicko family's running round having sex with everybody else. I mean, gross. It's all over the Net that my mom was fucking her *father*. And my sister was . . . Ah, forget it." His face went crimson.

"Your sister was what?"

"My sister was *murdered,* in case you don't remember!" Which was not what he'd begun to say, but Pan/Poppins was not meant to go there—and she didn't have the nerve to jump the traces.

"Come on, let's grab a slice of pizza at the stand and then head for the beach. If you don't take to combat Korean style, you can just throw a few American punches at me."

He did take to the squats and whirls and kicks, despite the tendency of his legs to get tangled in each other. He did not take to a few gingerly delivered prods from me to complete what he'd begun to say about Calista and sex. When the sky began to darken, it was Jared who said, "We have to get back. Grumbach's coming to shrink my head." His attitude was changed—it might have been Tom speaking. The glint in his eye was Tom's, too: reckless Tom, preparing to do something outrageous. Time does not heal all wounds, I remember thinking, as I started the car on its way back. Time also allows disease to set in and take over. Time can be the worst of enemies.

CHAPTER

29

I wanted to say these things to Nate tonight at dinner, but he canceled the plan. After his session with Jared, he found me and begged off, pleading a sudden, fierce headache. "I get them occasionally, real killers. I'm good for nothing at all. Sorry to bug out on you."

"Me, too," I said tight with tension, unreasonably peeved with his headache.

"I know there are things you're bursting to talk about. But we're going to be cooking together Wednesday, if that's still okay with you. We'll have all afternoon together, plenty of time."

Instead, I spent the evening back at Barney's house, tying words into confounding knots of doubt and fear: Melanie, Tom, Nate—the new factor, Tonya—and always Jared. In the midst of telling Barney about Jared and me on the beach, the new reckless look when he'd mentioned his shrink session, I *did* burst— not into an impotent scream as I had with Melanie, but into sobs, which commandeered my body like a convoy of barreling tanks. "I'm scared," I repeated in syncopation between spasms. "God, I'm scared." Even swaddled in his arms, my face burrowed in the rough, smoky warmth of his sweater, I did not lose the queasiness of that fear. Time was ticking away, not on our side.

As I was readying to leave, Barney said gently, in the way one might speak to a person balanced on a window ledge, threatening to jump. "Lex, the Tonya thing. We know Calista looked up to Tonya. Let's even say she had a crush on Tonya. You are working at constructing a lesbian child molester out of a kid's homework assignment. It's a long, wild shot in the dark."

"I know," I said, my head feverish with caroming thoughts. "But I need a long shot. That weapon worries me. It looks like something a child might put together— a precocious child. Maybe the child was Calista. Maybe." I kissed him hard and left.

It was close to midnight when I returned. No sign of activity downstairs. I knew Tonya's routines fairly well by now; she would be in the kitchen. I found her there, semi-slouched on a chair, feet up on the kitchen table, engrossed in a newspaper. At first look, I thought it was a tabloid; it was that size. But no, it was *Barron's* she was reading.

"Buying long or selling short?" I asked, exhausting my lingo on the subject.

She lowered the paper and her legs, straightened herself in the chair and said, "Both. If I told you the reasons, would you get them?"

"Probably not. My grasp of the world of shares and bonds is, put kindly, limited."

"And you're surprised mine isn't?"

It would have been more patronizing to deny it. "Yes, I am surprised."

"You stereotyping on race or job description?"

"If I were doing it on race, I'd hardly admit that, would I?"

"Sump'm Ah kin git you, Miz Cavanaugh?" she drawled out minstrel-style.

"Get off it, Tonya. What is your bloody problem with me? That I asked you a few tactless questions? Right, I did. I'm going to ask another one: Just how friendly were . . ." I hesitated and then decided to go ahead. ". . . you and Calista?"

My eyes were fixed on her, ready to notice any nuances, any flicker of anything. And they did. The changes were subtle, but they were there. With the first words of my question, her face froze, its bravado gone; I could swear she was scared. But then after I'd finished asking it, she relaxed.

"I told you first time I met you," she said rote-like, "I liked Callie. She was a good girl, a smart girl, a girl who wanted a lotta lovin' and got it."

"And did she get it from you? Did you love her?"

She stared back, sussing out where I might be headed. "What the hell you talking about? I said I *liked* the child; that's all."

Okay, let's see how you lob back this one. "Saw a great deal of her, didn't you? Those nighttime visits, just the two of you."

"You mean . . . What *do* you mean? I work here. She was here a lot. She'd talk to me sometimes. Here in this kitchen while I cleaned up."

"What about when you went to her house?" I asked softly. Just fishing, but sometimes you get a bite.

She answered just as softly, "I baby-sat there a few

times." Then her voice dropped down past mezzo-soprano into the tenor range to add, "You are one evil little bitch, you know that? First you try and pin the tail on Vin. Then when that doesn't fly, you decide, how 'bout the colored girl. Anybody but your precious family."

She was standing now, fists clenched at her sides. She'd have liked to hit me, and I could hardly blame her; in her place that's what I would have felt like doing. She was only average height, which made her less than half a foot taller than I, but she looked a good deal stronger—those long arms, muscled legs. If she took a fair punch at me, I'd go straight down. But since martial art had made its way back into my physique, I calculated what it might take to throw her and moved my feet into position to have a go, if it came to that. Her fists stayed clenched, but she made no move toward me.

I said, "Would it surprise you to learn that Calista admired you more than anyone else she knew?" Her look said it surprised her mightily. Her fingers uncurled. "Tonya, might we sit down and just . . . talk?"

"Why would I want to do that?"

"You might learn something—something that would come as a surprise if you heard it later. From the police."

Point out to me a person who could walk out on that and I'll show you someone with no imagination and nothing to hide. We sat.

"Calista had a school assignment to write about the person she admired most. She chose you, because you do what you want and no one owns you—that's what she said."

"Well, she was right about that," she said, but her tone was sadder than the words. She looked confused and troubled; near tears. "What else did she say?" she asked.

"She said that you were very clever, and that you'd be rich one day from investing in the stock market," I improvised. I saw the smile. "And that she loved your smile."

"Ah, shit!" Her fist pressed hard against her mouth, as though to kill the smile—and perhaps stanch unconsidered words? "That poor little girl," she mumbled, fist in place. "Damned mess!"

Her distress seemed real, but the pitch of it was wrong. If it was remorse I was hearing, it seemed off-key and muted for a murderer.

I was no specialist in this sort of interview: my camera and I were quiescent observers, active editors. I thought of how Tom would rough up such a subject, and knew that if there was a time to strike, it was now. "Did you visit her late Halloween night?"

She shook her head, no.

Quick second blow: "Where were you then?"

"In my bed."

"Can you prove it?"

I'd made a catch—that's what Tom used to call it—I saw her bite the hook, suffer pain, lose hope. She stared at me for a long beat, undecided what to do. When she spoke, she was calm, yet filled with the scorn of the righteous.

"I can, if I have to," she said. "But not to you. Bring on the police. I'll give them two alibis for the price of one." She probably *was* good at trading shares; she had good nerves. Before I could sort out my own thoughts, she was up the back stairs, presumably to her room. I did not try to follow her.

* * *

SOMEONE HAD BEEN in Tonya's bed. I did not think she was bluffing. Of course her companion could have been anyone: butcher, baker, broker. But in an instant, a pair of fragments found each other as though magnetized, glided into place for me easily, their contours a snug fit: Tonya, angrily stubbing out her illicit cigarette, glaring at me in dislike and distrust; Courtney, going rosy while describing her postcoital wakefulness, her sated husband asleep beside her. The common element here: Vin.

Tonya, who'd been voluble about everyone—even Calista—had gone up the spout at my mention of Vin as a possible suspect. Courtney, whose blush I'd put down to maidenly modesty, I saw now as an unaccustomed liar, rattled. Vin had left her bed. To visit Tonya's, I would wager, unless Tonya was lying for him, too.

I called on Domingo at her office, reputable as I could make myself in newly pressed black trousers, pressed white shirt, and proper shoes. It was a calculated risk— and I was far from confident about the chances—rather like what American footballers call the Hail Mary pass: it likely won't work, but you've nothing to lose. She seemed less surprised to see me than I'd imagined.

"I have some observations for you," I said. "Still interested?"

"Of course."

"Vin Anacleto was having it off with Tonya Baynes, their maid."

"Yes?" She cocked her head politely at me.

"You likely have Courtney and Vin down as each other's alibis. I'm saying that Vin left Courtney's bed for Tonya's, or so Tonya will say."

"Where are you going with this, Lex?" I watched her interest wane.

"Well, don't you see? It seems to me that both women are rather eager to cover for Vin."

"Or themselves?"

"I don't think so—even though Tonya and Calista . . . Well, Calista had a sort of girl's crush on Tonya." I told her about the school homework assignment.

"And how did, let's say, Vin get himself back into the McQuade house that night?"

"Calista let him in," I said. I outlined the secret friend theory. Her attention sharpened.

"*Other* than Vin Anacleto, do you have someone in mind as secret friend?"

"Not specifically," I said, warming to her interest, "but she had classmates, gymnastics mates—perhaps one of them was closer to her than we know. And what about the adults at the Halloween party? What about the McQuades' day help or former day help? This was a compelling child. . . . Whether she meant to be or not, she was a sexy kid!"

I saw a flicker of protest in her face—there and gone quick as a passing snowflake. Was her own daughter a black-eyed, raspberry-lipped Calista? She nodded, seeming to consider a fresh possibility. My breath caught on a speck of hope.

"Jared's almost a teenager," she said, with pointed nonchalance, "a very susceptible age for a boy. Might *he* and Calista have been closer than we know?" The cincture round his neck was tightening as surely as the garrote round Calista's; I imagined I could feel its press against the pulses in my own neck, making the blood pound like surf in my ears.

CHAPTER
30

Courtney stopped me in the vestibule on my way out Tuesday morning. She was no games mistress at that moment, but a Victorian headmistress, prepared to administer a well-deserved caning. "I have some things to say to you, *my gel.*"

She led the way into her study, no clubby offers of breakfast this morning, though I felt a crave for food. "Where do you get the idea that the private matters of this household are any of your business?"

She wanted an answer. I gave her one. "Dunno." It was as good a password as any to get into what was on her mind.

"Your sister and your brother-in-law are a pair of irresponsible sexual sociopaths, and that may be merely the tip of their iceberg. I am sorry I ever laid eyes on them. And you, masquerading as a slip of a waif, you're no better. All you've done here is damage. Tonya is gone. *You* are to blame."

What did she know, or think she knew? "Do you mean she's quit or that you've fired her?"

"*Fired* her? Tonya has worked here for twelve years; her aunt brought me up. Of *course* I didn't fire her."

"Why did she quit?"

"Because you've humiliated us. *My* arrangements with *my* husband and *my* maid are *my* business. Now you've thrown us into the same mucky trough your diseased family seems to thrive in."

"So Vin and Tonya—that's *your* arrangement?" She stared at me cold-eyed, the red splotches rising from neck to cheeks: twin flags of war on her plump face. "I was trolling for Tonya's alibi," I said. "The rest is none of my concern. I understand that."

"You don't understand anything—you with those big eyes always watching, judging everyone! People make their accommodations, my little friend. I've been very good to Tonya. She'll have a future with her investing. Who do you think got her started?" The landscape of her face began to tremble, threatening a small earthquake. "We were doing fine! I had it all arranged. I will want you out of here, all damned four of you, by Monday."

My big eyes watched her, all right: a quivering piece of privileged humanity, ready to disintegrate because the private puppet theater she called her life has been rechoreographed by other lives. "I don't think there'll be any problem about that," I said.

THE SAME DAY, Melanie, up out of her sickbed, went off to run the gauntlet of lenses, lights, and mikes, bearing herself like Joan of Arc in yellow tweed armor. Tom, at her side, was on this round a supporting player, but would costar next week. She was scheduled to occupy the hot seat as the first guest on his newly resumed television show—taping Friday, airing Sunday night. She would discuss, with tantalizing innuendo, her checkered past. Tom would publicly forgive in the name of love, citing his own checkered past. They would beseech their daughter's killer to give himself up; they would demand the police pursue new avenues of investigation.

A whiff of suspicion would cling like smoke damage to them both, especially to Melanie, but nothing more substantial than a whiff. This was the strategy: playing the cards they held, the stakes, their son's safety—gamblers, both of them. They were a matched set, Melanie and Tom, alike in their risky souls. They excited each other. Why had I never appreciated that?

LATER THE SAME afternoon, the police released information on the scrubbed-away drawing of planets on Calista's hand. Both parents claimed it was a Halloween decoration, painted on by Melanie, washed off by Calista herself before going to bed. No guest at the party or neighbor on the trick-or-treat round noticed it, either to corroborate or refute the family's account. A nonevent.

I managed to catch a private moment with Tom, long enough to ask whether he still regarded that piece of evidence as dangerous.

"Dangerous? Why would you call it dangerous?"

"You thought it was, remember?"

"Did I? Guess I was wrong." He laughed the devilish laugh I'd worshiped at one time. "Things are looking up, Lex. House goes on the market soon as the cops give it over to us. Meantime, we're out of here next week. I've found us an apartment in Fairfield—room for you, too. We are going to make it. Jared's going to be okay."

* * *

JARED DID SEEM closer to okay. There was a new, almost manly, resolve to his step, a light of purpose in his eyes these last couple of days. No more did the haunted urchin skulk about his bedroom, trying to crawl inside his computer screen, coming alive only during his lessons with Barney, dreading Nate as though he were Dr. Mengele. Now he exhibited a zest for tae kwon do, learning it quickly. He practiced daily and was coming along well, hardly tripping over his own feet at all. The movements were taking on a crispness. I fancied bringing him back to London with me, when all this was over, introducing him to my *sensei* in the Chalk Farm Road studio.

Early Tuesday morning I had come upon him downstairs in the conservatory, enveloped in a large chair, bent over a book, his head propped on one hand. He sat perfectly still, utterly absorbed. A cold, bright sun shone through the frosted windowpanes, outlining him like a classic statue: Boy Reading. I assumed it was one of the scientific tomes Barney'd brought—there seemed to be a new one every day, not only on astronomy, but on oceanography as well, in which Jared had begun to take an interest. But when I moved closer, I found that the book commanding such focused attention was *A Wrinkle in Time*, the book he'd shied at my head weeks ago— the book I'd given him for his sixth birthday.

"Enjoy it still?" I asked, stifling the impulse to hug, which would have embarrassed him. "I've kept my childhood books, too. Of course, I don't have any that go back to when I was six. That's the year I left America with my mother, and nothing from the old life came with us—no possessions, anyway."

"That's how Mom wants it to be when she sells the house," Jared said, looking up. "Leave everything behind, she says. We'll get it all new. I asked her if she was going to leave all those pictures of Calista behind, too, and her mouth pruned up like she was gonna blast me—you know, like I was being snotty. But I wasn't; I just was curious. Anyway, she just gave me that ray-gun look she pulls sometimes, and she said, 'I don't need pictures. My head has its own pictures.' "

And what pictures did Jared carry in his head? The words "Jared, please tell me. Tell me and I will understand and be with you" sat in my throat, begging for release, almost taking my breath away. Before I had the chance to say something safe and inane, Jared said, "Maybe she's right, my mom. That's why I was trying to kind of memorize parts of this book, you know, pack my head with the pictures I want to keep there."

Tuesday evening at his house, Barney and I did battle. He greeted me with a right tongue-lashing: teacher to a child who has seriously misbehaved, savaged a classmate on the playground.

"I hate what you did to Courtney yesterday. What do you think you accomplished, except to rip the skin off a fragile woman who's abased herself to hang on to what she feels she needs?"

"*Fragile*? She runs a small totalitarian state, everybody hopping to her tune, doing what she thinks they ought to be doing for their own good—oh, and by the by, for *hers*."

"Yes, fragile. Courtney's no dictator, just a woman raised to be sure that the only thing desirable about her is her money. You ought to be ashamed, Lex. I know I'm ashamed that I was the one who loaded your damned gun with the bullets to shoot down Tonya."

"Oh, stop being a sanctimonious ass!"

"When you stop playing Dirty Harry." His face was

crimson with the Warden family flush. "If what you're honestly after is helping Jared, then ask yourself what's really going on with him—why does he suddenly seem so much better? Discuss it with Nate, why don't you, while you make your chestnut dressing and cranberry sauce. It seems to me like a false dawn; I don't trust it. Something is up with him. *Jared's* your interest here, remember? Not blowing to hell the life of a woman you hardly know and won't even try to understand."

Butbutbut . . . I might have taken a whack at reminding him that blowing Courtney to hell was no intention of mine, that I'd merely stumbled on Courtney's *ménage à trois* and didn't give a fart for it. I might have assured him that I remembered quite well, thank you, what my interest here was. Instead, I yanked on my jacket and slammed myself out his door.

THE NEXT DAY, the afternoon before Thanksgiving, I took myself to Nate's house to fulfill my duties as *sous chef*. The fact that we were going to be preparing food posed a predicament for me. Since the beginning of the week, I had been beating back the stirrings of a binge by almost ignoring its presence. Almost. I observed the rules of prevention: eating with Jared or Barney or at a lunch counter crowded with strangers; choosing bland food, chewing each boring mouthful till the count of ten before swallowing it. But last night's skirmish with Barney had left me feeling shaken, guilt-pricked, and desolately alone.

Nate had begun the work before I arrived, so the house was fragrant with browning onion and sage, tangy with orange and cranberry, rich with butter. He embraced me in greeting, tight hug—a surprise: we'd greeted each other before with a touch of hands.

Equally surprising, I did not want to pull away. I had come in colder than the weather warranted, chilled to the bone. The lotion-scented warmth he radiated was welcome as . . . as a father's embrace: *There, there, darling, it's all going to be okay.* Does anyone get over anything, ever? Or do we just keep recycling the same dreams and disappointments until they distort into things barely resembling what they were: quirks, cranks—eccentric, useless.

He released me with a small push away, like a good leader on a dance floor signaling his partner to swing round, and gave me a full, face-rumpling grin. "You've been causing a fair amount of havoc, I hear."

"I suppose I have. Is there anything that goes on you *don't* know about?"

"Probably." He took a deep breath and exhaled it, letting his cheeks puff up as he did so. "Look, Lex, I want us to have a good day together; I've been looking forward to it. Suppose we get our Jared talk out on the table and over with for starters. That okay with you?"

It was like pushing hard at a door, and having it suddenly flung open: one falls smack on one's nose. "Yes, it is," I said in a voice smaller even than I am.

He poured the inevitable coffee and began sipping it. "We're getting someplace," he said. "Have you noticed a change in attitude the past few days?" I nodded, my heart waiting for instruction on which way to leap. He nodded back. "I can't go into clinical detail, you know that, but Jared is gearing up to look his ghosts and devils straight in the face. He's building muscle for the next step. It's not going to be a walk on the beach, but he *is* going to take it very soon now, wherever it goes."

"Barney is worried about where it's going," I made myself say.

"Barney sees depression from the inside. That affects how he sees what's outside. I don't say there's nothing to worry about, but to me the view looks a lot brighter than three weeks ago."

Innocent? I knew better than to ask it aloud, but my facial muscles didn't.

I fancied I could see myself in his black eyes. "I don't know, Lex."

Later, as I took a masher to the huge bowl of boiled potatoes he'd assigned me, I felt my mouth begin to water uncontrollably. I swallowed hard.

"Taste them, why don't you?" he said, his hand directing a serious knife in quick, professional strokes against carrots destined to join raisins in a salad. "I've got sauteed onion, garlic, and a bit of chopped spinach to put in there, plus a little butter and cream. You know, some cooks insist on doing the potatoes at the last minute, but I swear by mashed potatoes done the day before, left to mellow overnight, then plumped up with extra butter and cream just before serving."

I bit at the inside of my lip and kept mashing. "You're preparing for a bloody army here. Who's coming?"

"Melanie and Tom, Jared, you, your friend Barney. Courtney."

"You're joking. Why would she want to spend a holiday with us? She's just evicted us."

"Maybe she wants to spend it with *me*. Of course, I *have* invited Vin. Do you think he might be the attraction?"

I laughed long and hard, the craving buried for a moment beneath a volley of guffaws. "You are evil," I said, catching my breath.

"Evil's in the eye of the beholder. Come on, taste 'em, give me your read."

"I'm sure they're fine." The sweat popped out now—neck, scalp, armpits, groin.

He quit decimating the carrots. "You don't have to fight it, Lex dear. You're safe here. If you need to eat now, you can. You can take the food upstairs, if you want to be alone."

"No. No, I can't—I mean, *won't*. I don't *want* to need to!" Saliva clogged my throat. "Help me. Will you help me?" He lunged toward me just in time to rescue the basin of half-mashed potatoes from crashing off the countertop.

His hot hands clasped mine, which were icy. "I will help you," he said with the quiet intensity of a hypnotist. "Now, sit for a moment. I'm going to go upstairs and get you a tranquilizer, Valium to calm the shakes. Then we'll sit down beside each other and I'll feed you some soup."

And he did, like father to child, one spoon at a time, talking in a soothing rumble all the while. Funny, I had no recollection of anyone having spoon-fed me, ever. I did not sit on his lap, but felt as though I were there. I remember his saying that Calista had called him Grumpa. I heard the word in my head; its echo made me want to laugh and to cry.

His voice came from far away. "I had a little girl once," he said, "a baby daughter. She died. She'd be close to your age . . ."

CHAPTER
31

Fingers worked at my scalp, washing my hair clean in warm water. At the same time, my back was being scrubbed. Warm, so very warm in the water . . .

"Lex. Lex. *Lex!*" Jared's voice.

My eyes opened to hot darkness. Except that I knew the voice—time, place, circumstance, were not to be fathomed. A second later, my eyes squinted shut against icicles of light, and all the heat turned cold. I sat up in bed. Thanks to Nate's magic, I had not binged, but in the aftermath, I felt hungover, as though I had—on something. "Why'd you ha' to yank the covers off?" I mumbled.

"Because you weren't getting up. You'd've suffocated with your head under that quilt."

"Lucky for you I wasn't starkers underneath. Time is it?"

"Almost seven." He was scrubbed up and fully dressed, including an outer jacket.

"Where d'you think you're going?"

"To Barney's with you," he said.

"I don't know that I'm going to Barney's." I had not seen or spoken to him yesterday. As I sat there in bed, my mind straining to clear the clouds, it seemed much longer than that. The day with Nate had spanned decades. I'd been the child I had yearned to be: cosseted, fed, stroked by a father who treasured me. Then I'd returned the favor, comforting him as he talked of his own losses: the slow dying from MS of a wife who'd understood him as no one ever had or would; the bewildering fast death of their infant daughter, unwakable from an afternoon nap in her carved antique cradle. He'd crumbled at this part, his deep voice grinding to a halt. I'd stroked his head then, as earlier he'd stroked mine. The gray hair felt like straw, the forehead beneath it leathery and cool as a shrunken head.

"Sometimes," he'd said softly, "I wake up at four or so in the morning and I jump out of bed panicked that I've forgotten to feed her, change her—that she'll die because of me. Those times, I lose track of whether the 'her' I mean is Zip or our little girl. I think you can imagine how that would feel."

"Yes," I'd breathed. "I really can."

"*Please*, Lex," Jared coaxed. "It's really nice out, and I thought . . . I thought maybe he'd take us sailing. We've got plenty of time before the Thanksgiving from Hell starts. Come on, please?"

The excitement in his voice was music I had not heard for six years and missed. It brought back Jared as he was: the keen-brained innocent, passionate to learn, to do, to master the next thing. I jumped out of bed at its call. "Go back to your room and give me five minutes."

It took me no longer than that to assemble myself.

When I appeared at his door, I found him hunched over his computer, his eyes perhaps half a foot from the screen. "Got to watch out for the tiny programmers who live behind there," I said. "It's a known fact that if you get too close, they make a grab and pull you inside."

The notion tickled him. "I'd like that a lot."

"Come on now, shut down. We'll leave a note downstairs saying we've gone hiking. I think I'm a bad influence."

WE ARRIVED AT Barney's just in time to catch him before his Jeep pulled away from the curb. Like Jared, he had thought it a fine morning for a sail. The silent messages the two of us traded were so deeply encoded that I didn't comprehend what I was sending, let alone receiving. The skin round his eyes looked bruised with lack of sleep, the cropped beard scruffy. Was it possible our row had nudged him off his tightrope into free fall? I saw what his doctor had meant in questioning my level of strength and generosity. I felt shriveled in spirit, stingily ill-equipped to be responsible for someone else's well-being.

Jared's "C'n we come?" got Barney's stiff "I guess. You want a ride?" He tossed the question my way.

"I'll take my car, thanks," I said carefully. "We're going to have to rush back and change clothes. Are you going to come to Nate's dinner?"

"Wouldn't dream of missing it," he said dryly: more code. I noticed that Barney was looking not at me, but at Jared, perusing him as though they'd newly met. "Ride with me, Jared?"

The invitation seemed to throw Jared off stride. "No," he said after a beat. "I . . . I'll go with Lex." On the way to the marina Jared was silent, deep in thought.

I asked whether he was all right, and got a *yes* that had a hollow, negative echo to it.

When we arrived, Barney was already there, waiting. He threw an arm round Jared's shoulder and pulled him close for just a moment. The gesture was intimate and intense: soul-mate to soul-mate. I expected Jared to stiffen or shake it off, but he did not. "Here, take Jasper's lead," Barney said almost gruffly. "Go on aboard. We're right behind you."

"You look awful," I said. "My fault, is it?"

"That's giving yourself a lot of importance," he said.

"Well, fuck you, too. I was trying to say some version of I'm sorry."

"Thanks," he said, looking straight ahead at the boat, hands not moving from inside his wind-cheater pockets. He strode ahead, then stopped to let me catch up. "Did you get Grumbach to talk at all about Jared yesterday?"

"Some. He said he thought things we're looking up. And they seem to be, Barney—or did till just now. You should have seen how alive he was earlier this morning. He came into my room and woke me up, dying to go sailing."

"Sailing was his idea?"

"Yes. And then at the sight of you, he wilted. Look, I told Nate that you were worried about Jared, and . . ." I stopped, reluctant to say what came next. He turned to me, his eyes asking no indulgence. "And he said that you were looking at depression from the inside."

"True enough. Can't fault him for that."

"Is there something I'm meant to see, Barney?" I asked. "Because I don't, and you seem to."

"I'm not sure. As the good doctor told you, my vantage point is different. It may be unreliable."

When we boarded, we found Jared squatting on

deck, looking out over the sound. Jasper sat beside him, Jared's arm draping round the dog's neck. They could have been a posed illustration for a child's book. Barney fetched a life jacket, which Jared obediently buckled into. "Okay," Barney said, handing him a ring of keys. "Now, remember what we do to get out of port?"

Jared responded with the all-purpose, "Duh," and started up the motor.

Barney came up behind him and placed Jared's hands on the wheel, with his own covering them. "Now, try and get the feel here. We're going to back her out, smooth and steady." It was a pleasure to watch teacher and student work in tandem under a bright, cotton-clouded sky, the sound of Jared's laugh in the wind. One of those perfect moments camera manufacturers single out for their TV ads.

Once in open water, Barney and Jared hoisted the sails and headed north into the wind. I stayed out of the way, from time to time giving Jasper's ears a scratch; I was still no fan of dogs, but this one would do. The air was peppered with Jared's staccato questions about the pull of the tides, depth of the water, speed of the current. I recognized in them a hunger not so dissimilar to my own: he wanted to eat the information, all of it—eat it fast, make it part of him.

Abruptly, the wind changed and freshened, spanking the sails as though they were drying laundry, the boat listing to its left. Barney took over, righting things quickly. It took perhaps three minutes, during which I watched him, fascinated and a bit envious of the authority skill gave him—every economical motion producing a desired effect.

"It's a treat to watch you handle that," I said. "And it's a treat to watch you with Jared. I wonder if he'll grow up to be a sailor, too. You are such a *damned* good teacher."

"Where is he?" Barney asked.

"Somewhere round. Maybe he's gone up front for the view."

"Find him," he said sharply.

The snap in his voice sent me scurrying. I heard Jasper's bark first—I think I did—and then I saw. Jared stood balanced on the bow of the boat like a thin bowsprit, no life jacket to bulk up his silhouette. "No," I said too quietly, I suppose, for him to have heard me in the wind's whistle. But I didn't want to alarm him into jumping. "Jared." Louder this time, but not the scream that was building in my throat. I was perhaps four feet from him, but knew enough not to make a grab. "Come down from there. Please."

"I can't," he said, his body not moving. Jasper's was though, back and forth, up and down, jumping and barking. I was terrified the dog's hectic activity would send Jared over the edge, but knew no way to stop it.

"You can, darling. You *can*. I don't . . . It's going to be all right. Really. You'll see." How entirely useless are words past a certain point—as useless as drugs when a pneumonia has reached full gallop. You suppose that if you can only pick out the right ones, they'll make all the difference. The truth is, of course, once it's too late, there *are* no right ones.

"I started to write you an E-mail, but I deleted it." So he'd planned this, counting on my being as stubbornly blind as I had in fact been. And I had sold him out, letting myself believe that Nate knew best what he needed. Had I in fact done it to get what *I'd* needed: a bowl of warm soup, spoon-fed along with fatherly affection just as warm?

"No!" My scream when it came out was something from a nightmare: full-throated in the terrified heart, a constricted mouse squeak out the mouth.

"Don't do it, Jared." Barney's voice from behind me. "I've been there, where you are. You can make another choice. It's hard, but I can help you. It's not *too* hard. You can make it." He moved quickly, just inches now from Jared.

"It *is* too hard. *You don't know fucking anything!*" At that moment, the boat listed, the dog leapt up, and Jared jumped into the water. His body broke the surface with virtually no splash at all.

CHAPTER
32

I pulled off one of my sneakers, readying to dive after him. He was just there, wasn't he? I fancied I could see an opening in the water. I could fish him right out. Smack him hard for doing something so . . .

Barney, who had already shed both shoes and anorak, grabbed my arm tight. "No, I'll do it. I'm bigger than you and a strong swimmer. Lower the sheets and watch for us. Got it?" No point to argue, and no time; Jared's best chance lay with Barney. I nodded and ran, blank of memory in brain or hand as to how the damned unwieldy sails got up or down. I heard Barney hit the water, Jasper going right after him.

One hears, reads, about the tricks time plays in crisis: accelerating to a blur of streaking color, freezing to a dead stop, stretching itself long enough to replay a life. It did none of those things for me; it simply kept moving, second by agonizing second.

How long does drowning take? It was something I

used to know, should know, though I couldn't remember why that might be—something to do with a film I'd once made, but I couldn't place . . . What did it matter, anyway? A stupid film. The acid taste of coffee and bile filled my mouth as I struggled with the spaghetti of damp ropes to find an operative one. When I did, my hands gripped it hard, as though they held Jared's mouth and nose, forcing the air to stay put in his lungs while Barney found him in the black water. *Just don't take a breath, Jared. Please. Concentrate on that. You've no reason to trust me, but trust Barney; when he grabs you, don't fight him.*

Once I'd got one sail to flap its way down to a heap at my feet, I tackled the other, which was stubborn in coming undone. The seconds ticked themselves off—many of them, too many. The sheet collapsed too quickly, swinging in the wind as it did, bashing me to the deck. *Tick, tick, tick.* I scrambled to my feet and looked over the side, ready to see them. I saw nothing. The damned boat bobbed and rocked as wind whipped the waves. But basically, it stayed put—waiting.

Time played all its tricks now. A proper circus of stunts. My head spun in a flood of blood reds and oiled blacks as the sun escaped its cloud cover to blast me full in the eyes. Behind my lids, the frank, brown gaze of a three-year-old took my measure across Fortnums fancy preserved fruit counter. The little boy wore a brass-buttoned navy blazer, dapper little thing. His smart, pretty mother held him tightly by the hand, making certain not to lose him. Melanie would kill me over this, and she'd be right to do it. I had come clear across an ocean to do nothing but help Jared die in cold water . . . *Tick, tick, tick.* It had been hours, certainly. Both of them were gone forever, no trace.

Ah! The film had been about a diver: a Hawaiian woman who'd begun the sport at forty-five, after she'd had a cancerous breast removed. She needed to control something in her life, she'd explained to my camera. She had held her breath for eight minutes underwater—eight minutes and twenty-two seconds. But that woman had wanted to live and win. Jared had lost and wanted to die.

The corner of my eye caught motion in the water. I spun left and spotted Jasper—his ears, eyes, and that doggy smile, all that were visible above water. Then I saw Barney, half his head above the surface, one long arm stroking through the water. "Have you got him?" I heard no answer, other than the echo of my own shriek.

Barney drew closer, raising his chin high enough to call out, "Rope. Deck, right by you. Knot to cleat and throw."

I scooped up the coil at my feet (heavier than I expected) and secured one end in what my numb, clumsy fingers remembered of the hitch knot he'd taught me. I threw the length far as I could manage in his direction. As he made for it, I saw—thought I saw—Jared's head lolling in the waves, the body pulled along under Barney's spare arm.

"Oh, my God, you *have* got him!"

But as Barney hoisted himself and Jared aboard—the sodden dog following a second later—I looked at the limp body, the still, corpse-white face, and knew that time had run out too soon. Jared was dead.

"Cushion. Under his head," Barney gasped. He gave a harsh, skidding cough as he knelt at Jared's side and flipped him onto his stomach, head turned to one side, propped a moment later on the cushion I'd fetched. Then Barney straddled him and began to pump vigorously at his back. *Tick, tick, tick.* Barney's shuddering grunts of effort; the whip of cold wind; the bark of the dog as he shook off the wet and pushed open the cabin door, knowing it was warmer in there. I did not speak, there was nothing to say. The next words would be Barney's: a verdict of life or death. All I could do was wait and watch and hope.

It was then that time stopped. This moment would last hours, years, decades, centuries, millenniums. This moment was all the time left to the world. Barney kept pumping and grunting and shaking with wet, freezing cold, while the moment hung, utterly still.

A faint cough. But not from Barney. Another cough. Jared's body twitched. Then it began to convulse violently, instinctually fighting for its life. Water and vomit spewed out his mouth. So much water inside such a slender vessel. The coughs raged now, turning Jared's face from white to red. Barney climbed off him and stood grinning for a moment. I spread myself on top of Jared to stanch his shivering.

"Cabin," Barney said. "You'll have to help me get him inside. I've got the shakes so bad I could drop him. Tarps, blankets. Whatever. Extra electric heater in there." We half dragged, half carried Jared, whose head and limbs flopped like a rag doll's, while his jaw chattered with the cold. "Shit," Barney muttered. "Should've taken him inside right away, I guess, but the only thing on my mind was getting him breathing."

Jared didn't speak. Then he gave another racking cough and one after that. His throat must have been strafed raw; perhaps he couldn't talk. His brain seemed in working order, though: he understood that he'd been thwarted and glared at me in silent fury while I stripped off his soaked clothes.

A few minutes later, he and Barney, wrapped in whatever sweaters, shirts, and blankets we'd been able to turn up, sat in the heated cabin, drinking hot, tinned beef broth laced with whiskey. Jared's first drink of alcohol: an unforgettable occasion—if he let himself live to remember it.

"Jared," Barney said, fondling the zonked-out dog whose damp head lay in his lap, "I'm not about to start questioning you, so don't worry about that. But no matter why you *think* you did this, the real reason, the only reason, was that the pain was so damned bad that you needed to make it stop." He paused. Jared's swollen, reddened eyes met Barney's swollen, reddened eyes, but gave nothing back. "I told you before you jumped that I've been there. You need help, and it's beyond what a Grumbach can do for you." At the sound of Nate's name, Jared's jaw began to work. He coughed hard and turned his head to the cabin window.

"Okay," Barney said, "I'll back off for today, but I'll be back in your face tomorrow. See, I give a damn about you, Jared. Your parents do, whether you think so or not. And Lex cares more about you than about anything alive. But you're the one who needs to care, because otherwise you *will* kill yourself, and nobody'll be able to stop you." Jared's right eyelid began to jump; that was all. After a moment, Barney said, "I've got to go topside and get us back." He eased the sleeping dog's muzzle off his leg, put on a dry pair of jeans and dry shoes and left the cabin.

"Jared," I said, whispering as though there were someone to overhear, "I've done a terrible thing—the worst thing in my life. I let you die." The blank stare turned puzzled. "That's right. Left to my devices, you'd be dead. I couldn't have rescued you the way Barney did. I'd have gone in after you and we'd both have died. But I won't let you die again.

"No matter what it takes, I won't. I am yours now. Yours; only yours, no matter what . . . No matter . . ." I didn't know what came after that. When words boil up, ragged, edged in the blood of a wounded core, they are likely to be true, as mine were. They are also likely to sound less authentic, be less persuasive than artful, cool-headed compositions. His face was turned away from mine, refusing eye contact. "I haven't done much to earn your trust, have I?" I asked miserably.

He shook his head left to right, and ended up still looking the other way.

"I will now," I said. "I swear." And how would I do that? My mind thrashed desperately as a trapped bird, but for only seconds: the answer was obvious. It had been standing in wait since almost the moment I'd arrived from London. I knew perfectly well what Jared wanted of me, why he'd summoned me. Every fiber of my instinct had wanted to act, and had been quashed, as instincts often are, by the more powerful muscles of desire or fear or good manners. In this case, it was fear of a sort: a cowing fear that the grown-ups, the professionals, must know better than I did—I, the perennial damaged child. I, whom Nate had aptly cast as Peter Pan, the boy who would not grow up.

I had stood passively by, while they—while *Nate*—had failed. Maybe Jared was guilty, maybe not. Right at the moment, I didn't give a damn. Maybe the psychiatrist Barney advocated was the right thing, but *not now*, were words that instinct, its gag removed, cried out. Now I would finally give Jared the trust he needed if he were ever to trust me back. *Just a while,* I prayed to who knows what. *Just give us a little time to regroup. I promise . . . Please!*

"I will take you away, Jared," I said. "You and me. When we dock, we will get into my car and just go."

"Yes." It was a tinny croak, almost soundless, but it roared inside me.

"Good. That's good." I reached for his hands, still water-puckered and white. I took them between mine and tried to rub the residual chill away—or perhaps I just wanted to touch him. "Now, uh, here's the thing . . . Making our getaway will require us to do something really rotten to someone who deserves the opposite."

CHAPTER
33

Barney thought we should take Jared to the hospital for immediate emergency room attention. "I figure we were in the water maybe as long as seven, eight minutes," he said. "There was a hell of a lot of it inside him and it was damned cold."

"But you pumped it out of him and we warmed him up with soup and grog. The cough's calming down and his head seems to be working right enough."

While we debated these points, Jared sat in my car clad in big-bummed jeans rope-tied at the waist and the Aran sweater I'd worn my first time on the boat. Both these garments were the former property of Barney's former girlfriend—an indication of divine providence, perhaps.

"Makeshift. He needs some real doctoring." He ticked off the reasons. "Hypothermia, possible oxygen deprivation—maybe pneumonia. These are real, Lex. And his head *isn't* working right. For Christ's sake, the kid tried to kill himself!"

I took a deep breath. This was a good man, the *decent thing*, his default position, a part of his hard wiring. I noticed, as I had not till now, that one side of his face was strafed with angry scratches, battle scars of Jared's rescue. I hoped it had not been Jared's nails that had put them there. "Maybe you ought to be checked on, as well," I said. "Suppose I follow you to the hospital and call Melanie and Tom from there?" On impulse, I threw my arms high, encircling his neck, and pulled his head down within my reach, down to where I could feel beard-scratch, smell salt skin. I kissed the damaged cheek and then his mouth, long and hard. I felt giddy, drunk almost. "I love you madly," I said, and sprinted toward my getaway car before I could say anything else, or hear a response.

I did follow Barney's Jeep for a bit, waiting for some covering traffic. It came soon enough: a file of cars, boots no doubt filled with pies and casseroles; families tricked out in holiday kit en route to join their kin in offering up thanks for God's bounty. When the critical mass was sufficiently heavy, I let myself fall behind. Moments later, I took the first turnoff and made my way to I-95 South. I accelerated to the sixty-five-mile-an-hour limit, but took care not to exceed it. Police attention was the last thing we required now.

"Where we going?" The first half-strangled words out of Jared since his "Yes" more than an hour ago.

"New York, for starters. Barney thought you needed to see a doctor and he was right."

Jared moved toward the passenger door as though to open it. "No doctor!"

"Get your hand off that door now!" I said, suddenly furious. "If you open it, you will likely kill and maim a number of people, including me. When I said doctor, I

meant *medical* doctor. I'm not taking you to a shrinker just now, okay? Your lungs took in water—it's why you're still coughing—and you might have hypothermia. That means—"

Cough. "I *know* what it means."

Intellectual arrogance: that's my boy! But his hand returned to his lap. "Good. I want to make sure and get you any medicine you need, so you won't get sick on the journey."

"To whe-ere?" His damaged voice skidded.

"Don't try to talk till it's more comfortable. To wherever. We'll head south, I suppose. No good reason, just because." I glanced at him, didn't like the skittish tension in his face. "I left Virginia when I was six, never went back for a look. Shall I tell you about that?" Nod.

I talked and kept talking. My intention was to engage his mind, move it off the impulse to bolt. But as I began, I recognized that diversion was only a minor part of what was necessary. These weeks had reminded me often how little I knew the boy I claimed to love so well. It occurred to me now that the converse was equally true: he knew me barely at all. The glue that joined us was made of a preserved mutual illusion: I recalled a small boy who was nigh perfect by any criterion that mattered to me; he recalled an odd little female—not his mother—who approved of him utterly. The illusion had held fast a remarkably long time, but had lately dried out, grown brittle under stress, shrunk to a mere indulgence, its power equal to a spray of dried flowers. For what lay ahead, we needed a bond of flesh and bone and muscle—lots of that.

I didn't tidy up the story of my early plucking and transplantation, nor omit the violence I had imagined visiting on my mother when I'd taken a knife, as well as illicit food, to bed. I had never told that particular piece of it to anyone—not Tom, not Nate, not Barney. Thinking Barney's name caused a cold ache in my chest. I reheard the clear pitch of his voice shouting out to Jared about how he'd been there himself, tried to die. Truth, or exaggeration—a desperate reach to prevent Jared's jumping? I felt it must be true, though I wished otherwise, and I knew it was quite possible my calculated deceit could send him tumbling. I cared about that, but not enough to have acted differently, or wish I had— which made the ache throb harder.

All the while I talked, Jared's head rested against the seat back, eyes shut, not in sleep, but in concentration. I glanced at his blue-veined eyelids with their trim of black fringe and resisted an urge to kiss them. A Mobil station sat at the side of the road just ahead. I annoyed my fellow drivers by cutting across two lanes to reach it. Jared sat bolt upright.

"Sorry about that," I said. "I need to use the phone."
"Why a phone?"
I pulled round the side of the station to a row of grimy, open glass booths. "I want to apologize to Barney," I said carefully, "and let your parents know you're safe. Don't worry. We're not turning tail and going back. I'm going to leave the car door open so you can hear what I say."

He scowled and hunkered down into his blanket.

I punched in his number and my charge card's. Lucky I had my wallet; unlucky I didn't have my phone, which lay on a bed in Courtney's house. I had no way to know where Barney might be—home, hospital, or Courtney's, spreading the news. I hoped I would reach his answering machine, and I did. "I know it won't matter a damn to you," I said to it, "but I didn't betray you casually. I just . . . I had to get Jared away. I promise you it was important. Look after yourself. Please." I moved to hang up, but my hand drew the receiver back into talk position. "I *do* love you madly—I didn't lie about that." Then I did hang up.

At Courtney's, Tonya's aunt answered, "Anacleto residence," with the barely withheld challenge of one who disapproves of her environment, but feels nonetheless obliged to stay. It was just noon. Since the note I'd left said we'd be back round that time, there would be no reason for alarm, unless Barney had sounded it . . . "Is Mr. McQuade there?" I asked. "This is Lex. I need to speak to him. Only him." I listened to room noise for what seemed a long time. Finally, Tom's tight, "Lex?"

I had no planned speech in mind, and I clutched. "Tom, uh, listen I'm with Jared and he's okay. I won't say where we are, but we're staying away from Connecticut until . . ." I had no length of time to quote. ". . . until we get some things sorted. It may be a while." Lame, quite lame.

"What in hell are you talking about? You're gonna have to do better than that. I'll press star fucking six nine the minute we hang up and I'll know where you are."

"Were," I snapped.

"Hey, my son is 'okay,' but you've got him in some undisclosed place for an unpredictable amount of time—that about it? Now let me have the rest, goddamn it. Did you happen to forget you're talking to someone who deals in facts here? Also, rotten as I am at the job, you're talking to Jared's father."

"And you're talking to Jared's *mother*." Melanie on an extension was icy. "Can't you keep your hands off what's mine, you reckless little bitch! You bring him home now. If he's not here in one hour, I'll . . ."

"You'll what?" Her contempt stiffened my spine. "Call the police? In the reckless honors list, you far outclass me, sister."

"Quit bickering," Tom said. "Melanie, hang up." She didn't and breathed into the phone to underscore her presence. "This is my phone call," he said tightly, "and if you're not off it in five seconds, *I* will hang up and so will Lex. Believe it." This time, there was a click. "Hang on a minute," Tom said. Dead air while I thought about how to begin, particularly in Jared's hearing. Moments later, he was back. "I've got Melanie where I can see her. There's no phone in her hand. So talk to me, Lex. If you give me any bullshit, I'll come find you and bust your ass. You know I will."

My hand clenched on the receiver. "Facts: Jared tried to drown himself this morning. We took him out on Barney's boat."

"We. You and Barney decided on your own to take him sailing?" The tone was dangerously mild. Had I been within reach, he would have hit me.

"Yes, but that's irrelevant." I turned my back to Jared and spoke as quietly as I could, lips almost brushing the mouthpiece. "Jared's been planning this, Tom. He'd have drowned himself in a bathtub, or jumped out a window, or cut his wrists. So whatever rosy assumptions we made about the success of Nate's so-called therapy were dead wrong. If I bring him back now, you and Melanie will put him under lock and key, one way or another, for his own protection—and that would be a disaster. He'd submit, just as he did to Nate—what choice does a child really have? But all the while he'd be planning ways to try it again, and the next time he'd succeed. Your son is terrified and angry and desperate. As you know, he is also smart and quite resourceful. If I bring him back now, I believe that he'll try it again and he will succeed. So we won't be back until he's . . . a little more ready to come."

"When's that likely to be? And how will you know what ready is?"

"I . . . I don't know. Look, it's up to you what you say to Melanie, but I wouldn't tell her about the suicide attempt—or tell anyone. Jared needs some time and . . . Tom, I don't have the answers you'd like, and I'd like. But something went terribly wrong and . . . Just a bit of time. I'm with him."

It was after a few silent seconds that he said, "Put him on the fucking phone."

I held it out to Jared and beckoned him from the car. "Your dad. Tell him what you like."

He took the phone as though I were handing him something live, a snake, perhaps. "Da-ad. It hurts to talk. I breathed in water and my throat's sore." Cough. Pause. "No, I'm okay. Look, I *need* . . . to be away. No. *No!* I don't want to talk about it anymore. Well, I don't want to see *you*—or her." He thrust the phone back at me.

"For Christ's sake, Jared, your mother and I only want to . . ." The grief slicing through his voice was terrible to hear, far worse than the anger.

"It's me," I said. "Tom, I'm not wrong about this, but you'll have to take it on faith, because I have no more facts to give you. Jared will be safe with me. I promise I will spend every minute with him, day and night. I promise you that. I'm sorry . . . I'm ringing off now."

As we drove into Manhattan, our silence had an electric charge to it: fugitives on the lam, kids feeling the dark thrill of flouting adult authority, excited to have made the break, yet too edgy to muck about with words—scared that talking about what they were doing would destroy the speedy, pumped-up confidence they felt. I'd pled the case to Tom with everything in me, and for the moment had won a shaky first round. But we were *not* two children. So truly, how dare I be so unreasonably certain I was capable of keeping Jared safe? What if I couldn't? What if . . . ? My stomach went queasy for an extended minute. Screw that, I thought, I will keep him safe because I must.

I took the Ninety-sixth Street exit and went down York Avenue until I reached New York Hospital at Sixty-eighth Street. I found a parking garage and bundled Jared in his rope-tied jeans, flapping Aran, blanket, and wet sneakers into the hospital entrance marked Emergency.

"We're going to need to lie again," I told him briskly. "Your name will be James Cavanaugh, address and phone . . . oh, I'll make up something East Seventy-fourth Street, how about that? Look, your parents are skiing in Switzerland; I'm baby-sitting you, and we went to try out a friend's new boat, and you, who swim like a salmon, were seized with a cramp. Got that?" He nodded, grinning broadly.

CHAPTER
34

Our Thanksgiving dinner arrived on a room service cart in the Hyatt Hotel, attached to Grand Central Station. Just in case anyone took a notion to locate my blue Avis car, I turned it in. We would take the Metroliner to Washington, D.C., the following morning, rent a car there, and head wherever fancy took us. No one is impossible to track, but we intended to make it difficult. This piece of indirection was Jared's idea, a ploy not unfamiliar to any fan of adventure films. Thinking it up seemed to buoy his spirits.

The emergency room doctor (a round-faced, round-spectacled man, whose fat wedding band looked like a tight fit on his ring finger) had pronounced Jared reasonably fit, despite his body temperature's being a bit lower than normal still. He prescribed a preemptive antibiotic strike against "opportunistic infection" and a good night's sleep. The throat would cure itself, though lozenges wouldn't hurt. He advised me with some sarcasm to give up boating until spring. His assessment of my performance in loco parentis was unspoken, but hung in the air between us. Quite clearly he thought the *loco* part said it all—I'd never get within a yard of any kid of his!

Jared and I reclined on twin double beds, finishing the last morsels of pallid sliced turkey, damp dressing, and cranberry-colored jelled stuff. I felt no twinge of voracious appetite. More significant was the absence of urge in me to force an answer to The Big Question. Nate had asked me weeks ago whether my feelings for Jared would change if I learned he was guilty. At the time, I did not know. Now I did. They *would* change; they would deepen with pity, grow viscous with the drive to shield him. I would not love him the less. Peculiarly, or perhaps logically, that certain knowledge made me patient.

Jared gulped down the last of a tall Coke and turned to me. "You did it with my dad," he croaked. The coughing had abated; he simply sounded froggy now.

That was no news to him. He needed to chew it until he could swallow it or spew it out. "D'you hate me for it?"

"No. But, well . . . I've been thinking. It's worse on account of you being Mom's sister, isn't it?" I nodded. "I mean, my . . . *he's* slept with anyone who has a steady pulse—that's what Matt Drudge said—so he's the main bad one about sex, but still . . ." He held his hands out, palms up.

"You're perfectly right about the 'but still.' Look, I was not forced, coerced, or even persuaded. It was free will all the way. And I'm going to be honest with you, though perhaps I shouldn't be, loving your father and having sex with him were the best things that had happened to me up till that time—apart from loving you, of course—so I can't feel purely penitent. Blame me; it's okay."

He made a face that might have been simple embarrassment, or might have been something more complicated. "But you don't love him anymore?"

"Or 'do it with him,' either, if that's what you're asking. No, I don't love him anymore."

"You told Barney on the phone that you love *him* madly. Was that the truth?"

"I told his machine, not him. It felt true saying it; couldn't swear, though. I can swear that I *like* him madly, but I shouldn't think the feeling would be mutual any longer."

He nodded, brow furrowing into a single vertical crease between his eyebrows the way Tom's did. "What would've happened if you hadn't woken up that night?" he asked. I was a beat or two slow following his quick change of subject. "When you were six. What if your mother'd just taken off without you?"

"Ah. I've thought about that a lot. If I hadn't woken up . . . If Melanie *had,* and stopped us going . . . If I hadn't played at hiding in the backseat of the car . . . If Tilt Schwartz had changed his mind and not shown up to meet her . . . I used to lie in bed at night plugging the possibilities in and out, because I was certain that if a single one of those moments had gone a different way, I would be someone else entirely. But, you see, I don't really believe that any longer. I think now that perhaps I'd just be me with a different accent."

"You can't say that! *Some* moments change everything! What about a plane crash, and everybody burns up? What about . . . a hold-up in a liquor store and someone gets shot?"

"You've got a point, of course," I said. "But I think I do, too. Death—by natural disaster or man-made disaster—obviously changes everything for the victim."

"What about for the perp?" In another universe, the TV cop jargon out of his mouth might have made me laugh. There was no laugh in me now.

"Many things change for the perp," I said quietly, "but not everything. He still is who he is."

"Yeah," Jared mumbled with an inmate's resignation, and clicked on the huge TV set. Mercifully, it was football that came up on the screen. He lay back on his pillows and stared at it, his face empty of expression. Within minutes he'd dropped into an exhausted, heavy-breathed sleep. His hand remained curled round the remote, but when I tried to slip it out of his fingers, he clutched the thing white-knuckled tight and issued a fighter's angry groan. I left him just as he was, covered him up, and turned the set off manually. I risked a kiss on his forehead. It was damply cool. He did not stir.

I spent most of that night looking across from my bed to Jared's, the room lit only by orange slivers of street lamplight round the edges of the draperies. Under the thick, padded spread, his body would flip side to side in an occasional spasm of movement. Then he'd lie still as stone. I would shut my eyes and when they stopped smarting, fuzzy amoebic shapes would dance before them. But no sooner would I begin to drift off, than I would wake with a sense of urgency, as though late for a flight I needed to catch. And I'd look back over at Jared sleeping and feel the cold blade of panic tickle inside me.

The pure elation I'd felt over his rescue and our flight had sustained a few arrows of self-doubt. Now it plummeted like a loopily soaring bird shot in its manic head.

Here in the quiet dark I was forced to revisit just how narrow had been the margin between his life and death; what a fragile thing his survival still was. And I could not escape knowing that, for all my bravado, I was a dangerously inadequate custodian of it.

But that was not all: while I lay there, an outside observer of Jared's unmonitored inner journeys, as mysterious to me as anyone's are to anyone else, I believed in his guilt. For the first time it had the heft of reality, and the other scenarios I'd been brandishing were brightly colored silk scarves out of a desperate conjurer's sleeve.

I thought of Melanie living one day after the next, her grief compounded by that same belief, but despite all, Jared's mother as well as Calista's: a fierce mother, willing to throw her body—or anyone's—in front of her child's. I had grabbed that child and taken him away: a child in grave danger, a boy who'd tried to obliterate himself. I had no right.

And I lay there and swore silently to the hotel room ceiling that in the tangle that bound Jared and me together, it was solely *his* need, not my own, that had sent us running. Then I felt my gut begin to rumble, and thought, "Oh, Christ, not now." Out beyond the ill-closing draperies, orange lamplight had given way to the pale gray of very early morning, and I recalled searching Westport at about that hour for spicy food, making do with bagels . . .

I must have dozed at about that point, because when I opened my eyes, Jared was out of bed and the bathroom door shut. "Jared?" I called, my knuckles rapping the door hard enough to punish them. "Yeah, be right out." The normalcy of his voice was a shock. When I drew the curtains open, bold sunlight mocked my night thoughts, beaming doubt on all questions of truth, lie and wish, playing no favorites. I found I was only moderately hungry for breakfast.

On the way to Penn Station to catch our train south, we passed a telephone shop, where I bought a cell phone with five hundred prepaid minutes on it. Jared didn't care for the idea and let me know it.

"Why do you need to carry a phone? You think I'm going to try something?"

"Do I think so? You know I don't, or we wouldn't be here. Am I sure? You're going to have to make me sure, but I'm trusting you to do that."

I stuck out a hand and he took it. "Deal?" I asked. He nodded, looking down. "I'm buying this phone so we can make calls we want or need to, without disclosing where we are. Your father mentioned star six nine. That's not in our interests." He looked up and smiled. "Come on, partner, let's get some traveling clothes."

We stopped at Macy's, which was alive with hunters and gatherers harvesting the bounty of post-Thanksgiving sales. Floor to floor to floor we scurried with the other ants, my Barclay card flashing like a fencer's foil. In the end, Jared and I were refurbished from the skin out—a renewal superficial, but in some part of it genuine: one can never underestimate the redeeming power of virgin underwear and jeans that fit.

The station, as train stations will, housed newsstands. Jared and I had an ocular conference. "Buy them," he said, his face taking on a Tom-like cast—not the devilish one, but the one that said, "I will risk anything to know."

"Okay." I collected five, ranging from the *New York Times,* whose front page ignored the McQuades in favor of Middle East bombings, Balkan uprisings, and congressional shenanigans, to the *Star*, which carried a cover photo of Calista and Jared, and the headline, "Big Brother Did It." Fortunately, the photo was perhaps a year old and Jared's face a bit blurred, which rendered him indistinguishable from any one of a random clutch of dark-haired, thin-faced preadolescents.

The *Post* late edition headline shocked. Under the banner "Exclusive," it read: "Jared Gone." The story inside allowed our hearts to resume beating—no national manhunt was afoot. An enterprising reporter had staked out the house trolling for a Thanksgiving heart-tugger, questioned Jared's absence, and learned from Tom that Jared was having a quiet holiday out of town. "He's very close to Melanie's sister, and we all thought a change of scene would do him good." Detective Domingo had no comment, except to say that Jared's parents "were accountable for his whereabouts and are responsible for producing him should we need to interview him." Which sounded at once starchy and ominous.

Once we'd settled in on the train—new canvas satchel, packed with new clothes and new toiletries, stowed on an overhead rack—we passed the newspapers back and forth between us in silence. As we read, this morning's air of optimism deflated in a slow leak. It wasn't that there was fresh news, but the steady rain of pressure on Jared—from a rehash of the scrubbed astronomical drawing on Calista's hand to various "experts" speculating on the sexual proclivities of twelve-year-old boys in general and disturbed, jealous ones in particular—sent an unmistakable message: You can run but you can't hide.

Asking the question finally was not difficult, an anti-climax, if one is thinking in cinematic terms. I simply turned to him and said, "Will you be able to tell me what happened that night?"

He looked at me with a dull misery, the whites of his eyes still a sore pink from his try at ending it. "I guess so." His mouth barely moved as he said it, but the lower lip trembled a bit.

The railroad car was half empty; the day following Thanksgiving was a continuation of the holiday for most people and an off day for travel. The seat backs were high; the lighting low inside the car and through the tinted windows from outdoors. Still, the setting was far from private, chancy for strong emotion and dangerous revelation.

On the other hand, this was the moment; we both recognized that. It was not ideal, but it had arrived, and if let go by, could vanish or explode.

He began to speak quietly, the hoarseness in his raw throat lowering and cracking his voice into a curious blend of the little boy he'd been and the man he might become. By tacit agreement, we did not look at each other.

He began not at the beginning. "Mom came into Calista's room . . ."

CALISTA'S DOOR IS wide open. What Melanie sees inside is nothing she expected. Jared lies on Calista's bed, his knees hugged into his chest by tightly wrapping arms, his face slick with tears and snot. Dark red stains like random inkblots stain his pajama bottoms. At the clack of his mother's high-heeled mules on the polished wood floor, he makes a noise like the squeak of a terrified animal.

She runs to him. "My God, Jared, what is going *on* here? Where . . . Where's Calista?"

More squeaks. His mouth opens and shuts, but words don't issue. Her hands grasp his shoulders and begin to shake him. "Jared, you're hysterical. Now stop gibbering and tell me. *Where is Calista?*" The sounds stop; he is still. His eyes try to deny he has ever heard that name.

"What have you done to her?" The question is quiet, muted by sudden terror. Jared does not answer, just stares, slack-jawed as a sleepwalker. On its own, her hand draws back and slaps his face, not all that hard, but hard enough to sting him into intelligibility.

"Downstairs," he says blankly. "Cellar."

She takes his arm, not gently. They descend quickly, Melanie having kicked off the yellow mules, their percussive beat a jarring distraction. Jared leads her to the wine cellar. On the stone floor sprawls Calista, her neck blue and swollen, the garrote beside her like a discarded toy. Behind her fanned fair hair, a red-black puddle is beginning to soak into the stone. It takes Melanie a second look to realize that this is not blood, but red wine spilled from a smashed bottle several feet away from the body.

For a moment, they stand, mother and son: waxworks. Calista is dead—dead despite the white T-shirt with the gold star, the red biking shorts and tiger-headed slippers she wears (current favorite items, chosen one by one, during a recent "girlfriend" shopping afternoon with Melanie). In Melanie's boiling brain it seems mightily strange, not possible that a corpse could be dressed in clothes so full of Calista's life.

Suddenly, Melanie comes to pulsing life. She shakes Jared now in earnest, as though trying to shake the filth off a soiled rag doll. "Devil. Devil. *Devil! How could you . . . ?*"

"Mommymommymommy," he keens as his head lolls back and forward, in macabre rhythm to her fevered thrusts.

Abruptly, she stops. Jared loses his balance and falls to his knees on the floor. "Mommy, I didn't. I just . . . I didn't mean . . ."

"All right, right, ri . . ." Melanie mumbles to herself. "Shh. Shh." Jared remains crouched on the stone floor, gazing up at her. For what seems a long time, she is somewhere else. Then, she leans down and takes his arm as though it were a delicate thing. "Jared. Jared, listen to me," she says quietly. "Did you draw that on her hand?" He nods and makes and indefinable sound. "All right, I'll take care of it. We are going back upstairs now. You come with me. Just lean against me. I'll help you."

And she does. Her soft voice, gentle touch are hypnotic—he feels half asleep. His mother leads him into the bathroom and runs the water in the tub. She removes his wine-stained pajamas and helps him into the bath. There is no embarrassment, though he has not been naked in front of her for several years. Tenderly, she bathes him with a soft, soapy cloth. And when she has finished, helps him back out and dries him carefully. She fills a glass with water and takes a bottle of Tylenol PM pills from the medicine cabinet (Calista would occasionally need one to go to sleep when she was keyed up). She places two of them into Jared's hand. "Swallow them." After he has done so, she takes him to his room and fetches fresh pajamas from his bureau.

"Put them on," she says. "Good. Now get into your bed." Once he has settled under the covers, she leans over him. "You will sleep now. Those pills'll help. I will attend to everything. Everything." He stares up at her, round-eyed, in the grip of emotions he can neither sort nor comprehend, but through the haze, he recognizes that he has not heard that gentle mommy voice directed at him in a very long time.

"You will say nothing," she says, the voice sharpening. "Nothing. To anyone. *Anyone.* This is important, Jared." Her hand touches his cheek, fingertips pressing hard into it.

"Mom, you don't know. I didn't . . ."

"Hush, now." Her eyes are hot and dry. If a tear touched them right now, it would sizzle and disappear in a wisp of smoke, like water on a griddle. "I'll say it one more time. You were sleeping. You heard nothing, know nothing. That is all you'll tell the police—and all you'll tell Daddy, too. Now, you will obey me in this, to the letter. Because, if you don't, they will take you away and lock you up—and I won't be able to do a thing about it. Nobody will."

"NOBODY WILL . . ." Jared's voice deserted him here; sobs took over. He cried hard but quietly in the seat beside me. I reached for him now with both arms and held him, my ear fused to his chest, so that his heart seemed to be beating inside my head.

CHAPTER
35

The train began to slow. The public address voice announced, "In approximately five minutes, we will be arriving station stop, Baltimore."

"We're getting off, darling," I said, my voice supported by not much breath. His sobbing had stopped, but I continued to hold him in my arms as though he might otherwise fly apart, or I might. He did not try to break free. I loosened my grip now. "Hang on to yourself just for a little while, okay? We're getting off the train here." My hand felt loose in its socket as it reached to retrieve the canvas satchel from the overhead rack; my other hand held Jared's tightly and did not let go. "Easy, Jared. It won't be long. Just . . . easy." I kept up the murmur. Like a lullaby of sorts, it seemed to soothe.

Fifteen minutes later, on the advice of a cabdriver, we were checking into the Harborplace Hotel. Our room overlooked trash bins rather than the city's picturesque

Inner Harbor, but the desk clerk said it was the last room available and we were lucky to get it.

Once the door was shut and bolted behind us, Jared sank onto one of the beds. He sat there, fists clenched white-knobbed in his lap, as though they itched to punch hard at something. I thought of Calista's funeral—how he'd run off to the parking lot and punished his knuckles against the bright black car fender. "Bash the pillows, why don't you," I said, my breath in short supply, like a spent runner's. "Scream, if you want to. Holler and kick and throw things. Whatever you need. But know this: I won't leave you or betray you or let you get locked up no matter what you did."

"I didn't," he said very quietly. His face tilted itself sideways, startled by a strange idea. "Did you think I did?"

It was tempting to disclaim doubt, to remain the steadfast Poppins/Pan, but that would have been its own betrayal. "Sometimes."

"Well, I didn't," he repeated. "I tried to tell her that. I . . ."

"Why didn't you try harder?" My voice ragged, angry. More quietly I asked, "Why didn't you keep on telling her?"

Several beats went by. He looked down at the carpet. "I don't know."

The investigator's imperative leaped its barrier and took the field like a hunting dog, leaving tender emotion far behind. Jared became a quarry about to slip away. "Yes, you do," I insisted.

"She wouldn't've believed me."

"Why not?" Silence. "Why *not*?"

"Because I was mad at Calista; I . . . said things." Now I didn't prompt. He'd tell on his own; the rhythm was going. "I said if she'd died, I wouldn't miss her. I said she was . . . disgusting." I nodded. "Mom came in and heard me. She smacked me. It made my lip bleed." He rose from the bed and walked to the window. I followed, but not too closely.

"What did you really say? I don't want the sanitized version. You didn't say 'disgusting.' What was it?"

"Dirty fucking cunt," he said, his mouth so close to the window that the words left small, frosted spots on it.

"And how long ago was that?"

"About a week before."

We stood side by side now, watching a white-aproned kitchen worker fill a large trash barrel.

"There are things you're not telling me, Jared."

He slammed a fist into his palm with a nice thwack. "I thought you believed me. I thought . . . you meant all those things you said on the boat."

I grabbed his arms now in tae kwon do grip, which held firmly and not comfortably. "Don't you manipulate me; don't toy with me because you know I love you and you think you can get away with it. It isn't fair, and more important, it won't help. What I said about keeping you safe, not betraying you—those things are true. Now let's talk about truth on your side. I believe everything you've told me so far. But now, you've decided to edit, to hold back. You didn't kill Calista. What *did* you do?"

"Bad things." The lack of embellishment made the two syllables all the graver.

"Things bad enough that if your mother knew them, she'd write you off." It wasn't a question; it didn't need to be. He nodded almost imperceptibly. "I think she wouldn't have, you know," I said. "She thought you'd killed Calista and she stuck by you, anyway." He shook his head no and looked about to weep again. "I'll tell you what. Take that easy chair over there. Turn it to the wall and sit in it, so you don't have to look at me or feel constrained by my gawping at you. Then tell me all of it."

He did as I said with the air of the about-to-be crucified carrying his cross to the designated spot.

"I touched her. Naked," he said to the white corner. "She touched me and I touched her. I got hard and then she laughed. That night was the first real time, and she laughed . . ."

IT IS VERY LATE, well past two A.M. Jared and Calista, lying in their own beds, both awake, both feign sleep when Tom comes in to kiss them good night. Ten minutes later, Calista pads into Jared's room. "His face was like sandpaper," she says. "I think I could smell sex on him. Like fish. Yuck."

"Would you shut up and get out of my room."

"Ja-*red* come on." That voice, the one he hates, like some girl in the videos he'd browsed into, first by accident, then not by accident. "Don't be so mean. Did you see what I did at Mommy's party? I saw you looking at me." He doesn't answer, unsure whether he can stand to hear about this. Wanting her to go; not wanting her to go. "He started to mess with my butt and I bit his ear. Hard. Then I jumped off his lap. I was so mad, I almost told her right there." Giggle, like a cat running across piano keys. "She'd've . . . It's a good thing she sent us to bed, right?"

"Does that mean you won't . . . you know, any-more?"

"Not with him. He's yucky and I hate him." She

smiles a private smile. "Let's go downstairs, okay? We could do the wine bottle game. And would you make stars and things on my hand? They look really neat." She lifts the covers off him and puts her hand on his stomach, way low down.

"Stop it. Would you fucking *stop* it?!" He jumps out of bed.

"I'll be good if you come down to the cellar and play. I'm not sleepy, are you?"

"No." What *is* it about this sister of his? It's like she's a spell-caster out of a sci-fi movie—which is a stupid idea for a scientist like him to let inside his head, even for a second. But how else to explain this power she has over everyone—even him? "Maybe for a while," he says. "Just a little while. If she catches us, it'll be me who gets blamed."

"She won't catch us. It's two floors down from her room on the other side, and we'll be back in our beds in plenty of time before she's up."

Barefoot and quiet, they take themselves down to the wine cellar. The house's former owner had installed it, and briefly, at Melanie's urging, Tom had begun buying some fancy wines. But he'd lost interest fast. "Your daddy's not the collector type," she explained to her children, her mouth turning down in that sucking-lemon way it had. "Wine is fine, but liquor is quicker," was Tom's own explanation to Jared. "I don't drink much, but when I do, it's for the payoff." So nobody goes down there much. Except the kids . . .

Jared has brought down his box of colored markers. As the two of them sit propped against the cellar's stone wall, he carefully draws Saturn on the back of her left hand: Saturn is Calista's favorite planet, though Jared has told her more than once that her choice is banal—a cliché. Tonight, she wants it drawn in black and orange, commemorating the holiday. "That's gorgeous, Jar. Now stars. Could you do three?"

It's all going well. It is. The first time in two and a half weeks he has not wanted to strangle her.

"If you want," he ventures, "we could choke a couple of bottles." She nods enthusiastically.

Jared has designed this wine-bottle garrote—a length of twine tied between a pair of pencils, really, but the physics of it are far less simple than they look. The length and weight and flexibility are optimally calculated for the task: You loop it just so and toss gently till you catch one of the suckers round its neck. Then you tighten the twine round the pencils till you've got a firm hold. The real trick is to lift it out of its nest in the rack, reel it in, and set it down on the floor, all in one piece.

"I'll do one first," he says, feeling big brotherish, "and then you can help me on the next bottle."

Just as Jared has hooked the bottle's neck, Calista steps into his line of vision. She smiles and begins to lower her red spandex bicycle shorts, slipping them down over her slim, white hips.

"Don't!" he yelps, jerking the garrote and sending the bottle into a tinkling crash on the floor. "See what you made me do, you bitch." He lunges to smack her, but she gracefully sidesteps and gives him a full-moon ass. Then she whirls front again and removes the pants entirely, dancing slowly toward him, her bare feet knowing to avoid the broken glass.

And a funny thing happens: Jared freezes in place. He feels the hot swelling in his pajamas and can't move, can't think of anything but the glorious feeling between his legs. Calista's hands reach out for the elastic waist of his pajama bottom. Quickly, she flips it down in front, releasing his stiffened cock as though it were a trapped bird waiting to escape.

This is different. They have touched before—down there. She, playing with the zipper on his jeans, then taking his all too willing hand and guiding it inside her underpants. But not naked; never naked.

She laughs, the brassy ring of it loud in the small stone room. "It's such a cute, little one."

He goes nuts. Propelled by fury, his wiry body moves like lightning, catches her off-balance, tackles her with all its anguish. She topples over onto her bared ass, right into the mess of wine and glass and gives a small scream of surprise and pain.

"Good for you, you piss-pants bitch. I hope you die right there!"

JARED STOPPED TALKING. The only sound in the charged air was his breathing: the heaves of an over-extended runner. He made no move to leave the small armchair facing the wall. I felt my professional discipline eroding. I had to steel myself not to speak, not to go to him.

He restarted, as I knew he must. He sounded calm, except for the odd shuddering breath. "I ran up to my room. I figured I'd . . . just fucking leave her there—like it served her right. She'd manage to get herself upstairs; she wasn't unconscious or anything, and she was good at . . . taking care of herself. I couldn't sleep; I was just lying in my bed, watching the clock, listening for . . . her to come upstairs. I waited an hour; when she still didn't, I went back down and . . . saw her. After that, I don't remember, not until Mom came and found me . . . on Calista's bed."

Relief felt like cool milk running in my veins. But

quickly it was supplanted by a hot excitement of imminent knowing. I went to Jared now, knelt beside his chair and asked the question. "The man, the one she bit on the ear. Vin?"

He shifted position so as to look straight down at me. "Vin?! How could you be such an *idiot!?* Grumbach was the one," he bellowed into my face. "It was *Grumbach.*"

CHAPTER
36

Guy Fawkes; Fourth of July; Quatorze Juillet. Fireworks popped inside my skull as of *course* sparked to ignite *impossible* and send it up in flames.

"You're hurting my arm."

I wasn't aware I'd been clutching him and promptly let go. "Oh, Jared. Oh, sorry." Still on my knees, I felt blown backward as though in the path of a storm. Torrents of tears collided with gales of laughter, but neither exploded. They fizzled inside my brain—struck dumb by the staggering power of the revelation: The Pied Piper of Westport, warm-smiled, hot-blooded, cold-hearted, as he charmed us all to dance to his tune.

A child molester; a child killer, once he'd been rejected, found yucky. He was the one. I did not know how he'd managed to get back into the house to kill Calista, only that he must have. And how brilliantly opportune for him the existence of Jared! Jared alive and terrified would do for a while, but ultimate safety meant Jared dead: cornered, nudged into destroying himself by a virtuoso playing his stops of guilt and despair.

"Right you are," I said unsteadily. " 'Idiot' is a dead accurate description of me." Beat, beat, beat: he was staring at me, panning my eyes for some bit of gold. It dawned on me what he was searching for. "Jared," I said, "you did not do bad things. Repeat: you did not do bad things. Kids make passes at sex—'you show me yours, I'll show you mine'; 'let's play doctor.' You're on the ragged edge of adolescence. That you could be turned on by your sister is . . ."

"It's incest," he said stonily.

"No, it isn't. You touched each other and you got a hard-on. Period. In fact, you exhibited a lot of resistance in the circumstances. One might almost accuse you of Puritan instincts." I gave him a shaky smile. He smiled back, sort of. "At your age, I'd have welcomed someone to dabble with that way. I depended on a pillow between my legs and my own right hand."

As those last words left my mouth, Calista appeared in my mind's eye—no connection with Jared this time, just Calista, on her own. And I found my senses flooded with feeling for this magnetic child, a child so unlike the one I had been. It was not her awful death that triggered my pity, but a close recognition of the solitary, rampaging hunger she had lived with—an unbridled hunger. The personal bargains one makes both to feed and to control it was something I knew intimately.

Tonya had called Calista's a big hunger for love. How benign, the sound of that, benign in its very banality. Hunger for love: infernal theme of pop ballads, romance novels, wet-hanky movies. Calista's hunger proved malignant, not because she couldn't manage to feed it, but because she *could*—so easily, with such powerful finesse, even as her appetite increased. And being ten years old, she wildly misunderstood the nature of power, her own for a start, and was innocent of the velocity and force of sex. In the end, it was she who was disarmed, defenseless, wide open to the pestilence that killed her.

Jared remained in his corner facing the wall; I was still on my knees beside him. "Come on, Jared. I've pushed you into a replay of hell, but the worst part is over for you. You don't have to be afraid anymore." He made no move.

"That's what you think," he muttered.

"What d'you mean?"

"He's gonna get me. He said so, and he will."

"He said that?" I thought of those sessions, fifteen minutes of terror a day, his mother standing guard, his father neutralized, his aunt a willing dupe. And he, helpless, a prisoner.

"No. No he won't get you." It sounded soft as a pat on the head—mild words meant to placate. But it was the plainest truth: he would not get Jared. And there would be no Domingo called in to mediate, to weigh Grumbach's word up against Jared's, alternative mounds of minced beef on a scale, the boy's version a bit tainted, the shrink's more reliable in color and texture. My body would be covering Jared's this time. I can't say to what degree my resolve in this was stiffened with outrage at a mosquito nip—less than a mosquito nip—when compared with murder, molestation, and mental torture: Nate Grumbach had played on my own hungers, toying with me, coaxing me bit by bit into making an utter and dangerous fool of myself.

"I will get him," I said, flat out.

"Right. How would you do that?" Jared asked, his lack of faith waving in plain sight. Not surprising: except for the past thirty hours, I'd done fuck-all to inspire credibility.

"Well, I can't know that yet, can I? But you're going to help me find out. In effect, *we'll* get him. You are a budding scientist; I am a journalist: we deal in facts. You've told me some crucial ones, and you'll tell me the rest. But first, I want to tell *you* something that you may not realize: You are brave and strong in your spirit. You withstood him better than the adults round you did."

"Bull*shit*. I'd've been dead, except for Barney."

An arrow straight to the heart. "True, but it took a lot to get you to that point. Come on, Jared, you don't need to look at the wall anymore. Unless you want to."

After a few seconds he shoved the chair back and rose. "Maybe we could take a walk or something," he said.

"WHY ARE YOU so sure he killed Calista?" Jared asked. We walked the Inner Harbor waterfront, famously developed a decade and a half ago into mall-like consumer-friendliness: a small woman and a tall boy, undistinguished in the holiday weekend crowd except for the baroque nature of their conversation. "You talk about facts, science. How did he get into the house? There's no way Calista would've let him in this time. She hated him."

"What do you mean, *this* time?" I asked sharply.

"She did the other time—the time I saw them."

Ping. I recalled Jared in his sickbed, trying to armor himself in a quilt. I'd asked him whether someone in the house might have let her killer in. He'd said, "Maybe," eyes glazy sad, and had quickly switched to, "No." I hadn't pursued it, honoring my promise to Nate to back off while he worked his psychological sleight of hand. Hatred filled me up as though I were an empty tumbler. I could feel the corrosion; I thought it might burn clear through the flesh like swallowed lye.

I reached for Jared's hand, and he gave it to me. Holding it seemed to stanch the poison's progress. "Tell me about that time, okay?"

"Okay." His hand gripped mine a bit tighter. He cleared his throat, and cleared it again.

"Does it still hurt a lot, your throat?"

"Not so much. Sort of. I guess I'm nervous." He cleared it one more time. "It was October tenth. I . . . like, I really couldn't believe what was happening . . ."

His hoarse monotone was a colorless backdrop, against which the events he described played themselves out in lurid color.

IT IS A TUESDAY night. Jared has been reading, which usually helps him fall asleep, but not tonight. He doesn't really know why. Things have actually been going okay, for a change. Maybe Grumble's right, he thinks, and I can't stand the good times because I know they're going to turn bad. Grumble is right about a lot. Grumble: that's his special name for Dr. Grumbach. And right after she found that out, Calista started calling him Grumpa (giggle, giggle). Of course she did—Calista, who always busts in, always sucks up the light and the air. Always.

He's been seeing Grumble since before school started—that's the way Mom puts it, "seeing." "You're going to begin seeing this doctor, Jared, if I have to handcuff you and drag you there," followed by "Admit it, wasn't I right? Since you've been seeing him, things are worlds better for all of us. I haven't had one complaint from your teacher yet—that's a whole month!"

Jared *sees* Grumble two times a week at five o'clock. But since the beginning of September he's been literally seeing him far more frequently: Grumble and Mom have become kind of friends, which worried Jared big time at first, and which he still doesn't much care for.

But by now, Grumble's at the house for dinner and they've eaten at his place a few times—which feels weird: all of them chomping lasagna in the same place where he talks about his fucking feelings, his worst secrets. No matter how much Grumble explains to him about "my vow of confidentiality" and "your need to be able to trust," he hates it.

All this confidentiality and trust shit wasn't supposed to be part of the deal, anyway. Seeing Grumbach was going to be about school stuff, not real stuff—about doing the boring homework and not blowing up in class. But it had gone way past that.

He'd told about him and Calista touching, spilled that one last week, and only because Grumble uncannily already seemed to *know*. Jared tosses in his bed, too hot under the covers, too cold when he kicks them off. He glances at his clock. It's ten past one. He needs something to get his mind off . . . whatever it is. Oh, come on, he knows damn well what it is: he wants to jerk off—jerk off and think about his sister, and feel his bottom half melting to hot syrup. Is that sick or what?! He sits bolt upright and wonders if he dares risk going down to the cellar, snagging a couple of bottles with his twine-and-pencil gadget. He decides he can: Dad's out of town, which means he won't be coming into Jared's room at some unpredictable hour with his sour-smelling good-night kiss.

Jared throws off the covers one final time and leaves the bed. He begins to descend the stairs and almost loses his balance when he spots Calista, dressed in a short red-and-yellow-striped sleep shirt, opening the kitchen door. He's about to cry out, "No, don't"—in fear that she'll trigger the alarm. But somehow he doesn't, and a split second later, when the door swings open, he hears no piercing shriek. Amazed, he watches Grumbach march into the house, lean way over, and plant a kiss on his sister's lips.

Calista gives her long, musical giggle, and Grumbach giggles back, a laugh different from any Jared has ever heard out of him. Jared, his mouth locked into a mute O of disbelief, creeps silently down the rest of the stairway, not fully aware that he's in motion. In some cranny of his brain he knows where they're headed. He follows behind, hanging back, taking care not to be seen or heard. He waits until the heavy door to the wine cellar closes, and then crouches beside it, bending his head to where the frame is slightly warped, enough to provide a lighted crack's worth of view inside, if you know just where to put your eye.

The sound through the door is muffled; anyway, they're not saying much. Grumbach smoothes his hand over Calista's hair and loosens it from it's ponytail, so that it falls silkily round her face, like a mermaid's. When he reaches down for the hem of her sleep shirt and pulls it up, Calista raises her arms high to help in getting it off. They know what they are doing, have done it before—anyone could tell that. Jared may strangle on his own bungee-jumping heart.

Calista stands, posing like a statue, one hand on her

hip, ass a bit stuck out to the side. In the dim overhead light, her rump cheek gleams like a peeled boiled egg. Grumbach, fully dressed himself, kneels before her like a worshiper in church and smiles right into her face. His hands run themselves like a pair of playful brown animals down her pale, stretchy, flexy body: neck, chest, hips—stopping to stay awhile on that shiny ass. Then one of the brown rats moves to her front. Is his finger in her slit? Jared, who cannot quite see, wonders. Is it messing round in there? And stunned, fevered with outrage as he is, Jared does not scream or faint or run to get his mother. Instead, his eye pasted against the viewing crack, he colludes with his own wayward hormones in an unthinkable response: the biggest, hardest, hard-on in his five months of experience with that phenomenon.

Calista stands still, but her pose is gone. Now, she's just standing, looking uncomfortable, like she'd like to sit down. Grumbach stands up and goes for a plastic bag he was carrying when he came in. He pulls out some blue cloth and holds it up to show Calista. A bathrobe. He helps her put it on and motions her to sit, and then sits beside her. His position blocks Jared's view of everything but his back.

The treble voice and the bass alternate, but Jared cannot make out the words. Then the talking stops. He imagines Grumbach unzipping the front of his pants, reaching inside his shorts, and producing with a magician's flourish a cock the color of a shrunken head and kind of flabby. At the mental picture, Jared's own erection wilts.

What if right now Calista's hand is being placed on the shrunken head? Does she pull back, reluctant to touch it? Or does her hand go right to the spot, knowing its business.

And still Jared does nothing.

But when his mind serves up Grumbach's brown paw capping Calista's head, beginning to guide it downward, he springs up from his crouch and throws open the door.

"Aaargh! Leggofuckinbastard*getout!*" The sounds come out of him in a garbled howl.

In an instant Grumbach is up; so are his pants, properly zipped. Calista, the blue robe hanging open, starts to move toward Jared, but Grumbach, his arm round her shoulder, restrains her. "Jared," he says, in the calm rumble that sounds so normal that Jared wonders for a split second what's real, what's in his own loony head. "Jared, pull yourself together, boy."

Jared stares at the two of them, his hectic breathing for a moment the only sound in the stone cellar. Then he manages to say, "You . . . get . . . out of . . . our house. Now." His voice is a shaky, down-the-well echo.

"Jared," Calista says. "Don't tell. Please don't. Mom will . . ."

"Jared won't say a word," Grumbach says quietly, his black eyes trained on Jared's, which are almost, but not quite, as dark. "For one thing, no one will believe him. Now, you know that's true, don't you, my boy?"

"Not your boy," Jared says through gritted teeth.

"Fair enough. And for another, we have our own secrets, you and I. I think you've imagined tonight, don't you? I think it all grows out of your own rich fantasy life about Calista, wouldn't you agree? Calista would agree." He gives her arm a little squeeze and smiles down at her.

"Jared," she says, "I know you think this is so bad, but you don't understand; it's not . . ." He can see she's scared. She looks sweaty and sounds like she can hardly breathe. "Really, I *want* to . . ."

"Who're you trying to convince, me or you?" Jared asks. His mouth has a funny metallic taste in it, and his knees are shaky, as though they're going to dissolve. "This is sick, Calista. Puke, disgusting." He makes himself look straight at Grumbach. "And it's a crime."

Grumbach nods slowly, not in agreement. "Don't take me on, Jared, I warn you. If you try, you will be one sorry boy, because I'll get you. And you know I can." All of this was said in a tone intimate, almost loving. This was the way he often sounded in their sessions together—like someone stroking your forehead with his voice. "Consider the things you've done with your sister, the things you've dreamed about doing. Maybe tonight is just a figment of your overactive imagination. I think that's it, don't you?"

Jared's voice did not waver in telling this last part, but his hand gripped mine painfully hard, like a battle-field casualty undergoing surgery without anesthetic. I would have believed him even absent the detail of the blue robe. Afterward, we walked wordlessly for quite a while down toward the quieter, less developed part of the waterfront. The day was ending, not sunny as it had begun, but gray cold.

"Dad was out of town a lot in September. That's probably when they started to do . . . this stuff. They must've planned it for those nights. Otherwise . . ." Jared beat back tears. "Otherwise, they wouldn't've *dared*, 'cause Dad would come home at strange times, you never knew when, and he could have . . . Mom would have said I was lying, if I told her—she's such a wuss for Grumbach, like he's God." The voice broke and some tears escaped. "I should've gone to my dad," he said quietly. "I should have at least tried."

His integrity sliced through the still air, pure as one

of those high-frequency notes with which certain rare singers are able to shatter glass. It made my head ring with thanks for the inner strength and last-minute good luck that had fused to keep him alive. "Yes, your dad. That would have been the thing. For what it's worth though, I don't think in your place I'd have been able to do it, either."

"You're saying that to make me feel better."

I stopped walking. Joined hand in hand as we were, he did, too. "Jared, you were mind-fucked by an expert. You didn't have a chance of outfoxing him. But he's had a bad break, you see. You're alive. He wanted you out, and he almost won that point. Almost."

"What's he gonna do now?"

I had no ready answer. I knew a fair amount about Nate Grumbach, if I set to piecing shards together in the way I'd do if I were researching a film. But every shard of his reflected itself back at me in fun-house-mirror distortion. Every word he'd said; every pithy observation, warm, homely smile; every squeeze of Melanie's shoulder, stroking of my hair; each had new shape, dimension, new texture, now that I knew he was a monster.

"I'll have to give that some thought," I said finally, weakly. "And we're going to need to be quite clever about what *we* do. He's a professional reader of people and knows us rather well, both of us. We shall have to find a way to surprise him."

The fear returned to Jared's face, giving it that pale custard look it had had when he relived the events in the wine cellar. "I don't want to go back now. I . . . can't."

I took his chin gently between my thumb and forefinger and lifted it, just a bit. "We're not going back now. We will go back when we're ready to make our move. The only way he's sure to win is if you scuttle yourself. Look at me and tell me I can count on your not doing that."

He swallowed hard; I watched his adolescent Adam's apple bob like a cork. "The second I jumped, I was so damned scared I wet myself."

"That is the best news I've heard in quite a long time."

"But wait, Lex, you never answered me. How *did* he get back into the house on Halloween? I told you Calista said she hated him. Besides, he didn't know when Dad was gonna come home. And . . . and then after he did come home, I went down in the cellar with Calista. *So how did Grumbach get back in the house?*"

"Can't say yet," I admitted. "But since I'm dead sure that he must have, I will find out. And that I promise you." I was doing a fair amount of promising, it occurred to me, unsupported by anything one could call a plan. But Jared was innocent and alive!

The empty rumble returned to my stomach. "Look," my voice was raucous with tamped down panic, "we've missed lunch and I'm bloody starving. I'll bet you are, too. We're in Baltimore—have you ever eaten a crab cake?"

CHAPTER
37

The hotel bathtub was huge; they often are. I crouched inside it, the tub empty of water, the cell phone in my hand ready for use. Jared, on the other side of the locked door, lay in bed watching an *X-Files* rerun marathon. Fortunately, the hotel room was large, walls and doors old and substantial, and Jared's bed was the one farthest from the bathroom. Not the ultimate in privacy, but as the alternative was to leave Jared alone for a bit, it would do.

I hunkered down lower in the shelter of the tub, punched in the number, and held the receiver hard to my ear. He answered almost immediately, as though he'd been waiting. "Grumbach here." It was what he always said, and it sounded no different. How remarkable. I said nothing, barely breathed. "Hello?" I stood there silent as the sweat moved down my scalp in tickling rivulets. "Hello?" he asked again, a bit more tense, though perhaps no more so than one might be with any crank caller.

Then, after a moment, a long one, he said, "It's no good this way; you know that."

He sounded almost wistful: a lover, a father. Small pause. "I'll bet you're on the edge of a binge right now, aren't you? I can help you with that. I did before, more than anyone ever has. I fed you, I soothed you, gave you what you needed. You can't be responsible for Jared, the state you're in—too dangerous. You're really such a child yourself. Why, you might run off and leave him, if you really had to eat." Salt sweat ran from my forehead to sting my eyes. I bit my lips together and waited. "Come on back, Lex. I miss you." He hung up gently, almost without a click.

He expected your call . . . He was waiting for it . . . He knows you so well . . . He'll know . . . No, no, go back to how well you know him. I made myself focus on the mechanics of calming panic: five seconds before inhaling, five more before letting out the breath; keep the mind in neutral. It took some time, crunched there in crash position, but my breathing began to slow and the heart followed along. I realized that while this call I'd been impelled to make had dealt me body blows, it had unsettled Nate, too. I knew him well enough to know that.

"You are working," I said aloud. The porcelain shell gave me back a faint echo. "You do not pollute work with your damned binges. And you promised to keep Jared safe."

I sat up now, still inside the tub, legs curled under in something resembling comfort. Then I made the call I'd intended to, before the impulse to hear Nate's sound took me over.

Barney answered his phone half a ring ahead of his recorded voice.

"Barney, it's Lex. Don't hang up."

"I didn't plan on hanging up," Barney said coldly.

Neither evidently did he plan on saying another word until he'd heard what I had to say for myself. I reckoned this must be good technique for a teacher dealing with a recalcitrant student; I know how useful it can be in interviewing a subject.

I thought to say again that I was sorry I'd had to lie to him. I thought to say that he'd placed his trust in unworthy hands. But I didn't say those lame things. I said, "Jared is innocent. And I know who's guilty."

"Let me guess," he said acidly, "Nate Grumbach, right?"

The power of speech left me briefly. "Is this a joke? Because if it is, it fails to amuse."

"For Christ's sake, Lex, don't you get what's going on? I'm going to bet that Jared told you it was Nate, and had a harrowing story to back up the accusation. Now, there's an outside chance that he pointed the finger at Vin, or even at me, but Nate's the odds-on favorite; he's the target for anger and fear. This is *rage* you're hearing from Jared, this is *desperation*. This is one very fucked-up kid, a kid who tried to kill himself. And he needs help that you can't give him, no matter how much you love him."

I could hear the voice behind Barney's words. "Are you quoting Nate to me?" I asked, the question unnecessary. "Does he know about the suicide jump?"

"I don't think so. Tom drove over to my place just a little while after your call, the one I didn't pick up, and said it was classified—his word, not mine. He said you'd called him from the road, and that he'd decided to skip telling Melanie, or Nate or anyone for now, and he'd appreciate my keeping quiet, too."

"Good," I said faintly. Tom's trust was not given lightly. That I had it meant a great deal to me.

"It was weird," Barney said. "There we all were at Nate's table giving thanks, and not one guest had a thing to be thankful for. So nobody said much of anything, except how good the food was, and mostly we kept our eyes on our plates. Of course, everybody was solicitous about my cough and hoped I wasn't getting the flu, and I should be sure to stay off the boat until it got better.

"Melanie explained that you'd taken Jared off for part of the weekend. 'Just a little break,' was how she put it. Your sister could play Lady Macbeth on my stage any time, but I think Nate knew something was up. You know, I made myself go to the damned dinner for one reason only: I was nose-diving into sad territory, and I was scared as hell to be alone." Having muted the call of chili and hot sausage for the past two weeks behind a baffle wall of constant company, I knew what he meant. Averting a crash of his sort must be harder, the stakes far higher.

"I'm glad," I said softly enough that he might not have heard. His grit did not absolve me from blame, nor should it have. I'd known quite well what my actions might cost Barney. "You are, though, quoting Nate. Aren't you?"

"Roughly," he admitted.

"What happened to the man who told me that he knew kids, had a *feel* about them, and that Jared wouldn't've done that crime—not in that way."

"I said I couldn't see Jared constructing a garrote to kill his sister. How many teachers at Columbine High School do you think would have predicted those boys planning and carrying out a massacre?" His voice had the plastic edge of a debater making calculated points against his own grain. "It's obvious I don't know much about much," he said in a different tone altogether. "Let's chalk my omniscience about Jared up to a rare case of postcoital enthusiasm." I could picture the quirked down corner of his mouth, the mocking half smile.

He was giving as good as he'd gotten yesterday. He meant to wound and did. "I know you're furious with me. How could you not be? But I plead with you, Barney, don't take it out on Jared. It's not his fault. And . . . and . . . and you saved his life; that means you're responsible for it." I drew a shaky breath and realized I'd best shut up.

"Why did you call?" he asked.

"Because . . . Can I ask you something first?"

"No, you can't." He held all the cards: he could simply hang up. And, all things considered, might.

"Because I need your help. *We* do, Jared and I. Nate Grumbach is good: I can give you chapter and verse on how very good he is. He had me programmed like a Pavlov dog, and he had Jared programmed, too, to kill himself. That's what this damned therapy was all about, driving Jared to check out." I heard a skeptic's exhale. "Look, you yourself questioned why a real doctor wasn't called in to prescribe medication for this depressed child. Nate didn't let that happen, right? It would have interfered with his *'process'*—bet your bloody arse it would have! Wasn't it you who found Grumbach a bit Rasputinish?"

"Quit it. All I've heard out of you is a mess of conjecture. It still boils down to he said /he said—and in this case you know how the weight balances out."

"What I know is that he's given you precisely the right arguments to discount the truth he knew I'd get out of Jared."

"How the hell can you claim it's true? Have you got a supporting fact, even one?"

I shut my eyes tight and prayed he'd see it. "I do, actually. There's this blue bathrobe . . ."

I told him what I'd heard from Jared—all of it, beginning with the night he'd found Nate and Calista in the cellar, Calista wearing the blue robe. And then I told him of my private encounters with Nate, excepting the phone call I'd just made, which might cause him to judge me entirely mad. I worked hard to lay fact upon fact, to delete editorial comment before it reached my tongue.

No sound at his end, just the swish of room noise that told me he hadn't left. A fresh track of sweat trickled down between my breasts.

"Barney, I never mentioned a word about Nate's giving me his wife's robe, my wearing it—not to you, certainly not to Jared; not to anyone. I was far too embarrassed about . . . the way it plucked my own strings."

"It would be a major coincidence, I suppose: you, Calista, the robe," he said, wanting—not wanting—to believe. He sounded flat-out exhausted when he asked, "What do you want from me?"

"More than I have any right to ask. For starters, I want you to keep to yourself everything I've just told you. And I . . . if you could—if you *would*—I'd be grateful for anything you can turn up about Nate's dealings with children in the school, anything that strikes you as odd. Oh, and he told me that his late wife was a dancer. She died of MS. He took care of her the whole time. Her name was Zip, proper name Zipporah. I don't know what last name she used, but she danced with the Martha Graham troupe and then with Paul Taylor, so she can't have been much younger than Nate."

"Are you implying that Grumbach killed his wife?"

"That would make a neat package, wouldn't it, all tied in ribbons? No, I'm just panning for gold. It's the way I'm used to working: sift enough, mine enough, eventually you get lucky. Just possibly, some facts about her—her illness, her death—might cast some light. You see, I think all this is about girl-women: Zip, Calista, me . . ." I pictured Nate spooning soup into my open mouth, like a father bird; recalled the sound of him not half an hour ago, *you're really such a child yourself*. A shudder snaked through me.

"Sorry, but that's going to need some explaining."

"Girl-women: childish women; womanly children. I don't know what his wife was like except that she was very small, like me. Calista was in some way quite a womanly child, and I doubt you need chapter and verse on my . . . lack of maturity." My voiced quavered, and I said no more.

"Would it be banal to suggest the police?"

"Worse than banal: disastrous," I said sharply. "Nate would run rings round us, serve Jared up like John the Baptist. You believed him; Domingo would, too, and our chance to get Grumbach would be shot. I don't think we'd get a second."

"Okay," he said tonelessly. "Got it."

"You mean you'll help? You *will*?" I squealed like a schoolgirl asked to a dance—the sort of schoolgirl I'd never been.

"I will do what I can."

"We're traveling, Jared and I. I'm not sure where to next."

"I think I don't need to know where you are. Just call me in a couple of days."

"Right. And one more thing . . ."

"I'm about thinged out."

"What I did to you—breaking faith—it didn't push you down the rabbit hole."

"You looking for absolution, my child?"

"Certainly not. I'm looking for the chance to tell you that you're a strong, well-woven piece of goods and I admire you."

"Thanks," he said wryly, "I'll make a note of that in my memoirs. What about you? Sounds like you managed to overcome the urge to curl up with a dozen take-out containers of curried goat?"

I laughed. It was a real laugh, quite spontaneous, but it died a quick death. "I haven't overcome it; I just haven't done it. Thanks for asking. Friend."

JARED WAS PROPPED in bed, eyes riveted to the screen—more specifically, to his grandmother's face, ever so slightly surgically tampered with, I thought, since the last time I'd seen it. It was a small shock for me now to note how very like Melanie she was in appearance, mannerism, even in sound; it must have been a larger one for him.

". . . not accusing Melanie, Barbara." What a kick she must be getting out of chatting it up with Barbara Walters. "Of *course* I'm not; how could I know what went on there? What I *am* saying is that my daughter was a dangerously reckless girl, and people don't change. Somehow, she put that child in jeopardy—and I mean sexually." Better than a quarter century in Britain and Australia had staked no claim on the shape of her vowels. Somehow, the soft accent of the American south lent a terrible credibility to her words.

"Jared, don't you want to turn that shit off?" As it happened, he didn't need to. *20/20* broke for a commercial: the segment was over. I went to him and ran my hand over his dark head, damp still from a shower. "She's dreadful."

He turned his head toward me. "She's right, though. My mom was always pushing Calista at him, laughing about how *cute* it was when she rubbed up to him. She'd call Calista 'Grumpa's girl.' How could she be so *dumb*? A mother's supposed to know stuff, isn't she? Great pair, my parents: she's fucking clueless, and he's just *fucking!*" The circles under his eyes were like bruises. The eyes themselves were blurry, as though he'd done some more crying.

"You can blame her from here to hell and gone, but I promise you it won't help. Think this about her instead: She believes you killed Calista, and she is willing to risk anything to protect you—even to leading the police into thinking *she* did it. You know, when I was six, she was my hero. I . . ." Tears threatened: old ones. How singular to be six, worshiping a hero—such an insular egg that all you knew of said hero were the embracing arms and dazzling smiles she reserved for you, and the fact that she would be yours forever . . .

He said, "The grandma from hell, she looks just like my mo-om," the word fractured by a wide yawn. "Sounds like her, too, sort of. She isn't one bit like you. Heredity or environment?" he asked, sleep-slurred.

"Complicated." It certainly was that. I pulled his covers up round his chin and snapped off the TV and the light.

"Why don't we go there tomorrow?" he murmured, eyelids at half-mast. "Norfolk . . . so I could see where they . . ." And he was off into a soft snore.

I felt a buzz of excitement generate at the base of my spine. "We'll see," I said to myself.

CHAPTER
38

We sped down I-95 on a gray morning in a red Honda.

Jared's finger traced the highway on the large road map spread across his knees. He'd peppered me with family history questions from Baltimore to Richmond. The answers I had were odd-shaped scraps that pieced together badly and tended to melt on the tongue like snowflakes. I did not volunteer the bathroom standoff scene with my father, but it jabbed inside my skull, causing an ache. I reminded myself that we were taking this journey to divert Jared's mind. My own initial enthusiasm for the expedition had overnight cooled to zero.

"You don't remember much about Norfolk, do you?" he asked, disappointed.

"Funny, I seem to remember smells more clearly than events. My mother wore a scent called Arpege, and my father, Canoe." Jared would have recognized Canoe, not by name, but from Nate's dark jowls; I did not mention that now. "Melanie's hair smelled of honey, and the kitchen of orange rind. I have the idea that orange juice was always being squeezed fresh."

"How will you know where to find the house?"

"I'm a reporter of sorts, like your dad. Do you think he could find it?"

"Yeah."

"Then so can I." I so wanted him to have more confidence in me than I had in myself at the moment.

His fist slammed the dashboard. "Why're we *doing* this, anyway? I mean, everything back in Connecticut's the same way it was: he's the shrink and I'm the nut-job. We're just jerking off here."

"Jerking off has its uses," I said.

"My parents think I killed her, and by now so does everybody else."

"Not everybody."

"I didn't mean you."

"Barney doesn't. Jared, I spoke with him last night." My eyes were trained on the road ahead, so I felt rather than saw his quick turn toward me. "I didn't tell him where we were, but I told him everything else—I mean I told him about Grumbach and Calista . . . and you."

"Shit! Why did you . . . ?"

"Because I wanted his help, and to get it he needed to know that you were not just a disturbed kid who'd tried to kill himself out of guilt." I paused and took a quick glance at him. "He believed you," I said.

"What do you want Barney to do?" Jared asked, sullen—about as pleased as I'd have been in his place that such a call had been made without his consent.

"Come up with facts we can use. He can look into things back there that I can't. He can ask round the school, find out if something similar went on with

another child. He's also going to try and uncover anything in Grumbach's past life that might ring a bell."

"What if he can't?"

A question I'd asked myself, when I awoke during
the night every hour or so. "Stop it, okay? This is thinking time, whether it seems that way or not."

"How did he get into the house?" Jared asked, yet
again.

"Dunno," I answered, one more time. My thinking
had not yet struck oil in that well. Nate's face appeared
in my mind's eye, crinkling into folds as it winked at
me, told me that of *course* I knew, if I'd only think
properly . . .

"He never told me I should confess, you know. Every
day in those *sessions* my mom made me have, he'd just
stare at me like some creepy hypnotist and repeat this,
like, mantra: 'The truth is your only hope to go on living.' But, duh, what he *wanted* was for me to say I
killed her." And Jared's stubborn conscience and orderly
mind, pushed farther into a corner daily, had decided to
quit living instead. I wondered how he could ever get
past this. Ever, no matter how it turned out.

As though reading my thoughts, he gave the dashboard another bash, but with less vigor. "Do you know
that hidden matter might make up, like, ninety-nine percent of our galaxy?" he asked.

"I didn't, no."

"Well, it does. They can tell, because the stars we can
see are sailing along at a hundred miles a second, but
the ones we can't, the ones in the outermost part of the
Milky Way, by redshift measurement, their average
velocity is twice that. So, what's the unseen matter?"

"I've got no idea."

"Neither do the scientists, even the famous ones.

Some of them say it could be plain old rock, or it could be exotic stuff no one's ever heard of. They just don't know." The scientific world might be in the dark, but Jared just cast light on something more personally vital to me than any galactic matter. He had given me the clue that the passion in his blessed fertile mind would help him recover. A passion to know: it was his strongest ally—had been, would be. And while this insight handed me no panacea, it did hand me something of worth.

"Have a look at the map, smarty," I said. "About how long before we get to your favorite stretch?"

"You mean the D.S.? Looks like only five miles or so." What was officially called The Dismal Swamp was an old, slow route going from Richmond through Newport News, but I turned off and took it just because its name made Jared laugh, and that was a precious commodity just now.

Norfolk is a peninsula, connected to the mainland at various points by bridge-tunnels. It is more sailor's town than anything else: the U.S. Navy is its largest industry, and many retired, as well as active, naval personnel live there. However, it also retains descendants of old families, some of whom are part of the self-designated piece of American royalty called First Families of Virginia. I'd researched the city exhaustively when I was an adolescent pining for some connection to it. I learned back then that prior to the 1860s, Norfolk's harbor rivaled New York's in its shipping activity. The port of Norfolk never quite recovered from the Civil War, a local grievance that continues to rankle in certain tradition-obsessed quarters.

"Boy, this bay's like an octopus," Jared said, as we drove over our third bridge inside the city.

I recalled that my mother had called them bridges to nowhere, suitable for her, really. An inveterate crosser of bridges, she: the most restless person I've ever met.

We drove into a minor traffic jam composed of people on their way to whatever amusements they'd chosen for the Saturday afternoon of a holiday weekend. I followed signs to the city's center and tooled round a bit. It was not a pretty place, and the boxy seventies buildings personified *anonymous*. On a rather crowded street I saw a car pulling out of a parking space, and nosed my way in.

"Where're we going?" Jared asked.

"To find ourselves a newspaper." Here, my thoughts had taken some useful turns. Perhaps. Melanie had talked of the Paper Boy—the one who had come to the house years ago. *His family owned papers. Society papers. Newspapers.*

Three minutes later I had what might be the right one off a news rack in a shop: *The Wire,* an independent weekly that according to its masthead had been serving Norfolk since 1897. In another quarter of an hour, we were parked in front of a large, self-confident Victorian brick house outside the commercial center of town in a section called Ward's Corner. The engine was turned off, but I made no move to open the car door.

"What's the matter?" Jared asked.

"Thinking." It would be easier to get what I was looking for if I went inside alone, and I was virtually certain that it would be safe to leave Jared waiting in the car for me while I did it. But *virtually* is no synonym for *absolutely,* and my promise to Tom was that I would not leave Jared alone. "Come on," I said. "When we go in there, don't say anything, okay? You may have to sit in a waiting room and study the society news of Norfolk while I do my research."

"Why can't I wait out here and listen to the radio?"

"Because I said so?"

"Shit, you sound like my mom." But he said it with a smile.

I FLIPPED MY BBC credentials at a desk clerk, said I was doing historical research, and asked if there was someone I might talk with who'd been round a while— knew Norfolk well. A few minutes later I was led across a near-empty newsroom of sorts into a small square office. At a comfortably messed desk sat a woman, fifty perhaps, with a crop of hair the color of tarnished heirloom silver and the face of a thoroughbred horse, her mouth not unlike Eleanor Roosevelt's.

"Holiday weekend; good time to catch up," she said, shoving gold-rimmed glasses up into her hair. "Lucy Baldwin. I'm the publisher here." The slightly nasal tone of top-class Virginia. I recognized that because it was the overlay my mother used to don for special occasions, until she realized that the effort was wasted: the Brits do not spend much time parsing the finer distinctions of American regional accents. "What can I do for you, Ms. . . . ?"

"Allie," I said in a quick temporizing with truth. Frances Cavanaugh, instant media celebrity, had made *Cavanaugh* a liability. "I'm doing some background research on the McQuade murder for the BBC."

She pushed the glasses back down into working position and took my measure. The lenses magnified the distaste in her hazel eyes. "I gathered from the way you presented yourself that the research you had in mind was history of a different sort. Frannie Miller has aired the human interest you're after ad nauseam, don't you think? Or shall we call it inhuman interest?"

"Do you know her?"

"Norfolk is not a large city; in certain of its circles, it's tight and tiny. My father owned this paper, as did his father," she said. "Look, if I can answer any specific questions for you that I don't mind answering, I will. But frankly I don't have a great deal of time I want to spare for this."

"Where did the family live?" Specific enough. A pallid query, asked with a tentative quality, as though my energy source had become partly unplugged.

"Fifteen Skilling Lane. College housing. Leonard Miller taught at Old Dominion University, but you probably know that." *Fifteen Skilling Lane.* I said it silently once, twice, trying to ring a familiar chime: *Allie Miller, I live at Fifteen Skilling Lane.* It meant nothing.

"Uh . . ." Power went dead. For the first time in living memory, I suffered a reporter's most serious affliction: a question blackout.

"Is something wrong, Ms. . . . Ali, did you say?"

The cover dropped away from me like the hastily grabbed sheet it was. "I am a journalist with the BBC, but I lied about being on assignment. My name is Alexis Cavanaugh. I'm . . ." The words *Frannie's daughter* might have tried my gag reflex. "Melanie's sister."

"Hmmm. The girl Frannie took away." She perused my face slowly, and made no effort to hide that she was doing it. "You resemble your father, now that I look, don't you?"

"I don't know. I never saw him or a photo after I was six. Melanie says I do. Did you know him, too?"

"Barely. I did audit a few of his classes, though. I went to school in Charlottesville, but my younger brother stayed at home and attended Old Dominion." Curtain up, another of Tom's expressions. My reporter's heart beat high as it sensed a key fact preparing to walk on stage. "It was Ned who knew your family," she said. *Your family* tasted rancid in her mouth, but she was too well-bred to spit it out. "He was quite a fan of Professor Miller's," she said benignly. I wondered where the bad bit had gone, stored under her tongue, perhaps. "You might like to know that your father was a fine teacher, Alexis, and a popular one. He sparked thought, excited controversy. Philosophy had blood and muscle for his students."

"Thank you," I said, uncertain whether thanks were what I cared to give. In an elemental way, it's far more satisfying for one's villains to remain unmitigated. "You said your brother knew my . . . family?" The instinct to know had regenerated itself.

"Why have you come?" she asked, visibly pulling back. "To confirm the things your mother's been saying? Refute them?"

"Probably neither. I came here mostly for my nephew. He saw his grandmother on the tube, which of course upset him but also piqued his curiosity—he's a very bright boy and a nice one. Anything positive he can take away from Norfolk will have been worth the trip."

"I see."

"I, on the other hand, now that I'm here, would be grateful to learn as much as I can, including the worst. You see, my life begins six years later than most people's, and lately bits of falling debris from the missing years have begun to bash my brain about. It would be easier to know." A nod that comprehended, then silence. "Will it ease your mind, Ms. Baldwin, if I tell you I loathe my mother?"

"Will it get me to talk freely, you mean?"

"Yes, that's what I mean, and I promise you it's for my consumption only. I'll tell Jared what you said about his grandfather, whom he never knew; he'll like that. But the rest is just for me."

"Ironic that you should turn up here today. I almost didn't come in, almost indulged myself and went riding instead. Ah, well, makes you think about fate, doesn't it?"

Fate: the gothic tower constructed by superstition to top its slapdash renovation of history—the whole mess plastered over with fear and exalted as spiritual high art. That's my view, but I didn't think it the moment to say so. Fact is, if Lucy Baldwin had chosen to ride today, I'd have come back here tomorrow, and *that* would have turned into fate. "Perhaps," I said, my pulses behaving in defiance of reason.

"Ned's hardly made a secret of it at the club bar," she said. "The relationship gives him a certain pathetic distinction these days. He's like a soldier who barely survived his youthful case of battle whim-whams, and decades later makes capital of war stories with martini in hand." Her equine mouth showed its gums in a laugh that resembled a dry cough. "My brother and your mother: third-hand, two-minute celebrities feeding off a child's murder. If I owned a paper that needed to support itself on that sort of thing, I'd shut its doors. At once. As it is, I told Ned that if he even considered going public with his fragment of ancient history, I would cut off his cash. My father left that in my control, as well as the paper. Unfortunately, my brother didn't make the grade as a philosopher—only as a gentleman drunk."

"Are you implying that my . . . family are responsible?"

"I'd say not, though for a good few years I did think otherwise. Ned lost his moorings when he was nineteen.

I can and do blame your mother for that, but I can't lay his whole life at her doorstep. He was a bright spark who lacked the flint to catch fire, and alcoholism runs all through my mother's side. Bad combination."

"What happened?" My imagination coupled with knowledge of my mother began to make some sketches, but I resisted leading the witness: bad practice in what I do. Tom used to enjoy pointing out that a reporter is not a lawyer—good reporters ask questions to which they do not know the answers.

"As I've told you, Ned was very taken with Professor Miller. Your father was apparently quite selective about students he invited home, but Ned was an engaging boy and I'm sure his hero worship was flattering. In any case, he did get invited and began going there a lot, encouraged not only by Leonard, but by Frannie, the climber's climber. After all, he was Edward Sayre Baldwin, FFV and all that rot. Poor Ned, before he knew it, he was besotted with them all."

"When was this?"

"Oh, six months or so before Frannie left—an eventful six months."

I pictured Melanie's honey hair brushing Tilt Schwartz's swarthy cheek, and wondered whether Ms. Baldwin had any idea of quite how eventful a period that was. "So Melanie was fifteen."

"And so pretty, a real sparkler. She was a talented gymnast, your sister; her picture had been in *The Wire* several times, winning competitions and whatnot. It was especially poignant hearing that her daughter had followed in those footsteps. Lord, what a world!"

"So, were Melanie and Ned mutually besotted?"

"Attracted. They'd have been a picture-book couple. She was a mature fifteen; Ned was a youngish nineteen.

And she was a strong-minded girl. That would have been good for Ned, I think. Even my parents wouldn't have minded. They weren't snobs in that way—you know, about Leonard being a Jew."

Big of them. "What went wrong, then?"

"Your mother"—the rancid taste had resurfaced in her mouth—"seduced Ned." She gave another of her coughing laughs. "It was like giving candy to a baby."

I did not need to ask what flavor candy might have been on offer. My mother's assortment was comprehensive. The summer I was thirteen there'd been an excruciating episode with a young man about the age of Ned Baldwin. George Washington Pie, she'd called him, with adorably intimate references to sturdy cherry trees, little hatchets, and private lessons in early American history. After she'd cut him loose, I'd answered a ringing phone more than once to a tearful Pie. "She's not in? Oh . . . Oh, Lex, tell her . . . tell her to please, *please* call me."

"And that preempted anything between your brother and Melanie, I imagine."

"It wasn't quite that simple. You see, there was another person involved. You may remember him: Howard Schwartz—Tilt, he was called."

Hearing her say his name filled me, absurdly, with something like shame. "I remember Tilt Schwartz quite clearly."

She pushed her glasses back up her forehead and leaned forward across the desk. "Alexis, I'm feeling somewhat guilty telling you all of this."

"Well, don't, please. You haven't shocked me, at least not so far. I barely remember my father, and I was out of touch with Melanie for a number of years, but I know my mother quite well."

"Sad to say, my guilt is not over your sensibilities; it's

about the rather unseemly satisfaction I'm getting from spilling the beans to Frannie's daughter."

"I absolve you; spill on. What I'm hearing closes a circle for me, just as it does for you, so our satisfaction is quite mutual."

Her lips curved in a toothy U of smile as she leaned herself back in her chair. "At the time Frannie horned in between Melanie and Ned, she—Frannie, that is—was deeply into an affair with Tilt. Now, Tilt was crass. Handsome, I suppose. Women liked him, certain women. Why has always been a mystery to me, but that may be a personal blind spot, part of the reason I never married. Of course, I've known Phyllis Schwartz for years—Ellenburg her name was, fine people. The family moved here from Atlanta two generations ago; mainstay of the symphony committee.

"Phyllis knew all about Tilt and Frannie and thought it would blow over; this was hardly her first go-round with such episodes. Of course, it *did* blow over, but the storm was fierce while it lasted. As you know, he ran off with Frannie, which was a huge surprise to Phyllis—and to me, I must say. I still don't understand that part of it, especially since he returned fairly fast once he fully understood his financial position."

And once Melanie's fetus had been safely aborted. "Things didn't get back on track for your brother and Melanie?" I ventured lawyerishly.

"No. She would have nothing to do with him; neither would Leonard. It was never clear what he knew or didn't. Both he and Melanie became quite reclusive after Frannie left. Melanie was a changed girl. It was sad: she dropped out of gymnastics, then out of school." She noticed my surprise. "Didn't you know that? Less than a year after her mother left Norfolk, she did, too. Predictably, Ned dissolved into a puddle of self-blame and alcohol over it: Melanie Miller was enshrined as the one love of his life, with whom all things would have been rosy. He reminds his wife, and anyone in earshot, of that often enough." Spectacles up; spectacles down.

"Now, your mother would have the world believe that Melanie got pregnant by Leonard. Nonsense. You try that one out on anyone who knew Leonard Miller at all, they'll say the same." She leveled her lens-magnified gaze at me. "If Melanie *was* pregnant at the time Frannie left, I'd sooner believe it was Ned's child she was carrying than her father's."

I was tempted: the closing of circles and all. *It was Tilt Schwartz's child.* The words made a small push, and promptly receded for lack of vocation. "Perfection is rare," I said, "but my mother does come close: an almost perfect monster." We rose from our chairs at the same moment, both as eager to quit each other's company as strangers who'd happened into a bed together. Nevertheless, I couldn't resist a final foray. "May I ask you one more question?"

"I'm afraid I've said enough. More than enough."

"This is about my father," I said quickly, "just about him." She flicked her hand out, palm up: yes. "You were so certain he could never have had sex with his daughter. Why? Aside from being intelligent and good in a lecture hall, what was he . . . like?"

Her finger tapped her lips. After a moment, she shook her head. "I met him twice at the college, and once at his home. My impression was of extreme self-containment—I mean *extreme*. I remember when Ned introduced us, Professor Miller stood there, stiff as a Buckingham Palace guard. I felt like an ass, I can tell you, effusing over his lecture with my hand stuck out.

He did put out his hand finally and let me shake it, but then I saw him surreptitiously rub his palm against his trouser leg to get rid of . . . the touch, I suppose. The contrast was amazing. This man who was bristling with passion in the classroom, virtually disappeared outside it. To answer your question literally, aside from the brilliance of that intellect, he was like . . . nothing."

Jared and I found the university, found Skilling Lane. We stood outside number fifteen and gazed. It was a small, rather austere yellow frame house with white trim. No sign of people about, or a car; likely the occupants were gone for the holiday. I wondered whether any children lived here now, and rather doubted it, as I saw no sign of bicycles or wagons or basketball hoops. I wondered whether the house had always been this buttery a yellow, and whether Melanie favored the color for some underlying nostalgic reason. I thought not, since yellow was also my mother's favorite color. I wondered how many peripheral items I could dream up to wonder about before wondering about the main one: the absence in me of strong emotion at the sight of this place.

It wasn't that I didn't remember it; it was that I *did*. Yet no drums rolled, no trumpets sounded. I felt dry and dead as a late autumn leaf. I felt the way Lucy Baldwin had described my father out of his classroom: like nothing.

"So this is where my mom grew up?"

I made a try at a good face. "Yes. And see, over there, that's the Old Dominion campus, where your grandfather taught. We can go over there later, walk round a bit. He was brilliant. He . . . Look, I expect I ought to be a good soldier—or in this town, sailor—and pretty the picture for you, Jared, but I'll say the truth instead. Your grandfather had a high IQ, as you do. He was apparently an awfully effective teacher. And he definitely did not molest or impregnate your mother. Those are the only positive things I can say about him. He was a mean-spirited, loathsome man, whom I hated and who hated me. He was a rotten father to Melanie, too. He . . . he made her squeeze oranges for him all the time. See, there now, I *have* remembered something . . ."

I didn't notice him make the move, but his arms went round me and his hand began to pat my back. "It's okay to cry, Lex. You said so, remember? Blubbing, you called it. Blub all you want. Then maybe we should just get the fuck out of this place."

CHAPTER
39

Washington was where we went. We were across the big bridge, Norfolk behind us, within half an hour. When Jared was grown, he might sometime be moved to pay another visit—to see his mother's childhood surroundings refracted through decades of his own experience with blame and forgiveness, pity and love. Then again, maybe not. Perhaps he would develop the same ambivalence that had kept me, a trained excavator, from my own dig—or at very least from trying to get a photo of Professor Leonard Miller from the university. Jared would do what he'd do. As for me, I would never set foot in the damned city again.

We arrived in the nation's capital just in time to catch the afternoon's last White House tour. As the guide was droning out a tactfully edited version of Oval Office history, an image flashed into my mind, a picture as sharp as though it had been placed with purpose just behind my eyeballs: Melanie mounting a staircase, a tweed-clad arm round her shoulder. For a fractured second I wondered whether I was dredging up more Norfolk flotsam, but no, this was *Courtney's* staircase I was seeing; the arm was Nate's—guiding her up to bed the first night I met him. Melanie had been exhausted at the dinner table, her neck and back aching. "Come on," he'd said . . .

And on the heels of that memory, the elusive fact clicked into place. I knew it for a fact straight off: I have heard that click before. It is unmistakable.

I tapped Jared's shoulder and whispered, "He didn't come back into the house that night; he never left." We traded conspiratorial glances. I continued. "You see, the others had gone home after the Halloween party blew apart. Melanie was upset. He must have walked her upstairs to her room, given her a neck massage or something. Then he hid himself, probably in the cellar, and waited."

"For what? Calista wasn't going to come down to him. She chomped his ear; she was *done* with him."

"Perhaps he meant to go up to her room and try to fetch her once your father had come home and everyone was asleep. But he didn't need to; she came down there with you, didn't she?"

"Yeah, and I just left her there for him. Is that what you're saying?" Heads turned at his raised voice.

"*Sssh.* No, that's not what I'm saying at all. How could you know he was there? Last I heard you had no supernatural powers." I reached out and scruffed at his neck. It was spontaneous, no second thought about the wisdom of touching him. His holding and comforting me in front of the strict little yellow house had broken new ground for us. He was no longer the designated patient, meant to be swathed in blankets, handled with tongs; I was no longer Poppins/Pan. It was lemon tonic for us both. "That's how it happened, Jared. I'm positive."

Behind us, a woman who seemed to have a cheese

grater stuck in her throat ground out, "Would you kids be *quiet* so's the rest of us can have a shot at *hearing* this guy?" I giggled, earning an offended snort. I couldn't help it. Suddenly, I was flying high as a kite. "Whyn't you and your brother go find a playground?"

Jared and I, sobered, exchanged looks as explicit as words. He was no one's brother anymore. After a second or two, I reached up and clapped his shoulder the way a teammate might on a playing field. "Come on," I said.

"IT'S LEX."

"I'm glad you called," Barney said, the way a doctor might to a patient if he were about to deliver news. "Where are you?"

"New York." We'd ducked into a hotel lobby, and Jared sat beside me on a plushy sofa in the most secluded corner we could find to make the call. "We've just got back here and seen the bloody paper."

"Yeah. She's off the wall and pretty mad at you."

It was Sunday afternoon. We'd only just garaged the car when Jared was clouted in the eye by the fat, black *New York Post* headline: "Where's Jared?" A full close-up, a recent one, of his face was directly beneath it. "I want my son back—yesterday," read a page three quote from an interview with Melanie. "I don't know where my sister took him. No, I'm not calling this a kidnapping, exactly, but I expected them back no later than Friday night. Jared is a high-strung child who's been through hell. I am very worried; he needs to be here with his parents. He needs to be close to us right now, and we need him."

"I'm pretty mad, as well," I said. Was this what it came down to, a terminal case of sibling rivalry? "Going to the fucking papers! Aping her mother even in *that*. I swear I . . ."

"She paid me an impromptu visit yesterday. She was sure I knew where you were. I was glad I didn't."

"Do you think Nate put her up to this?"

"Indirectly, I'd guess, whipping up her urgency about getting Jared back into therapy. Listen, I think you should come here. I've heard a few interesting things. The question is what to do with them."

"Tell me." If anyone ever bothered laying a tombstone over me, those words would be the ones to engrave on it. They seemed to be the keynote of my life.

"It isn't telephone talk, Lex. Come to my house," he said—the firm sound I'd first admired on the school playground. "You'll be hiding in plain sight. We'll stick your car in the garage. Melanie won't come again. No one will know you're here."

"I . . ." I looked at Jared staring at himself on newsprint. His hand holding the paper trembled. "Jared may not be ready to do that." The issue at hand was simple and momentous: a leap of faith, or not? Civilizations are built and destroyed on the question. "Hang on a moment, okay?"

"Jared," I said quietly, "Barney wants us to come stay with him. He will not call your mother or anyone else. He promises that, so we'll be as safe there as anywhere we could go. If we trust him."

"Do *you*?" His eyes were black and wary as a hunted refugee's.

A second betrayal, even an inadvertent one, would deny me a third chance with him. My whole life did not flash before me, only the days and nights with Barney, his sea-water eyes, Chekhov smile. My innards rode a wave of something akin to seasickness. "Yes, I do trust him."

"Okay," Jared mumbled.

CHAPTER
40

We arrived at the blue house with black shutters. After I'd told Jared the scant bit Barney had told me—that he'd learned something of interest and was unsure how it might be put to use—our drive was largely silent. Both of us were hot-wired with curiosity, yet too tense to speculate, too stretched emotionally for small talk. In this state, the sight of Barney standing in the open doorway made my eyes fill with tears of quite unreasonable joy.

Jared bounded out of the car and into the house quick as a wood animal going to ground. We'd spoken almost not at all on the ride up. I knew that in his mind his mother had turned active enemy—a figure frightening in the most primal way. I understood too well, but had no comfort to give him.

Barney ran his hand over Jared's hair—precisely the right amount of touch, I thought. Any more right now, a hug, for example, would have prompted recoil. "We'll get through this, Jared," he said. "One foot in front of another and we'll get there. Your mom's scared for you. She doesn't mean you harm; try and remember that."

Jared didn't answer, just knelt down and buried his face in Jasper's neck.

Barney's left cheek had a deep vertical crease running down its center into the red beard. Had that been there before? Maybe it was just shadowed in a particular, new way. And there was a stretched look about his face, eyes and mouth narrowed, as though subjected to a spate of hard weather. "I don't know that I've ever been gladder to see anyone in my life," I said. "Will that do for hello?"

"Yes," he said. He reviewed my face as if it were new to him. I put out my hand. He nodded and took it.

Not long after, we sat in a semicircle on the living room carpet, three campers ready to tell ghost stories round the fire. Barney had placed a plate of generic sandwiches on the mantel beyond Jasper's reach. Jared took one. His body was tensed, face blank of expression, but his jaws seemed to welcome the task of chewing. I was hungry only for information.

"I'm not going to censor anything for your ears, Jared, okay?" Barney said. "With the shit you've been through, it would be an insult." Jared didn't smile, but I saw him begin to unclench. It was almost imperceptible, but I'd begun to learn his smaller signals. "First of all, school. Nothing there: a spotless record for Grumbach. From time to time, he's opted to not take on one kid or another—said the compatibility wasn't there; he wouldn't be able to help. But for ones he has treated, all A's; whistle clean."

"How can you know that this fast?" I asked, attacking the words because they were other than I'd hoped.

"If you're talking 'know,' as in a court of law, I can't.

But yesterday I talked with an authoritative source—the guidance counselor. She's the one who refers kids to Grumbach, and I figure, she's the one who'd hear complaints. There haven't been any. Lot's of praise, but no complaints."

"That was efficient. Did she think it was peculiar, you calling about that on a holiday weekend?"

The one-cornered smile. "Not really. She owns the sweater you asked about. The one you wore on the boat?"

"Oh." That shut me up good and proper. Sexual jealousy breaks and enters where it pleases. I saw a flicker of satisfaction cross his face, and couldn't blame him for it.

"What about 'second of all'?" Jared asked, impatience with man-woman banter curdling his disappointment at no news.

Barney continued. "Second of all, I did manage to contact someone who danced with Zip and more or less stayed in touch over the years."

"How'd you do that?" I was impressed and surprised. The surprise, I'm afraid, was more evident.

"You want to watch out for intellectual arrogance, both you guys," he said. "It wasn't so hard, actually. We teachers are methodical beings. I went on-line and checked out her name in some modern-dance sites. It was there from the Martha Graham years, as well as the Paul Taylor ones. Then I E-mailed and phoned round until I hit some live humans. They were glad to talk. Performers are, especially dancers: too many of them, too little attention to go round. One would put me on to another, and so on. Finally, I got hold of the right one, a Norma Testa, a friend of Zip's from the old days.

"Norma's got arthritis and a two-pack-a-day Camel habit now, but back when Paul Taylor split from Graham, she and Zip were two of the lead dancers who went with him. We kind of hit it off on the phone, Norma and I, so I drove over to Brooklyn last night, took her to dinner. Best date I've had in a while, present company excepted. Zip and Norma roomed together for three years, so they knew each other pretty well, and of course Norma knew Nate."

"Is she likely to call him? Tell him someone's been nosing about?"

"Wouldn't think so. I borrowed a leaf from your book, told her I was looking into a possible TV film. I said I'd heard about this outstanding little dancer, whose career was ended by MS, and thought her story might have possibilities. That gave her a laugh. 'Baby, you don't know the half of it,' is what she said, and then proceeded to tell me some things. I don't know in practical terms how you might be able to use this, but it's another slant on Grumbach: Grumbach in love . . ."

Barney told us. Perhaps these were not his words—almost certainly, they were not, as he took pains to make it straightforward, a history lesson. But Norma's story, as I heard it, reverberated in me. It came alive in my mind, which, while it made no additions of substance, did apply brush strokes of color. All by way of saying, the language in this retelling is mine.

NATE GRUMBACH AND ZIPPORAH Selansky had met in Brooklyn College, a classic case of an awkward misfit drawn to a glamorous opposite. There was a whiff of the tropics in Zip's tiny, pliant body, her heart-shaped lips, glossy, black hair long enough to sit on. Her mind was restless, her tastes adventurous veering toward wild. Dance, sex, combat: all three seemed to satisfy a craving for strong sensation, which perhaps was why partners found her as much a dazzler in bed as she was onstage—and why thwarting her will, or trying to, could be dangerous sport. Scorn and ridicule were her weapons; her aim was precise. But she gave quick first aid to her wounded: hot, erotic balm strategically applied, and so they came back for more.

Nate lived with the grandmother who'd raised him— it was unclear what had become of his parents. He was a loner, shambling round the edges of this crowd or that, not disliked, but without specific friends, male or female. Except for Zip, whom he adored. Zip would twit him, tease him, called him *"Bubbeh's* boy," or "Frog-face," or sometimes, "Lo-*ver,"* and he'd grin, glad for the glancing beam of her attention.

Zip dropped out of school to accept an apprenticeship with the Graham Company, the *sine qua non* of the time for a modern dancer. Nate would arrive after his classes and hang round till late in the night when she was done performing or rehearsing for the privilege of having a cup of coffee together—if she didn't have other plans. Meantime, there were boys and men; men and boys, and perhaps the occasional girl for Zip (she had hinted at this, but no one was certain). She played with them, and tossed them when she was tired of them. Through all, there was Nate, never a boyfriend, just always there.

Once he'd completed graduate school, begun practice as an educational psychologist, he took on visible polish. The same Nate who five years earlier had been sporadically inarticulate, ungainly in his awkward slouch, clad in shirts too large, jackets too small, had developed a gently authoritative professional manner, laced with humor. He had acquired tweed jackets, tailored just so, and ten pounds in well-distributed body weight. In sum, he had coalesced into an *attractively* homely man.

By then, Zip was dancing leads opposite Paul Taylor, the beautiful young man who was Graham's star. When

Taylor left to form his own company, Zip was the first one he invited to go with him. Unlike many of Zip's choices, the decision to go with Taylor was not motivated by sex: Taylor was gay, as were most male dancers. In any case, it wasn't artists, actors, writers, nor doctors, lawyers, accountants, who appealed to Zip. It was football players, truck drivers, cops—the rougher trade. Yes, there was the occasional black eye. On one such occasion, Zip was seen in a coffeehouse with Nate, his hand clasping hers across the small table. It was he who was weeping.

Norma saw him in tears again: this time a storm of them, punctuated by thunderous bursts of indefinable words, as they drenched a face purpled with rage. It was backstage, after a performance. He and Zip had been talking quietly in a far corner near the back wall, when all of a sudden, the man the company wryly called "The Gentleman Caller" exploded. As they watched, motionless in their sheer surprise, Nate lunged at Zip. His hands gripped the base of her slender neck, and began to shake her like a rag toy, her head flying back and forth to bash against the corner's brick walls with each shake. Within seconds, the stage manager and a few dancers sprang into action, pried him off her and bum's rushed him out the stage door.

Zip, leaning against the walls for support now, was openmouthed, eyes glazed, a trickle of blood running down her forehead. Quickly, Norma was at her side, trying to guide her into her dressing room. "Who would've thought?" Zip asked groggily, smiling like a sleepy baby. "My head. Is it cracked, Norm? Feels cracked like Humpty . . ." In fact, she'd suffered a mild concussion. Overnight in the hospital, and she was fine.

Nate didn't show up for quite a long time after the incident—many months. But eventually he did, just at about the same time Zip's odd symptoms began: the episodes of sudden leg weakness; right arm refusing sometimes to obey. MS: the initials had a muted dignity to them, stately, slow, lacking the immediate menace of cancer, for example. There'd be years, the doctors said, before it got bad. Perhaps that prognosis would hold hope for some, but not for a dancer, not for Zip. For a short time, she binged on sex and motion. She bought a motorcycle and gunned round the city. She danced with a frenzy, until the time her leg collapsed under her onstage, landing from one of the astonishing leaps that were her trademark.

And then she gave it up, all at once, completely: dance, adventure, sex, even the teasing laughter, and married Nate. Twenty-three years they'd been together day and night, almost to the silver wedding anniversary, when Zip died. A docile wife, tended through a long, slow decline by her devoted husband. Death, when it came, was peaceful. And why not? In any way that mattered to her, she had already been dead quite a long time.

"NORMA KEPT UP with visits and all," Barney said. "She was really very attached to Zip, though she and Nate tended to be uncomfortable with each other. On one visit not so far from the end, she said something to him about how tough it must be for him, you know, tending a total invalid. He got this peaceful smile on his face and said that caring for Zip was the center of his life, and he regretted not one hour, one moment he'd ever spent with her—except, of course, the death of their daughter. Which kind of left Norma floored, hanging there, ready to say, 'What daughter?' But she saw this look in his eye—a look that reminded her of a girl from back in fifth grade who had sworn that she'd seen Mary wheeling baby Jesus down Flatbush Avenue in a plaid stroller—and she decided it was better to let it go."

As I heard the story, I felt bathed in a murky, gray fog. It was a sense of being off-kilter: deeply dissatisfied. I looked at Jared and saw that he'd been taken in similar fashion. I don't think he could have identified its cause, but I think I knew what it was: our towering villain had been shrunk down to mundane proportions, his superpowers hacked off at the knees. The reduction didn't mitigate Nate Grumbach's crimes, it merely demythologized them. It made him mortal, subject to bleeding if his flesh were cut.

I thought of Hannah Arendt's book about Adolf Eichmann and the banality of evil—a book dead on the mark, much vilified for that reason. The drama of omnipotent malevolence grips the imagination, while letting the rest of us off the hook. Awe is a habit-forming drug, quite as potent in ritual obeisance to our devils as to our gods.

"Where's your computer?" Jared asked sourly. I doubt he'd ever heard of Arendt or Eichmann. He didn't exactly know why he was pissed off, only that he was.

"Upstairs," Barney said. "You want to use it?"

"Yeah, I just wanna get away from all this stuff before I puke."

"Good idea," I said. "If you really don't want to puke, I'd stay off any site to do with your relatives." He glowered at me, eyes ignited with anger, then turned to leave.

"A fact," I called after him, just to, I don't know, calm him a bit, I suppose. "Come on, Jared, tell me a fact."

"You want a fact? *Here's* a fact. He's a fucking *dweeb*, and I wish I'd taken a shot at killing him instead of me."

CHAPTER
41

Though much of my early life is a blank, white screen on which the stored images refuse to show up, there are moments as sharp in detail as though they'd only just happened, one of them the first night I spent in London.

Both my mother and I are rank and cranky following an endless, bumpy plane ride during which I'd thrown up, only partly into the small sack provided for that purpose. Approximately fifteen minutes after we get settled in a musty bed-and-breakfast in South Kensington, she is showered, wrapped in a threadbare towel, and on her way to falling fast asleep, dead center in a sagging double bed with large, blood-red roses on its scratchy coverlet. I want to smash her face, and might, were I less scared.

Instead, I curl myself, still dressed in my vomit-flecked clothes, into the coverlet's top corner and hug the flaccid, lumpy, pink-cased pillow to my face as though it were a pet. I do not cry, but I am certain that when the morning comes, I will be dead. And I don't mind so much.

But here I was in Barney's bed, alive. One doesn't die easily—not of grief or fear or hate; nor for love, either.

As I lay here, this night, my brain churned itself into a butter of dread at what it was contemplating. And then, a fevered urge to act made the butter froth and spit with its heat; the cycle repeated over and again, making focused thought impossible. I knew what was required of me, and I knew how to do it. Of course I did: it was what I do, have done a dozen times in the service of a dozen films. Except this time I could not seem to begin. I could not concentrate. I could not open myself, ready to receive a consciousness not my own—receive it and feel it inside out, without judgment or blame. Absent that framework, nothing would be possible.

Finally, still unsuccessful, I rolled out of bed trying not to wake Barney, who lay beside me lightly snoring. The damned dog, stretched across the foot of the bed like a great, hairy rug, jumped off when I did. I grabbed my bag and sprinted, closing the bedroom door almost on his snout to prevent his following me.

Once safely locked inside the hall bathroom, I sat on the cold tile floor, back against the door, thinking of another bathroom: Nate's. I saw myself that first afternoon at his house, taking off my rain-soaked clothes in the room where he shaved, brushed his teeth, used the toilet. I'd stood there naked, remembering my father, and then I'd sheltered in the dry, comfort of a blue toweling robe: Zip's robe; Calista's robe. As a shudder shook me, legs to shoulders, I clasped my hands together hard and stared down at them. They looked like praying hands;

perhaps they were, praying that revulsion would not stymie me, nor fury, nor fear—praying that I could approach this subject as I had the snake charmer, the trapeze artist, the self-mutilator, as someone ready to enter his personal universe as his guest and make it my home for just long enough to understand . . .

After a minute or three or four, I fetched the cell phone from the bag and dialed. It was well past midnight, but he answered just after the first ring.

"Grumbach here."

"Lex here," I said. My voice was small, but managed to keep even.

"Lex. Are you all right?" The question was asked with a warm concern that sounded authentic and was, in its own terms—the only terms relevant here and now, Nate Grumbach's terms. All else must be cordoned off.

"More or less. Are you?"

A rumbling "Sure," its ironic undertone asking for notice.

"Tell me really. It does matter to me."

After a long wait, he said, "No. I'm not all right. But you know that, don't you?"

"I do."

Laugh. "And I do, too. I now pronounce us . . . What do I pronounce us, Lex? Man and what?"

"Man and woman who know each other quite well. How's that?"

"Where are you?" I felt a ping of self-confidence at a sudden ragged urgency in his voice. I pushed the *end call* button and turned the phone off. This was enough for a start. My heart rang like a gong. He would . . . ? What would he do? Nothing, I thought. He would wait, longing to see me.

Later, back in bed, as I drifted in and out of a state

that mimicked sleep but was far from it, I felt soul-soaked in toxins. I could not bring myself to reach for Barney's hand, which lay curled just beside my temple, certain my touch would infect on contact.

"You're going to make a play, aren't you?" he asked. It was my first clue he was awake. He did not reach for me either; perhaps poison glowed out through my skin in the semidark. Or perhaps it was just that we'd grown to know each other unreasonably well in this short and awful time.

"Yes," I said.

"Soon."

"Quite soon. Do you think you could take the day off, keep an eye on Jared?"

"Sure. For what it's worth, I'm with you on this."

"It's worth a lot, Barney. You're worth a lot . . . to me." About as expressive as the peep of a constipated chicken.

"But you're not asking for my help, right?" His hand brushed my hair, then reached in deeper, raking my scalp, not all that gently. The tracks of his fingers reproached my skull, resenting the goings-on inside it.

"There's nothing more you can do," I said. "I wish there were. You're my mate, you know? Maybe the best one I've ever had, and . . ." I couldn't go on, not and keep my purpose firm. I rolled away and bounded out of bed. "Hey, it's probably morning. Want to run?"

We did, the two of us and Jasper, of course. In the early quiet, all that was heard was the faint whistle of wind, the soft scuff of rubber sole on the ground, and the occasional unseen car—those sounds and our own breathing. After we had showered and dressed, we clasped hands, tight and brief. "Good luck, mate," he said. "I worry about you."

"I think that's the best thing I've ever heard," I said, and meant it. And held him tight round the waist, my face pressing into the lower part of his chest, nourishing myself on his smell of salt and soap.

Shortly after, I walked in on Jared, who sat in his underpants and T-shirt, mousing about on Barney's computer, traveling God knew where in cyberspace. He looked rested and calmer than he had last night.

"I've left cereal out in the kitchen," I said. "There's also orange juice in the fridge and milk and some sliced ham and . . ."

"You going someplace?" he asked, looking up.

"I am, yes. I'll be gone awhile, all day, in fact. I'll be back sometime this evening, can't give you an exact time, but Barney will be here with you. He's skipping school today."

"You're going to see *him*, right?"

I nodded. "Not just yet, though. I've got some . . . things to do first." His brown velvet eyes widened. He might have been seven years old, hearing the start of a ghost tale.

"Well, what is it then, the plan?"

"It'll dissolve like spun sugar if I talk about it. Can you understand what I mean? It's not that it's a secret, just that . . ." I shook my head. "I can't. But I do know what I'm doing. I promise you that."

"What if . . . What if he hurts you?"

"He won't." The assertion caused a chill deep in the bone, reminding me how thin was the ice under my feet. "Look, this may sound like a dumb question to you, but what would you say is . . . ? Put it this way, what did you used to find Nate Grumbach's most positive quality—what did you like best about him?"

He didn't snap back with a bitter wisecrack. I

watched him separate thought from feeling like the scientist he was becoming. "He knew who you were behind the bad stuff you did," he said slowly, "and he liked you. He . . . could make you think you were really something special." His eyes shut for a split second. What he'd said had caused him pain. It occurred to me that for years I had taken as a given my love for Jared, when all I'd actually loved was an idea: my own version of a boy custom-tailored to suit me. Now I knew better. I knew this particular boy well enough to love him. And I did.

I kissed his forehead and stifled an urge to wrap my arms round him, because I knew they would clutch too tightly. "It'll be over soon."

CHAPTER
42

Six o'clock. I walked down his street slowly, as though each step might have something to teach me. The streetlamps shone like moons; the lighted housefronts welcomed. Halloween decorations were a month gone, and some eager families had jumped the gun on Christmas. Otherwise, Westport looked just about the same as it had the night Calista died: a fine place to live, a fine place to grow up.

I had spent much of the day at Compo Beach letting the wind slap my face, turn my ears icy, enjoying the pulsing pain. From time to time, I'd stop my walk or run for a whirl here, a kick there: tae kwon do moves executed by a runt who had never been—would never be—much good at them. Could I defend myself in a street mugging? Perhaps, if the mugger were less than skilled at his craft.

For hours I grouped and regrouped shards of my subject, the vessel called Nathan Grumbach, PhD: a man whose chosen career was helping children become their better selves; a man who had been impelled to violate and kill a child; a man who had appreciated the Jared behind the "bad stuff" he did; a man who had systematically driven Jared to attempt suicide; a man who had been Melanie's rock and redeemer; a man who had robbed her of one child and tried to rob her of the other; a man who had adored a dancer, suffered gladly any abuse she'd cared to serve up, nursed her through a long, slow death—and in a long-ago moment had been gripped by a fury so powerful that he'd publicly tried to smash her brains out.

And then there was his effect on me. I had basked in his personality and been glad for the heat of its beam. I'd laughed at his jokes, eaten his food, engaged him in debate, and, in the end, abided by his judgment. "Don't be a stranger," he had told me; I had been no stranger. In fact, Nate was the only person in my life who had gentled me out of an incipient binge—fed me spoon by spoon, dosed me with soft words and calming medicine.

My good dad.

After a final long run that frost-burned my face and cleared my head, I climbed into my car. It was coming up on five o'clock. I had not eaten since breakfast, and knew that my gut needed food, though no other part of me had a taste for it. On Route 1, I almost drove past the Dunkin' Donuts where I'd shopped before daylight for a carton of bagels and cream cheese and pepper, what was it, three weeks ago? Four? Time had lost its precision.

It being early evening, I had my choice of lunch counters, pizza parlors, delicatessens, but found myself backing up to park in front of that Dunkin' Donuts. Call it superstition or a longing for symmetry, perhaps both. I almost expected to see the same voluble man behind the counter, but of course this would not be his shift. Instead, a tired young woman wordlessly took my order by fixing her eyes on me and raising her brows.

"A large orange juice and a bagel with cream cheese. Just one," I said, and noted her mildly puzzled look.

NOW, FOUR HOUSES away from where Nate Grumbach lived, an odd thing happened: I seemed to shrink inside myself; I felt very small. Of course, I *am* very small, but usually that is not at the top of my mind one moment to the next, any more than I suppose it is on a toy poodle's marching down the street in the midst of humans and Alsatians.

As I turned into his driveway, a question asked itself: Does Nate in his deepest recesses feel like a good man driven to commit the occasional evil act, or like an evil man who has managed most of the time to pave his true nature over with good deeds? I felt certain, you see, that it was one or the other. He had a hold on reality—he knew what he had done.

No car in the driveway. Good, no visitors. His Volvo, automotive hallmark of prudence, would be in the garage as usual. I walked round to the side. From where I stood, before the kitchen door, I could see him puttering, pouring himself a mug of coffee. The sight of him, the actual sight, gave me a turn. It was his back I saw, a three-quarter view, the same angle, it occurred to me, that Jared had caught at the cellar door, where he had watched Nate and imagined the brown paws he could not see caressing Calista. No, I told myself. You must not think of this now. But a wave of revulsion hit anyway. I waited, breathing hard, and willed it to break and recede.

I knew the door would be unlocked. He didn't lock the back door when he was in. I turned the knob and opened it.

"Hello, Nate. I'm here."

His fingers gripped the mug's handle. Though the large hand did not visibly tremble, coffee slopped up over the edges of the mug onto the brick-tiled floor. He stared, just stared. His deeply pleated face, its accustomed color gone, loomed like the chrome bonnet emblem on a fast car aimed at my body. His black eyes blinked finally, as though to swallow me whole. I grew smaller by the second, mouse-sized.

The urge to streak out the still open door at a dead run had a go at winning me over. I shut the door behind me, quite carefully, my hand as unsteady as his. "Did you think I wouldn't come?"

"No," he said. I noticed now that he looked older and at the same time younger, exhausted and tallow-faced, but with a vulnerable blur in the eyes, a softening at the mouth. "No," he repeated, "I've been expecting you. Just not so soon." Then he gave a husky, almost merry chuckle.

The first BBC film I did focused on a naturalistic actor. My minicam and I shadowed Albert Quinton onstage and off during six weeks of *Hamlet* rehearsals. For the first four, he tried everything from scream therapy to self-hypnosis to find, as he put it, "a way into the perverse motherfucker." Then, one late night in the fifth week, backstage at the Donmar, Albert suddenly disappeared inside the prince. There he was, he told me later, waiting for Ophelia to speak his entrance cue, and the next breath he took was Hamlet's. At the time, observing through my lens, I did not get precisely what was happening, just that something was. Later, when I reran the tape, sure enough I saw it: in subtle but essential ways the man had altered.

For the past twenty hours, I'd have done damned near anything to find for myself a way into Nate. Now, all at once, I felt something starting to happen. I was not in his head, not breathing his breaths—nothing that dramatic. But face-to-face here, the puzzle of him expanded to fill my mind and heart so completely that fear and disgust were smothered in ravening curiosity. I was no longer a mouse, nor a cat either. No camera was in my hands, but I was in the state I strive for with a subject: open to embracing what he was and learning how he worked.

He said, "Your cheeks are so red, like a kid who's just finished making a snowman." He was enjoying the sight of me; I could tell that. It was in no way feigned.

"I was walking on the beach, for quite a long time. I love it when it's bleak and empty."

"Figures. You see yourself as an isolate, the little observer who so easily could become invisible. But that's not the way you really are. It's not your nature, just what you've become because you had to." I knew he was talking not only about me.

"And what is my nature?"

"Strong. Powerful, even. You're like a small missile. Years of anger tamped down and stored because you didn't dare express it—oh, except through sneaking food. All that fury's packed into your warhead." He smiled, proud of me: a that's-my-girl kind of smile. "You shoot with your camera, right? Your targets ought to beware."

And yours, I thought. "Hard to differentiate though, as the years go on, between nature and what one becomes, in self-defense or otherwise. And *is* there any real difference in the end, Nate?"

He considered the question, reading my code as well as I read his. "In the end, maybe not," he said sadly. Then he put an arm round my shoulder and leaned down to kiss my forehead. I did not flinch. "Come on, let's have your jacket." He hung it on a peg and then took a piece of paper toweling and stooped to mop up the spilled coffee. "I've got some made fresh. Would you like a cup?"

"I think I'd rather have wine, actually. Red would appeal. Will you join me?"

"Good," he said. "Very good." I had pleased him. "Go into the living room and light the fire; it's laid, just a match'll do it. I'll be right in. I've got a bottle of cab here. Australian; supposed to be good."

"I need the loo first," I said. There was one on the main floor, just down the hall from the kitchen on the way to the living room. After I'd used it, I peered into the mirror above the sink. Reflected in the glass my hair looked wild, my eyes far darker than usual. My cheeks were red as Christmas.

When Nate walked into the living room, I was sitting, legs curled under my bottom, on the sofa. The fire had begun to dart forked orange tongues. On its surface, the scene was as it had been on my first visit here—except that that time I had tried briefly and *pro forma* to resist relaxing into intimacy. He put two glasses down on the coffee table and filled them two thirds. After a moment during which I watched him consider sitting beside me, he took his glass and the bottle to the wing chair at the far side of the hearth. Once seated, he sipped. "My wine guy was right. Not bad."

"Not bad at all," I agreed. I knew it would be better if the first move was his. The subject who takes the lead has a sense of control, which frees him to go farther than if pushed. My role is to speak as little as is necessary.

"It was a dangerous thing to run off with Jared that way," he said, matter-of-fact and kind, the way he must sound to a patient. "You've made him look guilty as hell and driven Melanie straight up the wall."

"Less dangerous than staying put, I thought."

"Umm." He might have been affirming what I'd said, or savoring the wine he'd just swallowed. "I knew you'd do it, take him away. It was just a matter of when." He did not know about the suicide attempt. At least I thought not.

"You sound almost as though you approve," I said.

He drew his hand across his forehead as though wiping something off it. "Like approving or disapproving the weather—it happens anyway. Ah, what the hell? Maybe I do approve." His body leaned forward in his chair now, angled toward me. "Let me ask you a straight question, Lex. If you buy whatever version Jared gave you, why're you here? Looking for proof?"

"I don't need proof. Of anything. I'm here to know about you—to understand."

"Were you scared to come?"

"Yes," I said quietly. "I've just told you something true. Suppose you tell me something true. Anything will do for a start."

"Right this second, you remind me so much of Zip that I want to lock you up and keep you here."

My mouth went dry. I wet it with wine and swallowed hard. "I believe that."

"You're not as pretty; you don't have the flash. And you're missing the flair for cruelty, but still . . ." He held his hands out palms up and shrugged. "But you're not bad—like the Australian cab."

"You had a daughter who would've been about my

age—you and Zip. Isn't that what you said? A baby who died?"

He nodded. "Babies die sometimes. This one shouldn't have. You wouldn't have let her die."

"How old was she when she died?" I asked it carefully.

"She was young," he said. "Very, very young. 'A woman's right to choose,' " he said bitterly. "And what the hell was *my* right?" His voice rang with rage. I saw the blood rise to his face, blotching it. He stood and reached his arm out at me, finger extended like an orator making a telling point. "I would have killed Zip to save that baby, but there was nothing I could . . ." His arm dropped to his side and his face went pale.

"Did you try to kill Zip?"

He shook his head. "Dunno. We were backstage at City Center when she tells me she's pregnant and she's going for the abortion next morning. First I heard of any of it. I lost it. I don't think I'd've killed her, but they pulled me off her, so we'll never know. The baby died on a Wednesday. I forget the date, but it was a Wednesday. I know because I was working with kids at the Walden School that day, and at about eleven or so, I thought, that's it—she's gone. You wanna talk about impotent? *That's* impotent!" I hadn't talked about impotent, but I'd bet Zip had.

"How . . . How do you know it was going to be a girl?"

He smiled, and it was only then that I noticed his eyes were tear-moist. "I just do. Look, I'd like to come sit beside you? Would that be all right? Don't be scared."

"I'm not." It may have been the truth, but not the whole truth, for my heart had begun to thud. He sat, but not before fetching his wineglass and refilling it. Perhaps a foot of space was between us, perhaps a bit less. I fancied I could feel the heat of his body, yet knew that was not possible. "Melanie will confess," I said, surprising myself, "or Tom will, rather than give Jared over."

"I'd agree," he said, his composure settling back round him like a cloak.

"And that bothers you, or not?"

"Parents do the damnedest things for their children . . . and *to* their children."

"You know, I've wondered about your parents? We've nattered on so about mine, we've never gotten to yours. All I've ever heard about was your *bubbeh*. I ought to learn to say that word better, being half a Jew myself. *Bub-beh*, is that how? Accent on the first syllable?"

"Sounds about right," he said almost curtly. I'd rattled him. Good.

I moved in now. "What *did* the parents do to you? Beat you? Leave you? Fuck you?"

A laugh of sorts. "Sharpening your teeth. Atta girl! Matter-of-fact, they died is what they did. Their plane fell out of the sky on the way to Miami Beach. It was the second flight of their lives. I managed to get the mumps and couldn't go. I was parked with my mother's mother. *Bubbeh*. And she inherited me. I enhanced her life no end. Satisfied?"

Far from. For the first time, *bubbeh* departed his lips absent its warm, folksy subtext. "So you became *Bubbeh's* boy," I said. His eyes widened in unpleased surprise. "So to speak," I added. "Tell me. Tell me about *Bubbeh*."

"Want to know? I'll tell you. She was nuts." His face was inches from mine, the wine and coffee strong and damp on his breath. But I did not pull back; that might have put him off, and I wanted to hear the next thing. "They called it manic-depression then. Now it's called bipolar. Soon there'll be some new name maybe even more neutral. The thing is they have pills for it now, fourteen kinds of antidepressant cocktails. Oh, they had meds then, too. Lithium. But poor, immigrant widows didn't take meds for mood swings; if they were lucky, they got prescribed insulin for diabetes. So she swung and I swung with her. When she was up, she was a dynamo: she'd cook everything I loved to eat for days at a time, we'd go see two, three movies in an evening, and then she'd come into bed and kiss me all over—I mean ass, cock, the works. And when she was down, she'd sleep day and night, and if I bothered her, she'd kick me across the room, or lock me in a closet, or tie me up, or . . . Well, you get the idea. She stopped when I got big enough to stop her. No, that's not accurate—when I got *brave* enough to stop her, and that wasn't until I was about fourteen. After that, her rage turned inward. She kept me close to home by running guilt trips and threatening suicide."

Through none of this did he raise his voice, but the words sprayed out of him like hard, stinging pellets of birdshot. Now he lay back against the sofa cushions, spent, his eyes closed. I felt an insane desire to hold him in my arms, and did not give in to it.

"So what was your true nature, and what did you become because you had to?" I asked quietly.

"It's always easier to read someone else's palm. That's one of the perks of being a shrink; you get to figure out other people. My true nature? I like to think I might have been a real healer—an important one—and a lover, and a father. On the other hand, my true nature might resemble poor benighted Jared's." Suddenly, he sat bolt upright. "Did you hear something?" he asked.

"No." I hadn't. Rockets might have gone off unheard by me, that complete was my absorption.

"I thought I heard a rattling back in the kitchen. I'm gonna go check."

He hadn't heard a rattling any more than I had, but if he needed a break from the emotional electricity, I needed to keep his faith by letting him have it. We'd come a long way, too far, too fast, perhaps, but the shards were fitting together: *Bubbeh* and Zip—subjugated by them both, impotent in a way far beyond sex. I had no trouble understanding the inchoate rage, nor the inevitable explosions—at least once with the high-flying Zip, and finally with poor Calista, who had strode in her arrogant innocence directly onto a land mine. A flash had gone off at his mention of Jared. I'd wondered why Nate disliked Jared quite as much as he did. Now I reckoned I knew. The boy I adored reflected back at him his most despised self: an emotionally impotent outcast.

I refilled the wineglasses and drank and stared at the fire. I am accustomed to waiting. In my work it is satisfying, the time spent letting subjects begin to reveal themselves, ripen to the point where my camera can pluck some bits of essential truth. But here I could sense myself growing impatient for the destination, dreading the rest of the journey. However we reached it, the next stop would be Calista; I hated the prospect of going there.

"Nothing going on. I locked the back door, just in case." He was back with a tray of crackers and Stilton. "I ought to be more careful about that, I suppose. You never know who might show up." He was working hard at being jaunty, at letting me know that the topic of *Bubbeh* was closed.

"No, you don't know who'll show up," I said. "Nor who'll decide not to leave. All that fiddle with alarm codes and things, so confusing. You put Melanie to bed that night, didn't you? Rubbed her back a bit to calm her? Then you decided to stay and hope, didn't you?"

He placed the tray on the coffee table and stood looking down at me in a way that told me I'd violated the rules. In my eagerness, I'd snatched control of his revelation from his grip. It was a mistake I'd pay for. "We all live in hope," he said deliberately. "You've thought about my rubbing *your* back, haven't you, stroking your little body? You've wanted to sit on my lap, have me bounce you on my knee like a good daddy does. Horsey, horsey."

My throat shut itself down in some sort of involuntary reflex.

"Still don't mind if I sit next to you?" he asked.

"I do, actually," I managed to say. "Go back to your chair." He did not move. I felt myself begin to surrender to the force of his cold, black stare and experienced Jared's terror with an awful, fresh clarity. It focused my attention and got my blood up. "You may be able sit beside me," I said sharply, "but not yet."

His faced pouched as he stuck out his bottom lip and nodded with something that almost resembled approval. He returned to his chair, a cheese-spread cracker in his hand. "Go on, have some. Good Stilton. Eat as much as you want." The knowing reference made me sweat. But the physical distance did help—a little.

"Thanks, the wine will suffice. I don't care to eat just now." Thoughts of Jared had got me over a bad moment, but dwelling on him any longer would work against me.

"Where do we go from here, Lex?"

"Where do you think we do?"

"Now, that's a shrink question if I ever heard one. I've got a return question for you. You wearing a wire of any kind?"

"What? Oh, no. No wire."

He clasped his hands at the back of his head and lolled. "Show me."

"Show you?"

"That you're, as they say on cop shows, clean." He raised his brows indicating that the move was mine, inquiring how far I'd go to get what I was after. But I sensed also that despite my gaffe in jumping the gun, his desire to tell me was quite as deep as mine was to hear him.

"Serious, are you?" I was wearing a dark blue sweat suit with nothing underneath it. I rose from the sofa, raised the shirt shoulder high, did a quick pirouette, and dropped it back down. I was not in the least girlishly embarrassed—too much was at stake for that. "Satisfied?"

"You'll do," he said with the old, warm rumble. "You'll do."

"Then tell me. Tell me about Calista now."

He could have demanded I leave. He could have picked up the fire poker and bashed me. He could have laughed. Instead, he said so softly I barely heard, "Let's try it." His eyes shut. They stayed shut. And he remained silent and still. To look at him, one might think he had fallen asleep.

"You can sit beside me," I said after some time, "if that will make it easier." He rose and made for me, a bit unsteady on his pins. I took a deep breath as he began to lower his bottom onto the sofa. "No," I said sharply, as though to a misbehaving dog. "*Beside* me, not on top of me." The voice did not sound like me, or like anyone I knew. It sounded like an animal trainer's, perhaps.

He obeyed, giving me a good eighteen-inch berth. "What do you want to know most?" he asked, his face weary, but the eyes hot, whether with his memories or with zest for a new game, I couldn't tell.

"How did you love her and why did you kill her?"

"Two things. Two separate things. You get to ask one."

"I get to ask both," I said evenly, risking it.

"You're a tough taskmistress," he said. "I loved her because she was amazing. She reminded me of Zip, but sweet, so sweet." He laughed, a two-note laugh like a rusty door chime, and threw his head back. "A sweet Zip," he said to the ceiling. "And she was so ready, so responsive to the touch, the way she'd squeeze back. See, what none of you can understand is that Calista wasn't really a child, not at her core she wasn't. Look, I can quote you neuroses, personality disorders, chapter and verse on oppositional children, ADD children—seductive children, too. I work with children day in, day out. I know what they're like, and I've never laid a glove on one of them, never even been tempted. *Calista was not a child.* She was the quintessential female *packaged* as a child. If you believed in God, you'd say she was a special project of His, an experiment. And she loved me, too, right from the beginning. It was her idea, you know, those late dates we had. She got such a kick out of pulling that off." He shook his head, chuckled, a boy again himself, remembering.

"Did you fuck her?"

He turned his face back to me now, confused, like someone who'd been suddenly slapped for no good reason.

"Fuck her? Of course not! That would've hurt her. I was gentle. Always. I celebrated her body, cosseted her. I . . ." He broke off and ran his tongue round parched lips. "What's the most exciting sex you've ever had?"

"We're not talking about me," I said.

"We are now. Come on. You've gotta give some to get some. Let's have it."

Something, some instinct I did not recognize,˙ made me say it. "There was a time I met a man in a pub, not my usual sort of bloke. Rough trade, I suppose you could call him. I went back to his place, and before we did it, he smacked me round a bit. I caught a good one in the eye, blackened for days, and I loved even that part. See, it wasn't about the pain or the bruise; it was about power surging right through me—like fucking in a lightning storm." Not a word of this was true of me, but it summoned up what I knew to be true about Zip. Nate listened, enthralled. I had him back. "Now it's my turn," I said. "Calista. Why did you kill her?"

"That's the wrong question—against the rules."

"This is my game," I said sternly. "I make the rules." Neither of us laughed—not at the absurdity of the exchange, nor out of sheer nervousness. I'd talked about sexual power, told him a lie I knew would titillate him. But it's no lie that power excites; even playacted power, if both sides buy into it, is no laughing matter. It is a ton of *plastique* inside you. I'd not possessed the power of this moment before in my life.

"Tell me why you killed her; tell me how that happened—and maybe I'll let you sit a lot closer."

"Yes," he whispered, his body beginning to lean over.

"No, tell me first."

"She wasn't herself that night," he mumbled. "When they first came back after the trick-or-treat, she was . . .

off. She bit my ear, squirmed off my lap. *His* fault. One way or another he got to her, horny little bastard, jealous of what he didn't understand. It was his fault she died." He lowered his head and stopped talking.

"Jared? *Jared's* fault?"

"Your precious Jared. She was playing with him. She was a playful spirit, a changeling. And he pushed her down into a pile of broken glass—left her there alone, with her pants down, crying. But when she saw me, when I tried to comfort her, clean the wine and blood off her legs, she fought me like a vicious little animal. She was holding that ridiculous rope with the two pencils tied to it—went for my face with the pencil, like it was a knife she had in her hand, almost got my eye. I took it away from her. I . . . She was screaming so damned loud, such terrible things. It got wrapped round her neck. I dunno . . . an accident . . ."

As his voice trailed off in a whining despair, his features seemed to melt one into the other, but perhaps it was the sweat pouring from my forehead dripping into my eyes, blurring everything in burning brine. "Stand up," he said, with a snap to it. "And drop those pants. You could be wearing a wire down there, you know."

In the skewed logic of the game, I rose; so did he. My hand moved to the waist cord of the sweat pants. Then I saw myself, pants down round my knees, helpless—and my fingers froze where they were. Mind racing to blur speed, I turned slowly before him like a studio model, stopping with my back to him, one hip stuck out a bit, head turned over my shoulder. I heard his breath catch, or was it mine? Then I imagined from far away the clink of breaking glass—or perhaps it was not far away at all, but something fragile cracking inside myself. "Beautiful," he said.

"Did you have her do this? Pose for you? Calista?"

"Yes, and she loved it. She'd laugh, make up poses of her own. She was . . ." Suddenly, he stood and reached out and made a grab between my legs. "You shouldn't have killed her," he hissed, twisting the hairy flesh. "She would have been such a fine baby, our baby."

Then the world exploded, inside me and outside too, all at once.

"It wasn't *our* baby!" I shrieked, high-blocking with my left arm and delivering a front snap kick into his groin, target of everything I wanted to punish. "Didn't you ever read a biology book? You can't make a baby if you can't get it up, *asshole!*"

The first and only tae kwon do move I had ever executed without flaw. As he stumbled backward from it, his yell was full-throated and loud. The gunshot from the direction of the kitchen was louder. Nate doubled over making yelping sounds.

"Stand up straight. I want to see the whites of your fuckin' eyes while you die." It sounded like a line from a gangster movie. Melanie, who had spoken it, stood tall as Gary Cooper framed in the arched entranceway, her gun in the two-handed grip familiar from screens large and small. Her yellow trouser suit and impeccable makeup turned the scene surreal.

He straightened up slightly, hands still protecting his crotch. His eyes streamed rivers onto his cheeks. "Go ahead," he said, a begging flagellant. "Do it. I killed your little girl."

The gun moved out, preparing to fire. I skittered across the room and raised my arms to tackle her round the knees. The crack of a shot beside my skull, and Nate went down with a muffled cry.

"Bitch!" Melanie hollered into my half-deafened ear.

I lay on top of her. With strength leased from desperation I pinned her arms at the elbows, knowing she'd throw me off within seconds, as soon as she got her bearings. I lowered my face and sank my teeth into her right forearm. She let go the gun and rolled over, dumping me flat. When she rose, I scrambled up as well and kicked it . . . somewhere.

"You sick little whore. I wish you'd never been born." Those were the last words I heard from my sister for a while. She spoke them just before her fist slammed my jaw and knocked me out cold.

EPILOGUE

No, Nate did not die, nor did Melanie's bullet mete out the poetic justice of castration. He bled a great deal into his rug from a thigh wound. When he recovered, his death wish had given way to an energetic campaign to save his skin. He pled not guilty to murder. Good Lord, he'd left the Halloween party after seeing the distraught Melanie to her room, gone home, had a cup of coffee, and gone to bed. His "confession" to Lex's sister had been bogus—part of a sex fantasy game they'd been playing—distasteful, but not illegal. "Why, Lex had come to visit me," he'd testified. "The two of us were in my living room drinking wine."

He'd been a bit drunk himself, confused, terrified of Melanie's gun pointed at him, when he'd exhorted her to, "Go ahead . . . Do it. I killed your little girl." On the charges of rape and child molestation he was also not guilty, in this case by reason of insanity. His team of lawyers and shrinks was eloquent in dredging up his tormented childhood with the lunatic *Bubbeh*, who in her manic kiss-and-caress mode, had placed no part of young Nate's body off limits.

He had not penetrated Calista. The lawyers hammered away at that: an aging widower, obsessed with a seductive child—they'd skirted, but only just, the trap of blaming the victim—a man with an unblemished career devoted to helping children, a man half mad with grief over losing the wife whom he had cared for through the long years of her decline. On the stand Nate was a touching figure, weeping uncontrollably for Calista and her family, articulate about his grief, his remorse over actions committed when he was "not himself." A vigorous cross-examination did not break him.

Once, just once, he and I made eye contact. His were the eyes of a Wimbledon winner, a bit of compassion in them for a worthy opponent.

My own testimony came off erratic: quirkily emotional, not entirely consistent. Melanie in the witness box was powerful, but her evidence was hearsay, all of it. The blue bathrobe was presented as the People's Exhibit A, and Zip's old friend, Norma Testa, was called to the stand. Our side thought she did really well, but of course the outburst she described had been more than three decades ago.

Jared on the stand was extraordinary. At times the words he was saying seemed to overpower him into choked silence while he labored to reclaim himself, but in the main he was clear and unwavering in his account, even the part of it that touched on behavior that shamed him. Under cross-examination by Nate's artful lawyer, though tears occasionally tracked his cheeks, though at moments his hot temper threatened to escape, he held his ground. I thought as I watched, listened, that this was Tom's son—that Tom's desire for uncovering the truth at all costs was at his core. And I was so proud of him it was hard not to stand up and cheer.

Now, nine months after Calista's murder, the jury is deliberating. Whether they saw and heard things the way I did, remains to be seen.

You may wonder how Melanie happened to recognize Nate's guilt and show up at the precise moment she did. No prescience was involved, no coincidence. It was simply that Jared had not sat passively waiting at Barney's computer. He had phoned up his mother. Despite the rents and tatters of their relationship, this child had wanted his mother—had trusted her more than he distrusted her, and with reason.

Perhaps the cool remove of telecommunication proved useful; perhaps it was her sheer relief at hearing his voice; perhaps seeds had been germinating unnoticed in her own mind—but whatever the reason, this time Melanie listened to Jared, heard what he said, and believed him. That border crossed, the result was unsurprising; it was, given those circumstances, what Melanie would do. And no, the phantom rattling Nate claimed to have heard in the kitchen had not been she; that had been nothing. But his locked kitchen door had posed her no problem. She'd simply broken its glass with the butt of her gun, reached inside, and turned the handle. The sound I'd heard while my body posed itself for Nate had been no figment of an overheated imagination, though his had evidently been sufficiently hot not to have heard it at all.

I wonder why it was I stopped her killing him. The question wakes me at night, or hits me as I'm walking down a street in the afternoon, or checking my E-mail, or listening to Jared explain something about black holes. Was it instinct that made me dive at her—the lack of killer instinct asserting itself as aggressively as its opposite? Or perhaps craven fear that she would kill her sick little whore of a sister, as well? But what haunts me is the possibility that some particle of protective feeling for Nate Grumbach set me in motion, something to do with a daddy. And if that were true, I would not be entitled to forgive myself for it.

MELANIE, TOM, AND JARED six months ago bought a house and moved in. Melanie, you may remember, is proficient at creating an instant home. This is quite a nice one—in Westport. Yes, Westport. Finally, it was easier to stick with familiar surroundings, familiar strangers than to cope with brand-new ones. The three McQuades, disparate though they are, have closed ranks among themselves; finally, they are all they've got. This fusion has resulted in some day-by-day chafing. Tom is one of life's soloists and, in the American slang I admire, a hard dog to keep on the porch. Melanie and Jared are, as ever, oil and water, chalk and cheese. And Jared's knot of anger remains tightly tied. However, it has been not quite a year; things are likely to improve. The aggregate strength of three such stubborn wills can move mountains—at the very least.

The red wagon disappeared, picked off perhaps by a souvenir seeker. Calista's wagon: Jared was not, nor would he ever become, a red wagon sort of boy.

I've stayed in Westport, as well. For Jared's sake would be the simplest explanation: far too simple. We do spend a great deal of time together, which I relish and he seems to. But there is a difference in the way we are: I'd promised him closure and something like justice; the promise, if not broken is badly cracked. In short, though Jared lacks killer instinct himself, he was disappointed in my lacking it, too. I am no longer a hero, just a kindred spirit. Maybe that part is all to the good.

The senior McQuades seem pleased to have me about; both of them do. Melanie calls me Allie sometimes, inadvertently or not. Tom often calls me sister with that twist to his mouth. I think I provide a sort of positive chemical effect on them: in some way I don't precisely understand, my presence just outside their triumvirate makes it a bit easier for the triumvirate to operate.

I am not in residence with them, though. No. For the moment, I live in a blue house with black shutters and a red door, with a dog I've grown passably fond of and a man I believe I love.

IMMEDIATELY AFTER Nate was taken into custody and I had given my statement to Domingo, I told Barney I'd be going to ground for a few days, and that I'd be in touch when I was ready.

"You're headed for an eating binge," he'd said flatly.

"What if I am?"

"I want you to do it here, in this house."

"I couldn't. I need to be alone—a motel or something. I . . . I've got in the habit."

"There's an attic; be the mad Mrs. Rochester, I don't give a damn, and I won't intrude on your space. I'll deliver provisions to the foot of the stairs, if you want. Until it's over."

"It's sick animal ugly when I binge. I don't do it often, and I probably won't give it up, but I can't be that exposed—to . . . anyone."

"I have seen you exposed down to the bone," he said, "and we're both here. If our places were reversed, I hope you'd feel the same."

I binged for three days. I did not do it in a motel. Since that time, the urge has come upon me three times. Twice, I've been able to hold the beast at bay with a bit of chemical tranquilizer and a lot of Barney's presence.

I'm making a film here. Not the one I was pelted with offers for, of course. This is a study of Tonya. Right in the spirit of the times, an American success story in formation: *Birth of a Day Trader*. Disappointed as they were not to have *The Calista McQuade Story*, the Beeb quite liked it.

Case in point about the resourcefulness of human determination in the service of human needs: Vin and Courtney are back together. She's found him a new student to Olympic-train—a boy, this time.

Oh, one last thing: I had an E-mail the other day from Australia. I pressed *Delete* without opening the document.

Visit
❖ **Pocket Books** ❖
online at

....

www.SimonSays.com

....

Keep up on the latest new
releases from your favorite
authors, as well as author
appearances, news, chats,
special offers and more.

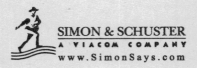